"*Uncharted* tells a story within a story. Readers will be forced to skate along the edge of suspended belief, eagerly turning the pages, hoping it all turns out to be true. A great read that will appeal to armchair sailors, romantics, and real adventurers."

~Carol Newman Cronin, author of *Cape Cod Surprise*

Uncharted

STORY *for a* SHIPWRIGHT

Second Paperback Edition

Copyright ©2012 by J. B. Chicoine
Edited by Diane Dalton
Cover and interior art and design by Straw Hill Design

Watercolor painting—*Marlena*—by J. B. Chicoine, based on image by Pascal Gentil; used with permission.

J. B. Chicoine's author website: www.jbchicoine.com

ISBN-13: 978-0615892405
ISBN-10: 061589240X

Printed in the United States of America

Acknowledgments

I'D LIKE TO THANK ALL THOSE WHO READ MY ROUGH DRAFTS and encouraged me along, especially my beta-readers who spent hours helping me refine this project, including Glenn Rawlinson, Douglas Noyes, Susan Mills, Scott Daniel, Liza Carens Salerno, and Laura Martone. Special thanks to Robynne Marie Plouff for her constant support, Jon Paul for all things Navy, Beth Zygiel, Peggy Heinrich, and Donna Morris for listening to me ramble, and Michelle Davidson Argyle for introducing me to Rhemalda Publishing, publisher of *Uncharted*'s first edition. Also, many thanks to the publishing team at Rhemalda for loving this story and investing so much in seeing it through to its first publication.

I also want to thank all those on *WoodenBoat* Forum who offered technical information and encouragement—boy, did I learn all sorts of things!

Most of all, thank you, Todd, for believing in this story even before I wrote the first word, and for keeping me grounded through all my ups and downs with it, and even providing a few great lines!

FOR MY TODD

Uncharted
STORY *for a* SHIPWRIGHT

J. B. CHICOINE

Straw
Hill
Publishing

Chapter 1

I EASILY LOST TRACK OF TIME IN THE BOATSHED, where minutes and hours hung in the air like fine sawdust, and so I couldn't say for sure how long I had been running my sander when I noticed the intruder. At a glimpse, I thought it was my hired guy. On a double take, the skirt was definitely not his style.

I doubt I would have noticed her at all, except she planted herself right in that place where the sun shot through that hole in the roof, which wouldn't get fixed for a month. No one had seen the sun for two weeks, but in that moment, it split the clouds, thrust a beam through that narrow fissure, and reflected off every hovering dust particle surrounding her. Filaments of wild curls circled her head like a halo. Even her skirt radiated. I hate to sound like a spiritualist, or worse yet, a romantic, but at first glance, she seemed like an apparition. If not for her quirky suitcase the size of a tackle box, I might have dropped to my knees.

She stood unperturbed, as if she had been watching me for minutes, studying me without concern over whether I would be so kind as to shut off the disk sander and acknowledge her. She wasn't local—I would have recognized most anyone from around here—and tourists wouldn't be showing up at our family's bed and breakfast for another month. It occurred to me that she could have been Mother's new "Girl," although we had talked about it after the last one left and agreed that this spring I would have at least some input in the hiring process. Perhaps Mother had made another one of her unilateral decisions and failed to mention it. Or maybe she did say something, and I tuned her out the way I often did when she began wringing her hands.

I didn't think I was straight-out rude to the girl, but I hated interruptions, and so I might have come across as impatient.

"Are you looking for the bed and breakfast?" I shouted, as though my equipment were still running.

She stepped forward into the shadows. "I found it but no one's around."

I remembered something about Mother taking Buck, my grandfather, to town. My eyes must have looked like they were rolling right out of their sockets when I responded, "Why don't you go wait on the front steps? Someone will be back soon."

In spite of my abruptness, she smiled and walked away. I pulled the respirator back over my face and continued scarphing the frame repair, but I did watch as she walked from the shadows out into the haze of the boatyard. I had never seen a girl carry herself with such nonchalant femininity. Just the same, I wasted no time, immersing myself in lists and deadlines. I would settle the hired help issue with Mother later. Within minutes, I had nearly forgotten about her altogether. I figured that if she stayed on, she would be no different from all of Mother's other Girls.

I worked without a break, right on through lunchtime, the way I always did once I was into a project, but even more so since my regular guy, Mitch, was recovering from rotator cuff surgery. When I quit—and only at the insistence of hunger pangs—I shook sawdust from my flannel shirt as I stepped into daylight. Mother hadn't returned with the car. Buck's appointment at the clinic must have involved an unusually long wait. There on the front stoop of our stately old Colonial, the girl perched an open book on her knees. *Oh, great!* Then it occurred to me that she had been sitting under the scant cover of the porch during intermittent downpours for at least several hours. I couldn't ignore her and veered toward the stoop.

As I plodded through furrows of mud, she glanced at me and smiled, as if only minutes had passed, not hours. I brushed sawdust from my thinning hair, forcing something like a smile.

She stuffed her book into a duffel bag beside her little suitcase and stood. My reaction to her outfit probably came across as a smirk, but honestly, she looked like an orphan in her full, just-below-the-knee denim skirt and fisherman's sweater that could have fit me. The anklet socks and muddied white sneakers with mismatched laces didn't help. Not that I qualified as any kind of fashion critic, but she was about as poorly put together as the crew I had seen climb out of the daytrip van from the County Institution. When I closed in enough to get a good look at her through all that wild hair, I didn't notice her outfit so much. Still, a pretty face was little compensation for slowing me down.

I shoved my hands in my jeans pockets. "I'm sorry. I really thought my mother would be back sooner. I'm surprised she didn't mention you were coming."

"I'm unexpected. I didn't make a reservation." So much for being Mother's new Girl. "Do I need a reservation to get a room for a week or two?"

"We aren't open to guests for another month." I squinted. "It's right in our brochure."

She winced. "I guess I don't have one of those."

How could anyone visiting the coast of Maine think she could just show up, preseason, and expect to get a room at a bed and breakfast? I stared long enough to make her fidget. "Well, sorry. Can't really help you there."

"Okay … I'll just come back in a month," she said as if it weren't any inconvenience at all.

"Sorry." I felt genuinely bad, but what was I supposed to do?

Her gaze dropped to my boots and traveled to my forehead.

"You're Samuel Wesley." She pulled her wild hair from her face.

I'm sure that if I had ever met her, I would have remembered those eyes—somewhere between gray and brown—not to mention the rest of her face. She had an exotic look about her.

"Yeah," I said. "That's me."

"You're the shipwright."

"Yeah."

Her smile widened as if she had just met a celebrity. It put me on edge, though it did tickle my ego a little. Perhaps a mutual friend had sent her.

I hoped for a clue. "What's your name?"

"Marlena. You don't know me."

It really bugged me that she seemed to know *me*, but I had no idea who she was or where she came from.

"So, I guess I'll see you in a month." She turned away, tossing her duffel bag over her shoulder as if it contained no more than her book and a pair of socks.

"How did you get here?" I called out after her.

"I walked from the bus station."

"You walked all the way from the depot?"

"It's not that far," she said, even though I knew it was at least five miles.

"You're not planning on walking back to the depot *now*, are you?"

"I can make it before dark."

I checked at my watch. I couldn't believe the next words out of my mouth. "Listen, it's late. I suppose I could give you a lift." At thirty-one years old, I still surprised myself.

"I don't accept rides from strangers, but thank you anyway."

I chuckled. I guess knowing my name and occupation did not disqualify me as an ax murderer. "You do realize the bus comes only once a day, don't you?"

"That's okay. I'll wait on the depot bench."

"You don't understand. They close up every day at five and don't reopen until eight in the morning. No overnight camping allowed."

Her shoulders slumped as she stood in a puddle with one bag in each hand. Wide eyes glanced up one end of the road and down the other. "Is there another place in town where I could sleep?"

As if only an imbecile would ask, I said, "No place in town opens until May."

She stood there staring at me. The blush tinting her face told me I had embarrassed her, which wasn't my intent. She looked barely twenty years old, and I hated to think of a kid hanging out on the street for the night. I sized her up as a low-risk inconvenience.

"Okay, listen, why don't you stick around until my mother returns?" I said. "I'm sure we can work something out." *There goes my afternoon!*

The naivety I had seen a second ago vanished, and a glint of suspicion shot from her eyes. Was she sizing me up? She must have deduced I was also low-risk because she gave me a nod, albeit with hesitation.

"C'mon." I gestured for her to follow me around back.

As I led the way, navigating between ruts, I glanced behind. Like a ballerina, she tiptoed along, balancing on high ridges between puddles, with one counterweighted bag in each hand. As graceful as she was, I still prayed she wouldn't take a nosedive. I was in no mood for whatever a rescue might involve. Once we arrived at a mound of newly sprouted turf, my concern switched to what I should do with her until Mother showed up.

From the looks of her, she wasn't a big eater. Just the same, I thought it polite to ask, "You hungry?"

She tipped her face toward the winking sun. "No. Not at all. If you don't mind, I'll just sit out here and wait."

"Suit yourself."

Inside, with microwaved lunch in front of me, I glanced up from the round kitchen table, expecting to see the girl on our back porch. She wasn't where I had left her. I had to admit, I hoped she had walked back to the depot, absolving me of any further obligation. Of course, my curiosity got the better of me, and I brought my plate to the door. The sight of her duffel bag on the steps dashed my hopes. She had wandered down to the sandy boat landing where guests would launch their kayaks and canoes, beyond the back yard and by the fishing dock. She clutched her little suitcase. If she thought I was going to rifle through her belongings, why didn't she take her duffle bag too?

Squatting at the water's edge, she bunched the folds of her skirt between her knees as the back hem gathered mud. The harbor was scarcely above freezing, but that didn't deter her from scooping a handful. She cocked her head, watching it drizzle from her palm. Then, of all things, she tasted it. With her fingers again in the water, she drew figure eights. I half expected she would go wading, sneakers and all.

As she stood, wrapping herself in the bulk of her sweater, I thought she might have caught a glimpse of me standing with my plate in hand. Appearing oblivious, she raked fingers through unruly hair and smiled at the glint of sunlight. I didn't regret my offer, but I wondered how much of my dwindling afternoon she would consume.

Fortunately, Mother returned while the girl lingered down at the water.

"Who is the young lady over by the landing? A friend of yours?" was the first thing Mother asked when we stepped into the kitchen, leaving Buck on the deck.

"No," I said, with my eye on the girl. "She's just some kid who got her wires crossed—just needs a bed for the night."

I should have broken it to Mother a bit more gingerly, knowing a day at the clinic made her testy. Those words barely left my mouth before her purse and keys clattered onto the countertop.

Her glare could have scared a lobster right into boiling water. "And where am I supposed to find time for this, Samuel? What were you thinking? You know we never take guests this early. I cannot entertain a guest, keep track of Buck, make up a bed, cook supper—"

More interested in Buck's appointment than indulging my unraveling mother, I set my plate on the table with a clank. "What did Doctor McKenzie say?"

"He says Buck is in great shape for ninety—in better shape than most seventy-five-year-olds."

"That's not what I'm asking."

Each hand vigorously massaged the other. "What do you want me to say?"

"I want to know what else McKenzie said."

"You want to know how Buck's cholesterol and prostate are?"

I sucked in a controlled breath. Why did she have to make these conversations so difficult? "Did he even ask Buck what year it is?"

She drew a strand of silver hair behind her ear and folded her arms. "Don't be ridiculous. Buck knows it's 2000, and yes, Doctor McKenzie did ask. Buck was exceptionally lucid and you would have been proud of him."

"Did you tell him about the wandering?"

"It didn't come up."

Buck's 'condition' was right at the top of the *Things of Which We Do Not Speak* list. I kept my eyes firmly planted, willing them not to roll. I flinched.

Her narrow jaw tensed and she fired back, "If you're dissatisfied with the way his appointments go, you are perfectly welcome to accompany him next time." End of conversation. She had such a way of minimizing the bigger issues and exaggerating the minute.

Talk of Buck's wandering sent me to the back door. To my relief, he had ambled down to the water, by the girl. Still able to stand erect, he towered over her as he talked. She giggled. He could be so charming with a new audience, especially a pretty one. He was at his best, and it made me glad to see him so happy. It also made me miss him.

From behind, I sensed Mother's nearness, the way her hand almost settled on my shoulder as some sort of concession or comforting gesture. Instead of a touch, she spoke. "You are not going to leave that plate on the table, are you?"

As if I ever do. I rolled my eyes. As usual, I cut her some slack. That's how it worked.

I headed back out to the shop, passing Buck and the girl on their way inside.

"How about a game of checkers," I overheard Buck say.

"What's checkers?" I stumbled, more at her question than the rut. She glanced at me as I recovered my footing. As I hurried on by, I could almost feel her stare all the way to the boatshed—not that I would ever turn around to check.

Chapter 2

I HADN'T ALLOWED THE GIRL TO BECOME MUCH OF a distraction while I worked that morning, but I had difficulty concentrating after lunch. It wasn't so much that she seemed to know me, or that she was nothing short of peculiar, but there would be repercussions for an untimely overnight 'guest.' I was not off the hook with Mother.

Just as I finally lost myself in work, our guest appeared in my doorway. I knew why Mother had sent her, but I waited for her to speak. She tipped forward to peek in, and then peered up and around the doorway, stroking the jamb, as if examining the building's structure. Slowly, her gaze moved to the contents of my shop. I picked a curled shaving from my hand plane, waiting for her eyes to settle on me. By the time she spoke, I'm sure I wore a full frown.

"Dinner is ready," she said.

I nodded, slapping the plane against my palm, waiting for her retreat. She held her ground.

"I'll be right in," I said, too uncomfortable to turn my back on her. She stood there staring. *Fine.* As soon as I put the tool down and stepped forward, she spun around and disappeared into the dimming light of the dooryard.

As I trudged toward the house, she waited by the door. I stomped mud from my boots and sidled past her, stepping into the spicy aroma of my favorite lasagna.

Mother hummed in the kitchen, her voice lyrical as she said, "Here, Marlena," and handed her a couple of ice-filled glasses. "Please, put these on the table."

I went to wash up, wondering at Mother's improved mood. When I returned, our dinner guest was pouring water from a pitcher into each glass. After filling one, she raised it, rattling the cubes as she held it to the light before setting it by a plate. She straightened the forks, then spaced each spoon and knife evenly. Mother's brow rose with approval.

As Buck pulled up to the table, he studied me for a moment. "Are you going with my soup for the brightwork on that refit?"

"Yup." Truth was, I had doctored up his "soup" recipe—one part varnish, two parts turpentine, and three parts tung oil—and sometimes, I even resorted to Ben Moore spar, but I would never let on.

Before Mother took her seat at the head of the table, Marlena placed a tidy little square of lasagna on her plate. Mother sighed and I thought for sure we were in for a lecture on manners. Instead of a rebuke, she said, "There's plenty," and heaped another slab beside the first.

With a grimace, Marlena looked up at me, as though pleading for intervention.

I shrugged.

"But I don't eat much," she said.

"Don't be silly," Mother replied with the firm smile that insisted upon obedience. "You're thin as a rail."

Marlena drew her shoulders back and glanced down at her body, as if it were in some way unacceptable, and then glanced up at me.

I urged Mother along. "Say grace, Ma, before everything gets cold."

While Mother recited her canned prayer, I sensed the girl's gawk. Obeying an impulse, I checked. She stared at me, unabashed, her gray eyes haloed in brown.

"Amen," I repeated under my breath.

The first few minutes remained quiet but for the clinking of cutlery against china. Marlena shifted her focus to Buck. He offered a big, toothy grin.

"I really like your teeth," she said. "Are they real?"

"Sure are." He clacked them like a ventriloquist's dummy. "Never had a cavity in all my days. They just don't make teeth like these anymore."

Clacking her own teeth, she returned to her plate. Buck inhaled another mouthful as his attention drifted to me. I watched a question form as he chewed. He didn't wait to swallow before asking, "You going with my soup on that refit?"

I glanced at Mother—her expression unchanged, as if she hadn't noticed his waning short-term memory—and replied, "Yup."

Buck finished chewing and swallowed a few more bites. Before long, and according to custom, he cleared his throat and began a story with familiar words. "You know, the interesting thing about the *Vanessa* was …," he continued with a narration from his intact long-term memory about our illustrious ancestor, Captain William Wesley, and his mighty schooner, the *Vanessa-Benita*. Tonight, his yarn included a damsel in distress and a mutiny, but often it entailed Confederate ambushes, pirates, mermaids, and renegade whales. I had heard this one often, although Buck did add a clever twist, a twist I nearly missed due to Marlena's most disconcerting habit. When not preoccupied with her fork and knife, manipulating them with infantile focus and frustration, she was again staring at me.

I'd had enough of her gawking and decided to see how she liked having someone's eyes glued to her as she ate. She returned my squint, as if formulating questions that never came. I got the feeling she had no idea how rude her staring was. Either that, or there was something terribly wrong with her.

Buck wrapped up his story with a favorite ending. I could almost recite it word-for-word along with him. "… Sheets of rain obscured an avalanche of seawater curling above the *Vanessa's* broadside. With the force of an ax, it sheared her foremast. Then, a final billow drank him down like krill in the maw of a whale, never to be seen again." Always in the end, with the ever-courageous Captain Wesley at the helm, the *Vanessa-Benita* succumbed to the watery depths of an angry sea. Buck's coherence when telling a story amazed me.

What fascinated me about Buck's tales was that one, or a combination of several versions, could have been true. No one knew for sure what happened to Captain Wesley. Reportedly, there were no survivors, not even a stray plank of the mysterious *Vanessa-Benita*. It seemed that once she left port she simply disappeared. Only vague accounts of her bearings or ultimate destination ever trickled back, with too many conflicting details to fill the gaps convincingly. We understood that those discrepancies gave Buck the right to take liberties with family history. We also understood that Buck made things up.

After dinner, while the girl retrieved linens for her own bed on the third floor, Mother informed me, "Marlena will be staying on."

So be it. Whether Mother wanted to admit it to Dr. McKenzie or not, we both knew that Buck was becoming less and less predictable. Early in the spring as it was, an extra pair of hands and eyes would be helpful. Even with Marlena's peculiarities, it would work out fine as long as she left me alone.

Back out in the boatshed, I hoped to get a few hours jump on the next day's project, but I had trouble motivating myself. Instead of picking up where I left off on the scarphing—now replanking—job, I pulled back the canvas from my favorite project, Buck's yawl, the *Mary-Leigh*. For years, she had been the product of neglect, but not for lack of desire. I ran my hand along her hull and whispered reassurance that I hadn't forgotten her. Lost in the moment, I was about to reposition the canvas when Buck appeared in the doorway. He hesitated, rubbing his forehead and surveying the shop before stepping inside and deflating my plans of getting any real work done.

"What's up, Buck?" I hoped he was only there to relay a

message.

He smoothed his hand over his bald head. "Just wanted to have a look at my old girl. You must've brought her in for her annual maintenance …."

My heart sank. The fact was, we had hauled her in for an extensive refit during the summer of '78, when I was nine, and she hadn't seen water since.

Before I could divert him, he began yanking canvas and scowled. "What the hell happened to her keel?"

I kept her covered to avoid that very reaction. Then, as if it all at once dawned on him, he rebounded. "Right—she foundered." He scratched his peppered chin, twisting his mouth. With a whistle to his words, he said, "Just looks worse than I remember … must be the light."

I nodded, knowing what he would say next.

"Philip Rhodes. A genius of an engineer. Couldn't wait to reproduce his *Pavana*. Fell in love with her the first time I saw her back in '49, the pinnacle of wooden boat technology, right before all that galblasted fiberglass."

"She is a beauty."

"Eight years it took me to build her." Pride curled his thin lips. "Twenty-one years she served me, and in only one night she foundered."

His devastation showed fresh on his face, and I began drawing the canvas like a curtain, back over his bad memories. Two years she had sat in the boatyard, garboards still sprung and varnish blistering in the weather. Then Dad was gone and I heard no more mention of her refitting. When Grandma Estelle died a year later, Buck had completely lost heart and wouldn't even talk about what would become of his *Mary-Leigh*. I hoped we weren't on the brink of revisiting those memories.

His large hand gripped the scruff of my neck with surprising strength. I hesitated to meet his level gaze. Too many times, his eyes appeared lost, as if searching for something, as if he would find what he looked for in my own eyes.

"Sammy," his voice crackled as his breath warmed my cheek. "When was the last time you went out on the water?

And I don't mean playing around on that dinghy of yours. When's the last time you had your sails stressed, took in some real water?"

"Buck ...," I wagged my head. He knew as well as I that I didn't have a serious boat aside from his *Mary-Leigh*. How pathetic was that for a shipwright? And the *Firefly,* my little racing dinghy—the product of my seventeenth summer—sure didn't count.

He tightened his grip. "When?"

I knew what was coming next.

"Sammy, you can't ignore it. The sea is in your blood, surging with all its turbulence—"

I finished his oft-repeated sentence with him. "... and as subject to longing and discontentment as the sea is to the tide ... I know, Buck," I said, patting his thinning shoulder.

I had heard those words for as long as I had listened to his stories, yet, while I was still in my twenties, I laughed them off as the romantic notions of an old man. I assumed that over the generations my seafaring blood had thinned, had been adulterated by the contented sort who stuck around. That I would be one of the guys who married some local girl and carried on the family business, placating myself with the occasional weekend sail. Now, I wasn't so sure.

Buck tightened his grip, as if trying to squeeze a response from me, but before the moment turned too sentimental, a cool draft rushed in. Mother's thin silhouette appeared in the now wide-open doorway, with Marlena—the new Girl—in tow.

"There you are, Buck." Mother sighed with melodramatic relief.

His hand slacked.

I released him. "See you in the morning, Buck."

He frowned. "You're gonna use my soup and not that poly crap, right?"

I sighed at his need to ask, as if I would be caught dead using polyurethane. "You bet."

Like a child, he followed Marlena to the house. Mother lingered, waiting until they were out of earshot. "You still plan on painting the house this spring, don't you?"

"Yeah, Ma. We already discussed this."

The hand wringing began. "I was just double-checking."

"Got it covered, Ma."

Her mouth opened and I intensified my stare until all she said was, "Alright then. Goodnight."

I glazed over as she walked away, vanishing into the dark. Mother took for granted my ability to handle it—after all, that was my job. Worrying was her job. In her defense, given all she had been through, it was no wonder. For that reason, I told her very little, strictly need-to-know information and never anything about how I honestly felt. Oh, God, if I did that, she would really come unglued. Therefore, she had no idea what I was thinking and hadn't since before my ninth birthday.

Giving the *Mary-Leigh's* shroud one last tug, I reviewed all that needed doing before the second week of May. At the same time, Buck's question begged an answer. When *was* the last time I had been out on the water—*really* sailing? For weeks, I had been suppressing some boisterous thing within me, rolling like a wave. The old man was right. In my heart, I was out beyond the shoals, beyond the touchstone of landfall, plunging and heaving, rising with exhilaration. Yet, in my mind, I was intent on crossing off the next task on my *To Do* list.

I tried not to think about it. I couldn't afford the slump it put me in. In fact, it had sapped me of motivation that evening. With no further ambition, I decided to turn in early, closer to ten than midnight.

As I made my way to the house, the first peepers of the season chirped. I paused, listening—enveloped by the promise of summer, of those carefree days messing around on the water and in the boatyard. In a fleeting moment, it evaporated. Childhood seemed like a lifetime ago. The kitchen light went out and I pushed onward.

Mother left the hall lamp on for me, as usual. As I went to turn it off on my way to the staircase, I heard quiet voices— that is, the murmur of a single voice—coming from the parlor. One of the French doors that we usually kept closed to conserve on the heating bill was ajar. When I approached, I caught our new hireling on the divan, staring—and mumbling—at the distinguished portrait of Captain Wesley over the fireplace. I stepped inside, silencing her and bringing her to her feet.

Even in the dim glow of the floor lamp, her eyes glistened. "I'm sorry—I just—I saw the painting ...."

"Yeah, well, I'm shutting things down for the night."

She didn't seem to get the cue. She just stood there, staring at me.

"I'm always the last one upstairs," I said. "And I'm heading up now."

Still, she didn't budge. She didn't even blink.

"My mother *did* show you where your room is, right?"

"Yes."

"Okay then ... I'll follow you up."

"Oh ... yes," she whispered and turned back toward the portrait to give it one last look as I held the door wide open. I tried to keep my suspicion in check, but this hiring someone right off the street made me uneasy. Usually we required at least a reference. Was this Mother's logic-defying payback?

I followed her unfamiliar, pleasant scent up the staircase. Dainty fingertips, peeking from her too-long sleeves, danced along the wainscoting. Her skirt and sweater hid much of what I assumed was a cute figure, and the way she moved made me wish she wasn't a hired Girl. All the way up to the third floor, I reminded myself of my strict hands-off policy.

She slipped inside her room across from mine—the only other bedroom on the top floor—and gave me one final stare. I offered a polite, "Good night," as her door closed without reply, leaving only the image of fixated eyes disappearing into her dark room. *Alrighty, then!*

I glanced at my alarm clock. Too wound up for sleep, I booted up my computer and changed into sweats. I should have been working on another article for *WoodenBoat* magazine. Instead, I clicked on my work-in-progress, my frivolous meanderings of a novel.

Earlier that morning, sometime during the scarphing repair, between lists and deadlines, I had worked out a new scene. Yet with all that had transpired during the day, my thoughts scattered. I focused on the screen, rereading a few paragraphs, visualizing what I wanted to say, and before I knew it, two hours had passed, giving birth to a new chapter. Really, who could resist a damsel in distress?

I shut down my computer, wishing I could shut down my mind as easily. Moonlight bounced from the water, reflecting on my ceiling. I tucked my hands between my pillow and my head. Another night pondering the state of my existence. What was life supposed to amount to for guys like me? As if there was a *Guys Like Me* category. If it existed, I would be clumped in with that handful of thirty-something men still living at home out of obligation rather than preference. What a frustrated and discontented lot, trying to navigate life in a boat that wasn't even ours and, worse yet, in want of a rudder. In irons—headed into the wind—going nowhere.

Chapter 3

MID-WEEK, I RECEIVED A PHONE CALL FROM MY best friend, Derek. He had just arrived back in Maine after six weeks in the Caribbean. Although I was still behind on work in the boatshed, he managed to wrangle me out of the shop and over to the local pub for a few beers. When we stepped into The Bilge, classic '80s music pulsed from the paint-chipped, rust-veneered jukebox. Before I had a chance to make my way over to the bar, Derek already had a mug of my favorite beer in one hand, and sipped from another. In two minutes, we had claimed the pool table. He hovered behind me as I blew a perfectly good shot, pocketing the cue ball.

"Scratch!" he gloated. "I can't believe you missed that! God, you're playing like my baby sister."

"You don't *have* a sister."

"And if I did, she'd play you right under the table." He raked his fingers through his tousled, sandy hair.

"If you did, I'd be playing under the table and having a *good* time."

As balls settled into a perfect lineup atop beer-stained felt, I retrieved my mug from the bumper and pulled at my neck muscles. Trying not to think of all the work waiting for me in the shop, I gulped from my third beer, hoping to hasten its effect.

"You're in a pissy mood." Derek eyed the orange ball as if it were a tough shot. We never used to call our shots, but lately he had become a stickler for the rules. "Couldn't have anything to do with one of your former Girls showing up here with her new man. Five ball, side pocket."

The cue ball clacked the five, driving it home.

Rubbing the sting from my eyes, I refocused on the nicotine-tinted green shade suspended above the pool table. Glancing around at The Bilge's décor, I wondered if there was anything more than grease and dust affixing the crossed oars to the wall behind Derek. That, and the remains of a fifteen-pound lobster above the liquor shelf, was the extent of the ambiance in our local pub. Down at the harbor docks, tucked between the lobster pound and the diesel pump, The Bilge was the place where only year-rounders dared drink, shoot pool, and throw darts. No one but those with an iron gut risked eating there.

I avoided anything more than a glimpse at the bar, where smoking ashtrays and smoldering grease somewhat obscured the view. The aromas of stale beer, fried fish, and cigarettes were more of an assault on my senses than the sight of her.

I glanced from Lindsey back to Derek. "No, I'm glad for her."

Derek raised his skeptical brow.

"No, seriously. I am." That was the truth. Lindsey was a perfectly nice girl, we simply weren't right for each other. Besides, I was the one who ended it. It wasn't as if she dumped me. Not that I was any great catch. I didn't delude myself about that.

I had always considered myself pretty average, but it was hard to be objective beside my older brother, tall-dark-and-handsome Billy, who could have stepped off the cover of *Gentlemen's Quarterly*, or Derek, who fit the profile of an *Eddie Bauer* model. I didn't repulse women, but I wasn't striking, either. Even so, compared to most of the guys hanging around the bar, I was in moderately good shape. No gut. No double chin. I was in good health. Had all my teeth. No loathsome diseases, and I had all my fingers—a real asset in a town of old lobstermen and boat builders.

"Eight ball, corner—You can't tell me it doesn't irk you, seeing Lindsey all happily married while you're as single as the day we graduated high school."

I huffed. "Look who's talking."

"Hey, at least *I'm* getting some action … and we both know how long it's been since you got—" With one decisive thrust, he planted the eight ball squarely in the corner pocket and gave me his evil grin.

"Change of subject. I came here to unwind, not to be reminded of my pitiable existence."

"What you need is to back away from that thesaurus, the boatyard, and your mama, and get out and mix it up a little."

"Okay, *another* change of subject."

"Alright. Tell me about the new Girl."

I shrugged, collecting balls. "I guess she's cute."

Every spring, Derek's big curiosity was the new Girl, but he always deferred first romantic dibs to me. We had been doing it since high school. I realized it was no less juvenile in our thirties, and most women would have considered it at least somewhat degrading and sexist. Honestly, we didn't mean it that way. At least *I* didn't. I just got bored by the end of winter.

"Cute, huh?" We understood that 'cute' encompassed face and figure alike. "Blonde? Brunette? *Please*, tell me she's a redhead!"

"Well, her hair's kind of dark brown and—" It was hard to come up with the right description for it. "Frothy."

"What?"

"You know, wild and curly, but not as if she had it done at a beauty shop."

"So, she's *au naturel*."

"That's one way to put it."

"How old?"

"She's fairly young. Twenty-two, Ma said." In my opinion, that was still on the young side. Derek's main concern was not getting in trouble with jailbait.

"She attached?"

"Didn't see any wedding or engagement rings. She does wear a gold band, just not on her left hand." Not that a ring on any finger would have deterred him.

"So, are you going to pass on her?"

I didn't have to think about it. I knew from experience that messing around with live-in help complicated my life exponentially. Once in a while, a Girl seemed like a good package deal, but by the end of the summer, she would already have us married with babies. Or I would find out she was only taking a break from her boyfriend or, worse yet, her husband. There was, of course, the temptation of convenience, given the proximity of our rooms, but that made it all the messier. Unless a Girl turned out to be my undeniable soul mate, not frilling up my bathroom with potpourris and candles or attempting an autobiographical discourse in the span of an evening, I would keep my self-preserving distance. Derek knew it, but he still needed to hear me say, "She's all yours."

Giving me one last opportunity to fix all that was wrong with my life in the sack, Derek-style, he asked, "You sure?"

"Yup."

Unfortunately, it didn't seem as if there were any 'fixing' my life. Sure, I griped about it, about how if I had been born eight years earlier, like my brother, with his looks and scholarship-worthy intellect, if I had escaped to college before Dad's accident, I would have been the one living in Boston with the beautiful wife. The truth was, I loved being a shipwright. The Wesley House bed and breakfast I could have done without, but it was part of our history, part of the town, part of its bronze-plaqued heritage.

Even if I had the option of looking for a different life, that was not what I wanted. I didn't aspire to anything near greatness, only something substantial enough to leave a wake. That didn't seem like too much to ask, but it sure didn't diminish my guilt as I periodically withdrew to my remote island of resentment and discontent.

I always passed it off as a seasonal thing, but this year, my restlessness pulled at me like a riptide on a windless day. Rowing against it was the right thing to do, and I had been doing it for weeks, but one distraction and I feared the current would carry me away.

Chapter 4

BUCK CARRIED THE STEPLADDER, FOLLOWING Marlena from window to window. Wavy glass panes squeaked beneath paper towels as she wiped. Buck rambled on, as usual, about ever-resourceful Captain Wesley, interspersed with old World War II stories. She paused to ask an occasional question, listening for a moment before beginning a new pane. Did she go about work at a slow, unhurried pace to accommodate Buck, or was it just that nonchalant way of hers? It didn't really matter—I appreciated the way she listened to him without glazing over.

During dinner, I sat through another one of her staring episodes, but when Buck cleared his throat and introduced a story, he seized her full attention. Afterward, he invited her to watch television.

"*Jeopardy* and *I Love Lucy*? I've never heard of that," she said. "I'd rather read."

Sure enough, when I came in at eleven, I found her in the parlor again, her knees up under her umbrella of a skirt with a book perched atop them. She read in an undertone. I paused and watched her read—and when I say read, I don't mean casually turning pages, I mean completely absorbing text—from a tired old hardcover from The Wesley House library.

A few days later, when Mother gave her a half-hour break right after lunch, when I returned to work, I stopped scraping paint and found myself staring. Watching her read, I could almost follow the story. Her immersion was so complete and uninhibited that every fluctuation of emotion showed on her face. Delight. Shock. Lust. Excitement. Horror. Grief. The whole gamut of human experience. She must have been reading the most incredible story ever written, and there it had been hiding in The Wesley House library the whole time. From then on, I took note of which stories she read more than once. She favored *Robinson Crusoe*. At the rate she was going, she probably intended to read every book in the house at least once. Except mine, of course. No one would be reading that anytime soon.

Fortunately for Buck, she loved stories. Having a new audience enlivened him. He smiled more and appeared less vacant. Marlena's company seemed to stall—dare I say reverse—his decline. She had no idea what he used to be, and that likely made it easier to spend time with him and tolerate his ever-increasing peculiarities. Not that she would recognize peculiarity in anyone else. She added a whole new dimension to the word.

For instance, while I scraped paint from the soffits, Buck invited her to fish off the dock. I couldn't figure out why she wanted to rummage through my cutoff pile.

"I need a scrap. Something long and narrow," she said.

From my ladder, I directed her to the rear of the boatshed. When she returned, she had a knife in hand, whittling the tip of some spruce.

"Find what you need?"

"Yes. Thank you." She offered a giddy grin.

Before I could ask what she had in mind, she skipped down the dock toward Buck and his pail. They exchanged a few words and tied fishing line to the blunt end of her stick. I nearly fell from the third story when she sent her tapered scrap flying like a javelin into the shallow water near the dock. At first glance, it was an amusing spectacle. Then, on her third attempt, she speared a cunner. Very peculiar.

🌊 FOR THE BETTER PART OF THAT WEEK, I SCRAPED PAINT during daylight and worked in the boatshed after dark. I had made some headway on the planking project, but by eleven at night, I needed a bit of hardware. I planned a trip to the chandler the next morning. Given the vice-like squeeze I had been under, I could have added a gronicle press to the list.

As soon as Buck meandered out to the boatshed with his new sidekick Marlena, it occurred to me that she might solve my hardware dilemma. Buck still knew everything he ever did about shipbuilding hardware. All he needed was a chauffeur.

As I opened my mouth to speak, Buck cut in. "You going with my soup on this project?"

"Yup," I said, holding my keys out to Marlena and gestured toward my beater pickup. "How would you like to take Buck for a ride?"

Her blank expression gave way to befuddlement. "I can't drive."

"What do you mean?"

"I don't have a license. I don't even know how to drive."

"You can't be serious."

She shrugged. "I am serious. Besides, I don't even like being in a car. They move too fast."

"But Mother said you came on a bus all the way from Kansas."

"That's different. I had no choice … and besides, I didn't drive the bus, did I?"

I couldn't refute that logic, but who above the age of sixteen didn't want to drive?

As she walked away, she turned and said, "You should paint your truck red with yellow and orange flames on the side," and then kept walking.

I climbed behind the wheel, chuckling at the thought of flames—or paint for that matter—on my old rust bucket. It didn't even merit primer!

Winding along the coastal highway to the far end of town, I made it to the chandler in no time. However, in six weeks the drive wouldn't be so easy. Halfway through June, Heritage

Week frenzy would jolt our sleepy little town awake. For over a century, we had been commemorating Wesleyville's founding, honoring my family's lineage, featuring, of course, our ancestor Captain William Wesley. It had become quite the tourist attraction, more like a county fair, with a parade and all sorts of competitions, culminating in a sailboat race. For those nine days, tourists booked every bed and breakfast, hotel, and motel within forty miles inland.

Fortunately, nothing more than showing up was required of me. In spite of Buck's short-term memory problems, I was confident that he still had enough presence of mind to ramble some dissertation at the commencement. The townsfolk expected it. Besides, no one seemed in a hurry for me to fill his shoes, and technically, Billy, the firstborn, should have been the one to step into them. Since Billy came home only during Heritage Week, he was in a position to carry on the tradition, but he wouldn't. Someday, Buck would pass on the so-called privilege, and I would embrace it about as well as I did all of my other conveniently-bypassed-by-my-brother obligations.

My truck groaned, heaving over solidified ruts in front of the boatshed. Settling into its familiar grooves, it halted with a thud. With my bag of bronze, I headed into the boatshed. That ray of light shot through the roof again. Something about the way it ushered a haze of light along a dark path made me hate the idea of repairing that hole. Breathing in wood shavings and varnish, I stepped into the beam of light and fell into a nostalgic lapse.

There was a certain romance to living on the water and being skilled in a centuries-old trade that was the backbone of the maritime industry. Too often, my harried pace distanced me from the gratitude I should have felt for my handed-down profession. As a seventh-generation shipwright, I had at my disposal decades' worth of accumulated lumber stock, well-equipped dry dock and trade-specific tools, little of which I had a hand in acquiring. Sometimes I took for granted the clientele and esteem bestowed upon me simply because of the Wesley reputation and skills I absorbed from the time I was old enough to walk.

Getting back on track, I grabbed the paint pail, a screwdriver, and a mixing stick. As I shuffled my way toward the house, Marlena's chattering drew my attention. I expected to see Buck at her side, given her animated discourse, but she knelt alone in Mother's perennial garden. When she spotted me, she quit talking, blushed, and then kept right on pulling dead leaves and loosening soil. Peculiar Girl.

Decaying mulch and tilled earth permeated the warming air—add salt, and it was one of the most pleasant aromas I knew. Bare trees stretched toward billowy skies, stark against varying shades of blue and beige. In a few weeks, Mother's flower gardens would spring to life, setting the town's standard for botanical perfection. Sightseeing women favored The Wesley House during Heritage Week's garden tour. During that week, I invited the men to peruse the boatyard and talk boats while I worked on an authentic rebuilding project, the *Mary-Leigh*.

My slow progress made her and me a standing joke with our regulars. If it weren't for Heritage Week, she would have scarcely seen progress at all. At least the regular boat-building enthusiasts and wannabees missed little in the restoration process.

The Wesley House also attracted architectural admirers and history buffs. Her sturdy bones were a credit to the shipbuilders who constructed her back in 1805. Antiques and family heirlooms appointed each room, all comfortably functional. People liked that they could sit in a chair where Captain Wesley had actually sat. I rarely gave it a second thought, probably because I rarely took time to sit. The master bedroom came with a steeper fee. Captain William Wesley took his first breath there. Later, he and his wife occupied the very same bed. However, he mostly slept in a berth, joining his English forefathers at sea, while his five brothers carried on the family business at the docks and in the boatyard.

That was the oft-repeated spiel I gave Marlena. I had been on my way upstairs and caught her in the parlor again, this time studying an old aerial photograph of the homestead. That's when she got me 'monologuing.'

"You sound just like your brochure and the Website." At least she didn't say I sounded just like Buck.

She turned to the mahogany-framed family tree.

"There's a William in every generation," she said, as if I didn't know.

"That's right."

"Even Buck is William?"

"Yeah. He picked up his nickname in the Navy."

"You and your brother were named after Captain Wesley's two sons."

"That's right."

Her slender finger traced the limbs of several generations past. "It looks as if Samuel's line died out."

"Yeah." I sounded inadvertently portentous. "He moved to New York to be a journalist when he was exactly my age. He never married."

"You have a wonderful history."

Her obsession with my family and our little town's past sparked my pride. She had likely read every passage of historical text in our house, and had even scoured our local library for any regional history she could lay her hands on. I liked that she looked to me to verify the truth of what she read or what Buck told her, as if I had some inside scoop on the past.

She refocused her attention on the Captain's portrait. "Have you ever noticed the dent on the side of Captain Wesley's telescope?"

I hadn't. "Looks like a smudge on the canvas to me."

"No. It's *definitely* a dent."

Now *she* was the authority?

She turned toward a glassed-in case of small metallic sailboats. "And these sailing trophies—they're yours?"

"Yeah." The Wesleyville race was nothing like those big-time regattas—we didn't even have a yacht club. All the locals knew it was a small-scale race that no one put a lot of stock in except those of us who competed.

Marlena returned her attention to the Captain and then glanced back at me, as if comparing our likeness. I waited for the often heard, 'Your resemblance is uncanny,' but instead, she asked, "Do you think *you'll* ever get married?"

If I appeared shocked, it didn't seem to faze her, nor did my awkward hesitation. Fidgeting with my earlobe, I looked her up and down. "At the moment, it doesn't look too hopeful."

To my relief, she left it at that. To my surprising disappointment, she exited the room without another word.

Just as well.

Chapter 5

EREK'S HUMMER SWUNG INTO THE WESLEY HOUSE dooryard, threatening to plow right into the boatshed. Did he hope to impress Marlena by humiliating my poor old rust bucket as he pulled in beside it? Given her opinion on paintjobs, perhaps she would be impressed with all that tinted glass and flashy lettering. Although he did make legitimate use of it in his line of work, I still thought a Hummer was overkill.

Derek climbed out, wearing only Ray-Bans and painting bib overalls. No shirt. Standard attire for him, but honestly, he looked ridiculous wearing that little on the first day of May, even if a warm front had moved in and he wasn't all pasty white, like me.

I slapped his bare shoulder as I walked past with a pail of paint. "Still saving up for the shirt?"

"Jealous?"

If I were jealous at all, it was only because he had escaped to the Caribbean whereas I was stuck in Maine. "No, but I love your new highlights."

He ran fingers through his hair and grinned. "Thanks for noticing."

With our preliminary banter out of the way, we got busy with paint.

"So, when do I get to meet her?" He scanned the yard and

peered through apple blossoms into second-story windows.

"Won't be long now."

We had been working outside for only an hour or so. It wasn't even noon and already sweat beaded on our foreheads. Right on cue, Marlena came out with a jug of water. She had this thing about hydrating. "If you're thirsty, you're already dehydrated," she would say, and wouldn't leave until I drank a cupful. We came down off the scaffolding together, but Derek moved quicker and accepted the first cup she held out.

With his eyes all over her, he accepted the glass with a wink. "I have the feeling this is going to be the best drink of water I've had in a long time."

Marlena smiled, focusing more on his chest than his face. For the first time since I had met her, she wasn't wearing her big sweater atop her full skirt—just a plain white T-shirt, slightly snug, and if she wore anything at all for support beneath, it wasn't much more than a whisper. She wasn't the only one staring.

She handed me a glass as I swatted the first black fly of the season. "Thanks."

"Where's your manners, Sam?" Derek nudged me. "Aren't you going to introduce us?"

"Yeah … Marlena, this is Derek," I said as Mitch's Buick pulled into the dooryard. I left Derek to work his charms with her and went over to see Mitch.

"How's the shoulder?" I asked.

He half-shrugged and his neck practically disappeared.

"How's your grip?"

His baby-face dimples deepened as a meaty hand enveloped mine. Even with diminished strength, he squeezed most of the color up into my forearm. I could have sworn my veins swelled.

"Jeez, Mitch," I said, and I wasn't exaggerating. I had never known a man stronger than him, or quieter.

It was hard to tell how much of him was padding and how much was muscle, since I had never seen him in anything less than a shirt and jeans. Most of the time, he wore a flannel shirt and his Carhartt overalls. Just the same, his grip didn't leave much to the imagination.

"Doc says I gotta wait to work."

"Think you could slap a little paint on with your left hand?"

"I 'spect so."

"Great." The extra worker would be helpful, but I also knew that since his wife had died a little over a year ago, he was looking to fill in some time. After an hour of painting, he went inside for the bathroom. That was the last we saw of him until lunch.

It occurred to me that he might have been more interested in Mother than painting. I suppose that shouldn't have surprised me. They had known each other for years. He and my dad had been best friends, and with his wife being gone and all, he was lonely. I wondered what Mother thought of his attention. Not that I would ask.

From the pictures of her youth, she probably could have had her pick of men. I suppose that even now she looked fit for her age, and she didn't wear her hair all piled up in teased curls like a lot of older women. She had a good head of silver hair with a youthful cut and likely still caught the eye of a few older gentlemen.

"What's with Mitch and your mom?" Derek asked, cutting in a second-story window.

I shrugged.

He shot me his raised risqué brow. I scowled, putting an end to that.

"Better question is what's with her?" Derek nodded toward Marlena, who knelt in the rose garden, weeding with Buck hovering at her side.

"What do you mean?"

"She's been pulling weeds in that same spot all morning."

"Yeah." I had noticed the same thing. "She doesn't move real fast, but I've got to say, she does get stuff done."

At that very moment, making me a liar, she leapt from the weeds, drew a good-size knife from the folds of her skirt like a sword from its sheath, and threw it at the ground, a little too close to Buck's feet. He reeled back but didn't lose his balance.

He picked up the knife, inspecting it. "What's a girl like you doing with a World War Two fighting knife?"

Her shoulders straightened defiantly. "Did you realize there are at least six hundred species of snakes that are known to be venomous?"

"Garter snakes are harmless." He eyed her and the knife before slapping it in her outstretched palm.

"I know." Marlena pushed the blade into her pocket. "But be careful, the head can still bite."

Derek looked at me, eyes agape. "This is the Girl you trust with your grandfather?"

"You'd just better watch yourself around her." I suppose I should have been a little more alarmed, but in my defense, I had seen her spear a fish. So what if she carried a knife. Maybe it was a Kansas thing.

At lunchtime, we all gathered at the picnic table on the deck.

Buck grabbed my arm as he sat. "You going with—"

"Yes, your soup, Buck." I said, taking my own seat.

Mitch nestled beside Mother, and I gave him a look. He responded with a timid shrug, as if admitting he had a thing for my mother. It was a subject we would never talk about. The reticence that made him so easy to work with out in the shop was the very trait that wouldn't allow us to discuss something so delicate.

Derek, on the other hand, was never at a loss for words. I couldn't wait to see what sort of conversation he might strike up with Marlena, or if he would strike out.

"Have you heard the one about the old couple who was speculating on what would become of the other at their death?" he started off.

Marlena looked at him with her typical befuddlement.

"Yeah," he continued, "the old woman said, 'Don't worry, Sweetie, I'll probably be acquitted.'"

I hadn't heard that one. I chuckled. So did everyone else, even Buck. She stared at Derek, her lips as tight as her brow.

Derek opened his mouth to explain. I wagged my head,

giving him the *don't bother* glare. I was no comedian, but I occasionally came up with some witty stuff. Marlena never got *any* of it and had none of the social grace to laugh anyway.

Derek tacked, adeptly moving on to his profession—his favorite topic, not just because it was all about him, but women did seem to find it entrancing. What could be more exciting than treasure hunting? I had known him long enough to realize he could embellish a story as well as Buck, but even if half of what he blustered was true, he had an enviable life outside of Wesleyville. He had enough booty stashed in the bank to be shamelessly casual about making a living. If he wasn't off on a hired hunt, he was back in town giving scuba diving or sailing lessons, or lending a hand on some project around the boatyard.

"Yeah, this kind of hands-on work, painting the old house, is a nice break from what I was doing all winter. I mean, diving off the Florida Keys is nice, but I really do miss home and my friends." He could sound so grounded.

Marlena perked up. "What do you mean, dive?"

"Just a hired treasure hunt off my cutter, is all." He snagged her attention like bass on a lure. "We took in a fairly good haul—paid for my vacation and then some."

Marlena's eyes continued on him, wide with interest. "How far south have you sailed?"

"Brazil's the southernmost destination, but Venezuela is by far my favorite." He was about to go off on a full-blown tangent about international waters and salvage rights, and she did let him go on for a bit before cutting in with another question.

"Have you ever found gold coins?"

"Sure, all the time."

"Are they worth any more than their weight?"

"Depends on what it is—"

"What if they once belonged to someone? Would they have to be returned?"

I cut him a look, hoping to squash his exuberance.

"Well, Marlena, I'd hate to commit one way or the other. It all depends."

"Depends on what?"

"It's all rather complicated and involved, but I think you'd find it very interesting. Why don't I explain it to you over a beer at The Bilge?"

"I don't drink beer."

I chuckled.

Derek persisted. "Then how about a game of darts or pool?"

I would have wagered good money that she had never even been in a bar or played darts, but she would beat him hands-down, given the way she could spear a fish at twenty feet and behead a garden-variety snake. I hoped she would take him up on it. Instead, she rose from the table and gave him one of her most genuine smiles. "No thank you."

Little fishy got away.

Marlena's willingness to converse surprised me. I attributed it to Derek's company—a common phenomenon. However, even more to my surprise, she didn't come back outside for the rest of the afternoon, completely deflating Derek, which I found all too gratifying.

I never would have said it to Derek, but his moving in on Marlena made me a little uncomfortable. I didn't see her being savvy with men like him. It was none of my business, but there were reasons why our town's most eligible bachelor hadn't married or even come close to it.

Chapter 6

I FLOPPED THE LAST BIT OF STILL-WARM APPLE crisp into my bowl, breathing in cinnamon as I carried it through the kitchen and out the back door. A breeze cooled my forehead. I made my way to the lawn swing—one of those wooden double-seaters—overlooking the bay and the tiny patch of sand we called 'the launch pad.' To the southeast, I had a clear view of the Atlantic through a narrow swath between islets. The boatshed partially blocked the most picturesque harbor scene, making it the *second*-best view in the area. The best view was my own private vista, visible from my bedroom window.

Polishing off my last few bites of streusel, I nudged the ground just enough to keep the swing in motion. When Marlena sauntered over, she hovered as if waiting for an invitation. I stopped the swing and glanced at the empty place beside me.

Marlena sat, hugging the far end, as if that might lengthen the six inches between us. She stared at the bay, pulling tangles of hair from her face.

"No dessert?" I asked in my friendliest voice.

"Too sweet."

Silence.

"Nice day," I said.

She nodded.

Another long, drawn-out, awkward silence. If she didn't want to talk, why had she bothered to come out and sit beside me? Resigning myself to quiet discomfort, I set my bowl between us and stretched my arms, clasping my hands behind my head.

From the northwest, shafts of light broke through heavy clouds at just the right angle, setting Cuttermann's Island aglow. About a mile out, it wasn't a particularly visible patch of low-lying land, but the way the light was hitting it made it look as if it were on fire. I wished I had my camera, or better yet, my *Firefly* up and running.

Marlena inhaled a deep, throaty breath and let it out, diverting my attention.

"I know you're a writer," she said. "I read your articles."

That was the last thing I expected her to say. I didn't have a chance to respond before she continued, "I can hear you typing in your room at night. Last night, I heard you for hours. You were typing fast. You must have had a lot to say."

I gave her a long look. "You know, I can also hear *you* in your room. Last night, you were talking to yourself, and I have to say, it was a bit distracting." I found her soliloquies alarming at first, but took consolation in the fact that I never heard her arguing.

"I don't talk to *myself*."

I folded my arms across my chest. "So, then, who were you talking to?" I thought she might say Captain Wesley.

"I talk to God."

I assumed she had at least some spiritual inclination, because every night before dinner, after Mother said grace, Marlena usually lingered in what seemed to be an extended prayer of her own. Mother must have also noticed, because one time she invited Marlena to go to church with her on Sundays, but she declined, not with her usually appreciative, *No thanks*, but instead, with an *I'd-rather-throw-myself-in-front-of-the-church-bus* eye roll. I found it amusing, because, honestly, that's how I felt, too. Not that I didn't believe in God or thought church wasn't worthwhile, but all that formality and the time—it seemed excessive and pointless in a life as busy as mine. I just hoped she wasn't going to get all religious on me. I acknowledged her admission with a stifling, "Oh."

Mercifully, she rerouted. "What are you writing?"

How could that one question catch me so unprepared?

"Just stuff." How lame was that? I had been hoping for conversation, she had hit on the one topic I would have loved to talk about, and that was all I could come up with. I wanted her to press further, to ask if it were another article or a short story. I wanted her to stumble onto the big questions: *Have you ever written a novel? What's it about? Could I read it?* Instead, she blushed and looked away. I ruined that conversation.

She sighed again. "If you had enough money to hire someone to do everything you do around here, how would you spend your time?"

I studied her face, as if assessing the wind's shift. She sure knew how to force a jibe. I smiled. "I'd write, finish Buck's yawl, and sail."

She tipped her head, squinting through dark lashes. "I think it would be better if you just wrote."

"Why's that?"

"Because writing is much safer, and so is simply building a boat."

"What's the point in building a boat if you don't sail it?"

She twisted her mouth. "Well, maybe you could build something else—like a house."

I grinned. "I already have a house."

"But don't you see? Boats are very dangerous."

"Boats aren't dangerous," I chuckled. "People are."

"Some boats are. Sailboats are. They seem like a very dangerous way to enjoy the water."

I couldn't help but laugh out loud.

"Why is that funny?" she asked.

"You've never even been in a sailboat, have you?"

"No."

"Well, I have. Hundreds of times."

Her eyes narrowed "Hundreds?"

"Well, I haven't actually kept track, but I can assure you, sailing is the most perfect way to enjoy the water. Besides, there's different kinds of sailing. The kind I do is perfectly safe."

"You've never flipped a boat?"

"Capsize? Sure I have, but that's why you learn to swim."

Her full lips thinned. "Hmm."

"You do know how to swim, don't you?"

"Of course I do," she shot back as wind pulled her curls in every direction.

I laughed again.

She grinned. "Do you think I'm funny?"

I smiled at the innocence of her question. "Yes."

"Why?"

"You just are."

Her mouth softened, blossoming into a full smile, and she erupted with a child's giggle. "I think you're the one who's funny."

Odd as she was, I liked her. I had compromised my indifference. At the very least, she would make her way into my journal that night.

Chapter 7

GRAY ALKYD-BASED PAINT SPECKLED DEREK'S bare arms. He wiped his brow, glancing from the scaffolding down to Marlena and Buck, tying knots on the yard swing, and then back at me. "Thought you weren't interested."

Craning from the third story, I caught Marlena's smile. She nearly threw my balance.

"I'm not," I said, although Derek probably detected how I had kept my eye on her most of the morning.

"Really?" he snorted. "That's not how it looks from here."

"I'm not interested in her *that* way," I insisted, but it felt like a lie.

Derek would make assumptions about my brief preoccupation, but that wouldn't slow his pursuit of her.

"Marlena!" he called out, performing a gymnastic dismount from the scaffold. His overall strap unhooked. "What does a guy have to do to get a drink around here?"

"All you have to do is ask," she responded with her usual willingness and returned to the house. We both enjoyed the view as a breeze caught her light cotton skirt, exposing the better part of her legs.

I landed beside him. "Nice dismount, Nancy—your booby's showing."

Derek flexed his pecs with a grin. Within seconds, Marlena

returned, embracing the sweating water pitcher and eyeing his half-bare torso.

He reached for both cups. "I'll hold them."

As she poured, they stared at each other's chests. She nearly watered his shoes.

He shoved a sloshing cup at me with a wink and ushered Marlena back over to the swing.

"You know, Marlena," he said, intentionally loud enough for me to hear and thus learn from the master. "You work awfully hard around here. You ought to take an evening off."

"I already have every evening to myself." She sat more opposite than beside him.

He moved in closer and she didn't back away.

"Tell me, what do you do with all that time?" He rested his arm on the back of the swing between them.

"Mostly, I read." She tilted her head back, tossing her hair over her shoulder, the way she often did.

Derek's hand tangled itself in her curls. She didn't seem to mind as he played with a few locks. "What do you enjoy reading?"

Her face lit up as she leaned toward him. "I like to read about all kinds of things ... about places, and people."

I hovered nearby, wondering how far he would get.

He winked. "I bet you like those romance novels too."

She shrugged. "Is that what you read?"

He chuckled. "Reading is fine, but I think experiencing is more fun, don't you?"

Moving in with precision, he traced her jaw with the tip of his thumb.

She squirmed, glancing back at me. "Maybe."

Moving in closer, he lowered his voice, but I could still hear him. "What do you say we go out some time and try the things you've been reading about?"

She didn't back off. She didn't act affronted. She didn't even blush. All she said was, "That's a lovely invitation, Derek, but I don't know you well enough to say yes."

With that, she rose and returned to the house.

"Smooth," I said as he stood in astonishment, "you got her

right where you want her—at home with a good book. I should be taking notes!"

"She's just playing hard to get."

"Well, this little fishy's gonna be really hard to get if she keeps spitting out your bait."

He shrugged it off.

We worked for another hour or so when Mitch joined us, just in time for lunch. Mother called us to the table right as the postal carrier stopped at our box. Detouring, I retrieved the mail. When I arrived at the kitchen table, I found Mitch beside Mother and Derek beside Marlena. No big surprises there. The surprise came at the bottom of the usual stack of flyers, bills, and other junk mail; a letter for Marlena. The return addressee was Capt. David Putnam.

I slid it past Derek, under his full attention, and placed it before Marlena.

Her eyes beamed. "It's for me?"

"That's right. Airmail all the way from the Mediterranean—Crete, to be specific, forwarded from Kansas."

An overseas letter from a man struck me as curious, though I didn't know why. Perhaps it was because of the way she brought her fingertips to her parted lips, as if feeling the formation of his name, "Dave ...."

She rose, clutching the letter to her bosom, and hurried from the room. Her footfall never slowed as she made her way up to the third floor. Not until Mother had cleared dishes and Derek went back outside did she reappear. I met her on my way out of the bathroom. Her usually lively eyes evaded mine. I wanted to ask about her captain friend. Perhaps he was a relative. I even tried to work him in as some sort of romantic interest, as if a preexisting boyfriend might add a little clarity to her profile and make it easier to remain detached. Even so, my ambivalence didn't keep me from remarking, "No bad news, I hope."

She shrugged, avoiding eye contact.

Derek and I worked until dusk, but he skipped out before supper. He said he had an appointment, but I think he was trying to match Marlena's hard-to-get tactic. By the time we sat around the table, Marlena seemed more herself, but not in her typical staring way. I detected some residual sadness in her downcast expression. Maybe I was looking for it, and that's why, when her eyes wandered to mine, she caught *me* staring. For heart-pounding seconds, neither of us looked away.

I had inched completely over the line.

Working in the hot sun all afternoon had sapped my motivation, and so what should have amounted to four additional hours in the shop ended up being only two. I didn't know what time I shut things down for the night, but when I came into the kitchen, Mother had the phone in hand. Her pinched lips drained of color.

Typically, Billy called later in the evening, at his convenience, and when I overheard Mother say, "Oh, you know, he's a little forgetful, but I'm thirty years younger and even *I* forget things now and then," I knew it was my brother.

As soon as she spotted me, she evaded any further conversation about her least favorite subject and said, "Sammy just came in. Why don't you say hello to your little brother?"

Billy hated being passed off on the telephone as much as I did. She registered neither of our protests and handed me the phone.

I gave the receiver an irritated glare meant for my mother. "Hey, Billy, how's it going?"

It was amazing how less than three hundred miles of phone line felt like three hundred *thousand*.

"Everything's great," he said. "Perfect, actually."

"How's Elaine?" I asked as Mother slipped out of the room.

"Great—real busy—just got that promotion to head of pediatrics."

"That's terrific … and how are things going in the psych ward?"

"Well, you know, rehab is a booming business. In fact, I'm putting my name in to head up the department."

"No doubt you'll get it." I tried to sound as if I cared.

After a stiff silence, he asked, "So, how's Buck doing?"

"What did Ma tell you?"

"She told me he's doing fine for the most part." I deliberated on how much more to say until he added, "But you know how she is—typical enabler response."

In fact, I did know how Mother was, but when he started diagnosing her as an enabler, a lecture on our 'dysfunctional family dynamics' would surely follow.

I yanked the tangled cord, staring out the back door at my reflection. Tired eyes stared back. "Yeah ... I guess he's getting along pretty well. His cholesterol and blood pressure are right where they should be, and so far he's pharmaceutically independent, so in my book, that says he's doing great." I would have mentioned the wandering issue, but that would only set him off, and with Marlena keeping Buck occupied, it seemed irrelevant.

Right then, Mother returned. "Hey, Ma wants to say good night—I'll talk to you later."

"Yeah, see you in a few weeks," he said as I passed the phone back to Mother and made my getaway.

Billy had a label for everything. And a solution. Maybe we didn't function as well as I would have liked, but it seemed to me that the biggest dysfunction had been between him and Dad—but that was another story. Billy was eight years my senior and left right after graduating high school, so he didn't really know me, although he thought he did. Admittedly, in a clinical sense, I didn't stray too far from the model of someone who had lost his father at eleven. Sure, I felt the need to fill Dad's shoes, but it wasn't as if I didn't have a strong father figure as I grew up. What I didn't have was a strong big-brother figure.

Billy had distanced himself from our life. It was ironic how he chose to visit during the one week that celebrated our provincial lifestyle. Likely, he picked that time because he needed the scheduled activities around town for convenient escape from the house and all its 'dysfunction.' He would come with his beautiful wife, Elaine, and no offspring or any plans to reproduce. Their professional lives didn't allow for such impingements. As it was, their life barely allowed for existing family.

Chapter 8

A S SOON AS WE FINISHED PAINTING THE HOUSE, things got even busier. Mitch's physical therapist gave him the okay to get back to work, which was a big help with the Memorial Day push. Even at half his usual output, he worked hard, but I doubted he would be his normal, focused self. There was no denying his preoccupation. In a way, it was funny to watch him trying to act inconspicuous while keeping an eye out for Mother.

Over the big holiday weekend, I entrusted Marlena with mending my jib sail, and while I worked in the shop late one afternoon, I thought about our conversations on the swing and around the house. The past month had been a blur, but one thing that stuck in my head was what she had said to me in the kitchen one morning, when she asked about my writing again. I had explained to her about revising and edits. She had asked, "Don't you like it the way it is?" I told her I wouldn't bother with it if there wasn't something about it I liked. She had smiled and said, "I think you and I bother with each other for the same reason."

That was the last time we had found any opportunity to talk, just the two of us. Ever since, Mother, Buck, Mitch, or Derek always interrupted or walked in on us. In addition, guests had been milling around for several weeks. I wouldn't have any real privacy again until late October. I didn't begrudge it per se—that's the way it had been my entire life, and we relied on the income—but this year I wished I could send everyone home. Therefore, I practically lived out in the shop.

I regrouped my work area, getting ready for the next project, sharpening a few tools. Sparks were flying like tiny shimmering daggers from my grinding wheel when I noticed her in the doorway, just like that first day. I had no idea how long she had been waiting, standing at attention with my folded sail in hand.

I flipped the grinder switch off. "Done already?"

"Yes. I'll leave it on your bench." She took a slow step forward.

"Bring it over." I moved toward her. "Let me see."

She had the mended area neatly visible for my inspection.

"It looks nice. You did a good job." I winked. "I may have to promote you to shipwright's assistant."

She blushed. "Well, I'll let you get back to work." With that, she spun and walked out.

Did she assume that when I worked in the boatshed I was too busy for her? That certainly had been the case over the past month. I should have been grateful that she wasn't eating up my time. Why was I even thinking about her, irritated that she walked off? If I had told her to stick around, I would have wasted far less time than I did trying to convince myself that it didn't matter. So what if I couldn't figure her out. So what if every time she looked at me I felt as if she were probing my thoughts.

Sitting across from her at the dinner table made it worse. Although several guests had joined us, no one demanded my attention. During a conversational lull, my imagination took liberty, leaping from the aroma of hot biscuits to the dab of butter dripping from Marlena's asparagus spear, down the front of her shirt … and on to thoroughly enjoying the way she licked her fingers. Well, it wasn't long before those thoughts had me immersed in some lewd fantasy. When I caught myself staring, so had she. It was impossible, but I swear she had intercepted my most intimate thought. It showed as a blush on her cheeks and a twisted brow. My heart rate spiked. Unnerved, I couldn't break away from those imploring eyes.

Later on, after I headed to my room for the night, I sat at my keyboard, trying to concentrate. I must have reread the same paragraph ten times before I resigned myself to shutting down the computer. After five minutes in bed, I counted off twelve strikes on the parlor grandfather clock. I knew that if I stayed in bed, I would be staring at the full moon for hours, so I crept from my bedroom, listening for sounds of her across the hall. Only the clock's pulse cut the silence. The second-floor landing creaked as I headed down. I grabbed my jacket from the hall tree and then slipped out the back door.

A light breeze had drifted in from the northeast, pushing out the balmy afternoon air. There wasn't enough chill to see my breath, but it raised goose bumps on my arms as I fumbled for sleeves. I stepped off the deck, heading to the swing. In five paces, I saw a curly-headed occupant in my spot.

I had to admit, the sight of her more than pleasantly surprised me. A patchwork quilt enveloped her, and beneath it I imagined she wore next to nothing. A very cozy sight indeed. She turned and smiled. I took my place beside her, and although she could have shifted over a bit, giving me more room, she didn't. Her eyes found mine. It wasn't long before I had envisioned every possible scenario for how our encounter might turn out.

I came right out and asked, "Why did you come here?"

She drew in her lower lip. Her gaze wandered. "I read about your town and wanted to see it for myself."

"There are hundreds of bed and breakfasts up and down the coast. Why come here?"

"Because of your history ... because of Captain Wesley."

I chuckled. "You've got a thing for him."

"I guess I sort of do." She wrapped the quilt tighter. In the bright moonlight, I thought she might have blushed.

"Why the fascination with him?"

"I think he's interesting, that's all." She glanced at me. "But you're far more interesting."

"Is that right?"

"Well, yes ... I mean ... you are alive, after all."

I laughed. "So, the fact that I'm breathing makes me interesting?"

"It's definitely an asset," she grinned.

I was more amused than disillusioned.

She looked straight at me. "You know how quiet people are, Samuel. We have a lot going on inside—things no one would ever imagine. I don't know what goes on inside your head, but it would be very interesting to find out."

Or so she thought. Most days, my brain felt like a hamster on a wheel.

She continued, "Of course, you don't know me well enough to tell me, but it makes me curious about what you write. What are you working on now?"

"It's a novel. Based on a captain lost at sea. About his family waiting at home."

"Is it about Captain Wesley?"

"It's a fictional character, but yes, based on him."

"What do *you* think really happened to him?"

"Well, Buck's pretty much covered all the bases—the noble and heroic ones, that is. Personally, I think he got caught up in something, and that's the slant I'm embellishing."

Her eyes widened. "Is there a shipwreck?"

"Maybe."

"I knew it!"

So much for originality.

"I guess it's a premise done to death," I said, struck by my own candor.

"I don't think so." Her eyes flickered with excitement. "I absolutely love shipwreck stories."

"I hope publishers love them as much."

"Could I read it?"

I expected that question, but it still made words catch in my throat. "To be honest, Marlena, I'm not sure if I'm comfortable passing it on to anyone until I polish it some more."

"Okay." Her voice wilted. "I hope it wasn't rude for me to

ask."

"It wasn't rude at all."

"It's just that I've been told I'm rude. I don't mean to be. It just comes naturally."

I didn't think she meant to be funny, but I chuckled.

"You think I'm joking," she said.

"No." I focused on the curve of her lips and then her unfathomable eyes. "I think you're being honest."

She looked at me, not just meeting my gaze, but scrutinizing every inch of my face as well, every line, every whisker, and every hair receding from my forehead.

"I am a very honest person," she said in a whisper that brought me nearer, just close enough to pick up the scent of her. She had to have seen what impulse I was restraining, because a quiver grazed her lips. When I moved in to kiss her, she turned away.

I took a deep breath, hoping to ease back into conversation. "Tell me about where you're from."

She stared off for several long seconds.

"Not much to tell. I lived in a rural prairie farmhouse in Kansas with my aunt and uncle and a cousin." She didn't look at me as she continued, "You know, typical stuff. Chores, schoolwork, church, and more chores. That's all."

"Do you plan on returning to Kansas at the end of the summer?"

"Oh, my goodness, no."

I wanted to ask about her plans, but I didn't. Her past interested me more. "No parents?"

She shook her head and stiffened, pulling the quilt tighter. Seconds turned into what seemed like minutes of silence as her brow remained furrowed.

Her lips finally softened. "Most of my life, I had no idea where I was, but I never felt lost. Not ever—not until I knew exactly where I was." She faced me again. "Have you ever felt that way?"

I found her statement odd, kind of a paradox. I wanted to say, *Yeah, I feel lost all the time*, but that wasn't entirely true. I only felt that way lately, so I said, "Sometimes." My admission made me brave, perhaps a bit reckless. "Tell me, Marlena, how do you feel right at this moment?"

She smiled. "I can't tell you."

"Is that because you don't know how you feel, or you don't want to tell me?"

She searched my eyes. "I know how I feel, but it's too soon to know if it will change, and too soon for you to hear it."

I wanted to contradict her. I wanted to hear it. Even though she was probably right, I was going for it—was about to say, *I want to know. I want to know everything about you,* when she stood, gathering the quilt around her. Her lips twitched with a wistful smile and she left.

I cannot explain the overwhelming mixture of frustration and sadness that twisted my insides as she walked away. I had an urge to call out after her, but I didn't. Instead, I kicked at the grass, wondering about a girl from Kansas who walked away every time the conversation was on the verge of taking off.

Sitting alone, I thought about the things she had said. I wondered about what might have happened to her parents. I knew how it felt to lose one, and I probably didn't even realize all the ways it had affected me, but it wasn't for the good. Whether her circumstances were the result of death or abandonment or whatever bizarre situation might leave a person parentless, they had shaped her and undoubtedly accounted for some of her peculiarity. I also wondered if she was now feeling lost. I sure was.

As I headed upstairs, I decided that the next day, when she was busy with something downstairs, I would leave my manuscript in her room. That night, while lying in bed, I was relieved I didn't kiss her, but it didn't stop me from imagining how it would have felt.

Chapter 9

EREK'S HARD-TO-GET PHASE DIDN'T LAST. HE HAD been showing up nearly every day for the past several weeks, trying to make headway with Marlena and monitoring my level of interest. I had to admit, since Marlena and I sat in the moonlight, she had me more interested than disinterested.

"Doesn't she ever leave the old man's side?" He hoisted a roll of roofing felt from the pickup bed to his shoulder. Perspiration fringed his hair.

I dropped a bundle of shingles onto the ground beside the boatshed. "Jealous?"

"Better believe it!" He grabbed the pail of tar and another heavy bundle. One glance in Marlena's direction and I knew why he had doubled his effort. She was on her way over with water.

I met her halfway as Derek dropped his load.

"Perfect timing, as usual." I accepted a glass.

Right as Derek caught up, she said to me, "You changed your mind."

It took me a second to realize she was talking about my manuscript. I smiled, leaving her words dangling for Derek's benefit.

Marlena handed him a cup with far less than her usual interest in his chest. "I'll leave the jug here on the tailgate."

She turned to walk away and then peered back at me. "I can hardly wait!" she said and hurried back to Buck.

Derek squinted in suspicion. "Can hardly wait for what?"

"It's nothing." I knew he couldn't leave it alone.

"You two got something going on?" His competitive brow shot up as he laughed, only half-joking.

"Give it a rest, buddy." I chuckled. "She just wanted to read some stuff I've written. She's giddy over it, that's all. Seriously, man, you need to chill."

His evil eye sparked and I stared him down for a second before returning to the shed. Not that I thought he had a chance with Marlena, but I had hoped some cute tourist would sidetrack him and he would back off. To make things worse, in two weeks our rivalry would come to a head at the sailing race. Each of us had won over the years, me more than him, so he wasn't liable to acquiesce on any other issues of manliness. If he was getting a little something in the sack, I could tolerate him much better, but this year, his frustrated obsession with Marlena would make him unbearable.

Already, I had to watch myself with her while he was around, knowing he wondered what I had been up to behind his back. Of course, he wouldn't say anything about it, not until he was on the verge of exploding. He always stewed on things for weeks. When he finally boiled over—watch out! I had never pushed him to that point, not that I ever had to be particularly careful. I guess that's why we were still friends—I didn't tend to get under his skin. Sometimes, I wondered if it was because he hadn't ever viewed me as a threat, and in those areas where it had been important for him to feel superior, he usually was.

He was the jock in high school. I was the assistant editor of the school paper. He dated the cheerleaders. I was so shy that I was grateful to get a date at all and usually with his assistance. Although my family was more prominent, his had more money. I might have pulled better grades, but he was the entrepreneur and knew how to multiply his cash, and still did. Just the same, the superiority gap had narrowed over the years. Now that we had both established ourselves as respected men in the community, the scales had balanced, but I wondered if it contributed to our increasing competitiveness. The bigger question was, how could one cute girl reduce me—an otherwise dignified individual—into a junior high blockhead, all too willing to spar with a tool like Derek? Sometimes I even wondered why we were still friends. I guess old habits were hard to break.

⚓TOO TIRED TO WORK AND TOO RESTLESS TO SLEEP, I stretched back in my chair, again staring at the cursor on my monitor. Household noise had quit an hour ago. Had Marlena fallen asleep? Answering my wondering, her bedroom latch clicked and a soft tap brought me to my feet, stealing my breath before I even opened the door. She stood, barefooted, still dressed in a long cotton skirt and T-shirt, clutching my manuscript tight to her chest. She'd had it for well over a week.

She handed it over. "I finished."

She peeked around me as I glanced at the stack of papers and back at her. "You want to come in?"

"I guess, for a minute."

I was dying to ask, but before I summoned the courage, she bailed me out. "I liked it."

I took that as generic *'it was readable'* feedback.

She continued, "I made notes on sticky papers and put them by the lines and phrases I liked. I hope you don't mind, but there were a few places where I wasn't sure what you were saying, and I put a note next to them too. But don't worry, there weren't many."

I thumbed through the pages. Nearly every one had a note attached. I was torn between wishing she would leave so I could read what she had written and hoping she wouldn't leave right away. I looked up as she scanned my room. There wasn't much to see. Aside from the usual furnishings, I had only a couple boat models and my computer against the backdrop of mismatching plaids.

I asked, "Do you want to sit down for a minute?"

Strange how I had never had a girl in my room. Even when I

was involved with someone, we had always ended up in her room. Mine had always been off-limits. Part of it had to do with Mother being in the house, but it was mostly a privacy thing. My one unequivocal boundary. I changed my own sheets, made my bed when I felt like it, dusted and vacuumed on my own schedule, though I did tend to keep it moderately tidy. Sitting on my made bed, I set the manuscript aside. Marlena sat at my desk with the chair swiveled to face me. Her intense eyes focused, as usual, on me. Her lips thinned, then softened and pursed again. I tilted my head, encouraging her to speak.

"I like your room."

"Come on, it's horribly decorated and smells like the workshop."

Her voice dropped to a lusty whisper. "It smells like you."

With unexpected impact, her words struck me as incredibly sensual.

"I know how to use a computer and I can type," she said, deflating anything rising within me. "I enjoyed the opening paragraphs. Even though I've never been sailing, the way you wrote about it made me feel like I was there. I even got a little nervous."

For the first time, my investment of energies had paid off. How could one insignificant girl's opinion validate me so completely? Now, I wanted to read every notation she had made. I had a hundred questions and her remarks would spark a hundred more.

Trying to mask my self-absorption, I asked, "Have you ever thought about writing?"

"Me? Oh, I just keep a little journal, but I'm no author." Then, after staring at me with so much concentration that it was almost painful to watch, she finally blurted, "But, I do have a story."

"What's it about?"

She bit her lip. "It's about what happens when a man pursues adventure over his family."

"Really." I had to wonder how a girl like her would come up

with a theme like that. I would have imagined she would have a coming-of-age story about a girl on a cross-country bus ride. She snagged my interest. "I'd like to hear about it."

"Well, it's a rather long story. Since it's so late, I probably shouldn't start telling it tonight."

"Then you should write it down."

"Perhaps. But for now, it's a story that I'd like to tell you face to face. It's just that it would take a while." She blushed again as her gaze dropped to her lap. "You probably don't even have time for it."

Without giving it a whole lot of forethought, I said, "I'll be taking my little sailboat out tomorrow for a test run before the race. You could come with me. We could pack a lunch and take it over to Cuttermann's Island. It would give us some time."

"I don't know … I'm sort of nervous about sailing. What if there's too much wind and we go too fast? We might flip."

"Speed isn't what capsizes a boat." I chuckled. "But I can make it go only as fast as you're comfortable with."

"Will you keep land in sight?"

"Yes. Land will be in sight at all times."

"As long as there aren't any storms coming in, I guess it would be okay."

I couldn't help teasing, "But you *do* know how to swim."

She smirked.

"One more thing," I said. "Because the boat's small, you can't wear that long skirt. It's liable to get caught in the lines. You need to wear shorts or a swimsuit."

"I don't have any."

"How about jeans?"

"I don't wear them either … they're uncomfortable."

I found that funny, but didn't laugh. I went over to my dresser, pulled out an old pair of canvas swim trunks, and tossed them to her. "They'll be pretty loose, but they should do."

"Okay." She turned and left before I could say another word.

What was it with her? Always up and walking off, leaving me wanting more. Was it some kind of strategy? Maybe it was a male ego thing, as if I needed to have the last word. Maybe it was one of her 'rude' little habits. Either way, I didn't like the way it left me feeling. It was worse than frustrating.

Chapter 10

I STEPPED ONTO THE DECK THE NEXT MORNING before the veil of mist lifted from the harbor. Diesel engines rumbled. Buoys tolled, rocking in the wake of lobster boats as they headed out. The palest orange warmed the horizon, and a light breeze grazed my forehead. Nothing like a lungful of ocean air and the image of a pretty girl to spike my anticipation of the day. The forecast was better than good. It would be the perfect day for a sail.

I tried to remember the last time I took the *Firefly* out for more than an hour. Probably not since last year's race. In fact, I couldn't remember the last time I took a day for myself. Vacation wasn't even in my personal vocabulary, let alone schedule, and so my irritation rose as soon as Mother gave me a look when I reminded her that I was taking the *Firefly* out. When I told her I would be taking Marlena, she squinted with disapproval.

"You be careful with her," she said. "She's not like the other Girls."

I couldn't blame her for being concerned. I didn't have a spotless record. Just the same, she had always been at least superficially tolerant of what she referred to as my 'indiscretions' with some of the Girls.

I guess I'd had more opportunity than follow-through, but there had been a couple of irresistible Girls—usually college students—and I was a whole lot younger then. Given that we had been hiring since Dad died, three out of twenty-one was not outrageous. I think Mother assumed I had messed around with more than that, and I suppose if flirting with or kissing a Girl counted, there had been plenty. And I did know that Marlena was not like any of them. I was sure Mother likely realized that. She simply couldn't help pointing it out. After I met her censure with equal glare, she walked out of the room, probably wishing she hadn't said it.

When Marlena appeared in the kitchen doorway, she stood barefooted, wearing my shorts. The crotch hung mid-thigh. Her plain white T-shirt topped it off, along with her hair cascading from a spout of a ponytail atop her head.

I smirked. "Nice outfit, but I think shoes would make a bold statement." I wanted to laugh. She looked ridiculously cute.

She glanced at her feet, as if they were deficient in some perplexing way, and then back at me.

"Sneakers." I was still suppressing a laugh. "You need to wear your sneakers."

She ignored my footwear suggestion and cringed. "Do I look that bad?"

I wanted to tell her she looked adorable, but Mother walked back in, so I only said, "You look comfortable."

Mother jumped right in. "Sammy! Those are your *swimming trunks*," she scolded, as if Marlena wearing them was somehow obscene. "I'll get her a pair of my shorts."

"I prefer these ones, thank you." Marlena tugged at the side seams. "The crotch isn't all bunchy up between my legs."

Why does she have to say things like that?

Within a half-hour, we pushed off in the *Firefly*, packed with a small ice chest, along with some towels and a blanket. As I unfurled the sail, Marlena fidgeted with the end of a line, knotting it into a Flemish figure eight. Buck must have been teaching her a few things.

As we headed out of the bay, the wind blew just right, a stiff breeze coming out of the southeast. I kept the heel to a minimum for her comfort, and although I could have been slicing water with some serious speed, I didn't mind restraining myself.

When we came about, she ducked and cleared the boom without freaking out, and before an hour passed, she was even willing to hold the rudder steady as long as I also kept my hand on the tiller. Of course, that required my arm behind her as we both sat windward. I doubted it was any sort of a maneuver on her part, but it seemed a convenient excuse to lean into me and I sure didn't mind.

Once she got the knack of it, she did surprisingly well. She panicked only a couple times when the wind picked up, wetting our faces with spray, but she stabilized the boat by heading into the breeze, the way I told her to. We didn't make a whole lot of progress distance-wise, but the longer we sailed, the more she relaxed and giggled. When finally comfortable with how the rigging worked and the way wind and sails interacted, she turned everything back over to me. "Make it go faster!"

Naturally, I pushed the boat and Marlena's limits. I couldn't resist making her squeal. As wind blew all those loose curls from her face, she appeared serene and exotic in one moment, and in the next, she grinned like a little kid.

After several hours, we made another pass near Cuttermann's Island. As we approached its banks, the tide was heading out. I lowered the sail and raised the centerboard. Before I even had a chance to drop anchor, her sneakers came off and she splashed into the water. As she traipsed through muck, I secured the boat out a little way so we wouldn't have to give the ebbing tide much consideration. I grabbed the cooler, and she transported the blankets through thigh-high water that most out-of-Staters would have considered too cold. She flicked water overhead and giggled.

"I think I feel clams or something under my feet," she said.

I dug my toes into the thick silt as I waded. "Yup! That's what they are."

Ahead of us, beach grasses and sparse shrubbery bent windward on about an acre of sand. Mussel beds fringed the north edge of the island, but I didn't mention those.

"I love to eat anything from the sea!" She left a wake as she slogged ahead. As soon as she hit sand, she spun around. "I forgot my knife. Do you have one?"

I pulled mine from my pocket, and at the sight of it, she couldn't retreat to the water fast enough. Within minutes, she had a half-dozen quahogs stashed in her pockets, lowering the waistband far beneath her navel. Between that and her soaked T-shirt—well, it would have been incredibly sexy but for the way she staggered ashore like an infant with a loaded diaper, trying to keep the shorts from slipping off her altogether. I laughed.

"Give me your knife." She dug a large clam from a pocket.

I handed it over. "You sure you know what you're doing?"

With one continuous and agile motion, she wedged the blade, cut the muscle, and sliced the big mollusk in two. With a final twist, she separated the shell into halves and handed one to me.

"Cheers." Through a broad smile, her tongue played with the pinkish flesh before she tipped her head back and it slid into her mouth.

I had never seen such ecstasy on the face of any woman as I did while she chomped that clam. With that one small act, she enthralled me, as if I had received my first glimpse of her true self. With my eye upon her, I downed mine with more pleasure than I had ever consumed any raw shellfish.

I had to laugh because most of us raised in these parts thought nothing of clams on the half-shell. I guess if we objectively examined the slimy mass we put in our mouths and thought about the fact that it was alive—or had been, until we gouged it from its happy home—it might have grossed us out. The only two locals who got the gag reflex were Billy and Derek. Even prairie girl devoured a clam as if she were a native. I added that to the list of her peculiarities.

I spread the blanket as she remained at the water's edge, digging her toes in the sand and facing the bay. When I came from behind and stood beside her, she startled.

"Sorry, I was someplace else." She turned and looked all

around the islet. "Now, *this* is a small island."

"How about some lunch?"

"Yes." She skipped over to the blanket.

Planting herself at one edge, she sat opposite and facing me as she arranged grapes, a jar of peanut butter, carrot sticks, saltines, and a can of kippers between us. Some lunch. I leaned back with a handful of grapes. She grabbed a carrot, scooped a glob of peanut butter, and bit the tip. She chewed with her brow raised, wagging the carrot at me.

"What?" I said.

She swallowed and licked her lips. "Your mother says your brother is coming home this week."

"Yup."

Apparently, Mother had mentioned that Billy was a shrink, because she asked, "Does he specialize in any particular field of psychiatry?"

"Yeah. Addiction is his specialty."

I guess she detected the disparagement in my tone. "Do you think he chose poorly?"

How would I know? It just seemed to me he had chosen that field to do psychotherapy on himself. Not that I thought he was an addict, but he was convinced Dad had been an alcoholic, among other things. That, however, was *not* a shared opinion. We used to argue about it but no longer did. Billy was the one versed in all the ins and outs, all the subtle nuances of addiction and mental illness, and I was merely the kid, eight years younger with a different set of memories.

I couldn't deny that I recalled a couple times when Dad had lost it and hit him. I hate to sound calloused, but if ever there was a kid that made you want to beat the snot out of him, it was Billy. Sometimes, even as an adult, I've thought it would be incredibly therapeutic to haul off and punch him right in the mouth.

Billy could be a kind of bully in his own way, only he used head games. My friends and even the guys that grew up with him had coined the phrase "Getting Billied Around." They called him The Bill-dozer. I couldn't condone it because he was my brother, after all, but sometimes even I used the term.

I didn't feel like getting into all that with Marlena, so I said, "I think his choice is perfect for him."

I cracked open a beer. Normally, I wouldn't have offered her one, but she hadn't taken her attention off it, nor had she shown any interest in the bottled water. I tipped the beer toward her. To my surprise, she took it.

"I thought you didn't like beer," I said.

"To be honest, I've only tasted it once with a boy from church, and I got in a lot of trouble." She took a sip, licked her lips, and then sipped again.

"We should probably share that, seeing as you're not used to drinking."

"You're probably right. I think I'll stick to water this afternoon, but maybe when we get home, we could share a beer or two sometime."

"Sure thing." I looked forward to it. Of course, Mother would think I was corrupting her and Derek would be glad.

She ate another carrot stick and a few crackers, and then reverted to watching me.

"You know, Marlena, people don't usually like being stared at while they're eating."

"I don't stare at everyone."

"Then should I consider it a privilege that you've chosen to focus on me for the last eight weeks?" I hoped she could tell I was mostly teasing.

"It's only that there's no other time when you're so up close. And you look a lot like the Captain, especially in the eyes. I like blue eyes." She looked right through me again. "You have his thick lashes too, and I like the way the corners of your eyes crinkle when you smile. And you have his nice straight nose, and that dimple in your chin. I think you're even more handsome than him, and he's *very* handsome."

I had never been told that before, not quite like that. I had always considered Billy the looker of the family, maybe because he was the one who seemed to be retaining most of his hair and I would likely go the way of Buck.

"I'm sorry … I've been rude. I don't mean to make you uncomfortable. I won't do it again," she promised, though her stare did not deviate.

"You're still doing it."

She laughed. I wanted to say, *I don't mind. Your eyes holding me captive is exquisite torture*, but it looked a lot better on paper than saying it aloud.

I stared back at her and neither of us said a thing. I would wait it out. Would she give in and finally break the silence or look away? She didn't. I wasn't sure what was passing between us, but it left me aroused. Her moist lips parted. I sat up, ready to move in, to pull her on top of me, and kiss her with more passion than I had ever kissed any woman.

As I was on the verge, she asked, "Did you read the notes I made on your manuscript?"

"Yeah …," I exhaled, curbing a whole lot more than my ego. "But we didn't escape to this island to talk about my novel. I want to hear *your* story."

Her smile tightened.

"You're nervous," I said.

"What if you don't like it? What if I don't tell it right?"

"Scary, isn't it? It's every storyteller's insecurity."

"Buck never seems that way."

"Yeah, but Buck's been doing it for *decades*."

She sighed. "I love the elegant way he tells a story."

I had always taken for granted his storytelling style. Though I had never given it much thought, her description nailed it. *Elegance.* Perhaps it sprung from repetition, but his delivery always sounded polished, as if he were reading from a well-rehearsed script.

"You'll do fine," I said, but I did wonder how she would measure up now that she had set the bar so high. To write out a story was one thing, but to orally convey it—that was another thing altogether. Before she even started, I wondered how *I* would measure up to Buck, who, as far as I knew, had never written down even one of his stories but could tell them nearly flawlessly.

I offered Marlena a reassuring smile and she nodded with a halting breath.

"Just remember, I'm a friendly audience." I prepared myself for something less than dazzling, given she was such a novice and all. I hoped it would at least be somewhat entertaining. "Take your time. Start whenever you're ready."

Chapter 11

AUGHT IN HER NATURALNESS, I LEANED BACK ON my towel and shifted to my side. As I smoothed the blanket in front of me, Marlena collected her thoughts. The sun overhead had bronzed her cheeks and her dense lashes barely shaded her squinting eyes. The purse of her lips relaxed as she brought her gaze again to mine. With a long, deep breath, she began.

"The Captain would have stayed at the helm and suffered his ship's fate, but another surge, like the one that moments earlier snapped the main mast in two, sent him into the heaving ocean where several of the crew already floundered. The lifeboat tossed aimlessly in the murky water. What had begun as an unexpected squall took on the characteristics of a gale, anomalous for winter months in the Caribbean. Whereas the skies had been blue and clear the day before, they had become indistinguishably black all the way to the depths of the sea. Sheets of rain poured upon them and into their small skiff. Billows dumped seawater much faster than they could bail.

"The crew scattered in the churning sea—some dead and some still alive. Each lighting strike came sooner than the last, illuminating the dark and distant hull of *Vanessa-Benita*. He watched her break apart against the rocks protruding from the sea like jagged claws."

I smiled, not only at her inclusion of the *Vanessa-Benita*, but also because her introduction was similar to so many of Buck's tales—that, and it had some heavy Daniel Defoe influence, which, given how she loved *Robinson Crusoe*, didn't surprise me. In fact, she conveyed her opening with such ardor and expressiveness that I found her a little distracting to watch. I hoped my smile didn't come off as a smirk. I rolled on to my back and stared up at the clouds as she continued.

"Her bow hung upon the ragged reef as the stern and quarterdeck broke away in pieces. In horror, with the sky continuously lit, he then watched the lifeboat meet a similar fate. A piece of her hull nearly struck him head-on and crashed into the water beside him. Relentless waves curled above him, and he took in what little breath he could as he clutched the board with all his diminishing strength.

"Within arm's reach, he made out the body of the Negro employed by Mr. Lawson, the gentleman who had hired the Captain's services. Another flash of lightning lit the whites of his eyes. Each man reached for the other. When their hands met, the Negro pulled toward him. The Captain's shoulder burned with pain, all the way down his side, leaving him with only one arm to grip the wooden floater.

"Had the seas not been so high, cresting far above their heads as they clung to the plank and each other, they would have made out the bit of land in the distance. Within hours, the limp bodies of the passengers and crew would wash ashore, some shredded and mangled by the coral reefs below the surface, and others miraculously transported over them by the waves that crested and crashed onto the shoals beyond. Warmed by the rising sun that showed through the breaking storm, only the living stirred."

Marlena paused and glanced at me. "Shall I continue?"

"Of course." I sat up. "Stop interrupting yourself. I was just getting into it."

She smiled with a terse nod and resumed.

The Negro, named Tomas, towered above the Captain and rolled his body like a barrel. The Captain groaned, peering up at the broad shadow of the young man. Darkness fell around him as massive hands at his armpits dragged him backward, farther ashore. It could have been for hours or only minutes that the Captain lay unconscious. When he awoke, Tomas stood at his side.

"Three dead have washed ashore," Tomas said. "And three alive—one of them barely."

The Captain sat, his head throbbing as the pain of his injury registered. "Where are the others?"

"Gathering ship parts." Tomas gestured southward, down the beach.

"Lawson? And his wife?"

"Lawson is dead on the beach. His wife—lost at sea. Briggs, Orvad, and Roberts made it, but Briggs—" he glanced toward a body leaning against a palm tree. "Briggs is bad off."

The Captain's heart withered. Briggs, his first mate, and two dead men still at sea were the only reliable hands among the crew.

The Captain came to his feet in slow, awkward stages, refusing help. He would have hit the ground if not for Tomas. The Captain acquiesced to his assistance, steadying himself against the youngster's trunk of an arm. Tomas looked to be a full-grown man in his thirties, yet the Captain knew him to be only twenty.

"Bring Roberts and Orvad to me," he dispatched Tomas, and in minutes they all three returned. The Captain gave Orvad, a deck hand, the order to find an appropriate gravesite. Roberts, the steward, he sent to find water.

Orvad found a sheltered place where the ground was sandy and free from the network of sea grape roots. It was a sufficiently spacious parcel of earth, adequate for burials should any more bodies wash ashore. It lay in a place somewhat hidden, protected by a near vertical rock hedge at the base of a large precipice, which jutted out to the sea and flaunted the perched remains of *Vanessa-Benita*.

As Orvad reported to the Captain, Roberts ran from the thicket.

"Snakes!" he cried, stumbling with fright.

The Captain grew pale. He could have dropped from fear, but he remained stalwart, hiding his utter terror of serpents.

"Snakes, hundreds of them, hanging from the trees and slithering under foot."

"But did you find water?" the Captain demanded.

"I could hear it beyond the mangroves, in the brush, but what's the use of water against venom? I should rather die of thirst than strangulation."

Orvad hid behind Roberts.

"I'll have none of this cowardice." The Captain drew in a lungful of courage. "I shall go myself."

Fooled by his own pride, he stepped forward only to stumble as pain gripped his thigh. Tomas caught him. Instantly, the Captain righted himself, pushing the young slave away.

The sun had risen high in the sky, and it beat upon them, wringing their bodies of any remaining moisture as their need for water weighed heavily against the terror of snakes. Roberts and Orvad quarreled over whose continued existence was of greater necessity, and it was Tomas who stepped forward.

"I shall strike the path. Snakes are no more than play things if you know which are venomous."

Orvad and Roberts bristled at the eloquent tongue of the Negro. His educated bearing overstepped the boundary of slaves—freed or not—and his bravery put them to shame. Yet neither of them was willing to risk his life for the others.

Tomas poured the last bit of rum from a jug into Briggs' mouth. He then affixed the empty vessel to his waist with a bit of rope and armed himself with a sword retrieved from one of the unfortunate crewmen washed ashore.

The first several yards beyond the palms and low shrubbery appeared clear, but sure enough, as Roberts had described it, a thick, spotty brown snake hung from a vine and there was one more within sight beyond it. All three men watched as he severed the first into halves. It hit the ground, writhing, and Tomas hacked the head from its body.

"Careful," he warned, flicking the venomous portion into

the brush near their feet. "The head can still bite."

Now, having slain his first foe, and with confidence borrowed from the sword, Tomas poked at every bit of ground, brush, and overhead vine within reach and disappeared into the jungle.

In angst for his safety, but more for their thirst, the three waited. Finally, Tomas emerged from the mangroves carrying the filled jug in one hand and a limp yet occasionally twitching length of a thick, headless brown snake draped over the sword blade. He told of many snakes, an array of slithering reptiles of various size and color, most of which, he warned, were the venomous kind.

He described how at the edge of the pool, he gave its surface several wide and fierce thrusts, dispersing those snakes which dwell in the clear waters. With his eyes constantly moving all around him, he reenacted how he had filled the jug with one hand, and with the sword in the other, had struck a yellow-spotted viper ready to lunge.

It was this bravery and willingness to secure essential water that made Tomas indispensable to their survival. The color of his skin became, to an effective extent, irrelevant.

Now that they had quenched their thirst, the burials could proceed.

With assistance from a stick of driftwood, the Captain hobbled to the site, gave it his approval, and instructed Orvad to carve the name of each deceased into the rock wall at the head of each grave. Beside each name, he inscribed the date, February 10, 1867.

Even with his right shoulder drooping at a peculiar angle, the Captain strapped his arm beneath his belt and used his left to help dig the graves. The Captain offered prayers for the crewmates washed ashore and for the other four lost at sea, among whom was Mr. Lawson's young Venezuelan wife, Vanessa Benita.

With two urgent tasks out of the way, it was time to see to another, but before the Captain gave orders, Tomas set a hand on his shoulder. "I've seen a dislocation, Capt'n—that's what this is."

The Captain eyed his crew, all two of them. "One of you men, set it straight," he ordered.

Roberts backed off as Orvad shook his head. "We ain't no surgeons, Capt'n—we'd only make it worse."

"I've done this before," Tomas said. "It'll hurt like the devil, but it'll be better than useless."

The Captain scowled at his men and looked at the young Negro, weighing his pain against his misgivings, his distrust.

"I have little choice but to charge you with its repair."

Orvad gave the Captain a swig of rum. He braced himself. With one violent maneuver, Tomas put his shoulder socket right, nearly buckling the Captain's knees. Orvad gave him another swig for the pain. The repair was not as he hoped, but sufficient to relieve his immediate anguish.

"Thank you," he uttered, more on principle than from gratitude.

In order to determine their true situation and if there might be any nearby land, the Captain then sent Orvad to scale the precipice, set barely inland above the graves. Meanwhile, the Captain, Tomas, and Roberts headed back to the beach to retrieve any bit of salvageable wreckage.

All three walked the shoreline, which curved outward from them in either direction, forming a pleasant lagoon. To the northwest, it abutted the rocky crags, and to the southwest, it crested at a dune and continued back around easterly.

They collected anything useful, gathering all they could carry or drag back to where they started. Much of it was from the quarterdeck, that is, the Captain and Mr. Lawson's quarters. They also retrieved some large sheets of sail, several wooden trunks containing utensils, a lamp and oil, Mrs. Lawson's wardrobe, and the Captain's own sea trunk.

Tomas carried the Captain's prized possession and set it nearby where they had set up camp. The Captain kneeled before it, retrieving a key from his pocket to unlock it.

"Praise be to God," he whispered when he had lifted the lid.

Specially constructed and watertight as a ship, the chest had transported his log, writing implements, and the Holy Bible as safely as Moses adrift on the Nile. He unfolded some cloth and lifted a dagger. Its blade flashed in the sunlight.

"Ruby," he called her—a gift from his father, beautifully carved and proudly bearing a single gem for which she was named. He stood and slipped the sheathed dagger into his belt.

At that moment, Orvad returned.

"What did you ascertain?" the Captain asked.

Orvad's survey revealed the island's irregular circumference of perhaps a league, that is, three miles or so. A conical mound near the island's center blocked its windward view.

"I saw a waterfall—well, more of a stream—falling from the mound. It no doubt replenishes during the rains."

The men speculated that given the small size of the island, it would not likely support predators other than snakes. It was good news, but also unfortunate, because it likely meant the island would not provide game for hunting. Nevertheless, Tomas said he startled at least one rabbit, which they hoped, given the prolific nature of the rodent, might not be the only one on the island.

They easily started a fire with driftwood and an intense beam of sunlight through the lens of the Captain's looking glass. All but the Captain partook of the roasted snake flesh. He merely satisfied himself with the meat of a coconut and sat with Briggs, reading passages from the book of Psalms, hoping to offer whatever comfort he could to the dying man.

A thin wisp of smoke ascended as the sun dipped into the sea. Under any other circumstances, the continuous whoosh of waves would have soothed even the most savage of men, but as the four sat, their minds churned. Orvad and Roberts bickered about provisions as Tomas's attention turned toward the southern dune where a figure collapsed on the sand. In an instant, he rushed toward the distinctly feminine form of Mrs. Lawson.

The Captain came to his feet and grabbed the water jug. By the time he caught up, Tomas was halfway back, carrying the petite woman. He laid her in the sand, stroking her face as the

Captain poured water into her mouth.

"Edward ... Edward," were her only words, once her tongue was wet enough to speak them.

"Quiet," Tomas whispered, helping her to sit.

"Edward ...."

Tomas pressed his forehead to her ear, caressing her silken black hair. He whispered words the Captain could not hear, and she let out a wrenching cry. Tomas pulled her to his bosom, trying to restrain her flailing arms and rocking her as she screamed. The Captain rose, knowing this was not his place, and left the two on the beach.

Roberts and Orvad watched impassively and soon resumed their quiet dispute. Not long after that, Tomas approached their campfire, supporting Mrs. Lawson upon his arm on their way to the grave. They exchanged no greetings as they passed by, but the arguing crewmen ceased their debate long enough to leer. For hours, she wept, sometimes whimpering and at times wailing. It sounded more horrid than anything the captain had ever heard, even in all his years serving on the blockades.

The two slept the night at the grave. Roberts and Orvad exhausted themselves into a stupor, each snoring with exuberance. The Captain, on the other hand, stayed with Briggs. He remained awake more from the idea of snakes and a troubled conscience than his desire to soothe the man near death.

In the middle of the night, furious winds again picked up. Palms rustled ferociously, crackling and dropping coconuts all around them. Trying to offer more shelter, the Captain yanked a nearby remnant of a sail, pulling it over him and Briggs. His first mate's body no longer radiated heat. In fact, one nudge and the corpse fell over. He knelt beside the body and pulled the sail up and over Briggs' head.

"Oh, dear God, forgive me." He quietly sobbed into his hands. It was then when the profundity of all that had transpired and all that still lay ahead of him gripped him with remorse. The blood of seven souls weighed against his selfish ambition, his restlessness, and, he had to admit, his greed.

Chapter 12

MARLENA HAD BEEN STARING OUT AT THE WATER as she developed the story, but now looked at me. She cleared her throat and reached for the water bottle. After taking several long sips, she sighed.

So far, I liked the direction she had taken with the plot, and now with a female character introduced—well, I anticipated the story taking an interesting turn. I found myself becoming impatient for more. "That's not the end of it, is it?"

She smiled. "No, that's actually just the beginning. There's a lot more. Shall I continue?"

I glanced overhead at the sun, high in the sky. "Absolutely. It's still early."

"Okay." She took another sip and then continued.

The next morning, they found the lifeboat washed ashore. Its starboard side damage, although extensive, was believed repairable, since the bow with its stem was still intact. Along with the boat, other useful articles had washed ashore, namely several good lengths of planking from *Vanessa-Benita's* hull, and with that, some bit of hope. It was noteworthy to the Captain that this hope seemed confined to Orvad, Roberts, and himself. Tomas remained at his employer's grave beside Mrs. Lawson and showed little interest in the boat.

Since the sea had calmed considerably from the day before,

the Captain dispatched Roberts and Orvad to retrieve whatever else they could utilize from *Vanessa-Benita*. In order to avoid the treacherous reefs, they traversed the rocks that led out to the crag that held her bound. Lines from her flailing foremast whipped to-and-fro across her splintered hull, and with the adeptness of the sailors they were, they seized the lines and scaled their way onto the remaining foredeck. When they returned with all they could carry or float ashore, they took inventory. If they perished on the island, it would not be for lack of resources.

By midday, as the Captain poked at smoldering embers, Mrs. Lawson and Tomas emerged from the brush near the gravesite. No longer did she use his arm for support. When they came to the beach, she walked to the shore whereas Tomas joined the Captain, whose eye was upon her.

"Shall I gather wood?" Tomas asked.

The Captain stared at her for a moment and then addressed Tomas. "Yes. We'll need plenty of it."

His attention refocused on the woman. She had a slight stature, yet erect—a lady's countenance, and a young lady at that. She was all of twenty-five, and figuring from the ten years Mr. Lawson divulged they had been married, she was but a child when they wed. No doubt, she thought of her husband as she scanned the horizon.

The Captain limped toward the shore. She did not turn to greet him. They stood side by side, and even though it would have served his comfort to avoid her eyes, he turned to face her.

Although she was native to Venezuela, her skin was as white as cream, yet her exotic features—black eyes, full lips, and glossy hair curled in tight ringlets down her back— indicated she was *mestiza*, of mixed blood. Grief had in no way obscured her beauty.

"I am so sorry for you—for your husband," he said. "I take full responsibility, I am utterly—"

She cut him off. "What's done is done. We shall not speak of culpability again."

"Mrs. Lawson, I—"

"Not ever, Captain. What's done is done." Her eyes, brimming with tears, flashed at his and she walked away.

The tide had gone out, and he stared out at the waves crashing over the shoals. At length, his focus came to rest upon *Vanessa-Benita*. He remembered the first time he laid eyes upon her. She was far grander than any ship built by him and his brothers. Their modest boatyard could never accommodate her girth. If he was ever to own a ship of such caliber ... well, an opportunity to sail a ship the likes of which he had commanded during the Union Naval blockades would, for a certainty, never again present itself. Financially, it would have given his family a sure advantage.

What Captain in his fiftieth year of life would not prefer to sail a merchant's route to the Caribbean in his very own vessel? It was that or wrestle the inhospitable North Atlantic, frostbit upon a hired barque in search of whale blubber. What Captain in his right mind would pass up a schooner for the trouble of transporting a wealthy speculator to the coast of Venezuela? In no longer than the time it had taken to drink a pint of ale in a tavern, he had struck the ill-fated bargain. He had completely inspected her from stem to stern, strake and deck, topsides and below. Yes, every plank and nail, every line and sail. Only then did he offer his guarantee.

It had not been merely a matter of her speed and agility. She was a first-rate beauty; fore- and aft-masted, gaff-rigged with a square foretopsail and staysail that stretched out far beyond her strongly raked bow to her slender bowsprit. She had begged his command. The seduction of her refined lines, sleek and elegant, had been beyond tempting. He would be satisfied only when she belonged to him, for he had fallen in love with her as surely as he had fallen in love with his wife. In his heart, the Captain had committed to her. She would know the hand of no other commander. The first time he saw her fully dressed in sail, it was as if seeing his wife on their wedding night—a sight he would never forget.

And now she lay a wreck. The man holding her papers lay

in a grave, as lifeless as *Vanessa-Benita*.

Returning to the camp under the palms, he inspected what foodstuffs his men had gathered. Quite a few crabs clawed each other, trying to climb from a salvaged boiling pot that sat upon a ring of large stones. Flames licked its sides as Tomas sat beside it, stirring the contents. Beside them lay a heap of coconuts. Then Mrs. Lawson came from behind and emptied several large tubers and shells from the folds of her skirt.

"Cassava," she said, "and a couple conch."

"Then we shall eat well tonight," the Captain said, contemplating their next need. Once they had all eaten to satisfaction, he again sent Roberts and Orvad to the ship's hull for anything else salvageable that they could not carry the day before.

Meanwhile, Tomas and the Captain undertook establishing better accommodations. They stood abreast each other, staring up at the south-facing precipice and the rocky ledge beneath it. Orvad had cleared a path, exposing several intermediate ridges that presented a plausible way up—at least for an able-bodied man.

The captain looked at the crag and then at Tomas. "Make an assessment and then return immediately," he said through gritting teeth. He loathed his weakness.

Tomas scaled the steep incline with ease. Once he landed on the upper ledge, he looked out over the beach then down at the Captain. Without a word, he turned to the crag and began hacking at vines. Wind and weather had scoured away rock, leaving a deep crevice. After stripping the concealing vines, a narrow opening revealed a small cave. Anticipating snakes, Tomas entered cautiously. In a minute, he emerged with another large, headless snake draped over his sword. He dropped it to the beach beside the Captain, who was barely able to maintain his composure. Several minutes later, Tomas again joined him.

"It appears deep enough for two men to stand or lie in any direction," he reported.

"Then it will make a fine shelter for those things which

should be kept dry. I will let you see to that."

Accustomed to receiving orders, Tomas nodded.

Over the course of the next few days, stretching into a week from when they had washed ashore, Roberts and Orvad made several more trips to what remained of *Vanessa-Benita*. At last, she yielded some hardware and hammocks, not to mention further murmuring between the two men.

One night, as all lay or sat around the campfire, the Captain sat alone, watching Mrs. Lawson in the flickering light. Tomas faced her as she spoke to him. The fact that he had been a member of her husband's household since his childhood seemed evident in their casual rapport. The Captain looked for some deeper confidence between the two but sensed nothing, at least, not on Mrs. Lawson's side.

Soon, all had fallen asleep. In the middle of the night, the Captain woke to the sound of hushed voices—Roberts and Orvad, again disputing.

"Where else could the gold have come from? And what do we know of the Captain, let alone Lawson?"

"You're suggesting piracy?"

"Piracy between gentlemen."

"Absurd."

"Then why was the money hidden, undisclosed on the manifest?"

The Captain thrashed in the sand. "Enough of you," he blurted, loud enough to stir Tomas but not wake him.

The two men ceased their murmuring, but the Captain vowed to deal with them in the morning.

It alarmed the Captain greatly that he should have such dissention between his remaining crew. However, he did not anticipate the violence that would erupt. Yet, it was not so much an eruption as a silent murder that could not be proven.

The following morning, both men had disappeared before the others awoke, and when Roberts returned, he said, "Orvad lost his footing at the precipice. It happened so fast that I could not come to his aid, and he fell to the raging sea below."

Fearing what Roberts was capable of, the Captain tread

carefully in his company, keeping Tomas nearby, if not close at his side.

On the following morning, Roberts had disappeared again. As if God himself demanded restitution for Orvad's soul, Roberts returned several days later, washed ashore— drowned—his pockets laden with ten gold coins. What recompense would God exact for the Captain's own bloodguilt?

It was only the three of them now.

They sat around the fire.

"We are fully into the dry season," the Captain said. "If we work diligently, we should have time to repair the skiff before the rains begin. It can be re-rigged with a sail and then launched at the proper time, putting us back in the trade routes and, at length, back to civilization."

Tomas was quick to proclaim, "I am no shipwright!"

"But I am," the Captain explained. Perhaps he was not of the same caliber as his brothers, but he could surely oversee the mending of a skiff. Why, he could do it himself if his arm had any strength but for lifting a fork or writing with a pen.

For the first time, Tomas spoke with force. "I am a free man, and if *I* choose to mend a boat, I shall, but as yet I am undecided."

Aghast, the Captain struggled to his feet, standing over Tomas. "Undecided? What decision do *you* mean to make? I have already made the decision! The boat's repair shall be undertaken immediately that she be ready to sail well before the season of tropical gales."

Tomas rose slowly, towering nearly four inches above the Captain. His nostrils flared.

"You are not *my* captain, nor are you my master. I am a free man." Staring into the Captain's unflinching face, he breathed deep and stepped back. "As a child of God, I shall see to your safety out of my compassion, yet I shall do as *I* determine I shall do, not as *you* determine." With those words, he set about feeding the fire for their next meal.

Later on, when only Tomas had fallen asleep, the Captain

resorted to pleading with Mrs. Lawson.

"Surely you can see that to stay on this island is suicide. We have a way off and we must avail ourselves of it."

"I have no more interest in staying on this island than you."

"Then you must persuade Tomas."

She huffed with what seemed like amusement. "Tomas has never been, nor shall he ever be, my slave. You think far more of my powers of persuasion than you ought."

He doubted so. "Just the same, you'll talk to him?"

"I shall do what I can."

Over the next several days, it seemed she was having no success with Tomas. The apparent delay provoked impatience, so that the Captain sought another opportunity to speak to her alone. Consequently, he joined her on the beach at sunrise.

"What seems to be the problem?" the Captain inquired.

She looked at him as if amazed. "You truly don't comprehend his dilemma."

"What dilemma?"

"What sort of life awaits him in the Carolinas or Venezuela? In either country, Tomas is a freeman by law, yet with negligible rights."

"Yes, but he can exist comfortably under your protection."

She laughed scornfully. "*My* protection? My husband is dead. He was my protection—the money was my protection." Her neck strained with emotion. "Look at me." She faced him. "I am *mestiza*. I do not have the *criolla* privilege of pure European blood. What's more, the disadvantage of my gender weighs as heavily against me as the blackness of Tomas' skin weighs against him."

The Captain's guilt-ridden eyes could no longer meet hers, nor could he find words to rebut. Nevertheless, later that night, he overheard her pleading with Tomas.

"… robbing the man of hope will benefit none of us, Tomas. Our own personal ambivalence should not, in the long run, rob us of future options."

Without waiting for a word from Tomas, the Captain set about doing what he could to gather whatever supplies and tools he might use. Working with little help from his injured arm, hoping to shame Tomas into assisting, he began training his left hand to do the work of his right.

Tomas finally approached. "I will help you mend it." He took the mallet from the Captain's hand. "But I will not help you sail it."

By the end of March, it became evident that the rainy season would arrive early, along with tropical gales. The Captain put progress on the boat secondary to securing better shelter. The cave provided an obvious choice, much to the Captain's displeasure.

With a window punched through a weak spot opposite the cave's narrow entry, better light afforded a cheerier environment. With their stash of supplies, it was close quarters, yet far better than remaining exposed during rain that fell continuously, sometimes for days. Below the window, a small bit of wood kept embers glowing, and a draft prevented smoke from collecting inside.

Snake became an infrequent meal. Tomas finally confessed that the vipers he smote on that first day were the only ones he saw on the way to find water. Since then, he had only occasionally seen others. His tale of their proliferation seemed a fair deceit to secure his value with Roberts and Orvad, who he deemed capable of doing away with him if commodities became too scarce. The Captain could not help but admire the young man's resourcefulness.

On days when the rain let up, or at least when it did not blow as hard, they collected mollusks and fished. Mrs. Lawson helped with her knowledge of edible and medicinal plants. Consequently, they ate a great deal of cassava, the stalks of which she cut into small sections and replanted, ensuring a new crop. They ate a tuber known as cush-cush, much like a yam, and replanted small bits of it. For several weeks, they also enjoyed eggs and the meat of a sea turtle, and after whiling away some time constructing bows and arrows, they killed a few rabbits. Additionally, they also raided several duck nests, which provided an occasional egg or two.

It was during that first rainy season, while confined to their tight quarters, that the three became well acquainted—that is to say, it became apparent to the Captain that Tomas was in love with Mrs. Lawson. In fact, even the Captain could not help but notice and secretly admire her feminine figure and charm. Although Mrs. Lawson evidently did not lack fondness for Tomas, she seemed not to reciprocate his love. She did not gaze at him the way he did at her.

Chapter 13

I WASN'T CERTAIN WHAT TIME IT WAS, BUT I HAD been sitting in the sun without a shirt for too long. Hoping not to distract Marlena from her story, I reached for my T-shirt. She paused.

"Sorry. I just feel like I'm cooking."

"I could just tell the rest later."

I quickly pulled my shirt overhead. "No. I'm completely engrossed. I like the conflict you've got going." The truth was she impressed me. I wondered how many times she had rehearsed her delivery. It was polished and without hesitation. She was stirring something in me, though I wasn't sure just what.

"Okay. Where was I?"

"Tomas has a thing for Mrs. Lawson, and I think the Captain does too."

"Yes." Marlena's eyes shifted bashfully as she grinned and continued.

*O*ne night, when a full moon broke through the clouds, the Captain woke. He lay restless as a beam of light shone in upon him. Rather than idly torment himself, he went to the ledge overlooking the beach. The sparkling water faded in and out of the moonlight as clouds waltzed like bridal gauze.

Before long, he heard the rustling of Mrs. Lawson.

"Finally, a break in the rain." She sat beside him. "Do you mind if I join you?"

The Captain peered at her. Although he was enjoying his solitude, he would be hard-pressed to find her an imposition. "Please, do."

"Tell me, Captain Wesley—"

"There is no need for formality. I am hardly a captain any longer."

"William, then," her voice lilted. "Tell me, what was it that woke you? The moon or your conscience?"

The Captain shot her a startled glance.

"Ah, the conscience," she deduced. "The conscience is such a troublesome thing—sometimes it betrays you, condemning when it ought not, and sometimes it's as lenient as an indulgent parent."

"I have never been a man at ease with my conscience," he said. "A calm conscience only serves complacency."

"And the provoked conscience, a handy device to send men to war—to protect and provide for their families. Tell me, what verdict does it offer when family—when children—are left to fend for themselves?"

Her words grabbed at his heart and squeezed blood to his neck. "What do you imply? That it is better for a man to stand back and watch while others defend and provide for his family? That he should coddle them at any cost?"

"You misunderstand my intent. I mean no accusation against you." She drew a solemn breath. "It is my own past that torments me."

"Tell me, that I may gain some perspective."

She turned to him incisively. "You want a woman's perspective, but I shall give you a child's." Her gaze drifted toward the beach. "I was only ten when the *caudillo* came and took our plantation. I lost my father, brothers, and uncles to the civil insurrections of those feudal lords. There was no one left to fend for me." Her voice tapered off, and her next words seemed to come with hesitation. "Had I not been a beautiful little girl, I would still be working the fields of those outlaws, used up like so many of the girls who had come of age."

The Captain stared at her, aghast.

"Don't be appalled," she said. "Things took a turn for the better when I was thirteen. A fine, rich gentleman visiting Venezuelan plantations noticed me, and it was he who essentially purchased me. He clothed me in the finest French silks and laces, placed me at his table and fed me exotic delicacies, and he educated me at the best institutions. Yes, he took my virginity, but my innocence was already lost. At least he had the decency to marry me."

Neither spoke for a moment.

"And Tomas?" he asked.

"He acquired Tomas three years earlier, bestowing upon him many of the same privileges."

"You make your husband out to be quite the philanthropist."

She laughed. "Oh yes, he loved to conceal his shrewdness behind humanitarian deeds—that was the guise for luring his investors. That and his charisma. Why, even you succumbed to it—to the gold, to the esteem."

The Captain could not refute her words.

She continued, "As for me, I was merely an investment, as good as a title deed to my inheritance once the Federalists took control again. A stock in commodities. With his beautiful wife at his right hand and imposing, fiercely loyal Tomas at his left, who would contend with him?"

"Did you love him?"

"I suppose I loved him as much as he did me."

"He didn't *love* you—he *used* you."

"And there you have it, William. Now can you see?" She glanced at him. "I am left pondering what a person is willing to trade for security—no matter if that security is in the form of esteem, a home, gold, or…," she looked directly at the Captain, waiting for their eyes to meet, "… or love."

The Captain exhaled, forcing his eyes from her arresting stare, reminding himself that he was a married man—not only on paper but also in his heart.

"I think the only security we can have is in God's

forgiveness." He stood, offering assistance. She rose with exquisite grace and faced him. She did not retract her hand, nor did he—not until it burned like fire, searing his palm. Immediately, he returned to where Tomas lay and she followed. The sound of her breathing from across the hovel was all he heard for the rest of that night.

Finally, the dry season came. By October, rain no longer confined them to the hovel, providing the Captain some relief from temptation. Mrs. Lawson spent considerable time alone, and without such close and constant contact with either man, all three seemed to fall into a comfortably amicable situation. This was especially true now that Tomas and the Captain resumed work on the boat. The Captain hoped that by January they might have stocked enough provisions and readied the sails in order to head, in his estimation, due west for the South American mainland.

Under the Captain's tutelage, Tomas silently worked beside him, lending his strength as they fashioned a mast and boom from salvaged spars. The Captain did not consider him capable of much more than menial labor.

"Tomorrow we shall fabricate a gooseneck from these spare parts," the Captain explained when they stopped for the day.

"Gooseneck?"

"A hook of sorts, and a channel, to stow the studding sail boom in. It lets the boom swing to-and-fro."

Tomas said nothing, and the Captain assumed the concept too complicated for a slave.

The following morning, he found otherwise. When the Captain arrived on the beach, Tomas had already stepped the mast, and on his own had devised a respectable gooseneck. The Captain cast him a skeptical glance as he inspected his work.

"Mr. Lawson provided you with more than a primary education."

"No, sir."

The Captain folded his arms across his chest and squinted in doubt. "No engineering?"

"No, sir."

"Humph."

"It's simple logic." Tomas bent over the boat to demonstrate the mechanism.

"Yes, yes, yes," the Captain said impatiently and walked away, over to where Mrs. Lawson prepared breakfast over the fire pit.

"It looks as if things are coming right along," she said.

"Yes, I think we'll be in good shape by January," he replied.

Mrs. Lawson watched Tomas as he walked past into the brush to gather wood.

She smiled. "Tomas is clever, is he not?"

The Captain huffed begrudgingly.

"Tomas has always been exceptionally bright. It's a shame that even with all that my husband provided him, he will never be allowed to achieve what you take for granted." She raised a brow at the Captain. "I dare say you've never given a second thought to the fact that you're a white man with a trade that has been handed to you."

His jaw tightened. "You imply that I have not worked hard at my achievements."

She laughed kindly. "You always assume I mean to accuse you."

"Don't you?"

"Why, William." She seemed perplexed. "You believe I hold a grudge."

"And how am I to think otherwise?" He looked away.

He sensed her stare but couldn't meet her gaze, convinced she would finally charge him with weakness of character, with greed, with recklessness and negligence.

"It's clear that you don't know *what* I think of you." The tone of her voice surprised him, but not as much as the way she closed the distance between them, leaning ever so slightly. "And you are too proud to ask."

The Captain admitted as much with a curious glance.

She smiled, her hands smoothing the skirt over her thighs. "In fact, I hold you in great esteem."

She had his attention. He waited, hoped for more.

"You are a man of admirable integrity, profoundly devoted to your countrymen and even more to your family." Her voice faltered as she continued, "To be honest, I'm jealous of your wife, of a woman whose husband truly loves her. I have never known the love of a man like you."

The Captain finally brought his eyes to hers, wishing he could catch her tear before it spilled.

From behind, firewood thumped to the ground, and Mrs. Lawson quickly wiped her own tear.

"I found what looks like a fruit grove, not far beyond where we last explored," Tomas said as he fed the fire.

"Then we shall set out on an expedition today," the Captain replied.

With Tomas striking the path using his sword as a machete, Mrs. Lawson followed with the Captain behind her. His hip ached as he labored to keep up. They pushed through the brush, canopied by vines and trees at first, and then thinning to lower bushes. Although they had started out early ahead of the full heat, they were no sooner into their hike before the sweltering sun had drenched the Captain's shirt, as it did Mrs. Lawson's. Had Tomas been wearing a shirt, it would have been as transparent.

Beyond a clearing, south of the farthest point to which they had previously ventured, Mrs. Lawson spotted a fruit tree of a sort she did not know. Tomas plucked a low-hanging fruit. Using his knife to peel back the thin green husk, he revealed a fleshy pulp. It was the first fruit, besides coconut, that any of them had seen since they washed ashore. Mrs. Lawson approached Tomas eagerly as he sampled it for safety.

"It's sweet." He cut another piece as she came near.

With her hand on his, he fed her a mouthful, releasing its juice down her chin, and she was so close to Tomas that it ran down his arm.

The Captain watched as Tomas fed her another bite, galled at the ease of their interaction.

In her spontaneous pleasure, Mrs. Lawson took the fruit from Tomas and brought it to the Captain, feeding him the way

Tomas had done with her. With his first bite, his gaze fell intensely upon her face, and as he took from her hand a second bite, his eyes were fully upon Tomas, whose stare met his.

It was no passing glance. Not an amiable exchange between friends, but the defiant stare between rivals.

After collecting several fruits in a sack made from one of the sails, they headed northeast up the windward side of the island. This side was more barren with the terrain nearly vertical in spots. Making their way along the bony soil of rocks and boulders, they found a nook in the watery crags where the crashing waves could not penetrate. In that semicircle, a wide, deep pool of less turbulent waters collected, along with many fish and several lobsters. With a nail bent as a hook on the end of a string, the Captain caught three good-sized fish in an hour. He placed them in his bag and they continued onward.

The northeast tip of the island proved to be particularly treacherous, and Mrs. Lawson depended much upon Tomas' arm for support. When they finally rounded the northern tip, the elevation again sloped gradually. Now the only visible rock was the precipice, which jutted up and then tapered for nearly a half-mile. Between the sight of *Vanessa-Benita's* bowsprit still pointed skyward and Tomas constantly at Mrs. Lawson's side, the Captain felt quite disheartened.

Although they feasted on more food than they had in months, the Captain did not share Tomas and Mrs. Lawson's cheer. He tried not to watch as they ate, sharing each other's food, but after eating only half his portion, he lost his appetite. He took the remaining bit of rum and left the two sitting at the fire pit.

The sun, low on the horizon, sank with the Captain's heart as he sat alone on the shore. He took a swig of rum as Mrs. Lawson came from behind and sat beside him. "Do you plan to drink all of that yourself?"

The Captain barely glanced at her. "Indeed, I do."

"That hardly seems fair." She reached for the jug. "It is, after all, the last of it."

"I've never known you to imbibe."

"Normally, I don't." She took a small swallow. "But this evening I'm in the mood."

Tomas came from behind and sat beside Mrs. Lawson. Knowing he did not drink liquor, she did not offer him the jug.

Warmed by the rum and Mrs. Lawson's nearness, the Captain glanced at her hands upon her outstretched legs, crossed beneath her tattered skirt. Although weathered and calloused, her hands remained elegant and poised. As much as he felt her presence, he felt Tomas' even more, especially when she leaned against the young man's shoulder.

That night, the Captain again sat on the ledge, but Mrs. Lawson did not join him. In his weakness, he wished she would. At the same time, he loathed his self-indulgent desires. There was no way he could ever have her. Not only was he married, but he was twice her age, and it had become evident that Tomas exceeded him in ways that were important to a considerably younger woman. What worth would he be even to his own wife in his enfeebled state? He yearned for her familiar touch, for her kiss, for the bliss of his marital bed and his ordinary life.

Not many mornings after that, when the Captain headed for the beach to resume work on the boat, he found Tomas binding bamboo shoots in some sort of small structure.

"What are you doing?" the Captain demanded.

Tomas did not look at him. He continued with his work and replied, "Making a cage. I'm going to snare several ducks so that we'll have plenty of eggs."

"We don't need eggs, we need a boat," the Captain shouted.

"The boat no longer interests me." He came to his feet and looked down to meet the Captain's glare.

The Captain walked away and commenced caulking the hull seams by himself.

For days, the Captain refused to admit defeat. It was not until one afternoon, while Mrs. Lawson cultivated cassava and cush-cush in her garden, that he began to doubt he would be leaving the island any time soon.

From the hovel's ledge, he caught sight of her and Tomas in

her little grove. She used a hoe Tomas had fashioned for her, but it appeared that he preferred to do the hard labor while she did the planting. She laughed as he tried to pull the hoe from her, and the more she resisted, the more he teased, pulling harder until she let go, sending him to the ground. He grabbed to pull her atop him, but she escaped, laughing, and he set out after her. He chased her out onto the beach, allowing her to evade him but not for long. Finally, he caught her, and once in his embrace, she acquiesced to his advance and more than allowed his kiss.

Their unabashed passion shamed the Captain and he retreated to the cave, not knowing how long or how far their passion took them.

Over the next several weeks, they would leave for hours, sometimes returning with more fruit or fish, and sometimes returning with nothing. In the course of those weeks, the boat project all but ceased as the relationship between Tomas and Mrs. Lawson progressed.

One February night, before the Captain marked their first complete year on the island, he woke from a deep sleep. In the dark, he heard sounds. One of them is sick, he immediately thought, but in a moment, he knew it was not that at all. A torrent of emotion shot through his veins as he came to his feet, and the sounds desisted. He said nothing as he stepped over their entwined bodies and stormed from the hovel. He slept the night on the beach, seething with repulsion.

For two days, he avoided them. On the third, Mrs. Lawson sought him out, finding him where he fished for his own food. She stood beside him as he drew in a line and cast it out over the pool.

"William." She touched his arm.

He ignored her.

"You can't pretend we don't exist."

The tendons of his neck stretched to his jaw.

She pleaded, "William—"

"Don't call me that." He refused to look at her.

"Please don't behave this way—"

Now he spun to face her and spat, "What do you want from me, *Mrs. Lawson*?"

She sought his eyes, begging him to understand. "I don't want you to resent Tomas and me."

"And why shouldn't I?"

The severity of his words made tears well in her eyes. She wiped them quickly and matched his tone.

"Why should I deprive myself of what *you* cannot give me?"

Her piercing words brought the acute realization that under other circumstances she might have been his, that she would have preferred him over Tomas.

His passion and rage took control and he grabbed her arm, yanking her closer. He wanted her, wanted to consume her. His frustration turned to cruelty.

Through clenched jaw, he rebuked her. "It is an unnatural and unholy union. That a dog like him should even touch you—"

Mrs. Lawson wrenched her arm from his grip and struck his face, matching every bit of his ruthlessness.

"You are despicable! Your own weakness has come back on you."

Before he could breathe enough to respond, she was gone.

Left with her deserved scorn, he wept.

Chapter 14

I DIDN'T KNOW HOW MARLENA HAD MANAGED TO make my heart ache along with the Captain's, but my whole body tensed. Straightening my back and massaging my neck, I sighed, probably sounding irritated. When she looked at me, I was overcome with self-consciousness. It was crazy. Why didn't I want her to see how her story affected me?

She cocked her head. "You don't like that Benita chose Tomas over the Captain?"

I shook my head, more to dispel my agitation than deny her statement. "No. It's fine. I just—I don't know. It's just the whole situation."

"Yes. It's tragic, really." She raised a brow. "What will become of the Captain?"

"I guess there's only one way to find out."

She glanced at the sun behind her. "Well, there's only a little more. If you want, I could continue."

Now I shook my head with resignation. She had hooked me. "Well, you can't leave me hanging."

"Okay," she said with a smile, and then turned serious.

The Captain did not return to the camp for days, and those days turned to weeks. Through the brush and from upon the precipice, he watched the young lovers. He watched Tomas build a hut in the fruit grove, and he watched Mrs. Lawson touch him the way his own wife used to. As he watched, he seethed, calculating ways he might do away with Tomas. Each scenario was ill conceived given that the young man's strength and agility far outmatched his. Besides that, Mrs. Lawson now despised him, and no matter what, she would never have him.

Just before the rains began, it became apparent that the couple had abandoned the hovel for their new hut. Glad not to share the space, the Captain claimed all of it for himself and rarely left. He fished alone, slept alone, ate alone, and as days passed, he fed himself less and less. By halfway through the season, he only left the cave to ease nature. As he stood on the ledge, a thin wisp of smoke rose from the midst of the grove, and with it the scent of roasting meat, agitating his own hopelessness and desperation.

On one particularly bad evening, one in a string of many restless nights, his fevered mind turned anger upon himself. He considered putting an end to his misery. He could not think clearly, let alone devise a plan, yet the idea ripened. His body ached as he stood in the pouring rain, urinating over the ledge. When he turned to reenter the hovel, he had a second notion and turned back to the ledge. He stood in a puddle as rain gushed from the precipice above him, streaming down grooves in the rock hedge and over the ledge. He stepped close to the edge, surveying the jagged rocks nearly thirty feet below.

One step forward, he thought, *and that would end it all.* His head ached and his body burned as he tipped his face skyward. The cool rain washed over his skin. *Just one step forward.* As fast as the notion came, it left, but as he turned back to the hovel, his foot shot out from beneath him. Slick mud and rushing water sent him backward and over the ledge. He grabbed a branch growing from a crevice, but it slipped from his right hand as his left grasped at a bit of protruding rock. His feet scrambled for a ledge, sending chunks of rock to the ground. He fought to live, though he did not know why. In an instant, he realized his life was about to end.

Something slammed into his forearm and gravel pelted his

head. He thought disorientation caused him to feel as if he were falling upward, and when he looked he saw the whites of Tomas's eyes. Sharp edges raked along his chest as he struggled to assist. With one forceful yank, his body slumped on the ledge. From below, he heard Mrs. Lawson.

"Is he alright?" she called out.

"Are you?" Tomas asked.

The Captain could not speak. He only nodded.

Thomas shouted above the pounding rain, "Yes."

"Bring him down," she said.

The Captain, weak from hunger, sleeplessness, fever, and injury, could offer no resistance as Tomas pulled his body up and draped him over his shoulder like a bundle of sailcloth. Blood rushed to and from his head as consciousness waned.

He had no idea how long he had been sleeping, but when he came to, Mrs. Lawson sat beside his cot. Droplets of rain danced on leaves outside the window but did not penetrate the thatched roof. Embers smoldered beneath a vent in the corner of the hut, and the room smelled of stew.

"Finally, you awaken," she said.

The Captain said nothing. He simply looked around and then tried to sit up.

"Don't." She put a cup to his mouth. "Not too fast. You've been very sick."

The Captain sipped, taking the cup from her hand. At that moment, Tomas entered, carrying wood in one hand and a large gutted fish wrapped in a palm frond in the other. He handed the fish to Benita, and then silently crouched to feed the fire. Benita stood and her rounded tummy became evident.

The Captain lay back, stunned at the sight. "You're with child," he whispered, remembering his own wife.

"Yes." She stood beside Tomas as he placed his large hand gently upon her stomach.

He could scarcely look at Tomas, not out of contempt this time, but shame and remorse.

"I will fetch more water." She grabbed the jug and exited.

Tomas poked at the embers and laid several sticks beneath a

hanging pot. The Captain's breath constricted as he inhaled. He swallowed hard and flexed his jaw, trying to retain his composure.

"I ...," he swallowed again as Tomas looked at him but remained squatting. "I owe you my life ... I have been indebted to you since we landed here, and I have done you a grave injustice."

Tomas said nothing, but he did not shift his gaze.

"Thank you is poor compensation, I know."

"I need no compensation. In fact, I need nothing from you," Tomas said without malice.

The Captain could no longer meet his stare nor offer another word.

"I do not mean to humiliate you." Tomas stood. "I mean only to relieve you of the weight you carry."

The Captain's eyes flashed back. "What do you know of the weight I carry?"

"I only know that while I had no choice but to obey my master's orders, to hide that trove of gold on the schooner, you *did* have a choice. You chose to overlook what you knew was contraband. You chose to leave your family for riches. You traded adventure and esteem for contentment. We are on this island because of greed—yours and Mr. Lawson's. We do not hold it against you. Benita and I have simply made the best of our situation. Can you hold that against us?"

Tomas's words burned in the Captain's ears.

"I cannot," he said.

Tomas then left the Captain with his remorse.

Weeks passed, and the Captain recovered. Although he reclaimed the hovel, the three shared meals and responsibilities. In some acknowledgment of the couple's union, the Captain no longer referred to Benita as Mrs. Lawson. Tomas remained somewhat aloof, still guarded but always kind.

In spite of their tentative rapport, the Captain could not help but admire the young man's devotion to his now claimed wife. He remembered the joy he and his own wife shared in anticipation of their first child and could not imagine bringing up a youngster in such wilderness. Nevertheless, no one spoke of their concerns for what might become of a baby born on such an island. Evidently, Tomas and Benita had no intention of leaving the island any time soon, and it was not difficult to understand why. Living on an island away from the oppression and judgments of others was an easier option. And as for the child, it was only a matter of justifying and fortifying their decision in their own minds, convincing themselves that it was also best for their baby.

The Captain's sympathies grew, and he resigned himself to the fact that if God sent him to the island as a punishment for his greed, he must accept his penance. In fact, he was determined that he should bear up under it and prove his penitence. With this in mind, the Captain set about building a high crib for the baby.

As April drew near, Benita became increasingly large until she could barely get around. Pains came and went over the course of days, and then weeks. As she neared a month past her calculations, both Tomas and the Captain could do little more than watch and hope.

"Another pain?" Tomas asked as all three sat outdoors around the morning fire.

Benita winced, reclining against his side. "More of a twinge."

The Captain looked at her with raised brow. Neither he nor Tomas took for granted that it was only another false alarm. Even in her distended state, the Captain could not help but admire her dignified countenance.

When she met his eyes, concern flashed between them.

"With our first, my wife went three weeks longer than expected," he said.

"Was she afraid?" Benita winced again and sat upright.

"Yes, and like you, she does not scare easily. Yet, all her worry was for nothing—she gave me a healthy baby boy."

"Was it difficult for her?"

"I'm sure I wouldn't know what it was like for her."

"But you were there?"

"For the delivery? Yes, but I cannot claim any bravery. I observed from the farthest corner of the room." He chuckled.

Benita seemed not to find any reassurance in his well-intended words.

All at once, she doubled over and let out a cry, gripping her belly.

Tomas immediately carried her to their hut. The Captain followed but did not enter with them. Her cries came at closer intervals with greater strength. It went on that way for hours. The Captain did not remember either of his sons taking so long. He reassured himself, remembering that his own wife screamed a good deal.

In a moment, it will all be over, he told himself.

Then he heard Tomas shout, "Captain, get in here!"

The Captain was aghast when he entered the hut. Blood, the likes of which he had never seen with his wife, seemed to cover everything near Benita.

"It won't come." Tomas moved behind Benita. Her face distorted with agony as she panted.

"What shall I do?" The Captain knelt at her feet. He dared not look.

"Do something!" Tomas cried out frantically as Benita let out another cry and bent forward.

The Captain had no choice and simply reacted. Amid all the blood, the baby's head became visible, and with another pain, it crowned. As soon as the Captain saw its face, he noticed the cord around its head. Quickly, he untangled it, ordering, "Don't push."

He released another loop about its neck and the child came out. Benita collapsed into Tomas's arms, pale and unrecognizable. As the Captain held the little girl, her arms and legs fell limp in his hands. He swatted her bottom, hoping to startle air into her little lungs, but she did not respond. Opening the tiny mouth, he puffed into her, but she did not stir. Beneath the blood, lack of oxygen had turned the baby blue, and as he looked at Benita, her own color waned.

"Let me see my baby," she whimpered. The Captain could not look at her. His own eyes filled with tears as he moved to Tomas. The Captain shook his head and placed the dead infant on her mother's belly as Tomas buried his face in his wife's hair. She continued bleeding as she let out one final cry of grief. Soon her body was as limp as the child's.

As Tomas rocked Benita in his arms, he wailed.

The Captain rose, his pants and sleeves soaked in blood. He left the three alone and staggered to the beach. Standing on the shore, he looked at his blood-covered hands and frantically wiped them on his stained shirt. At once, he rushed into the shallow water, stripping clothes from his body, scrubbing his skin and choking on his own bile. He fell to his knees as the surf pummeled his numb body.

Once he had exhausted himself, he went to the burial ground, and with his one good arm, he dug a grave. He then returned to the hut with a large section of sail and found Tomas where he had left him. The Captain stood over him, waiting in silence. Finally, Tomas rose. He carried Benita to the water, and the Captain brought the baby. Laying his love in the shallow water, Tomas let the surf wash her body, dispersing her blood until it ebbed from her, as if it were her last bit of life.

He placed her body on the outstretched sail, and then the Captain handed him his child. Cradling her, Tomas took her out into the water. As he knelt, he washed her perfect little body, kissing her head and fondling her tiny fingers, sobbing all the while. The Captain could not help but cry with him.

Together, they brought them to the gravesite. The Captain spread the sail in the grave. Tomas laid his wife upon it. He then placed the baby across her breast.

Both men gazed upon their bodies until they could no longer bear it, and then the Captain folded the cloth over them. The Captain spared Tomas the gruesome task of shoveling earth over the bodies.

Afterward, he recited the twenty-third Psalm, "Yea, though I walk through the shadow of darkness ...."

Weeks passed, but neither knew how many. If not for the steady rains, they would not have noticed the passing of a season. During those days, both retreated into the darkness of the hovel. Strange, the Captain realized, how in the dense gloom, one does not distinguish the color of a man's skin.

In the hovel one evening, while rain poured outside, Tomas could ignore the Captain's stare no longer.

"You've been quiet for a long time, Captain."

"Indeed."

"Shall I leave you to your thoughts? Or will you tell me what you're thinking?"

A wave of a smile passed over the Captain's lips. Tomas had learned to read him well. "You remind me of my son, Samuel—"

"The quiet one."

"Yes. Quiet but insightful, even at a young age—the cleverer of the boys."

"He was your favorite."

The Captain smirked. "A father must never show favoritism."

"He may not show it—"

"It was hard not to favor him."

"Then, I do not reckon your esteem lightly."

The Captain thought a moment longer before continuing.

"If you were a white man, there would be nothing unattainable for you."

Tomas looked away.

"I can give you a shipwright's apprenticeship."

The young man's eyes flashed at him with disbelief, but the Captain did not relent in his stare or the intent behind it. Every evening, he brought up the issue again, and each time it seemed to dispel a bit more of Tomas's skepticism. As a result, by nearly halfway through the rainy season, they had completed repairs on the skiff.

Only weeks remained before safe launching weather. The Captain's excitement had diminished his perceptions of reality, of the poor reception Tomas would likely receive once they returned home. It would be one thing to hire him and provide accommodations outside of the Captain's house, but to invite him into his home—to give him a white man's apprenticeship and pay him white wages—even the most liberal-minded Northern white family would balk at the arrangement. Nevertheless, Tomas had come to trust the Captain. At any rate, anything was better than the life they presently shared.

Finally, the day arrived. Provisions filled the boat. The mast stood erect with its sails furled and ready to hoist. An easterly wind blew in, and the Captain prayed that the fluctuating currents so close to the equator might fortuitously send them directly west.

The evening before departure, the Captain battened down their supplies.

"Looks like good weather for tomorrow." Tomas gazed out over the water.

"Yes. We'll leave at high tide."

"Will you miss this place?"

The Captain paused, contemplating Tomas's question. "No. Every moment here reminds me of my worst weaknesses." He looked at Tomas. "But you'll miss it, won't you?"

"I have never known such pleasure as I have here. I do not expect I shall ever be happier anywhere else."

"I do not take for granted your willingness to leave."

"And I do not take for granted your confidence in me."

"It has been well earned."

Tomas took those words with him as he picked up two empty jugs. "I'll fetch water," he said, and headed to the jungle.

Coiling the lines, the Captain watched him go, wondering what reception his own sons would give Tomas, a young man he knew better than his own offspring.

With anticipation, he surveyed the palms. Tomas seemed to take longer than expected. As he went to investigate, the young man staggered from the brush. The Captain's heart lurched in his chest as he rushed toward the faltering man. By the time he reached him, Tomas had collapsed.

His neck swelled. Within seconds, Tomas could barely breathe. The only words he could speak were, "I'm sorry."

The Captain clutched his friend's head to his breast when he saw the two puncture wounds. Never had he felt so impotent as during those moments, which seemed like hours as he clung to Tomas, who writhed in pain as he slowly suffocated. The man's life left his body and it went limp, taking with it the Captain's own spirit and hope.

Night came and went before the Captain gained enough strength to roll Tomas onto a piece of sail and drag him to the gravesite where eleven other souls lay in rest. All the guilt he had ever known revisited him in the hours he spent weeping over his companion's grave. He cursed God for allowing such a good and guileless young man to die and leave him, the one worthy of death, to bury yet another innocent victim on the island.

In fact, death seemed his only recourse. He would come to his end on the island or at sea. He determined that in spite of his incapacitation, he would somehow set sail, and if he should die at sea, then he deserved it—he would welcome it.

He waited sleeplessly for the first light of dawn and then for the tide to come in. Feeling like no more than a corpse himself, he used his weight to push against the small hull, inching it toward the water. Once the skiff was buoyant, he boarded. With his right hand on the tiller and his left drawing in or letting out the sheet, he made some progress heading west with a strong easterly wind. As he put some distance between himself and the island, he came into a strong crosscurrent before the shoals and a sudden gust of wind out of the west. With fury, it sent the boom athwart, striking him violently in the shoulder as the sheet released and swung the boom back again to strike him across his temple. The pain of the injury sent him to the floorboards in unconsciousness. He awoke sometime later to the hull slamming against jagged rocks. Had the deviant current and winds not sent him so near the shore, he would have sunk at sea.

In utter defeat, he waded ashore with a wrecked boat and no

hope. His throbbing shoulder masked all the pain of spirit that rushed upon him as soon as he set foot on dry ground. He had not even a morsel of dignity and even less strength. He could not even let out a cry in his pitiful state.

Nevertheless, the fact that his right arm and hand were of no use to him at all did not prevent him from making a final entry in his log. On October 23, 1869, he gave a concluding account of his second shipwreck, his debilitation, and his resignation to his hopeless situation. With words barely legible, scrawled by his left hand, his final sentence was: "My efforts to leave this forsaken island have failed—I am at last alone, with all that I deserve, and I shall die here with no one to bury me. May God have mercy upon me."

WITH A LONG SIGH, MARLENA GLANCED BEHIND HER AT THE sinking sun and then back at me without another word.

My shoulders ached as I hunched, clenching my knees to my chest. I was lost in the Captain's anguish and swimming with agitation over her awful ending and her unexpected ability to draw me in. My jaw wouldn't relax as I stared at her in disbelief.

How could *she* tell a story like *that*?

Chapter 15

MARLENA'S STORY OF DESPERATION AND DEFEAT magnified all the futility in my own life. As I lay in bed that night, I almost wished I hadn't listened to her version of The Captain Lost at Sea. Her ending ran round and round in my head—there had to be more of a payoff for all the Captain's struggles, some benefit to having sought his life of adventure. I related to him in more ways than I cared to admit.

Our conversation as we packed up our picnic didn't help. Even though I had pressed Marlena for a more conclusive or satisfying ending, she would only say, "He died alone on the island."

"So, how did he die? Did he jump from the precipice or get bit by a snake? Or what?"

"I suppose he died of loneliness," she said, as if she couldn't alter it even if she wanted. The real clincher came as she shook sand from her towel. "I should probably save the rest for some other time."

I rolled my eyes, lifting the cooler. "They all died. What more could there be to the story?"

"There's a lot more. That was only the prologue."

That was no prologue. That was a full-blown, calculated, researched, and impressively delivered work of enviable fiction. "Do you even know what a prologue is?"

She stood at the water's edge and glanced back at me. "It's the setup for my story."

"That's some setup."

"Well, the rest of it won't make any sense without it."

I faced her, searching her eyes for some hidden agenda. "Why do you have such a burning need to tell me this story, anyway?"

Her gaze flashed away for a moment. "Who else would I tell it to?"

"Well, I'm not sure I want to hear the rest of it."

She hugged her bundle. "Does it bother you that I told a story about your Captain Wesley?"

"No." I squinted at the sun behind her. "Well, maybe. Though I'm not sure why."

"I didn't depict him in the most flattering way."

"Well, neither did I in my story."

"Yes, but he's *your* family, your blood."

In that moment, I realized my agitation didn't spring from her borrowing my character, doing what she wished with him. Rather, it was the fact that her story, ending aside, was good—really good—maybe better than mine.

We made our way home in silence as the sun sank into the tree line, dispersing flickers of light as we beached the boat. Although predictably quiet, Marlena never waited longer than a moment between glimpses and never moved farther than arm's distance. Yet she always seemed just out of reach.

I suppose it didn't help my mood when we came in the back door and Mother, who was cleaning up after supper, said, "Derek came over earlier, looking for you."

He knew I would be taking a test sail, but I guess he didn't expect me to be gone the whole day. Honestly, neither did I. I didn't ask, but I assumed Mother also told him that Marlena went with me. I doubted he would say anything about it. He would hope that I would bring it up, but I wouldn't.

He took far too seriously our worn-out policies regarding women. Maturity should have suggested a renegotiation. At least, I should have informed him I was no longer playing by those rules. Even having to take a stand seemed incredibly juvenile. I had a whole week of Billy and his head games to look forward to, and I was in no mood to start that with my best friend. If Derek pressed me on it, I would tell the truth. I had no idea what my intentions with Marlena were, but if he still wanted to sway her his way—have at it!

I left Marlena hanging around the parlor while I went out to button up a few things in the yard. The clock struck eleven when I headed upstairs, and when I reached my bedroom door, she came out of our bathroom at the end of the hall.

Thick ringlets framed her face and hung in loosely coiled tendrils, wetting the front of her T-shirt, apparently the only article of clothing she wore. Moving toward her door, she didn't try to hide herself at all. Perhaps she didn't realize how much of her anatomy showed through. My eyes came back to her face, taking much longer than they should have. She rested a hand on her doorknob.

In that low, lusty tone of hers, she said, "This was the best day I've had in a very long time."

"It was a good day," I had to agree, although now my insides swam tighter circles than earlier. She had brought me to a surrealistic setting, stirring unexpected turmoil, and then yanked me back, leaving me as discontented as ever. Now, my restlessness swirled into a brew of lust and irritation. I shook it off. "I hope you will finish telling me your story."

Her hand relaxed and dropped from the knob to the hem of her shirt. My gaze dropped with it. I swallowed hard.

"You weren't bored?" She smoothed clinging fabric against her thigh.

Focus, Wesley—back on her eyes. "Nope. I wasn't bored— not at all."

"But, you didn't like the ending."

"No, I didn't." I tried to remember the reason why. "I can't help it. I guess I prefer a happier, less morose ending."

"Like Buck's? Where even if he does kill off the Captain, he is valiant and courageous to the last?"

Had she meant to provoke me? "That's right."

"Then, I guess you're more of a romantic than you let on."

"Yeah, and maybe you're more of a pessimist than I would have imagined."

Her brow twitched. "That's the thing with quiet people, isn't it, Samuel? We're terribly complex. Or did you imagine I would turn out to be a simpleton?"

She *had* been reading my mind from day one. "I've never thought that about you."

"Not ever?" her brow arched, exposing my lie.

"Maybe at first."

"I could tell." She stared through me again. "I may not be very experienced, but I do know a lot of things."

I no longer doubted it, given all she had divulged that day. "I'm sure that's true."

We stood, staring at each other. I wanted so badly to kiss her, but it wouldn't have been the tender or gentle kiss I had imagined earlier.

She reached behind her for the doorknob. The door pushed opened and she slipped inside. I stood in my doorway, suppressing a frustrated shiver as I watched her watching me until she disappeared.

My body pulsed with the Captain's lust while visions of Benita and Tomas fused with Marlena and me. How many times would she evoke those desires before I acted on them? I had never felt more frustrated. Under any other circumstances, I would have kissed her, perhaps gently or even without restraint, but I wouldn't have hesitated. And I wouldn't have stopped at that. How far might one passionate kiss have taken us? Would she have been in my room for the night?

I reeled myself in. I knew Marlena wasn't like that—why else would I hold back? Was I afraid for her tenderheartedness, afraid that I would get careless and she would get all busted up? For sure, it was one of the worst feelings—calling it off with perfectly nice girls when I couldn't even define why and had to offer some lame excuse like, *It's not you, it's me.* Did I get bored? Maybe I had difficulty seeing beyond the immediate—couldn't picture myself with whomever it was ten or fifty years from now—couldn't imagine she wouldn't get bored with me.

More to the point, why did I jump from thoughts of a first kiss to freaking out over a commitment?

Why do I have to overanalyze everything? And why did she have to tell a story like that?

None of that mattered. I couldn't leave her alone.

Chapter 16

EREK CAME OVER EARLY THE NEXT MORNING TO help get the boatshed leak repair underway.

"So, how was that little skiff of yours?" He pushed a course of asphalt shingles up the pitch of the roof toward me. I was surprised it took him well over an hour into the project before he broached the subject.

I yanked a stubborn nail. "She was great. The wind was perfect. It was a beautiful sail. All my lines worked perfectly."

"Must've been … seeing as you were enjoying her for the entire day."

"She was exactly what I needed."

He raised his evil brow. "Do you really think your day out with her is going to give you the advantage?"

I scraped bits of old tarpaper, sending them in his direction. "Can't hurt."

Sweat trickled from his hairline to his jaw. "So, I guess Marlena's over her fear of sailing?"

"Oh, now we're talking about sailing? You'll have to ask her about that."

Once he realized he wasn't getting the better of me, he dropped the subject and we got some serious work done in spite of my distraction. I hadn't stopped thinking about the Captain, Tomas, and Benita—mostly about the Captain and the choices he had made, about the consequences of those decisions. Did it really boil down to family over adventure? For that matter, could Tomas and Benita have existed as a complete unit, free of all else? Could family be enough? Had Marlena intentionally run that theme through her story? Pondering it made time pass quickly. Sooner than I expected, she appeared, notifying us that lunch was ready.

As we gathered around the table, Marlena smiled at Buck, attentively seeing to his needs—much to Derek's envy. Unaccustomed to vying with the old man when it came to pretty young women, he had a hard time getting in a word. When Buck filled his mouth with coleslaw, Derek wasted no time.

"So, Marlena, I hear you're no longer a virgin sailor." He grabbed her attention as if it were her *derrière*.

It took her a moment, but a full blush rose from her neck and she glanced at me. "Well, Samuel and I did sail over to Cuttermann's Island yesterday."

That was the perfect response to his question, for the remote little island, with its tall grasses and easterly facing beach was favored for its privacy. One could get away with almost anything out there, and Derek often had.

He gave me *the look* and, with perfect timing, she uncovered a bowl of quahogs left over from yesterday.

"See what we brought back!" She waved the clam knife, threatening the big mollusk in her grip. "They're better fresh from the sea, but"—she slid the blade in—"that won't stop me from eating it now." She nearly shoved half the clam under Derek's nose. "Here! Have some."

"No … thanks, I'm full." He turned away, trying to mask his utter disgust.

She then offered it to Buck, but he was more intent on getting to the bathroom and followed Mother into the house. Then, with the dainty tip of her tongue, she coaxed the glob from the shell, past her sensuous lips and into her mouth. With sounds of primal ecstasy, she savored it with sheer delight. Derek nearly gagged at what would have driven him over the edge with lust had it been anything other than a clam. I had to laugh. She shared the next one with me.

Undeterred, Derek reclaimed some headway. "I know where the bed is. If you want more, I could take you out there tomorrow."

"That would be so fun." She looked at me. "Do you think your mother would mind if I took a few hours so Derek could take me out to dig clams?"

"No problem. Buck will be occupied with the parade and all, so you may as well take advantage of the opportunity." I even said it as though it were a great idea.

With all innocence, Marlena smiled at Derek. "Promise you won't go too fast."

Derek winked, dividing his attention between the two of us. "We'll go at whatever pace you want. Personally, I love taking it nice and slow."

"Slow is good," Marlena agreed with a glint in her eye that left me wondering.

Admittedly, those plans didn't thrill me, but I couldn't say they bothered me, either. Derek was aggressive but no predator. He knew when 'No' meant '*No*.' Just the same, Marlena was so very ambiguous. Could Derek have met his match? It seemed unlikely. Although what she had revealed of herself on Cuttermann's Island did give rise to some second-guessing. Even so, I still had a hard time believing that Marlena was anything other than what she presented.

No. I wasn't worried about Derek taking her for a sail, in spite of the gloating smirk I caught when I glanced up from my plate.

"We should probably get back on the roof," I said as Marlena followed Mother inside. "Billy will be here in a few hours, and I want to get it done."

Derek pushed away from the table. "Don't be sore, Sam. I'll be gentle with her."

"It's not her I'm worried about. Did you not see her knife?"

He followed me off the deck. "What's the matter, did she threaten *you* with her little knife?"

"I'm not like you, Derek—I wouldn't give her reason.

Remember? I'm the kind of guy who actually gets to know a girl first."

"So, how's that working for you?"

"It's working just fine."

"And yet she's so eager to go with me tomorrow. Perhaps she's interested in comparing the size of our keels."

"You don't want to disappoint her on your first date. Trust me, you'll have plenty of opportunity for that." I returned his evil eye with a smirk. "I'm telling you, she's not as gullible as you think."

He met me eye to eye as his face reddened and a vein at his temple swelled. For a second, I thought he might rebut square on my jaw. I braced myself. He wanted me to react—instead, I backed off and stepped onto the ladder. "Oh, don't get your panties in a wad. Grab that stack of shingles."

He followed me up, forcing a lighthearted chuckle. We would let it pass—for now.

Several hours of sweltering atop sticky tar did not improve my mood, and when Billy's BMW pulled into the dooryard, I suppressed annoyance at his early arrival. I checked my watch. In fact, he had arrived right on time. He emerged from his car wearing vacation-appropriate L.L. Bean khaki shorts and a polo shirt, smoothing his glossy black hair. Pressed perfection.

Although Derek purportedly found Billy as annoying as I did, he quickly abandoned the job, greeting my brother first.

"New Beemer?" were the first words out of Derek's mouth.

Billy spared only a moment to acknowledge me before he joined Derek in admiration of his latest acquisition. I came off the ladder and greeted Billy, extending my hand. I understood his hesitation; after all, a trouser-wipe did not constitute a clean hand. I withdrew, pulling a turpentine rag from my hip pocket, smearing more of the mess as he gave me a congenial slap on the arm.

"Good to see you, little brother." He smiled as if he meant it, while Derek took advantage of Billy's distraction to flirt with Elaine. She always acted as if she found his trifling rude, but that never stopped her from playing along.

"How was the drive?" I asked.

He smoothed his Ken-doll hair. "Perfect."

"Hello, Sam," Elaine called out from a safe distance. "I'd give you a hug, but …." If I weren't covered in tar, she probably would have. She was from the South. I liked her well enough, and I didn't so much mind that she was a hugger, but I always feared for her hair. I'm not sure why. Whatever varnish she used was virtually impenetrable. I would have loved to try it out on some mahogany planking.

In less time than it took Billy to rattle off his new baby's accessories, Mother hurried from the house to greet her firstborn. Normally, she restrained the hugging part of her personality—until Billy came home, of course. After all, she saw him only once a year. No doubt, Elaine's influence on Billy made reciprocating look surprisingly natural on him.

"You should go clean up now, Sammy," Mother said to me as she escorted Billy and Elaine toward the deck. Derek, who never got as filthy on the job as me, followed.

Using the lavatory at the back corner of the boatshed, I washed up while suppressing a twinge of something a single beer wouldn't squelch. The frayed denim shorts and crumpled T-shirt I climbed into were less offensive, but I still smelled of turpentine and tar.

Shards of laughter cut across the dooryard. The sight of my loved ones, all sitting together enjoying the moment, churned some emotional mixture—part jealousy and some other fleeting pang. I choked back the heat of it and forged ahead.

Guests had been trickling in for nearly a month, but on the eve of Heritage Week, they came and went like drones on a hive, with Mother playing Queen Bee. Amid the coming and going, I looked for Marlena.

"Grab me another beer, would ya, Sam?" Derek interrupted his banter with Billy as I stepped inside. Marlena stood behind the counter with Mother.

"Have you met Billy yet?" I pulled a couple beers from the fridge.

"No, I've been a little busy in here, helping."

"Oh, honestly, Marlena." Mother patted her shoulder. "I told you I have everything under control."

"Yes, but there's so many people tonight, I just wanted to—"

"Don't be ridiculous! Go sit with Buck. He's probably thinking you forgot all about him."

Marlena winced. "I suppose I could see if there's anything he wants."

Mother pushed a bowl of shelled peanuts toward her. "Bring these out, dear."

I gave Marlena a nudge and a wink. "Come on. Billy won't bite. At least, not right off."

Her eyes widened as she drew in a breath and grabbed the bowl. With my hand comfortably on her back, I ushered her onto the deck.

"Billy, Elaine," I said, "this is Marlena, the new … um … Girl."

She hesitated before looking Billy in the eye. "Hello."

"Hello," he said, immediately distracted by some remark from Derek. His greeting came off as incredibly dismissive.

Elaine nodded politely, the way people do with hired help.

Marlena offered a twitch of a smile and traded places with Mitch, who joined Mother inside.

To my relief, none of the guests gravitated toward the deck where the six of us sat. It must have looked like a private party. That was fine with me. I preferred not having to be on my best behavior after a few beers, even though outsiders were bound to be hanging around and wanting to make small talk. Derek, on the other hand, didn't mind socializing. He was always looking to promote his business, especially if the potential diving or sailing student was female and at least somewhat attractive. Married or not, it didn't matter to him. He seemed to prefer the married ones—more of a challenge and no commitment.

We all listened as Derek brought Billy up to speed on his life and most recent Caribbean adventures while Billy restrained himself, awaiting his turn to flaunt his latest exploits.

That accounted for Derek's higher-than-average Billy tolerance. They each provided a new audience for the other, someone worthy of impressing, not like the rest of us who lived our sheltered, ordinary little lives. Derek also enjoyed the way my brother stirred things up, how he brought emotions closer to the surface where he could pick at them. Maybe I was being too analytical and cynical, but Billy rarely made Derek a blatant target, in spite of his observable flaws. He preferred him as a pawn. Even if Derek caught on, he wouldn't care. He liked the banter, whereas I preferred quietly observing human nature.

Speaking of which, I couldn't help but notice the way Marlena set her attention on Billy. Her expression was difficult to read, but the way she jiggled her foot beneath the table and dug at the label on her sweating beer gave her away. After only a few minutes, she jumped from her seat, asking if anyone wanted a refill. Only Derek said yes. No more for Billy. His limit was one beer. He wouldn't want us to conclude he was going the way of his 'alcoholic' father. Did he really think that his perpetually menthol-freshened breath didn't rouse suspicion? Or that I didn't know about the flask in his cargo shorts? I wasn't going to call him on it, but his hypocrisy sure rankled me.

After Marlena had appeared a few times, Billy fixed on her each time she stepped onto the deck. His attention volleyed between Derek and her and Buck. By then he must have realized she was more than an inconsequential hireling.

It was still too early in the visit for him to pass judgment. He usually spent his first day or two in observation mode. Then the questions would come, and finally, the verdict.

Chapter 17

A PARADE MARKED THE BEGINNING OF HERITAGE Week, a tradition my family considered next to sacred. In homage, we would gather at the curb of the fully decked-out Wesley House, waiting. Mother, Billy, Elaine, Derek, and I, along with Mitch and the current Girl and a number of guests, would stand or sit on fold-up lawn chairs in some reverent version of frivolity. Today was no different.

"Is it time yet?" Marlena leaned forward between Derek and me and peered down the state road.

I checked my watch. "Just another minute."

"But I can hear the music."

"It's only the bagpipes warming up," I told her for the third time in a half-hour. Those sounds sent me back to some fragment of my life, some place resembling carefree. They visited only during a few fleeting minutes every year, hanging on each moaning note, dissipating in an exhalation.

"How long will that take?" she asked.

I showed her my watch and assured her that the parade would begin at precisely ten o'clock.

At the edge of our group, Billy chatted with a fellow BMW owner. A wide grin stretched across my brother's otherwise expressionless face. The guests saw him as charming and out-going. All I saw was a performing bundle of overcompensating nerves.

"I've never been to a parade." Marlena's attention darted between the road and us.

"What? No parades in Kansas?" Derek slung his arm over her shoulder.

"Not any that *I* ever went to." Just then, the '59 convertible Caddie pulled out of a side road. She slipped away from Derek. "Look! There's Buck in the front seat!"

I chuckled as she burst out waving at Buck riding shotgun beside the Mayor with Miss Wesleyville waving from the rear seat. Even though it was all plainly visible, Marlena stood on her toes as if she were a child trying to get the best possible view.

In about twenty minutes, they had all marched past, heading for the fairgrounds, otherwise known as Wesley Park and the beach.

"Now what?" Marlena asked.

"Now we walk to town."

It was only a mile or so, and since tourists had inundated Wesleyville for several days, finding a parking spot wouldn't be easy. So, we strolled down the state road, which spilled into the main drag through town, where quaint shops lined the narrow streets and sales racks crowded sidewalks beneath handsomely carved signs.

I hung back as Derek did his best to walk beside Marlena as she wove her way between window shoppers, always a few steps ahead. Neither of us had any chance of talking to her or anyone else as we funneled our way through oncoming tourists. She glanced back frequently, like an overeager puppy, afraid the throngs might sweep her away.

Arriving in our little group, we gathered toward the front of the park, under the red-and-white-striped pavilion near the bandstand where live music played every night. Later in the evening, similar tents would shelter rows of white plastic-covered tables and fold-up chairs beneath a web of tiny sparkling lights.

Depending on the day, some of those tents housed the Arts

and Crafts Fair, the Baking Competition, the Quilt Show, flower arrangements from the Garden Tour, the Whose Pet is Smartest, Whose Kid is Most Musical … and on and on. The carnival also came to town and set up between the tents and the beach. At night, I would row out on the water where colorfully flickering lights of the revolving Ferris wheel shimmered on the harbor. Stunning.

The week culminated on Saturday with the sailboat race. Regulations permitted only small boats. Skiffs, dinghies, catboats—a few fiberglass, but nothing high-tech. In effect, full-keel boats were excluded because all boats had to beach and re-launch with manpower alone, and we sailed in shallow waters. We kept it on the technical low-end so that anyone could compete. Only a few of us took it halfway seriously. Often it resembled a free-for-all—a bunch of tadpoles swimming circles. A desire to stay upright and avoid collisions governed the competitors more than the actual rules.

I also enjoyed the evening dances but usually attended only one or two, depending on who would be there and which band would be playing. Marlena promised Buck she would go with him on Saturday night for the Big Band music.

As the crowd filled in, Marlena sought me out. On tiptoe, she kept her attention on Buck, as anxious to see him up on stage as she had been for the parade to pass. Derek cast an evil eye in my direction. I'm sure it irked him that Marlena glued herself to my side, but I didn't plant her there—that was all her.

When Buck took his place in front of the mic, my heart rate spiked. He squinted at the audience and tapped the microphone a few times. He gnawed his lip and scanned the crowd. His eyes found mine and I smiled. He didn't smile back. How much of a risk had we taken, putting him up there in front of a crowd? Heat came up my neck.

This is where he really shines—he'll pull it off, no problem.

He cleared his throat and scratched his chin while I prayed he would do us proud. I hoped he wouldn't say or do anything a little off, something that might give Billy ammunition. But I was more concerned for his dignity.

He inhaled and then welcomed the crowd with a broadening smile and crackling voice, moving right into his usual dissertation. I exhaled, relaxing a kink between by shoulder blades. He gave us the same spiel we heard every year, but I listened more carefully than I ever had.

His admonitions on community and family values struck me afresh, stoking heat that rose from my core. All at once, the pride swelling in my chest pushed air from my lungs, leaving me bereft. His words muted. Short on breath, I heard nothing beyond my thumping chest. *What if this is his last time?* I swallowed back a choking sensation as my body radiated heat. Marlena patted my arm, and I focused my blurred vision. What did she say?

Applause broke through. I joined in, my breath coming back. Marlena rubbed my arm. It was over. Buck must have done okay.

🪢 As soon as we arrived back at the house, Marlena went upstairs to change for her big clam-digging day out. She reappeared on the deck, wearing my trunks, her T-shirt, and sneakers. She had piled her hair atop her head like coiled metal shavings springing out in all directions. Derek looked her up and down, one brow arched. He then glared at me as if I were her fashion coordinator. "No skirt today?"

"Samuel says skirts are dangerous on a sailboat."

"A skirt might be dangerous on something as tiny as his little dinghy, but we're cruising in luxury today." He tossed a glance toward his cutter, *Trigger*.

Without acknowledging his pomp, she stated, "Well, we're digging for clams, and this is my clam-digging outfit."

He again glared at me. I shrugged. I still thought she looked adorable.

In spite of her appearance, he took her by the hand.

Billy chimed in, "How about a tour?"

"Sure thing." Derek knew me well enough to be certain that I would have no interest in the bow-to-stern particulars. After the first two times, the tour bored me.

Derek escorted Marlena and Billy around the back of the boatshed to the moorage. They reappeared halfway out on the planked walkway. When they reached *Trigger's* slip at the end of the dock, Marlena waved.

Admittedly, *Trigger* was a beauty; forty-five feet of relatively new fiberglass, fully decked out with a gourmet's galley, wide master berth, and every nautical, direction-finding, course-plotting, map-reading, depth-gauging gadget available. Derek had little appreciation for the romance of the old wooden boats—he liked things shiny and a little ostentatious, and she was all that. I was envious only from the standpoint that he had a serious cruising vessel in the water. *Trigger* had navigated offshore seas, sailed the Caribbean, all the way down to Venezuela and back, while mine remained on stilts in the sick bay. But once the *Mary-Leigh* was up and sailing, I would take her over *Trigger* any day.

From my chair on the deck, I watched Derek as he assisted Marlena aboard and then gave Billy the full rundown, as much for her benefit as my brother's. I'm sure Derek hoped to convey how much bigger his was compared to mine, as if the *Firefly* and *Trigger* were in the same category. What Marlena didn't know and probably cared less about was that mine, that is, the *Mary-Leigh*, was a good twenty inches longer. I preferred to think she remained unimpressed with all that fiberglass, which was more than I could say for Billy.

Once the tour ended, *Trigger* purred out of the harbor amid a bay buzzing with motorboats and dotted with multicolored sails. That's when Billy and Elaine slipped off to the craft show. Mother, in her usual whirlwind, returned to the kitchen to prepare more food, so only Buck and I remained.

We walked down to the launch pad and stood at the foot of the fishing dock. He said, "How about we cast a line or two?"

"Nothing's going to bite today, Buck, not with all the racket out on the water."

"Oh, we'll outsmart them, sure enough." He winked. All Buck really wanted was to spend some time, the way we used to.

We strolled to the end of the dock where we kept a couple of rods at the ready. I picked up a can of crawlers, holding it as he plunged his knobby hand inside and fumbled with a squirming specimen.

As if I hadn't fished with him a hundred times, he pinched it in half. "Like this, Sammy." He grabbed the hook and pushed it through the worm. "Here." He handed over the other half of the bait and watched as I pierced it through. He patted my shoulder. "Good."

I looked him in the face as he focused on his reel, letting out a little more line. His eyes held the same fixation I used to see while he sailed. I wondered where he went in his own mind, appearing so detached from anything in the moment.

I continued watching him until he cast his line off the end of the dock. He then looked at me, gesturing that it was my turn. I did as he did, the way I used to as a boy. I cast my line away from his, remembering how his huge hand once felt, settling on my small shoulder—how he never stopped talking, but even in midsentence, he would smile at me and say, "You're a good boy, Sammy."

The sound of it hung in my memory, and I glanced at him. He smiled, staring ahead at where the line danced on the water. His pleasure roused warmth—but not the anxious, heart-pounding sort I experienced earlier. I was fine with the silence—would have preferred it. Then his eyes returned to mine. They watered more than usual. He wet his lips as if restraining their tremor, and with all the sincerity his voice had ever carried, he said, "I'm very proud of you, son."

I didn't know how to respond, and I guess he didn't expect me to because he quickly went back to fishing as if he hadn't even said it.

What prompted him to say that? And why had he chosen that moment? I only knew that his words resonated somewhere deep inside me, some place where a young boy thrived on any scrap of approval. I wished that in all his words, in all the stories, that he was the kind of man who could talk about those things that men in my family never discussed. *The sea is in your blood,* he had always said, *restless and turbulent.* I thought that meant he understood me, that we understood each other. But he never talked about how that restlessness affected him, how he dealt with it. I wanted to ask but I couldn't. It seemed as wrong as reading the last page of a story when you're only halfway through—like cheating. A man needs to navigate uncharted waters on his own. I again thought of the way Marlena depicted the Captain; his torment shuddered through me afresh.

Chapter 18

ROUND MID-AFTERNOON, BUCK WENT TO TOWN with Mother to pick up some last-minute groceries. I offered to go, but I think she was afraid that if I knew how much prosciutto cost, I would come back with shaved ham. Just for the record, I wouldn't.

So, it was Billy and me. Just the two of us. All alone together, sitting on the deck. Up until then, he had remained in observation mode. As we each took a long draw from our beer, I knew he would segue into interrogation.

"So, what projects have you been working on around the house?" he asked, as if willing to lift a finger on any of them.

"Just the usual."

Then he volunteered, "Let me know if I can give you a hand with anything."

"Sure," I said, but I wasn't buying it.

Then came the expected, "So, what do *you* think of the new Girl?"

I wanted to say, *the* Girl *has a name*, but all I said was, "She's been a big help to Ma."

He responded with his typical, "Hmm." He was getting primed.

Right then, Elaine came out onto the deck. "William, we need to decide on tomorrow's itinerary."

Mother found it annoying that Elaine called him Will or William, and even I rolled my eyes the first time I heard it. I always called him Billy unless I really want to tick him off. Then I called him Bill, which is what everyone used to call Dad.

Elaine ran down their list of options as Mitch pulled into the dooryard. I excused myself and went to chat with him for a few minutes. Before long, *Trigger* made harbor, furling her main sail and heading for her slip. She was hard to miss as she headed inland and docked. Even at several hundred yards, I noticed Marlena's hair, now loosely pulled back to the nape of her neck. When she rose and accepted Derek's hand to debark, the difference in her outfit became apparent. She now wore something distinctly girlish—a dress, to be specific. How long had he had that number stashed?

She walked the whole length of the dock, barefooted, hips swaying, and swinging her sneakers by their laces. Derek carried the bushel of clams and what I assumed were her clothes. He was, in every way, the operator I would never be. It irked me that somehow he had managed to manipulate her into something more to his liking. Even more, it irked me that she had allowed it. They walked out of sight behind the boatshed and came into view a moment later as they rounded its corner into the dooryard. Now I got a good look at her. I had to admit, Derek did pick the perfect dress for her. It wasn't the trashy style he usually went for, though its snug fit did show off her figure better than anything I had seen her in, other than her wet T-shirt. The pale blue contrasted her tan shoulders and legs, and the short skirt flared inches above the knee. And that puckered white fabric across her bust—nice accent. It wasn't very low cut, but definitely more revealing than her typical outfit. Quintessentially feminine. She was all smiles when she came up the back steps under the climbing wisteria vines of the pergola.

She said, "He bought this for his sister but it didn't fit. Do you think it's pretty?"

"Sure," I said with feigned indifference. "It's nice."

She grabbed the bag of clams and stepped inside as Derek shoved her clothes at me. He smirked, "Yeah, I got her out of your nasty swim trunks."

"You probably ought to get a sister if you're gonna keep using that line," I said as he chuckled. I asked if he wanted a beer. Of course he did.

In the kitchen, as Marlena rinsed clams, I came up beside her. "How was the sailing?"

"Good, but his keel was too low to get as near the bed as we got." She gave me a nudge and smiled. "To tell you the truth, the whole time I was wishing you had come along."

"Then we'll have to make sure we take the *Firefly* out again sometime."

"Promise?"

"Yeah, I promise."

With only the hint of a conceited grin, I returned to the deck and parked myself at the end of the picnic table with my fresh beer in front of me. Derek, Billy, and Mitch sat across the table. When Marlena came out carrying a bowl and a knife, she sat right beside me and revealed the bowl's contents. She looked like an excited kid showing me her candy stash.

She rubbed her hands together. "Derek says the smaller ones, cherrystones, are better on the half-shell." As if he knew. She slid the blade in, twisted off the top shell, and gestured toward Derek. "Would you care for one?"

Derek waved it off and she frowned. "Well, I know *you* want one of my cherrystones, Samuel."

"Hell, yeah, I do." As she passed it to me, I cut Derek a look, probably not unlike the one Captain Wesley gave Tomas as Benita fed him.

Then she opened another for herself and drizzled lemon juice over it. Derek and Billy tried their best to avert their eyes, but I think even Derek got over enough of his initial repugnance to appreciate her sensuous consumption of it, especially once she started the 'yummy' noises.

When she had his full attention, she reached over to *my* beer and took a long swig, wiped her mouth, then passed it back to me. I could actually see the dagger plunge into Derek's gut. To give it the twist, I took a long gulp after her and strategically placed the bottle right between us.

Billy was quick with his observation. "You don't sound as if you're from around here. Where did you grow up?"

"I came from Kansas."

"You didn't learn to do *that* in Kansas."

"What?" She glanced at the beer and back at Billy with a friendly grin. "Drink beer from a bottle?"

"You know what I'm talking about."

"Oh, the clams." She bristled. "You think people from Kansas aren't capable of learning surprising things?"

"No, but how would a girl from the Midwest learn to do that?"

It was a question I had pondered myself.

"It hardly seems important how I learned, but I'd be glad to open one for you. Or perhaps I could show you how to open your own. It's really not that hard."

"No. Thank you," he said with disgust.

"Well, you and Derek are no fun at all," she said as Mother pulled into the dooryard. Marlena rose. "I'll go help carry things in."

"You can sit." I stood with her. "I'll get the groceries."

"No," she grabbed my arm. "I haven't seen Buck all day. I miss him."

I stepped aside and followed her, watching her sway the way she did, and as I stared, I felt them stare. I overheard Billy ask, "So, who exactly does this one have her eye on? You, Sam, or the old man?"

I didn't hear Derek's response.

As I grabbed the paper sacks from the trunk, Marlena threw her arms up and gave Buck a hug, revealing dark wisps of hair under her arms.

Mother cringed. "Marlena, dear, if you're going to go sleeveless, you really need to shave your armpits."

"They're my armpits and I'd just as soon keep my hairs right where God made them grow." She locked her arm in

Buck's and headed toward the deck. I followed with a chuckle. Personally, I thought she looked sexy in that *au naturel* way of hers, though I did wonder how it went over with Derek. He had very particular opinions about women and body hair.

I brought the groceries inside, left them on the counter, and then left Marlena in the kitchen with Buck.

As I sat out on the deck, Derek commented, "You were right about her, Sam, she's not nearly as … what was the word you used?—*gullible*—as she seems."

I raised my brow, waiting for the punch line.

"Yeah," he winked, "especially now that she's seen enough to make a comparison."

"Really? Then I guess you haven't shown her your *short* attention span," I said as Buck and Marlena stepped back through the doorway.

Buck sat beside me at the table and Marlena placed a bowl of chips in front of him. As she rounded the far end, reaching for the dip, she brushed past Derek. He grabbed her hand.

"Why don't you sit down, Marlena? Ol' Buck's got everything he needs for a few minutes, don't you think?"

"I suppose." Her hand obeyed his lead. She glanced at me as she sat beside him, her fingers withering from his grip.

Derek didn't know it, but he did me a favor. If she had sat at the picnic table beside me, I would have missed the view of her knees relaxing and spreading in the most unladylike manner as she crossed her ankles. I had to wonder if her aunt had ever taught her how to sit properly in a dress. Apparently, someone had given her some sort of instruction, because when she caught me noticing, she blushed and daintily raised one knee over the other, exposing the underside of her thigh as she crossed her legs. *Very nice.*

Sitting for only a few minutes until Buck polished off the dip, she was again on the move, twirling toward the kitchen. She returned to the seat beside Derek, repeating her knee crossing performance, but never sitting long enough for him to complete a maneuver. I wasn't the only one noticing his thwarted efforts.

For the rest of the evening, questions formulated behind Billy's judgmental eyes. Aside from watching Marlena interact with Buck and Derek trying to interact with her, Billy's astute eye would also pick up Derek's borderline, if not overt, hostility toward me. Perhaps I was being a little paranoid. What difference did it make if he figured out Derek and I were after the same girl and that we had hired Marlena as Buck's summer companion?

"THAT MARLENA—SHE SURE KNOWS HOW TO PLAY DEREK and you against each other," Billy baited me after everyone had retired for the evening. Crickets chirped in the dark. "You know, some women really get off on that sort of thing."

I should have slipped back into the house when I had the chance. Agitation rose in my chest as I stared at the citronella candle's flame. I wanted to lay into him, and I almost did, but it was pointless. I didn't feel like playing that game. Besides, it was only his usual; analyze behaviors—especially the deviant—and label them.

I passed my finger over the top of the flame. "You don't know anything about her."

"And you do?"

"I know that she's a big help around here."

"So, what exactly *does* she do around here?" As if it were any of his business. He had figured out that she didn't fit the role of all the previous Girls, that her primary job was Buck—proof that he had gotten worse since Billy's last visit.

I exhaled, making the flame flicker. "She helps out with the usual stuff, and she likes to listen to Buck."

"What sort of background does she have? Any medical training? Can she at least perform CPR?"

"She's not Buck's nursemaid. He doesn't need one. She simply provides him with company so we can get things done without worrying if he might wander off." *That* was the wrong thing to say.

"What do you mean, wander off?"

I wiped perspiration from my forehead. "You know what,

Bill? It's late and I'm tired. We can talk about this some other time." I pinched the flame, extinguishing it, then stood and headed for bed.

Yeah, it was immature to walk off that way, and it wasn't as if I didn't realize those were issues that needed discussing. I just really resented that Billy had walked out on our family and then, for one week out of fifty-two, he sauntered back in and thought he had any idea of what our life was like or how it was for us right after Dad drowned. It would have been nice to have had a big brother around when I needed one, but those years were long gone. Buck had stepped in where I needed him to, and I would be there for Buck until the day he died.

I would have loved to tell Billy what he could do with his PhD.

Chapter 19

OR THE NEXT FEW DAYS, I WORKED OUT IN THE boatshed, away from all the bustle. As I worked on the *Mary-Leigh*, my mind drifted back to the night she foundered, so many years ago. I had awakened to the sound of thunder, heavy rain, and window-rattling gales. I thought I had heard some scuttle downstairs and told myself that it was only wind twisting branches against the house. I was barely nine, much braver than a seven-year-old now that I could explain away most of the creaks, groans, or even the occasional crash in the night.

The following morning, limbs had fallen throughout the neighborhood, causing power outages. High winds had tossed a few boats in the harbor, but only the *Mary-Leigh* had pulled away from her mooring, slammed into the dock, and taken on enough water to leave her bow tipped skyward, listing like a half-full bottle and lodged in the mud.

The summer I turned nineteen, I removed her ballast in the yard and then brought her inside, intent on burning right into the project. I was already trying to pull more than my own weight at the boatyard while keeping up with maintenance and repairs on the house. Consequently, Mother's agenda had relegated the *Mary-Leigh* to after hours and one guaranteed week each summer. I had made progress, mostly on her keel and frames, but paying projects kept her at the bottom of the list. Therefore, this was the week I always devoted to her.

Billy had little or no sentimental attachment to the *Mary-Leigh*. When we were growing up, he had always said, *Sailing is boring—I like motor boats*. Although over the years, and especially since he had achieved a certain professional and social status, he liked the way sailing looked on him. Just the same, the whole boatbuilding business never interested him. For that reason, I would have a little peace away from him out in the shop.

He and Elaine came and went throughout each day, always by themselves, never including Buck. Once a day, Marlena and Buck walked to the fairgrounds together, returning a short time later when he went in for a nap. That's when Marlena checked on me, usually with a glass of water. She watched me drink. As soon as I emptied my glass, she took off. Perhaps she assumed that in the shop I was all business and didn't have time for her. In fact, I would have welcomed a little interaction, but when I finished for the day, I knew she would be looking for ways to engage me. I especially looked forward to that.

Each day, Derek showed up for at least lunch or dinner, and of course, so did Mitch. That wasn't unlike either of them during Billy's visits, but Derek had the added Marlena incentive. For me, it was nice to quit earlier in the day and not have to get back to work after eating. It took a couple of days, but I enjoyed the more leisurely pace my life took on. I also enjoyed the repartee when we all gathered on the deck.

Usually the bantering was evenhanded, and all of us took our fair share of abuse, but this year it had gotten a little lopsided. Billy had been his normal obnoxious self, easily caught up in Derek's attempts to make me look foolish to Marlena. To my own amusement, even if she got any of their jokes, she didn't laugh. She merely sat there with her baffled expression, and they were so preoccupied with their own wit that they didn't even notice how her eyes often found mine. I loved the way her eyes smiled.

I guess if any part of Billy and Derek's alliance irritated me, it was that my best friend was supposed to be *my* ally, not my brother's, and that didn't even cover what brothers were supposed to be.

I understood what was going on with Derek, but our growing competition was so stuck in high school. In all fairness, given some of my own ineffective ways of handling relationships, I didn't have any legitimate right to expect our friendship would move beyond that, but I wished it would. At any rate, I wasn't playing anymore. When that finally dawned on him, if it hadn't already, maybe we would talk about it, but probably not.

On Tuesday, when Derek didn't show up for lunch and then supper, I was a little disappointed. Thanks to the diversion he had been providing, I had managed to avoid almost all one-on-one interaction with Billy. What I had not anticipated was how Marlena would become Billy's focus in Derek's absence.

During dinner, Marlena sat opposite me at the picnic table. After helping Mother clear dishes, she returned and sat beside me, close enough to bump elbows while we shared a bowl of peanuts in front of us. She crossed her legs in that particular way, and every so often, her foot nudged my calf. I would have enjoyed our comfortable rapport a whole lot more if Billy hadn't had his eye on us.

He shelled peanuts, popping one after another into his mouth, allowing us a few minutes to relax. As soon as Marlena leaned into me with an unguarded sigh, Billy swallowed and started in. "Marlena, you seem to have a real knack for handling Buck."

She no longer leaned as she looked at him for one of her long moments, scrunching her brow. "I'm not sure I understand what you mean by *handling*."

"Handling—you know—effective way of enlisting his cooperation."

"I don't *handle* him. I spend time with him," she said, without the irritated spin I would have put on her words.

With perfect timing, Buck appeared on the porch. "Marley, I have something I want to show you,"

He slipped back inside and she followed. Derek came up the

steps with a six-pack in hand and set a cold one in front of me. "What have I missed?"

"Not too much yet," I said, cracking a peanut shell. "But I think Billy's about to enlighten Marlena with a dissertation on The Elderly: How to Manipulate Them without Their Knowing It."

Derek chuckled, taking a seat.

"I was about to do no such thing." Billy adjusted his collar. "I'm only curious about her, and since *you* seem to have little information to share, I thought I'd get it directly from the source."

"Then why beat around the bush? Why not simply ask her?"

At that moment, Marlena returned with Buck and a smile.

Derek's face lit up. "Beer, Marlena?"

She hesitated and sat. "Okay."

"Let me open your top." He winked and twisted it off as I rolled my eyes. She thanked him, and he turned his attention to Buck. "How about you, old man?"

"Nope, I'm headed off to bed." He turned to leave. "And I don't want to be up in an hour to pee."

"Goodnight, Buck," she said for all of us, leaning into me and grabbing a handful of nuts. "And thanks for the book."

After she sipped her beer a few times, Billy started in again, but with a calculated, affable tone. "So ... Marlena ... do you mind if I ask you a question?"

She glanced at me, crunched a peanut shell, and then looked back at Billy. "No, I don't mind."

"I was wondering if you have any background in geriatrics."

"In *what*?"

Both Derek and I laughed. Guess not.

"Well," he continued, "what sort of education do you have?"

"Is this your question?" She paused and then responded with all sweetness. "What sort of education do you think I should have?"

"I should hope at least a high school education."

"Oh," was all she said, in such a matter-of-fact way that it would come across rudely for him to press the matter, and of course, he did.

"You do have a diploma, don't you?"

"Do I need one of those to be Buck's friend?" The subtle shift in her demeanor belied the sweetness in her voice as she pushed peanut husks around the table in figure eights.

Billy's lips tightened with a pretentious smile. "Let's be honest." That particular phrase always made me cringe. "You're not being paid to be Buck's friend. You're being paid to keep track of him."

Before I could set him straight, she came right back at him. "Are you saying I wouldn't be Buck's friend if I didn't get free room and board?"

"I'm saying you wouldn't get free room and board if they didn't need someone to keep an eye on Buck."

I jumped in. "You know that all the Girls we hire get free room and board, Billy."

"And yet, it's quite obvious that she doesn't perform the same function as all the other Girls, does she?"

I was about to come to her defense when Marlena interjected, "So what exactly was it you wanted to know about me?"

"I want to know if you're qualified to assist with Buck."

"Oh, I thought this might be more about Samuel's qualifications. After all, he's the one who sees to this family's needs."

Billy's mouth dropped, but not for long. "You're quite clever."

"Is that what you think? That I'm being clever?"

"I think that you're far more clever than you let on."

His arrogance galled me. I said, "Back off, Billy," and they ignored me.

She took a deep breath and squinted. "Are you saying I'm dishonest about my intelligence?"

"I'm saying you're not nearly as naïve and inexperienced as you would have us believe."

"You can choose to believe whatever you want, but since

we're being honest, how does any of that matter to you?"

"It matters because I'm concerned about the caliber of person hired to look after my grandfather."

She stood, pressing her beer bottle into the table, crackling peanut shells. "Had I known how little stock you put in Samuel's judgment, I would have sent *you* my résumé. Or do you also require an IQ test and a Multiphasic Personality Inventory?"

He glared at her. She stared back, but not long enough for him to rebut. In an instant, she left the table and the door open behind her.

I glowered as he chewed a nut with his eyes on me. "I didn't mean to sound as if I don't trust your judgment, Sam."

"Well, ya did. And you couldn't leave her alone, could you. You just had to get your psychoanalytic crap all over her." Before he offered his usual justification, I too up and left.

I could have stayed and told him off. As good as that might have felt, I was more interested in Marlena. I had a hunch she would be in the parlor, communing with the Captain, and that's where I found her.

I came up behind her and stroked her folded arm. "Don't let my brother get under your skin. He can be a real jackass sometimes—just gets too full of himself."

My own tempered words surprised me.

She glanced in my direction. "He doesn't like me."

"I don't think you care."

"I don't."

"Then why let him get to you?"

Her nostrils flared. "Psychiatrists just want to put people in hospitals, even if they don't belong there." She turned to walk away.

"Marlena," I said before she stepped through the doorway.

She spun toward me.

"Why do you always do that?" I asked. "Just up and walk away when we're in the middle of a conversation?"

"Is that what I do?"

"Yeah, all the time."

She shrugged. "I guess I don't have anything more I want to say about your brother. Was there something more you wanted to say?"

"Well, no, nothing at this moment, I guess."

"Okay, then." She exited through the doorway and ascended the stairs.

It wasn't until I had gone to bed that I began to process her exchange with Billy and his accusations. In all honesty, I had difficulty reconciling Marlena's usual introversion and lack of sophistication with the young woman who had held her own against The Bill-dozer.

I couldn't deny that he did bring up some issues that even I had wondered about. I couldn't be sure, but it seemed her hostility was as much toward his profession as toward Billy personally. Might she have had a bad experience with a shrink? I could only hope that if she had, it was secondhand and not first.

As a general rule, I tried not to attach a stigma to the mentally skewed, but an alarming notion did occur to me. Maybe Marlena was on leave from the funny farm. How would we know? That might have explained a few of her peculiarities, but I hated to start labeling that as mental illness, otherwise a whole lot of us were in big trouble. So what if Marlena was not as naïve as she seemed … as long as she wasn't psychotic. Sure, she talked to herself, but that didn't mean she was responding to voices in her head … did it?

Besides, 'odd' made for interesting characters. Marlena's peculiarities intrigued me as a writer. I considered myself insightful when it came to human nature, but the intricacies of the brain, that was Billy's forte, not mine. Still, I pondered the line between reality and imagination—how it sometimes blurred. I saw it in Buck. Had all his storytelling gotten the better of him? Considering how much loss he had experienced, it wasn't surprising that he escaped into the realm of fantasy. The scary part was, I completely related to it.

When I worked out a character, when I wanted him to seem real to my reader, he first had to feel real to me. During that time when I brought him to life, he could be as consuming as the guys I drank with at The Bilge. I never wrote everything about him, but I knew him far better than I knew even my best friend. When I completed the story—and it never felt entirely complete—I missed him, and sometimes I would reread my favorite parts where he shined just to visit for a while.

Now, that was a scary admission, though it was scarier wondering if the affliction eroding Buck's lucidity would one day erode mine. If Billy was right, if Dad had been a drunken lunatic, I supposed that should have frightened me even more.

Was I concerned about Marlena's sanity? Not particularly. In fact, I found her all the more attractive. Perhaps that said volumes about my own grasp on reality—or lack of it. One thing was certain. Billy was thoroughly primed, and next he would corner *me* about Buck.

〰️ I HAD ARRIVED AT THE COUNTDOWN PRECISELY ON TIME. Billy was scheduled to leave in three days. On Wednesday, after Marlena and Billy's go-around, he and Elaine conveniently slipped off first thing in the morning, right on through dinnertime. Later that evening, some hot jazz band played at the fairgrounds, so for the entire day he spared both Marlena and me any unpleasantness. Thursday, Mother and Buck consumed most of Marlena's time, while I stayed safely busy at the boatyard. I'd had two Billy-free days, but he was closing in on me.

That evening, quite a few guests socialized at the house, so I grabbed a quick sandwich and ate it out behind the boatshed by the old marine railway. We called it the working side of the yard, where we hid away the Travelift and wintering boats so as not to clutter up the view from the bed and breakfast. Its seclusion offered the illusion of privacy, a good place for quiet conversation or silent meditation. Sometimes Derek and I would hang out there when guests overran the house. Back in high school, we used to light up a joint every now and then, as if we could get away with anything when out of my mother's sight. Tonight, I just wanted some solitude.

The summer solstice had approached, so it stayed light until around nine o'clock. A little later than that, Billy appeared with a six-pack. I was sure he intended the gesture to soften me up, and I had to admit, it did slightly temper my dread. We each drank our first beer in silence, and I waited to see if the next four were mine. When he reached for his second and took a long gulp, I joined him and felt the alcohol diluting my resentment. He stared off and seemed to have no agenda—not that I believed it for a minute, but at least he deferred the pace to me. I took another swig. "How are you enjoying your visit?"

"Good."

Beside us sat a dilapidated pram, fallen over on its side and half-buried in weeds. Tipping my beer toward it, I directed Billy's attention. "You remember that summer when Dad helped us build that?"

"Yeah." He stared off. "I remember ... but it was Buck who helped us build it."

"No, man, I distinctly remember Dad—he had on that red hat and a plaid shirt."

"Didn't say he wasn't there ... he was, passed out in the corner. Remember? Buck was the one who taught us how to use the drawknife, because Dad cut himself and had to sit down."

I vaguely recalled it ... remembered how Dad didn't get up from that chair for the rest of the day. Billy didn't say anything more about it.

Crickets and peepers dueled in a chorus. Water slapped against the old railway only a boat's-length away. Wispy clouds reminded me of 'bridal gauze waltzing' in front of the moon.

"You know Buck's not doing well," Billy said.

I choked down provocation. "Yeah, I know he's slipping."

"He's doing a whole lot more than slipping, Sam. We need to bring him to a specialist."

Offense rose in my chest. "Ma just took him to the clinic last month." Or maybe it was two months ago.

"I know. Doctor McKenzie is an adequate family

practitioner, but Buck knows how to schmooze him. What he needs is specialized attention."

"Just because he takes off and forgets to tell us doesn't mean he's completely losing it." I couldn't believe how much I sounded like Mother.

Billy shook his head. "He doesn't forget to tell you—he's disoriented and gets lost."

"Listen, Billy, I'm not trying to be a jerk about it, but when was the last time you spent more than five minutes, just you and Buck? How can you possibly presume to know what condition he's in?"

Billy couldn't say anything to that. We both knew the answer.

We drank the last beers in silence. When he finished, he said goodnight and I sat outside in the dark for a long time. I had drunk only three beers, but my head splintered off in a hundred directions. I just wanted it to stop.

Chapter 20

FTER HALF A NIGHT OF STARING AT THE ceiling, I fell asleep. Two minutes later, the alarm went off. My only real rest came during those ten minutes after I hit the snooze button. I hit it three times.

I didn't lie in bed obsessing over anything in particular, but perhaps the whole Billy and Buck issue unsettled me more than I wanted to admit. The thing with Derek also nagged at me. And then there was Marlena, but I couldn't categorize her as stress—not really. I simply couldn't follow through on any one thought with any degree of continuity. Instead, my mind trolled all over the place. I hated that out-of-control feeling, and that's probably why I woke up in a mood. Not even the wonderful aromas—coffee, bacon, sausage, home fries—could entice me as I envisioned the looming 'Breakfast Table.'

If there was any upside to having strangers in the house, it was that none of them paid much attention to me first thing in the morning. They all preoccupied themselves with food and itineraries. I was merely another occupant at the table, unless I could manage to slip out of the house undetected. Unfortunately, when Billy came home, I couldn't.

On my way downstairs, I stretched my back and massaged my neck, hoping all my kinks—mental and otherwise—might dissipate before I had to look anyone in the eye.

I sat at the table with a pasted-on smile and glanced at Marlena. I wished it were only the two of us. Scanning the table, seeing people I scarcely knew, family members included, I cringed at their infringement. God, I missed my usual morning routine. Maybe after so many years, I didn't like all those intruders in my house. I didn't like the formality of the social breakfast event. I missed my two-cups-of-coffee mornings with no breakfast to slow me down, and the jaunt to my secluded boatshed.

Stifling an exasperated sigh, I settled my sights on Marlena, the one person I cared to share my morning with. I focused on her. Actually, we were mutually absorbed. She smiled, coaxing my reaction to the way she licked syrup from her fork after a bit of pancake tumbled back onto her plate. She brought out the sensual in even the clumsiest act. I'm sure Mother found our little staring game rude. She cleared her throat in that particular high-pitched way. Only Billy and I detected its intended reprimand.

"So, what is everyone planning today?" Mother asked.

I jumped in. "I'm taking the *Firefly* out for a sail. And I'm taking Marlena with me."

It sounded completely premeditated but it wasn't.

I added, "We'll be gone until late, so don't expect us back for lunch and probably not even for supper."

Marlena's eyes shot back at mine, beaming like an eager accomplice. "But, what about Buck?"

Without hesitating, I looked straight at my brother. "Billy's going to spend the day with him."

What could he say? I didn't feel the least bit manipulative. He had backed himself into that corner.

Within twenty minutes, Marlena was wearing my shorts and had packed a lunch. At the launch pad, I steadied the *Firefly* as she boarded with a co-conspirator's glint in her eye. One big shove, as I hopped aboard, and we were off.

The occasional whitecap spit water at the bow as we tacked out of the harbor. Out beyond Cuttermann's Island, the bow lifted and slapped against each swell. Marlena's eyes widened.

"We won't flip, will we?"

I smiled in reassurance. "I've sailed in a lot rougher waters. This just makes it more fun."

The wind picked up, I adjusted my tack, and we listed to nearly forty-five degrees. She grabbed my hand. A sliver of water spilled over the rail and sprayed the front of her. I waited for her reaction. She squealed, leaned back, and flung both arms overhead. When the boat was at full heel, when Marlena laughed and looked at me without any fright—I never felt more manly and more in control.

Although constantly aware of her, I handled all the rigging the way I did when alone. Never once was she underfoot. Anticipating every shift of my body, she responded as if we had sailed together a hundred times. She knew when the boom would swing and moved where I wanted her. If I could have sailed and made love to her at the same time, I would have. I knew exactly how far out to take her, how far I could push her limits.

I dropped anchor at Cuttermann's Island where we previously had. Before I even gave the word, she slid into the water, dumped the blanket on the beach, and then returned to the clam bed. As soon as I set the cooler in the sand, she giggled behind me, and I felt a splat on my bare back. She had lobbed me with a glob of mud.

Within seconds, black muck slung all over the place as we traipsed clumsily through thigh-high water, falling all over ourselves. Mud covered us, head to waist. It fell in clumps from her coiled hair and all over her no-longer-white T-shirt. I wiped it from my face and dug it out of my ears as she smeared it all over my bare chest and retreated, only to go at it again. I couldn't remember the last time I laughed that hard. I was defenseless as she pushed me down into the water, and I pulled her muddy body down on top of me. If the thought of a mouthful of muck wasn't so revolting, I would have kissed her then and there. Instead, I grabbed a huge handful and held it over her. She begged for mercy. When we caught our breath and called a truce, we swam out to deeper water and rubbed off as much silt as possible.

She submerged and then resurfaced out a bit farther. "Turn around. I need to rinse my top."

She lifted the hem of her shirt, exposing her waist, and then paused, giving me the opportunity to do the gentlemanly thing. I lingered in her teasing smile before she turned her back on me.

Finally, my restraint kicked in, but it did not curtail my imagination as I headed to the blanket and collapsed on my back. I glanced out at the water for a peek, but I had missed my chance.

Soon, she lay beside me, still trying to catch her breath. With the most natural and easy gesture, she slipped her hand into mine. A perfect moment. I dared not alter it in any way. I lay there, reveling in the incredible convergence of childhood, adolescence, and full-grown manhood. I didn't look at her face, but I heard her smile with each exhalation, and squeezed her hand. *Could this be what love feels like?*

After a while, she rolled to her side, her knee nudging my thigh. I glanced at her body beside mine, the curve of her hips dipping to her waist and then rising again to her breasts and shoulders. It was hard to keep my eyes on hers as I shifted to my side. Her head, resting in her hand, cocked with a question.

I tucked a stray lock behind her ear and asked, "What?"

"Um ...." Her attention wandered from my face to my chest and back as if she were having as much trouble concentrating as I was. "Uh ... your grandmother's name was Estelle, wasn't it?"

"Yeah."

"You know, sometimes Buck talks about someone named Mary, as though she were his wife. I was wondering if he's confused."

I ran my finger over her hand between us. "The *Mary-Leigh* is the name of his yawl." Her fingers responded, playing with mine. "The one he built, that I've been working on. She's named after his first wife."

She re-secured the stray curl. "I didn't know he was married before."

"It was only for a few years. She was the love of his life. She died not too long after they married."

"That's so sad." Her fingers returned to mine, and her gaze to my gaze. "How did she die?"

"I'm not really sure, but it tore him up pretty bad."

"How did he meet Estelle?"

"Shortly after Mary died, World War Two broke out, so he enlisted." I caressed her forearm, struggling to follow through with my thought. "He met Estelle in France. By the end of the War, he married her. A few short months after that, my dad was born."

Her fingers pressed her lip. "Do you think that Buck *had* to marry her?" She lowered her voice as if discretely shielding their reputations. "That she might have been pregnant?"

I found the innocence of her reaction astonishing. The shameful stigma attached to the circumstances surrounding my father's birth struck me afresh, even though they wouldn't raise a brow these few decades later. That stigma was something I had thought about, but not until years after my father died— after I finally did the math. "No one's ever admitted as much. But that's the way all the dates add up."

She sat upright, drawing figure eights in the sand. "Hmm ...."

I pushed myself upright so I wouldn't be staring directly at her chest. She opened the cooler and unpacked lunch, all but the kippers this time. As we ate, I watched her as much as she did me, although neither of us focused exclusively on the other. We said little but exchanged a whole lot in those long moments. Was she reading me again? Could she tell that I was thinking about the story she had told, about how I envisioned her and me, shipwrecked alone on an uncharted island, without any restraints of propriety? Was her coy smile inviting a confession? I withheld.

She drew in her lower lip, slowly moistening it as she again nudged my thigh. "Do you still want to hear my story?" she asked in her low, lusty tone.

It took me a moment to refocus. Of course, I wanted to hear

the rest of her story, but I hesitated to bring it up. What if it didn't meet the standard she had already set? Ending aside, what if she didn't pull it off as well as she had the first?

"That's why we're here," I said, though I might have had a few other activities in mind.

"So, you didn't forget."

"You know better."

She wiped her lips with her fingers. One lingered at her mouth as she licked it.

Now, how was I supposed to concentrate? I forced myself to look her in the eye. "Tell me the rest of your story."

Chapter 21

MARLENA SAT ERECT, CRISSCROSSING HER LEGS as she faced me. She drew a deep breath, looking more excited than nervous. "Ready?"

I nodded, directing my attention toward the bay, like last time. One more deep breath and she began with a poem.

The Sea possesses authority.
She calls and men obey.
She churns the desires of his heart.
Lust for an adventure,
Love for a woman,
Merge in her capricious bosom.

The Sea is sly,
Baiting a man's pride,
Tempting his arrogance,
Allowing him great feats.
She leads him on,
Draws him with her exuberance,
Into her vastness.

She howls,
Bring your lover to me,
I shall sway her heart toward yours,

And she will remain yours
Forever....

"I'll love you forever," Miguel whispered to his bride as they stood at the helm. A fresh breeze from the east filled their sails. Sophia nestled into his embrace. Their future spread out before them like the spray of stars above. Each night had brought wonders more splendid than the last, honeymoon-bliss for weeks under the Atlantic sky.

Their forty-five-foot sloop, *Anna-Bella*, had already navigated an early tropical storm and high seas out beyond the Virgin Islands, past the French West Indies. Fearlessly, they continued on to the Windward Islands and left St. George's, Grenada far behind.

"I wish we could just keep sailing," Sophia said. "Could Venezuela possibly be better than this?"

He kissed her neck. "I suppose my barrage of relatives could wait a day—perhaps even two, but we can't be late for the banquet."

His suggestion required no reply as she pushed her fingers through his black curls and drew him to her lips.

That night, the sea lulled them to sleep, and in the morning, she enticed them with promises of fair weather. By evening, she turned fickle.

Years of offshore sailing as a member of numerous expeditions and races gave Miguel some advantage over his jealous mistress, but when a squall began at dusk, she tested his prowess. As tropical winds blew in from the coast of Africa, the sea unleashed them upon *Anna-Bella*. Sophia and Miguel wrestled to furl the sails and donned their life jackets as a precaution. Just before sunlight disappeared, they braced themselves on *Anna-Bella's* deck as her bow tipped skyward. Waves crested above them. Thunder rumbled in the distance.

Lightning split the black skies. Torrents of rain pelted Miguel's face as he kept to the helm. Sophia struggled with the storm anchor as it fought against her balance. As soon as she heaved it over the side and the line pulled taut, *Anna-Bella* righted herself with a tug. Now, if they could ride out this storm just like the last, they would write about it in the log and again marvel at their seamanship.

"Done!" She braced herself to stand.

In an instant, a sudden, twisting gust heeled *Anna-Bella* to leeward. Sophia stumbled as the mast snapped, twirling like a baton overhead. She glanced up as the beam struck Miguel at the base of his skull. As if in slow motion, his body spun, toppling overboard along with the mast. Horror seared Sophia's veins as she scrambled for the life ring and sent it into the swells, only to watch him disappear under the pulverizing billows. He resurfaced some distance away, his arms flailing against not only the waves, but also the lines of the mast and boom. Another swell mounted above and then crashed overhead, swallowing Miguel and the mast, filling the hull and nearly taking Sophia overboard.

As water continued rising and surging in, *Anna-Bella* listed. Sophia grasped at the locker as her footing gave way. Another surge filled the deck, lending her enough buoyancy to reach for the lid, grab at the life raft's cradle, and grip the ripcord. She clung to the burst of orange that pulled her overboard as the undertow sucked *Anna-Bella* down, compressing her own lungs.

In a frenzy of adrenal strength against ferocious wind and waves, she shot back to the surface and kept with the raft, praying the ballast chamber would quickly fill, so the wind would not lift the vessel and send it crashing down upon her. Within seconds, the canopy loomed above her, but another billow nearly ripped her from the safety strap. Unable to catch her breath, she struggled against disorientation and roiling waters, making her way around to the entrance flap. With what little strength she could rally, she pulled herself inside.

In the dark, she lost all equilibrium as the forces outside threw her against the canopy. The raft had all but capsized, and it would have but for the ballast, which quickly righted her. Again and again, she tumbled inside, like clothes in a washer, her own vomit mixing with seawater. Overtaken by exhaustion and shock, her body shut down. She had no idea how much time had passed before the wind and sea abated, when sleep finally subdued her and black took over.

As consciousness trickled back, light crept in where a breeze lifted the entrance flap. She scooted toward the opening where the horizon bobbed over the edge of her raft. She cast her gaze to the blue sky above as her body sang with fatigue. Sleep came and went for a day before she gained enough clarity to sip from bottled water in her survival kit. When she finally came to again, she rummaged through the kit and tore into a protein bar but ate only half. As she peered out the porthole, she scanned the unending ocean for any remains of *Anna-Bella,* but mostly for Miguel. She saw nothing—only the undulating sea and the scorching sun. Under the circumstances, she could barely scrounge enough emotion to cry, let alone feel gratitude. Had it not been for Miguel's insistence on spending the small fortune for the 'raft the astronauts use,' she surely would have perished. Even so, it was supposed to transport both of them, not her alone.

Don't despair, she told herself. *Stay positive. Someone will surely find you. This is the Atlantic, after all—not the Pacific.* For two days, she drifted eastward, rationing her portions and trying to no avail not to think of Miguel. For three years, he had been her constant companion and soul mate. How could he all at once be gone? They had always managed to pull through any situation, be it on land or at sea, in the wilderness or in some back alley. As an individual, he had always been the stronger, always goading her daring, fearless side, and together they had been invincible. How could *he* not survive?

On the third day of consciousness, as she sipped water, she lazily scanned the horizon. Adrenaline whipped lethargy to excitement as she spotted a small immovable mass rising above and then sinking into the ocean. With sudden enthusiasm, she paddled toward it. Her confidence grew in leaps. Even as she approached the now discernible island, she could not make out the incongruous structure projecting toward her like a crooked, beckoning finger. Not until she neared its scant remnants did she recognize it as a once-mighty vessel, wedged into ragged rocks. The sight of it turned her stomach with foreboding; ragged rocks above—ragged rocks below.

At once, she met cross currents above the unseen reefs, where breakers mounted and then crashed over shoals below the surface. The tide rushed her toward the island, and she could not keep the raft from rising and then thrusting forward, tipping to near vertical and throwing her against the canopy. It righted but seemed to be hung up on something. Another wave tossed her, and water gushed in through the flap. The ballast must have caught a reef, and if she didn't abandon the raft, she would continue to flail in her little dome. Just the same, she did not relish the idea of the reef tearing her to shreds.

First, she tied her survival kit to a length of line and affixed it to her waist. Through the porthole, she timed her escape, waiting until she could catch the wave at its crest and ride it past the shoal or reef. Taking a deep breath, she lunged into the oncoming wave, but she should have waited a split second longer. The waters crashed down on her as she roiled below the surface, scraping her thigh. Then, in a fortuitous twist, the undercurrent drew her toward the island and away from the coral.

With blood streaming from her wound, she waded through shallow waters and limped ashore with her kit floating behind. The solid earth beneath her feet seemed to shift and undulate, sending her to the sand. Even as she rolled to her back, the ground rolled with her. The gentle surf and a stiff windward breeze cooled her skin, yet she should not remain exposed to the midday sun and willed her body to stand. The earth would not hold still, and she nearly fell back to the ground. From a sitting position, she examined her thigh. Blood streamed from what looked like a scrape.

"Oh, great," she muttered. On closer inspection, the scrape was in fact a deep gash that needed more than a butterfly suture from her first aid kit. She unhitched her lifejacket and tossed it aside. Then she pulled her T-shirt over her head and wrapped it tightly around her leg. For several minutes, she applied pressure to the wound and then, tugging the line, she drew the survival kit to her. As far as first aid went, Miguel had not packed much more than bandages, antibacterial ointment, Band-Aids, and hydrogen peroxide, but he did include a sewing kit. If she could muster the strength to wade back into the water to flush the wound, she could steady her hand enough to stitch her leg.

As soon as she cleaned the gash, she rewrapped it in her shirt and stumbled back to shore before wooziness again sent her to her knees. She lay back down, knowing she had no choice. She needed only a few minutes to stabilize herself before she sat again. When her hand steadied enough to poke thread through the needle's eye, she was ready. Spreading the wound, which barely bled, she doused it with peroxide and closed it quickly. She remembered the time she and Miguel had climbed Torres Peak in New Zealand, and she had to stitch his hand. She had flinched more than he had, but now she didn't dare. She exposed her thigh, took a couple deep breaths, pierced her skin, and drew the needle through one side and then the other. Tears welled, blurring her vision, as the thread seared its way through; she swore, hating to take time to wipe them. She tied off one stitch and repeated the process five more times, wiping tears between.

Flopping to her back, she closed her eyes and let the tears come, though no emotion accompanied them. It was as if her body—independent of her heart—needed to cry and she let it, but not for long. As soon as she was able, she hobbled with her kit up to the shade of palms and fell asleep beneath them.

When she woke, the sun had peaked and long since begun its descent. Her raft no longer bobbed. Deflated, with its canopy half-collapsed, it rolled with each crest and tumbled with each breaker. If the reefs didn't shred it by morning, she hoped to salvage at least enough to make a shelter, but that would have to wait. The most she could do for now was find a makeshift crutch and collect some driftwood for a signal fire.

As the sky darkened, she sat upwind from the ascending smoke, but still her eyes and nostrils burned. As she warmed herself in front of the flames, she pushed visions of Miguel from her mind.

"Stay calm. Be positive." She repeated the words like a mantra, keeping her from the brink of panic. Sophia's inherent fearlessness was her greatest asset. Others often remarked at how daring she was, without apparent fear of consequence. It wasn't that she never considered or ignored how poorly things could turn out, she simply knew she could handle whatever came up. She held to the motto, *Fear weakness, not experience.*

As if time held any relevance, she glanced at her wristwatch—identical to Miguel's. One in the morning. She had better get more sleep, for she had a big day ahead of her. Behind her, off in the brush, the cacophonous chirps and caws of birds filled the night air. Though eerie, their song was beautiful—an indication that somewhere on the island, fresh water likely existed.

As soon as she awoke, she fed the smoldering coals, adding palm fronds. Blackened smoke ascended as she ate an entire protein bar and peered out at her raft. It had drifted a short distance from the shoals, but apparently, something still held it bound. It extended and retracted with each wave. Distracting herself from the sight of her foundering raft, she took inventory. Aside from the first-aid kit, she had several more small water bottles. Three protein bars. A flare. A lighter. Waterproof matches. A signaling mirror. A small compass. Fishing line and several hooks. Water purification tablets. Several condoms for water storage. Chap Stick. A small pocketknife. Her lifejacket. Needles and thread. She gathered all that back into its pack.

She drank a few swallows of water and then, with the help of her new crutch, she rose on her steadier leg. Her wound throbbed, but she ignored the pain and headed back to the beach. Crabs scurried sideways with the ebb and flow of each wave. Staring out over the horizon, where the water no longer seemed to move at all, she hoped for Miguel. With a harsh shudder, she tried to rid herself of the notion that her husband was likely dead. The sight of cormorants circling over the lagoon and perching where the old shipwreck wedged at a torturous angle offered even less hope.

Turning her back on the sight, Sophia walked down the most approachable length of beach, which wrapped around to the southeast. When she crested the dune to the southern tip, she found nothing but more beach and more cormorants.

"Time to find water." She headed back toward the signal fire.

Less than a minute into the thick, creeping foliage, a snake slithered across her path, startling her. Overhead, a large bird swooped from a tree and crossed in front of her. She steadied herself with a sigh and continued following what appeared to be a natural course through the brush. It was difficult to hear much over the twitters and caws, but the tricklings of water lured her ahead.

She parted a bushy vine, and the sight of clear water brought a tear of relief. Keeping an eye upon her surroundings, she bent to fill a bottle. There, to her side, she noticed something as out of place as a schooner on the rocks.

She gasped. "What the …?"

There, erect at the water's edge, a long, rusted sword stood perpendicular, plunged into the ground. She filled her empty bottles as she stared at the peculiar sentinel. A corroded tin cup hung from its crossguard. Pocketing her bottles, she yanked the sword from its place.

"Who did you belong to?" she asked, as if the blade would speak.

She returned to the beach. Her situation had taken a positive turn, albeit a small one. She pointed the sword toward the horizon and circled the tip of the blade, cutting through air.

"And what else has your owner left for me?"

A scan of the beach brought her attention to the weathered hull out on the crag. Cormorants launched from splintered wood and flew to the precipice.

"That's a place to start, but it'll have to wait." The climb would have been easy if not for her injury. Instead of investigating the precipice, she waded out into the water to see if she could do something about her raft.

After the initial burn of saltwater on her wound, she pushed through the gentle surf and found it felt better after a minute. She continued on, conscious of any undertow that might pull at her. All seemed safe and so she made her way into waist- and then chest-high water. It didn't take long to find that the reef still clung to several lines. Now, in water to her chin and with her pocketknife in hand, she swam behind the raft. Hoping to salvage as much of the line as possible, she dove under and followed the line as far as she safely could. She quickly sawed through the line when the waters around her pulled toward the shoals. When it gave way, the force of the raft pulling toward shore in the upper current drew her to safety.

The canopy remained mostly intact and could act as a shelter. She slept under it that night. The next day, she ventured past the southern dune, wishing she knew the actual size and layout of the island. If only she dared climb the precipice, but even as well as her injury seemed to be healing, it would likely be days before it was wise to test herself. She continued onward, keeping track of her direction with the compass. She risked walking only as far as where the beach turned into bony ground and rocks, always keeping an eye out to sea. She then turned back, but not without a supply of crabs tucked in a sack constructed from raft remains. Every day, she ventured a little farther, building her strength, and by the fifth day, she decided to try the initial slope of the precipice.

To her surprise, after clearing away a few vines and a little overgrowth, she uncovered several tread-like carvings notched into the rock. Using the sword to clear away more of the overgrowth, she placed each foot with care, ascending until the steps ran out at a ledge. There, she decided to call it quits before a wall of vines, not quite halfway up the summit. Poking with the sword at a strange bit of light behind the overgrowth, she loosened a tangled mass. There she found a cave's narrow entrance.

Cautiously, she peered inside. A disturbed snake slithered over her foot and sent her reeling backward. With a shiver, she breathed in courage. The cave's southerly exposure lent light to the first few feet inside. She stepped forward. Some small bit of light came across from the opposite wall. She approached and poked at the small carved-out window. More light eked in and she gasped. There in the shadows, she made out other occupants, dead and alive. A small snake slithered through the eye socket of a skull, part of skeletal remains upon a dilapidated cot. As a precaution, she poked at anything nearby with the tip of the sword. She grabbed a trunk small enough to drag by its side handle and scooted it out into daylight. The latches had rusted shut, yet they were no match for a rock and her determination. With several thuds, she broke the fastener and slowly lifted the lid.

Inside she found a large volume. Barely legible, its gold lettering spelled, *Holy Scriptures*. It lay atop another volume. At its side sat a compass, a ruby-embellished dagger, and a pocket watch. She lifted a wad of cloth and ten gold coins tumbled to the ground. While they likely had substantial value, the looking glass is what won her gratitude.

"You see? All is not lost. You have water, and now you have a way to start as many fires as you wish."

With what items she could carry, she made her way back down to the beach and caught crabs for dinner. Skewered and roasted, they made a tasty meal. All the while, she kept her eyes to the horizon, unable to fathom that her beloved husband was possibly, yes, very likely, dead.

"Don't think that way. He could be alive …," though after nearly a week, it seemed unlikely.

She gathered more palm branches and twigs and added them to the smoldering embers as thick smoke ascended. The following day, she claimed a little more space in the cave and brought more of her cache down to the surf. With sand, she scoured some rusted-out utensils, a lantern, and four glass jugs. She rinsed some tattered linen garments with care and laid them upon a boulder to dry. The remainder of an ax head and a grinding stone did not need anything more than dusting off.

Handling those items, those things that assisted another

survivor—she knew not how long ago—connected her in some way to the stranger on the cot. Every time she entered the hovel, she looked upon him with pity and then with admiration, even gratitude. It was as if he were nudging her along, offering reassurance. His skeleton still bore strips of the material that had once clothed him. Tufts of hair lay about the skull. Long, brittle fingers overlapped his ribs. One of those intertwining bones bore a gold band. She stood over him, imagining a peaceful demise, and touched his blanched skull. It rocked upon what was once his pillow.

"Who were you? And why did you so carefully pack that trunk? Were you expecting someone?" She smiled. "Perhaps you were expecting me."

Hunger pangs demanded she collect more crabs, but before she left him again, she promised, "Tomorrow I'll give you a proper burial."

After enjoying her tender bits of crab, she sat beneath a palm and opened the skeleton's trunk. She picked up the Bible and set it aside, now focusing on the worn and stained journal. She stroked its soft leather binding. Gingerly, she opened the cover and found it well intact with pages not nearly as brittle as she would have expected from such a relic.

She read aloud the first line, "'Captain William Wesley—in command of the schooner Vanessa-Benita—January 5, 1867.'"

After that, she read for hours, page after page. At first, it read typically of a captain's log, not unlike what her husband had recorded in *Anna-Bella's* log. Then, on the date February 9, it all changed.

"'We are shipwrecked. Six of us remain.'"

She continued reading until the words, "'We buried Roberts today. Only three of us remain.'" That was as far as she read before her eyes tired.

Chapter 22

ARLENA DIDN'T OFTEN INTERRUPT HER STORY to add commentary, and so I was a little surprised when she paused for a moment, bringing her eyes to mine, and said, "I just love Sophia. Isn't she brave and fascinating?"

I chuckled. We storytellers do become enamored with our characters. "Yeah, she's pretty cool. Fearless. And beautiful—at least that's the way I see her."

"Yes, very beautiful." Marlena's lips curled in a wistful half-smile as she stared out at the water. She sighed and then continued.

Early the next morning, she transported the Captain's remains after locating the burial site as per his description. Out of respect for those already interred, she cleared creeping vines from the communal headstone. She read the names as if seeing each face. Each one a life, long forgotten. Surely, someone mourned them, once upon a time. As she read, she halted at the word *Baby*—carved beneath *Vanessa Benita, Wife of Tomas. April 10, 1869.*

"A baby ...," her fingers stifled the words in her mouth. "There was a *baby* ...." Her tears fell upon the grave of strangers, yet she had not cried for her own husband. As she dug the new grave, she choked back her emotion. By the time she had him arranged and buried, she had regained her composure.

"There." She patted the ground over him. Brushing sand from her hands and knees, she stood, strangely at ease with so much death surrounding her.

"Well, Captain, I'd say a prayer for you, but God and I aren't exactly on speaking terms." She sighed. "I want to thank you for leaving your things. I think you were probably a kindhearted man. Perhaps a romantic, like my Miguel—" Her husband's name cut through her denial.

Covering her mouth, she let out a cry and fell to her knees, unable to hold back the pain and the tears. She would never again see the only man she trusted implicitly, the one person who saw the best in her, who didn't consider her independent spirit a threat; in fact, he had nurtured it. With him at her side, she could conquer any mountain, desert, jungle, or sea. Without him, isolation would put to the test all he had taught her.

She sobbed for hours, her tears mingling with all the anguish of those who cried before her. Over the next several days, she ate little, and with what scant strength she had left, she decided to climb the precipice, for better or for worse. If she could scale the rock face, she could prove herself adequate without Miguel, and that she was competent on her own—or she would die trying.

Standing at the ledge before the hovel, she looked out over the sea at the haunting remains of *Vanessa-Benita*. Would the rocks also claim her? She had a hard time caring as she started up. With her injured leg, she struggled on what would normally be an easy climb, relying more on her upper-body strength. Even as her muscles burned, her confidence sparked as she imagined Miguel above her, waiting, telling her how amazing the view was.

As she pulled herself up and over the top, Miguel was not there to offer his hand, but she hoped she might feel him beside her as she looked out at the ocean panorama. She came to her feet, and as the view struck her, she never felt more solitary or obscure. Slowly, she turned, hoping for anything on the horizon. The line that should have set the boundary between earth and sky blurred. Her eyes would not focus on so much nothing.

The stiff wind whipped around her and tousled her short hair. Would she lift from the precipice as she edged closer to the brink? She looked out at the crashing waves, at *Vanessa-Benita*. How would she come to her own end? Would the time come when she wished she had ended it now? She looked down and thought of Miguel. Had she believed in an afterlife and the possibility of joining her husband in eternity, she might have stepped off. Miguel was likely dead, but there was still a chance *she* might be found, and whether she would be dead or alive was up to her. She couldn't give up—she had it in her to live.

When she returned to the beach, Sophia roasted a few crabs and continued reading the Captain's log. At least she had this dead man's company. With his help, she learned the island. She located the cassava and cush-cush and harvested some seaweed. She also dug for mollusks in the shallow water and found duck eggs in the low-growing mangroves. She even ate snake one evening.

With the Captain's direction like a guiding hand, she set out on a small expedition. Hacking her way through the lush greenery, she finally found the fruit grove. So much of it had overgrown that she nearly walked directly into what remained of Tomas and Benita's hut. A breeze wafted strands of delicate vines to-and-fro from a slanting beam and former doorway. She parted them like a curtain and stepped inside as birds cawed overhead, singing an eerie tale of despair. Most of the roof had blown off or caved in, yet for the most part, the side structure still stood. She turned slowly, imagining all that had taken place in the little dwelling.

She stepped forward and nearly stumbled over something at her feet. The remains of a tall, leaning cradle startled her, and she could almost hear the screams of a woman laboring over an infant she would never nurse. Sophia's heart raced. A large bird swooped overhead and sent her out of the hut, crying and gasping for breath, horrified at the thought of bearing a child in such a wilderness. She found it so difficult to shake the melancholy it put her in that she delayed her search for the fishing hole until the next day. It was three days before she could read the captain's journal again.

While all the details he provided helped her survive, it was the Captain's personal observations and confessions, which drew her back time and again. To read his torments of conscience, of his various lusts, his love and sometimes-explicit remembrances of his wife, and his growing respect and friendship with Tomas—it was better than anything she had ever read. With each reading, she fed a bond between her and this very real yet long-dead man. His intensity and passion were akin to the temperament of her own husband and made her miss Miguel all the more. She stretched her imagination, trying to hear her husband's voice in the Captain's words, but she heard only waves relentlessly crashing on rocks and lapping the shore. She missed his companionship—his strong and gentle hand.

Weeks passed. Each morning and each evening she stood on the beach and peered through the Captain's looking glass as the surf licked her toes. She spotted the occasional dolphin, and sometimes, farther off on the horizon, a distant storm.

How many more days?

One night, she bedded down in the Captain's hovel, staring into the dark as wind rushed through. Each lightning strike flashed images before her, drowned only by deafening thunder. Gales turned to hushed voices, swirling around her, and distorting to the weeping of a woman. Her own chest heaved, and she realized the cries were her own.

I'm losing my mind ….

In the morning, she looked for her husband again, but only seaweed and a few stray planks had washed ashore. Day blended into day, and she wondered how many weeks had passed. Maybe a month, she thought as she carried several speared crabs to her little fire up near the palms. Then again, perhaps it had been longer. She picked meat from the shell. It didn't taste as good as it had however many days ago it had been since she waded ashore. In fact, after she ate, her stomach turned with nausea.

"Well, it's not as if your shelf life could have expired," she muttered at the crab remains as she flicked them into the brush.

As soon as she stood, her breakfast was about to come back up. She made it as far as a palm tree and leaned against it, retching into the thicket.

She had no trouble keeping her dinner down, but the next morning, her breakfast again came up.

"Oh, God." She tried to remember when she had her last period. "You can't possibly be pregnant."

Days passed and the sickness continued. It was one thing to battle the tangible elements of nature, but to have her own body turn on her—to be defenseless against something growing within her and the accompanying hormonal surges—she had never known a more daunting foe. Each night, she staved off the tears as long as she could until they encroached upon her without restraint. She loathed her weakness and hated the parasite that robbed her of her dignity. She could no longer give herself pep talks, nor did she speak to Miguel as if he could hear. Only the Captain's words provided any reprieve.

Several more weeks passed and still no period, though her sickness had subsided. She tried not to think about it, but with little to occupy her time but finding food, she thought of little else. And she couldn't deny her swelling abdomen. She sat on the beach, staring at her rounding tummy; she could not comprehend it. It seemed unreal, as if she were host to a tumor.

Night after night, she awoke, unable to erase visions of Benita in her pangs of childbirth. Sophia feared little, but the thought of pregnancy and childbirth churned something in her that loomed large and ominous. The only births she had ever seen were on her family's farm, but calf birthing interested her as little as having children of her own. Even when some of her friends had babies, she had no desire to hold them. In fact, she and Miguel decided to forego a family. Travel and adventure would be their baby. What would Miguel think now? It didn't matter. He had left her, and he left her pregnant. She tried to imagine his shock if she had ever told him the news. She could scarcely remember what he looked like.

Life continued as it had for the past weeks, only now she marked off days. Many nights she lay awake, trying to calculate how much longer she had. Once, when the moon shone through the hovel window, she woke to voices somewhere outside. Alarm spiked through her body as she rushed to the ledge overlooking the beach. She no longer heard voices, but she something crested on the dune at the southern tip. Her heart raced as she called out, "I'm up here!"

She stumbled her way down the carved steps and fell onto the beach. In the moonlight, she ran to the dune and then beyond it, calling out the whole time. No one answered and no one came into sight. Falling to her knees, she collapsed and lay there until the morning. She saw only her footsteps in the sand.

The following night, she heard the voices again, so clear she could almost make out words. This time clouds hid the moon as she looked out over the beach. She someone stood on the shore at the sea's edge and she called out, "Here I am! I'm up here!"

The figure moved toward her, and once again, she scurried her way down the steps to the beach. When she landed, she called out "Please! Wait for me!" as the figure moved toward the water. "Wait!" she cried as she followed it into the surf, and then she could no longer see it.

"Wait … Please don't go!" she whimpered and dropped to her knees in the surf. "Please come back …." She wailed, throwing her head back and sobbing into her hands.

She wept in the water until sunlight, when cries of winged creatures filled the trees, taunting her. *You are losing your mind! Losing your mind!* they cawed. Exhausted, she tripped through the surf, back to the beach, where she saw only her footprints. The voices had been so clear. How could her mind so vividly conjure her deepest wish, only to dash her to such despair? How could her own psyche betray her so?

She heard the voices again the next night, and nearly every night after that, but she simply rolled over and cried herself back to sleep.

Around the time when her shorts no longer fit, she lay on the beach one afternoon, watching a cormorant circling above.

"What are you looking at?" she yelled at it. "Why can't you be one of those birds who learns to talk? The whole lot of you—you're a waste of bird flesh!"

She closed her eyes, and at that moment, something moved across her tummy. Her eyes flew open. She saw nothing, but then she felt it again, only to realize it was something inside her moving. For the first time, it occurred to her that she was not alone. She had wept many times since she landed on the island, but never for sheer joy. She leapt to her feet, rubbing her tummy and danced on the beach and into the surf. Her arms flailed as she kicked arcs of water into the breeze. If anyone but the cormorants had seen her, they would think she had gone mad. Finally, she had someone to talk to.

With her renewed spirit, she began making plans for her baby's arrival. Now that her appetite fully returned and she thought of each meal as feeding her child, she spent most of her time acquiring and eating or storing food. When she fatigued, she read.

During one late afternoon, near the end of her pregnancy, she sat in her favorite reading spot, propped against the rock hedge outside of the hovel's entrance. There, the south sun warmed her belly and lent light to faded words. As she read aloud to her baby, she came upon the account of Benita's pregnancy. She continued reading about how they had prepared for the baby's birth.

"This will be helpful." She patted her tummy, glad to reread things she had forgotten.

"'She grows larger by the day,'" Sophia read, and paused at the words, "'her pangs began ....' Well, you don't need to hear about that."

Silently, she continued reading the account of the baby's birth and, of course, her death. She wished she had not reread it. The Captain, bitter of heart, provided no solace.

Sophia slammed the book shut, tossed the journal atop the Bible, and wept. She thought of death, of the horrible burial. She thought of the Captain's words—'*Yea, though I walk through the valley of death, I shall fear no evil, for thou art with me.*' The Captain had written those words, and when she had first read them, she had thought him an eloquent poet. But those words rang from somewhere earlier in her life.

She glanced at the Bible, drumming her fingers upon her large stomach.

"He has no use for me," she said to the child inside. "I've been a heathen since I left home. I suppose it's your father's fault. He never had any use for church, but you won't ever have to worry about sitting on those hard pews."

Using the trunk for leverage, she stood with difficulty and glanced at the Bible one last time before shutting the lid. For the remainder of the day, she seemed as preoccupied with the notion of an unseen God as she was with her unseen baby. The following day, rather than grab for the Captain's log, she lifted the large book—the one book that made her more uncomfortable than all others—the book she had avoided for over half her life.

"At least it will be something new to read."

Forging ahead through 'thee's' and 'thou's,' she grew to enjoy the archaic language—it seemed so literary, a challenge for keeping her mind sharp. The verses in themselves were not void of meaning, but it was more of an intellectual rather than spiritual exercise.

As her time drew closer, she tried again to calculate her baby's arrival, but she could only guess at the day based upon how she felt. With several false alarms behind her, she had everything ready. A clean cloth, jugs of clean water, fishing line to tie off the umbilical cord, her pocket knife to sever it, and a great deal of food stashed for her recovery.

One night she woke to a gripping pain that stole her breath. She lay in a wet cot and her abdomen bore down.

"Oh, God!" she cried out, holding her belly, in the worst

pain she had ever known. The pain relented only to come again before she had caught her breath. Prodding around in the dark, she located her kit and pulled it near. After the next pain, she tucked the cloth beneath her bottom. "Oh, God," she screamed again.

However, the baby did not come. All that came were more pangs and more screams. She begged, "Dear God, let me have my baby—please don't take it from me."

Still the baby did not come, nor had the worst of her pains.

Believing she would suffer Benita's fate, she swore, "Dear God, this child will be yours—don't let us die."

All at once, as the sun rose, she opened up and the baby came out. As her child cried, she scooped it from between her legs, and with it wriggling upon her belly, she tied the cord and cut it. Weeping, she nestled her baby girl to her breast. Her bird-like mouth gaped, searching for milk, and with scarcely any help, she found it. Sophia could not have imagined the sweetest little cooing her baby made as she sucked, nor could she have imagined the blissful satisfaction of giving her baby what she needed. She fell in love.

"You have your daddy's hair." She kissed her head, wetted from her own tears. Her tiny little fingers gripped her with such strength. As she nursed, Sophia checked for all her parts, amazed at her perfect formation, that her own body could produce something so wonderful. She was beyond a doubt a miracle.

For several hours, the two slept. By midday, Sophia regained enough strength to carry her baby to the beach. The sun beat upon her shoulders as she waded out, letting the water wash her daughter's little body as she wriggled, kicking her feet and fanning her arms. It was as if she wanted to swim. She didn't cry, she simply looked up at her mother. "Baby, you're as fearless as your Mamá."

Chapter 23

THROUGHOUT THIS PORTION OF MARLENA'S STORY, I had taken to studying her face. Although she appeared to be gazing out to sea, I could tell from the distant look in her eyes that she was imagining a place far away, as vivid in her mind as the story she relayed. Several times, her eyes misted over and I thought I detected tears welling, but she restrained them with a deep sigh. Although she didn't glance at me, she must have known I was watching her. I was glad my stare didn't throw off her rhythm, especially as her excitement intensified, talking about Sophia's baby. With a big smile, she elaborated on island life.

With her infant to care for, time passed quickly. How had her desperation so completely transformed in only weeks? No longer did Sophia hear voices at night. The sweet cooing of the baby at her breast turned into the giggles of a toddler who could swim before she mastered walking. Little by little, Baby learned the island.

"Mamá." Baby floated her ragdoll on a small driftwood boat in the shallow water. "Tell me again about *Vanessa-Benita*."

Mamá sat in the sand, peering up at Baby, who gazed out at what remained of the Schooner. "She didn't look anything like she does now. She was once a sleek beauty, as swift as a dolphin's fin, and her sails as full as billowing clouds."

Baby poked at a jellyfish. "We built a hut. Perhaps we could build a boat, just like the Captain."

"And what happened to the Captain?"

Baby pursed her lips, thinking about the shipwrecks. A crab tumbling in the surf distracted her. She chased it ashore, snuck up, and grabbed it from behind. Holding it inches from her face, she stared into its beady eyes. "You'd like to pinch my nose, wouldn't you? But I'm faster than your claws!"

Mamá stood and laughed. "Play with him for a little while and then add him to the dinner pot."

As they ate, Baby picked crabmeat from the shell. "Tell me about when you were my age."

"When I was eight, I lived on a farm."

"F-A-R-M …," Baby wrote the letters in the sand.

She had heard the stories so many times she often filled in the details, but she always asked for something new. *Was it as big as the precipice? As small as a grain of sand? Sweet like fruit? As vast as the sea? Soft as a rabbit?* Baby tried to imagine a different world, forming complex images of all textures and dimensions from sand, rocks, trees, water, and wind. One story blended into the next—stories from the Captain's log, from the Bible, from her mother's life before the island, and from their own imaginations—just as each day blended into the next. Only variations of seasons marked the passage of years.

One year might provide an unusually strong storm or longer season. However, even those markers tended to blur as cycles repeated themselves. Then, about ten years after Baby's birth, in the middle of the rainiest week, Mamá and she sat under the palms in a little lean-to, telling stories to the patter of rain.

"Mamá, look there!" Baby pointed out to where the sky and sea merged. "Is it a large dolphin or a whale?"

Mamá pulled the looking glass from her belt and peered out. She came to her feet and moved toward the surf.

Baby followed. "What is it, Mamá?"

Mamá gasped. "A ship!"

She passed the looking glass to Baby and ran toward the

hovel. "Stay here! I'll get the flare!"

Baby's heart beat fast. If only the rain hadn't soaked everything burnable. For days, they hadn't been able to light a fire. Only a few embers smoldered in the hovel. Soon, Mamá returned to the shore. She fumbled with the pen flare, loading it and holding it away from them as she pulled the trigger. Nothing happened. Mamá tried again and again until she finally threw it to the ground and used words Baby had never heard before.

"What about the mirror, Mamá?"

"What good's a mirror with no sun?" she shouted as their only chance of rescue disappeared on the horizon.

"Will they come back?"

"Not today." She covered her face.

"Don't cry, Mamá." Baby had never seen her mother cry. Her own eyes burned. "Aren't you happy here?"

Mamá did not respond. Baby pulled her mother's hands from her face. Seeing her tears, she cried too.

"But Mamá, you said God has blessed us with each other—that we should be happy for what we have."

Mama wiped her own face. "Yes, Baby …."

Although Mamá affirmed it, for the first time, Baby wondered if it was true.

More time passed and Baby continued to grow. Womanhood came upon her gradually, and if not for the arrival of her own monthly cycle, there would have been nothing to mark that spring as out of the ordinary. In fact, during those years, only three occasions stood out in the adolescent's mind.

The first was during the earliest summer of her young womanhood. Baby and Mamá stood atop the precipice as they watched a storm come up in an unusual pattern from the west. Thunder crashed in the distance. The display sent tingles up Baby's spine. When the breeze strengthened and pushed against them, they retreated into the hovel. From the ledge, they watched wind whip with such force that it stripped fronds from the palms, uprooting many of them. That's when they blocked the hovel's entrance.

Before the day was over, the thunder passed to the east. Near sunset, when the ferocious winds abated, they stepped out onto the ledge. Gales still sent water surging toward the island, and when they looked for the beach, it had become part of the sea. Sitting on the ledge, their dangling feet nearly skimmed high water as they stared out at the crooked rocks of the lagoon. Wind and sea had washed away the last bit of *Vanessa-Benita's* hull.

Baby wiped tears from her eyes. "It's as if the Captain's no longer looking over us."

Mamá sighed. "But God still is. He gave us the Bible to comfort us, the Captain's log to keep us company, and our courage, our brains, and our hands to put to good use. Never forget—no matter what may happen—you can always get by. Just keep learning and keep experiencing." She looked deep into Baby's eyes. "And what's the most important thing?"

A hint of a smile curled Baby's lips. "Never give in to fear."

The next morning, they waded through what remained of their beach. The day after that, when the water receded even more, they sloshed their way to the water hole. Even though water gushed rather than trickled from the spout at the island's center, when Baby scooped a handful, it tasted like seawater. Collecting fresh water from the falls was a lot more work, but without that, they would not have strength enough to rebuild the hut in the fruit grove. Imagining they were the Captain and Tomas, they cut trees with the old ax and fixed the fallen roof and slanting walls as well as they could. They again enjoyed the shelter of a hut, but it was not what it once had been.

The next milestone proved even more profound. It took place during the fourth rainy season after Baby entered womanhood.

One afternoon, after they had eaten a nice meal of crabs and cassava, Baby gazed out over the ocean and imagined her island right at the center of the sea. Although Mamá sat beside her, Baby felt like their little island—all alone and isolated. She stood and walked toward the south dune.

"Where are you going?" Mamá called out after her.

"For a walk."

"Wait, I'll come with you."

"No. I want to walk by myself."

"Don't be silly." Mamá caught up to her.

Baby whirled around. "Why must you always walk with me? I'm as grown as you are—I am not a child who needs constant watching!"

Stunned, Mamá came no farther as Baby turned and walked away.

Baby regretted her tone, even though the words were true. She continued walking and crested the dune alone. She did not look back. She marched ahead, but not as far as the windward crags and fishing hole—only far enough that she could not see the hovel or hear the surf on the beach. Lying outstretched on a boulder, she stared at the sky and thought about a world she had never seen and could not comprehend.

She thought about the Captain. She wondered about Tomas and Benita and the love they shared. She wondered too about her own parents. Mama had explained about how men and women made babies, and she tried to imagine her mother and father together, making her on a boat in the middle of the ocean. She thought about the warmth of lying close to a man instead of her mother. Even though curly dark hair now grew from parts of Baby that used to be smooth, she could not picture it growing from a wide, flat chest. Nor could she imagine whiskers, like coconut hairs, or arms as thick as her thigh, or fleshy parts hanging between tree-trunk legs. Her insides fluttered as tears slipped from the corners of her eyes.

As the sun dipped behind her, she sat hugging her knees. The vastness of the sea—infinity—stretched out before her. A different world existed beyond her imagination. Limitless experience. People. Men. If only she and Mamá could build a raft. They had repaired a hut. They could certainly make a raft! She could talk her mother into it. Why, she could start building it all on her own! Baby remembered Mamá's disappointment when the ship passed by. If only they could drift out to where the big boats were. The thought of it made her insides tingle even more.

Baby had been away for half the day, and it felt good to be out on her own. Just the same, she couldn't wait to get back to the beach and tell her mother all she had been thinking and feeling. Somehow, Mamá would understand, and she would forgive her for behaving poorly. Mamá always understood. She seemed to know what Baby thought and felt before she even said it.

As she trudged toward the sandy dune, she found a perfectly shaped seashell—a gift for Mamá. Baby smiled as she hurried up the dune. As she stood upon its crest, she spotted her mother. She lay halfway between the palms and the surf. Baby could snuggle close to her, waking her gently, and apologize. Then they would prepare a nice supper and tell stories under the full moon, and Baby would tell her about the raft and her plans. Her heart raced with happy anticipation, but as she neared, Mamá no longer looked as if she were napping—the awkward angle of her body sent Baby running toward her.

"Mamá," she cried, but her mother did not move. At her side, the seashell fell from her hand as Baby dropped to her knees. She nudged Mamá and then shook her. That's when she saw her swollen leg and the two small puncture wounds ….

MARLENA'S VOICE DROPPED TO A WHISPER AS SHE SPOKE THE next words. "She was dead."

She blinked. Biting her lip, she caught a tear before it escaped. As she wiped it, mud smeared at her hairline. Her gaze lowered.

"I need to stop there …," her voice tapered off.

A gull called. The breeze whooshed through rustling grasses. Water lapped the shore. The sun heated the back of my neck. I couldn't speak. If I had tried, it would have watered down her ending—her whole story.

Marlena had stirred my agitation again, but it wasn't the same as before. It didn't spring from disenchantment with her ending, or from envy, but from somewhere deeper. It ended too abruptly. Still bound by her final words, I studied her face. I forced back the tightening of my throat.

My own eyes burned as another tear welled in Marlena's. Before it wet her cheek, I wiped it away. Her face warmed my palm as her eyes met mine. They begged for something, for some deeper comprehension. I couldn't look away, couldn't even blink, let alone talk. I could only linger in her gaze, crumbling a bit of dried mud from the tip of a curl. She leaned into my hand as her pursed mouth relaxed. My thumb found her lower lip and the caress of her tongue. I wanted my mouth there. Drawing her face toward me, I met her halfway, but she pulled back even as she was kissing my fingertips.

"We need to leave now," she said without breath and without conviction as her chin left my hand.

"Marlena … We could stay right here on the island, all night if you want …."

Her eyes flickered, I thought with desire, but she said, "No."

She came to her knees and then stood, staring at me the whole time, leaving me unsure of what she really wanted. I rose with her, fully intent on kissing her, on testing her resolve, but she kept out of arm's reach and started packing up, keeping her eyes on mine.

In my frustration, I followed her into the gentle surf, and as we waded back out to the boat, the coolness of the bay took the edge off my desire. The air and water had calmed and the tide had come in. I hoisted myself up and inside first, and then gave her my hand, careful of where I placed it. Now she was close enough to kiss, but the moment had passed, had transformed into something more intimate.

Barely enough wind kept us moving, and enough remaining sun provided safe navigation. Water slapped the hull, insisting on silence. In the diminished daylight, Marlena's distant gaze pacified my desire to interrupt her thoughts. The feelings she inspired made it difficult to focus on our destination.

As soon as the harbor came into view, I headed into the wind, stalling our momentum. We drifted inland, barely rocking at all. Carnival lights intensified as darkness fell. The distortion of eerie music waltzed toward us—a medley of bluegrass and carnival organ.

She whispered, "How strange and beautiful."

Looking directly at her, I had to agree. She was both.

I suppose it was my staring that prompted her to ask, "What have you been thinking, Samuel?"

I didn't reveal the tangled emotions for which I had no words, nor did I divulge my more immediate sensual thoughts—but along the way, I had been wondering about her story. "I was thinking about the girl, Baby. That's what Sophia called her, but did she have a real name?"

She smiled, looked away, and then brought her eyes back to mine. "I suppose, if you like."

"What was it?"

"Can't you guess?"

"I would name her Marlena."

"Then Marlena she is."

I chuckled. "Tell me, what happened to her?"

She shrugged. "Maybe a snake came out of nowhere and bit her, or in her grief and guilt, she threw herself off the precipice or swam out to sea and never came back. Or perhaps she simply died of loneliness, like the Captain."

"Why does there need to be such a sad or tragic ending? Why not rescue her off the island, have her live happily ever after?"

"Can you imagine what this world would do to someone like her? Do you really think she could possibly live happily ever after?"

With that question, I set my course toward the yard lights of the house I knew so well, toward the only place I had ever known. I thought about the island as a perfect metaphor for the isolation experienced by someone who didn't fit—who couldn't find her way. What *would* this world do to someone like her 'Marlena'? Could she possibly find her way?

I maneuvered with almost imperceptible progress toward the landing. Marlena's face fell dark in the shadows, but I still felt her eyes.

As I beached the *Firefly*, we continued in silence, and as she climbed out, I saw two silhouettes under the pergola. "Looks like Billy and Derek." I wasn't in the mood for their company, and I doubted she was either.

She climbed out. "Could we sit down here—just for a few minutes?"

"I was hoping you'd say that."

We sat where the sand met turf, and she leaned into me. It was dark, but I knew from experience that we were visible from the house, so I refrained from putting my arm around her. In fact, on a still night, conversations carried across the yard, and too often I had overheard guests divulge things never intended for an audience. If Marlena had been inclined, I might have attempted a hushed conversation—maybe even a kiss— but she seemed content to ride out the silence. We sat there ruminating for I don't know how long. I only knew I didn't want my day with her to end.

When she yawned the second time, I said, "We should probably head on up."

As we carried our things, and before we were within earshot of the others, I said, "Why don't you go ahead and shower first?"

I knew she was eager to get inside, to avoid conversation, but when she stepped onto the deck, Derek detained her. "Looks like Sam's kept you out past your bedtime."

"I don't have a bedtime." She smiled innocently. "But Samuel did sort of wear me out."

With that, she walked into the house without apology or any 'good night.' I guess I wasn't the only one she did that to.

I stepped into the dark kitchen along with her and placed the cooler on the counter, debating whether I should follow her up or sit with the guys for a minute. I returned to the open door. Neither spoke. Derek would barely look at me.

After a stiff silence, he stood. "I guess I'll be taking off."

"See you at the race," I said.

On his way off the deck, he slapped Billy on the back.

Using that as my opportunity to bow out for the evening, I left Billy alone. The time—11:49—glowed from the digital clock on the range. It was hard to believe how fast the day had gone by. I smiled at the thought of Marlena as I opened the refrigerator and put some leftovers inside. The smile left my face when I turned to grab one last item. In that moment, the appliance light reflected off the edge of Billy's flask as he brought it to his mouth, tipping it until it emptied.

I shut the refrigerator and went to my room.

Sitting on my bed, I heard Marlena in the shower. I waited for the water to stop running, for the emerging fragrance of whatever she used in there. I waited until the bathroom door opened, listened for her footsteps in the hall, and didn't leave my room until her bedroom door clicked shut.

It wasn't that I didn't want to see her. I did. I simply didn't want another awkward hallway encounter—didn't want to excite anything more intense than what already stirred, not until I could sort it out. I wasn't sure what line we had crossed out on the island, but we very definitely crossed one. The day was so perfect, the moment so intimate, but she didn't let me kiss her, and I didn't know why. Just the same, what happened with her felt like far more than a kiss.

I don't mind admitting that it was the most sensual encounter of my life.

Chapter 24

AYBE I WAS OVERTIRED, OVER-BILLIED, OR JUST plain over-stimulated from all the storytelling, but, once again, I had the worst time falling asleep. At some point, in that vague place between sorting through the day's events and slipping into unconsciousness, I was rescuing Marlena from the island. She was the beautiful virgin, and I was the heroic sailor, fighting the wind and high seas. Buck was with us. She jumped overboard and became a mermaid. He dove in after her. Then, just below the surface, a blur—some sort of sea monster—pulled them into the turbulent depths. I wanted to dive in after them, to save them both, but couldn't move. Trembling, I stared into the water. Then Dad's bloated body broke the surface, his face gray and oozing. I woke in a cold sweat—my heart throbbed in my ears and even my skin hurt.

As if that weren't bad enough, when I finally dozed back off, I slipped into something more akin to a recollection than a dream. Dad clenched a beer. Empty cans cluttered the floor around his chair. Billy stood in the shadows. Dad muttered something like, *where's that little puke—where's Sammy?* He spotted me hiding in the corner. He came toward me, his face red with fury. Billy stepped between us and started mouthing off at him. Then Dad let him have it. In terror, I ran to my room but tripped on each step. That's when my eyes shot open. I was safe, in my own bedroom.

I could not put into words how that felt. Had it actually happened or had I just dreamt it? I choked even to think of it, yet I couldn't *stop* thinking about it. I had to shake the funk before I went downstairs, before I had to look at Billy. I sat in my bed, aware of my conspicuous absence at the breakfast table, but I didn't care.

I headed to the bathroom, shaved, and took a long shower, forcing myself to focus on something else—anything else. Marlena came to mind, in my now favorite setting, Cuttermann's Island. Marlena. Me. Lying in the sand beside her. The breeze carrying away every worry. The day had been all about the story and us. Nothing else mattered. Immersed in it, in the sound of her voice, her skin against mine—the sensation of it ... I soon imagined how it would have been, making love to her on the beach, the kinds of things I would have dreamt if she had been beside me last night and beside me this morning. I would have made love to her as if she were the girl in her story. As I visualized her in my arms—not her imaginary Marlena, but the real one, the one downstairs whose face would light up at the sight of me—I could finally breathe. I couldn't wait to be with her again.

I headed down the stairwell, plowing into a wave of aromas—gourmet coffees, sausages, biscuits, and maple syrup. My appetite squashed any lingering reluctance. As usual, we had a full house for breakfast, including Billy, Elaine, and Buck, in addition to guests, but no Marlena. She wasn't in her room. I had heard her bounding downstairs long before me.

Everyone seemed to know I was looking for her, and directed me to the docks. I grabbed a biscuit and took my coffee to where she sat at the end of the fishing dock with her feet dangling. She peered over her shoulder and smiled, pushing my uneasiness aside.

I plunked down beside her.

"How'd you sleep?" she asked, pulling hair from her face, wrestling with the insistent breeze.

"I've slept better."

"Me too. I barely slept at all."

I glanced at her. "Why's that?"

"I guess I have a lot on my mind."

"For instance?"

"Well … I've been thinking about my story, about the ending—I meant to tell you the rest of it yesterday, but I guess I got kind of emotional." In fact, her eyes appeared glassy even as she said that.

I moved a wayward wisp of hair from her brow. "I'm still all ears."

"I'm glad you still want to hear it."

"So, when are you going to tell me?"

She took a deep breath and smiled. "When you can no longer stand not knowing."

I laughed. "I can't stand it now."

She giggled. "Well, I'd tell you right now, but it's as long as the other parts."

"Then we probably won't have time today, will we?"

"No, but maybe tonight. I could come over to your room."

How much storytelling would we actually get done? "Okay, but maybe we should wait and see how late we get back after the dance."

Her feet swung back and forth, kicking at the water like a little kid. She smiled with promise as I sipped my coffee.

"You know, Marlena, there's something I've been wondering about."

"What?"

"Where did you learn to spear a fish?"

She looked at me with an innocent tilt. "On my island, of course."

"Be serious."

She shrugged. "It's as easy as learning to throw horse shoes—we did it in Kansas all the time."

What did I know about what went on in Kansas?

There were so many other details I didn't know about her, so many questions and things I wanted to say, but I couldn't get the words out. I had no trouble coming up with words when writing, but around this girl, I got all jammed up. Something froze inside me, like an engine that wouldn't fire. I kept cranking—and nothing.

Caught in mid-thought, I heard a faint and happy, "hmmm …."

A flush rose in Marlena's cheeks. She glanced at me, biting her lower lip, smiling at the same time. From the way she moved her mouth, I knew what she was remembering. I saw it in the spark of her eyes. The wily breeze whipped her hair, obscuring my view. Before I could bring my hand to her face, she had those loose strands pulled back and under control. Her eyes sparkled.

Three crazy words came into my head. There was no way I would say them—I had never said them to any woman. A lot of guys threw them around, simply to get what they wanted. But I had never done that. It was the kind of thing you had to be really sure about before you said it, and lately, I didn't trust myself to be all that sure of anything. Instead of speaking, I took her hand in mine. She leaned into me, the way she always did. It was, again, perfect in all its silence.

THE *FIREFLY'S* BOW POINTED TOWARD THE BAY. SHE dipped and bobbed beside the fishing dock when I boarded and sat on the port side. Cinching her main sheet, I gathered it in a tidy coil on the floor planking. Bare feet padded toward me. I glanced over the boom at familiar canvas trunks, half-hidden by an oversized Madras plaid shirt. It didn't show off Marlena's figure quite so much as my favorite barely-there T-shirt, but she still managed to pull off cute.

I winked. "Experimenting with a new orphan fashion line, are we?"

She smoothed the buttons down her front. "Buck gave it to me. Isn't it pretty?"

I clutched the boom in front of me. "It's pretty, alright."

She squatted at the edge of the dock, her face bright.

"Hey, lady." I waggled my eyebrows. "You wanna take a ride with me?"

"Just what sort of a girl do you think I am?" she replied like a line right out of a cheap romance novel.

I responded in kind, "I don't know. Why don't you come aboard and show me?"

With that, she hopped in, tipping the boat. She reached over the boom, gave me a peck right on the lips, and then sat. I was so stunned, it took a few seconds to remember what I was doing.

Like another bad cliché, I asked, "Are you in the habit of going around kissing strange men on boats?"

"You're not all that strange. Besides, wouldn't I have to do it more than once to make it a habit?"

I took that as an invitation and moved to kiss her.

She recoiled. "You'll tip us."

In truth, if she had offered any resistance at all, we could have both ended up in the drink.

She sat to starboard as I pushed off and raised the mainsail. Once we caught some wind, she ducked beneath the boom and sat beside me.

In that pensive way of hers, she focused her sights on me. "Are you going to be sailing fast in the race?"

"Not very fast, but faster than everyone else, I hope."

"You want another one of those shiny little sailboats to put behind glass?"

I smirked. "Sure."

"That's important to you?"

I pulled in the main sheet. "Tack." We both ducked beneath the boom as I released the sheet. Now we sat starboard. "It feels important right now, but after the race it'll only feel important if I don't win."

"I don't understand."

"If I don't win, I won't like knowing I didn't sail well enough." I steered the bow toward the beach. "If I do win, it won't be because I worked all that hard."

Her toes pressed against my sneakers. "Why not just let someone else win?"

"Because that's not fair." I looked at her sideways. "Don't you know anything about competition?"

"Yes," her brow narrowed. "I've read about the Olympics. It's just like that."

"Yes, well, in principle." I lifted the centerboard and dropped the mainsail, letting our momentum take us ashore. "You don't have a competitive bone in your body, do you."

"Nope. I don't need one." She steadied herself on my shoulder and climbed out.

One of the locals came over to chat, and Marlena lingered for a minute and then slipped off into the milling crowd. I wasn't sure where she might have gone off to, but I had been hoping for another one of those kisses for good luck. I scanned the swarm of people but didn't see her anywhere, though I sensed her watching me the whole time.

I looked around for Derek. Perhaps he had homed in on her. He was an easy find, with his gregarious guffaws. I spotted him amid several attractive young women, with his arm draped over one of the girl's shoulders. What might have previously evoked a tinge of jealousy now put a genuine smile on my face. The entire universe seemed in perfect alignment. Peace and harmony prevailed. I headed toward him, and by the time I reached earshot, I had convinced myself that Marlena would be mine, free and clear.

"Hey, Derek," I greeted him as if things between us were never better.

"Well, if it isn't Sam." He ignored his hovering fan club. That should have been a red flag, but I persisted. "Ready for the big race?"

He stepped closer, right in my personal space, almost nose to nose. "You think you're going to do better than me today?"

Heated by my miscalculation, I chuckled. The ladies had drifted away and he didn't seem to care. "C'mon, Derek, we're competing with fifteen- to seventy-year-olds out there today. This is only supposed to be about having some fun."

"Since when?"

"You know, the race doesn't have to be about anything more than just a good time."

"You say that now, but once we're out there, we'll see

who's having a good time."

I reeled back as if he had shoved me, and off he went to the other side of the beach.

I stood alone for a moment, stunned at my lack of discernment, and then went back over to the *Firefly*. All the boats lined the shore as the master of ceremonies ran through the basic rules. Some of the newbies were even paying attention. At the far side of the group, Derek gave me his before-the-race evil eye, but with a little more evil than usual. It should have been about having 'fun,' but Derek was right— and so was Marlena. I wanted the shiny little sailboat. Mostly, I didn't want him to get it.

I pushed off the beach and jumped aboard, hoisting my sail. We all vied for position during the starting countdown. I looked Derek in the face. We both knew it was on.

At the blast of the horn, his fiberglass sloop took the lead by a breath. As we tacked toward the first mark, he took the windward position. For the length of the broad reach, we made our way through most of the other sailors. One had already capsized, which was ridiculous. The wind was stiff but predictable. Our familiarity with the more favorable currents out by Cuttermann's Island gave us the advantage as we passed a kid in catboat and an old guy in a Seaford skiff—neither of them local. Derek was clearly ahead until we neared the island, where we over-lapped. With a quick reversal of my boom, I swung sharp and thought for sure he would foul me as we rounded the island. He yielded. I took the lead, keeping my sights ahead, smiling at the recollection of Marlena and me on the beach blanket. The wind stayed consistent as we reached the next mark, a buoy, but somehow, Derek found a better puff and we were soon neck and neck.

As I rounded the gybe mark, it was downwind to the finish, and I was able to steal his wind and overtake him just before the line. We crossed it together. At least, that's how it looked to me.

Some debate ensued, but consensus gave Derek the victory. When it came right down to it, winning the race mattered less than I expected. Coming in first with Marlena made it an easy concession. As that thought occurred to me, a pang of self-accusation speared my ego. Marlena was more than merely some prize, but all at once, I felt like a participant in something undignified and somehow demeaning to her. That's when Derek swaggered over with his little gold sailboat.

"Congratulations." I extended my hand, trying to be a good sport.

He latched on and squeezed. "And the better man wins."

His jaw clenched and our grip tightened.

"Of course, next year, I'll reclaim it, so enjoy it while it's yours." I tried to keep it about the race and withdrew.

He held his ground. "So, where are you keeping Marlena today?"

"Excuse me? Keeping her?"

"Yeah. I know you're trying to keep her away from me."

"Don't be ridiculous."

"Yeah," he huffed, raising the trophy, pressing it into my chest. "And *this* isn't supposed to be some kind of consolation prize?"

"So how does *that* feel?" God knew I had suffered it a hundred times.

Derek flinched and pushed off my chest. "This isn't over, Sam."

In the crowd, I caught sight of Marlena. "And I'm done playing."

I sidled past Derek as she approached. Her lips matched her tight brow. Had it finally dawned on her that Derek and I were a couple of juvenile morons? Although I hated getting caught up in his contest, it felt good—*really good*—to have a girl prefer me over him. Could it possibly have taken her that long to realize he had wanted her from day one and couldn't stand the idea of losing her to me?

I didn't know what all happened out on *Trigger*, but Derek never spared a maneuver. I mean, for God's sake, the dress and everything—how could she not know? Well, if she hadn't figured that out before the race, she had at that moment. She wouldn't even look at me.

"Hey," I said. "Where have you been?"

She ignored my question. "Derek won. Why is he mad at you?"

"That's just Derek. He's always getting his shorts in a bunch. Don't worry about him. He'll get over it."

She looked away and then flashed a glare back at me. "Did he think that if he won the race, I would like *him* better than you?"

"I don't know what Derek was thinking," I lied.

"But he's your best friend. You mean he's never said anything about me?"

My gaze shifted. "Marlena …."

She squinted. "He likes me the same way you do."

"No. *No*, he doesn't like you the same way I do."

"But I think he might have wanted to kiss me, out on his boat—the way you wanted to."

"That's different."

"How?"

"Are you serious?" I couldn't believe she needed me to explain the difference between guys like me and guys like Derek.

I immediately regretted my tone, because she shut down right in front of me. Her eyes dropped and her chin quivered. She wouldn't look at me. She walked away, and like an idiot, I just stood there and let her.

That would have been a nice time for the proverbial engine to turn over. I ended up smacking the steering wheel instead.

Chapter 25

S I WIPED MY FOREHEAD, RUNNING FINGERS through salt-laden hair, I glanced over my shoulder, scanning the southwest sky. Thunderclouds gathered far off, their mushroom tops billowing. The wind had died to an inconsistent waft, hardly bowing my sail as I nudged the tiller toward home. Humidity hung like granules in the air, diffusing the usually vivid array of colors on the harbor and bay. If thundershowers dumped on me right then, it would have been a relief, but it looked as though they would hold off until later, as forecasted.

Firefly floated toward the boatyard and rounded *Trigger's* slip. Buck and Billy fished off the end of the launch pad's dock.

"Anything biting?" I asked.

"Yeah, right," Billy winked, reeling in his line. As I passed by, I caught a glimpse of my brother giving Buck's shoulder an affectionate squeeze. Buck smiled as if Billy were twelve again. Could one gesture so easily dissolve more than twenty years of distance? For Buck, maybe. He could never hold a grudge. Perhaps he had forgotten how Billy walked out on us. Or did Buck's age provide the perspective I lacked?

Rather than beach the *Firefly* and compete with the steaming clambake pit for space, I tied her off at the dock. As I made my way across the back lawn, past the swing and several long tables, a dense pocket of aroma—lighter fluid and charcoal briquettes—enveloped me. Mitch poked at the grill as I bounded up the stairs to the deck.

"Need any help with the pit?" I asked.

Keeping a vigilant eye on his glowing coals, he wagged his head. "I got it."

"You seen Marlena?"

"Nope."

As several guests stepped outside, I scooted inside. Mother stood over the sink, whittling away at feast preparations.

"Has Derek been by?" I asked.

"Haven't seen him."

"What about Marlena?"

She shot me one of her impatient glares. "I don't know. Check with Buck."

I wasn't about to interrupt Buck's time with Billy. Besides, I would probably find Marlena upstairs. I hoped to apologize—for what, I wasn't even sure. I headed for the hall, and as I passed the parlor, a guest waylaid me, curious about some artifacts on display. That ate up the better part of half an hour. Marlena trotted downstairs before I could break away, still barefooted and wearing her orphan outfit. She hesitated, as if she might join the conversation.

Mother called from the kitchen. "Oh, good! Marlena, I need your help."

Marlena shrugged, resigning herself with a timid smile as she followed Mother's voice. I excused myself and trailed behind, hoping for a moment to tell her how I felt, to make her understand that Derek and I did not feel the same way. As I came up beside Marlena at the counter, Mother nabbed me, ushering me to the back door, and pointing at bushels of corn and rinsed mussels.

"Bring them out to Mitch—he's out at the pit. And make sure he has plenty of fresh seaweed!"

Being assistant clambake chef wasn't so bad, but Mitch wasn't the company I had been looking forward to. I didn't know who was more distracted—him or me.

When the call to dinner came, we transported steaming clams, mussels, lobsters, crabs, and corn on the cob to the center table. From the array of additional salads, grilled shrimp, steaks, burgers, and clam pie, I piled my plate high, keeping an eye out for Marlena. When our gaze met, she tossed a glance at the deck. We met at our usual place at the picnic table. A number of guests joined us, along with Buck, Billy, and Elaine, but no Derek.

Salivating, I sat, breathing in sweet, salty aromas.

"Did you try the crab cakes?" Marlena sat across from me. "I made them."

"They were gone before I got to them." I said, feigning irritation.

Her foot nudged mine. "I already took a bite." She passed her cake to me, sliding her toes to my ankle. "But you could have it if you want."

How could I refuse?

As I prepared to break open my lobster, Marlena already had hers dissected. She scooped a glob of green—that sweet bit of innards that most people discard—and licked her finger in that particularly delectable way. As I chewed, we reverted to our staring game. Her smile said everything between us had returned to normal. Again, we required no words as chemistry passed between us, saturating our senses, mixing and swirling like the medley of flavors and textures. *What I wouldn't do for a real taste of Marlena.* As soon as she swallowed her last bite, she stood, gathering empty dishes from the table. When she made her way to my side, she wedged herself between me and my neighbor, grabbing my plate. She stood so close I could have bitten one of her buttons clean off. God, she smelled good.

"Marlena," Mother appeared. "Why don't you go on up and get ready for your date with Buck? I have everything under control."

Marlena shrugged, peering down at me.

Perfect. I could follow her up. Perhaps we could talk, or maybe even get a taste.

"And, Sam." Mother's hand weighted my shoulder. "Mitch could use some assistance on the lawn."

Great.

We waited for the last guest to finish eating before we cleared the tables. How had I been relegated to bus boy?

As soon as I wiped my hands, ready to head upstairs, Buck came out of his room, struggling with his tie. He stood before me in his best right-out-of-the-seventies suit. I tied him a nice fat Windsor knot and bounded upstairs. As I stepped onto the third-floor landing, I heard Mother in Marlena's room. *So much for that!*

An hour later, wearing my best jeans and a polo shirt, I joined my family, gathered on the deck. Mother sauntered out under the pergola in something new—it was the first time I had seen a public display of her cleavage. I didn't find it embarrassing, per se, but it definitely confirmed her interest in Mitch.

I turned my attention to Buck. "Big date tonight, huh?"

His grin trembled. "Tie me a nice fat Windsor knot, would you?"

I glanced at the knot I had tied earlier, stepped forward, adjusted it, and patted his chest. "All set. You look very suave."

He turned the most delicate shade of pink, all the way to the top of his shiny, bald head, and smiled.

"You did get her a corsage, didn't you?" I teased.

His eyes flew open; pink turned red.

"Take it easy, Buck. I've got just the solution." I flipped open my pocketknife and led Buck to our own personal florist—Mother's garden.

"This one." He pointed at a large yellow rose.

I envisioned it in Marlena's hair. "Yes. That's the one."

When we returned to the deck, Marlena stepped through the back door. She had brushed her hair away from her face instead of letting it do its normal gyrations. It showed off her eyes. Locks of it came around to the front, framing her chin in curls. It was an admirable attempt at getting her unmanageable mass of hair under control, especially since humidity would send it in all directions within an hour. And, of course, she wore that dress. She turned awkwardly, shuffling her feet. I had never seen her in anything other than sneakers.

"I don't think your sandals fit me." She grimaced at Mother.

"Don't be silly, of course they do. And they look perfect."

"They hurt."

"That, my dear, is simply part of being a woman."

Marlena's frown did not abate as she bent at the waist to massage her heel, oblivious, as usual, to ladylike decorum.

Nice.

Buck cleared his throat and held out the rose. Fumbling with it, he avoided her chest and pressed it to her shoulder. "I need a pin."

"I have a pin right here. I'll take care of it," Mother cut in front of him.

I intercepted. "I'll do it."

Snatching the rose from Buck, I refused Mother's pin and moved in close. At first, she resisted looking at me until my fingers slid into the hair at the nape of her neck. Her eyes met mine. I pushed the stem deep into the silken nest that curled above her ear. I swear, if she wasn't Buck's date—if he hadn't been standing guard over her—I would have kissed her the way I had been wanting to, right in front of everyone. I would have erased all questions about the difference between the way Derek and I felt about her.

Chapter 26

BUCK OPENED THE PASSENGER DOOR TO MY OLD Dodge pickup, and Marlena scooted beside me on the bench seat. She immediately removed Mother's sandals. Buck climbed in after her. I would have tried to hold her hand, but Buck had already seized one, and to grab the other would have seemed a little cheeky. *He puts the moves on faster than Derek.* I laughed to myself. My grandfather had demoted me to chaperone.

We started out quiet on the short drive over, and although she leaned into me in her familiar way, she tensed.

I returned her lean. "You nervous?"

She nodded. "I told Buck I don't even know how to dance— not *with* someone—but he doesn't believe me."

"There's nothing to it," Buck insisted. "Benny and Duke will teach you."

"Who?" she asked.

I laughed.

Pushing her thigh against mine, she sank further into my side. I stretched my arm across the back of the seat. She fit just right in the crook of my arm. I glanced over at Buck as he felt for his Windsor knot for the tenth time.

Fortunate to find a parking space in the beach lot, I pulled in before Billy's BMW could claim it. Marlena's full weight shifted toward me during the ride, and if I had made for the door as quickly as Buck did, she would have fallen over onto the driver's side. As she righted herself, we caught each other in an attempt to have one brief, private moment between us. Her expression seemed a mixture of nerves and anticipation, but I doubted it had anything to do with the dance.

"Your rose is lopsided," I lied, bringing my hand to her hair, keeping my gaze immersed in hers. She drew in her lower lip, moistening it. Had Buck not poked his head back in the truck and grabbed her hand ....

I shifted uncomfortably and climbed out my side just in time to catch sight of her bending over and slipping back into her sandals.

At the tent, we met up with Billy and Elaine near the dance floor at one of those long tables covered with white plastic that stuck to our bare arms like the mugginess in the air. Buck rambled excitedly but didn't have my attention. I couldn't shift my focus from Marlena. That's when Mitch and Mother arrived together—as a couple—not that it was some big surprise, but now I needed a beer for sure.

I bought two plastic mugs filled from the keg, one for me and one for Buck. When I returned, the band had already started playing some Benny Goodman. By then, several couples danced out on the floor, kicking it up. Marlena studied them while Buck took a few sips.

"Ready?" he asked.

"You'll do fine." I gave her a nudge, hoping to erase some of her jitters.

He grabbed her hand. "Don't worry, I'll teach you all the steps."

She stood. Off came the sandals.

Buck and Marlena remained at the perimeter, watching other dancers for a minute, and then he pulled her in. For a ninety-year-old guy, he was amazingly nimble. It wasn't too long before she caught on to the Lindy and he moved her petite body all over the dance floor, maneuvering between couples and twisting her, making her giggle. They were quite a spectacle, putting a grin on many faces, my own included.

Buck surprised us all.

After each dance, they sat one out and then returned to the floor. I would have asked for a dance, but he completely monopolized her attention. That was okay. I enjoyed watching Buck having such a great time. He seemed twenty years younger.

Billy and Elaine also took their turn on the floor and so did Mitch. I think it was the first time I had ever seen him dance. He wasn't bad, although I didn't pay much attention to him. The weird part was *my mother* dancing. She smiled and laughed like a carefree kid, not like the proper, uptight Mother I knew. I had never seen Mitch with that wide a grin—and the way he held Mother! The way she *allowed* him to hold her! Not what I would have expected for a tentative first date. I worried about her virtue and what the church ladies would say. I sensed a certain familiarity between them, the kind of unspoken intimacy that comes from more than a casual or even flirtatious friendship.

Oh, my God, they've been sleeping together.

I didn't know how I could be so positive, or when they had even had opportunities, but I knew they were.

When Mother returned to the table, I looked her in the eye. She glared back with all the defiance of a teenager. Mitch took the chair to my left and she snuggled up beside him.

While trying to process that, I spotted Derek at the perimeter of the floor, watching Marlena. She and Buck were dancing their first slow number of the evening. He had to bend a bit, and for the first time since they started dancing, she stiffened. Thunder rumbled in the distance and her rhythm faltered. I thought about cutting in, but Derek ambled over to our table. With his eyes on the dancers, he dropped to the seat beside me, in Marlena's place.

Rocking the chair backward on two legs, he breathed the words, "So ... Sam ...."

I got a strong whiff of gin and beer—not a good combination for him.

He slurred, "Why aren't *you* out smooching with Marlena?"

The nerve in my neck pinched. "Listen, Derek—"

The music quit and the crowd offered a quiet applause, muffled by another round of thunder as the tent heaved with a strong draft. Derek joined in with a few sloppy claps, keeping an eye on Marlena as she returned to the table. A gust played at her hem.

She appeared pale and didn't meet his eyes when she said, "Hi, Derek."

"That dress looks great on you." He gave up the chair.

She seemed to ignore his compliment as she took her seat and Buck sat behind her.

Derek held out his hand. "C'mon, Marlena, dance with me."

"I want to sit for a while." Her attention focused more on her tightly clasped hands in her lap than on Derek.

"Let's go, Marlena. I've seen you out there all night in that dress. It's my turn—" he slurred even worse.

"Maybe later."

He grabbed her hand. She recoiled, but he didn't let go.

Buck sprang from his chair. With all the force of a thirty-year-old, he bellowed, "The lady said *NO*!"

Derek dropped her hand, giving Buck an incredulous glare. "You can't be serious, old man."

"Come on out back and find out how serious I am," Buck said as if he meant it.

Derek started to move toward him. Mitch's big mitt pressed against the table, as if he was ready to launch into action.

With fire in his eyes, Buck said, "Come on!"

For a second, I feared Derek would take him up on it. I grabbed his sleeve. "It's Buck, man. What the hell's the matter with you?"

With a firm tug, Derek reclaimed his sleeve and backed down. Mitch sank back into his seat.

"Apologize to her," Buck ordered.

Distress twisted Marlena's face. She couldn't even look at Derek when he said, "Sorry, Marlena. Maybe later," and walked away.

She trembled as her gaze darted all over the place.

Once Derek stepped outside into the dark beyond the tent, I nudged her hand. "You alright?"

"Yeah, I just need to use the restroom." She excused herself.

She didn't seem alright, and to tell the truth, I didn't feel all that great, either. I didn't know if it was the heat or the tension, but my sight blurred and my chest hammered. I could hardly breathe—like a wave, the sensation came and left. A few minutes later, Marlena hadn't returned. Buck got ready to send out the posse.

"I'll go find her," I said, needing some space.

I stepped out from under the tent into a rush of cooler air as a light drizzle moistened the atmosphere. I filled my lungs. It felt good. Fluorescent mist glowed under the buzzing bulb hanging above the Ladies' room door. Dodging a kamikaze June bug, I asked an older woman if she could check for a girl wearing a yellow rose. She said no one else was inside.

In the short time it took to check the parking lot, my damp shirt clung to my body like ocean spray on a humid August afternoon. She wasn't there—that would have been too easy. Certain she wouldn't leave without telling us, and figuring she would want to be away from the crowd, I headed across the turf for the beach.

A young couple sat in the sand, and several others gathered at tables in the picnic area. All were on the verge of taking cover as drizzle turned to droplets, dimpling the water surrounding Marlena. She stood, knee-deep, facing the bay with arms tightly drawn about her waist. Her hair had returned to its wild ways and stirred with the breeze. The rose stayed intact. I walked toward the shoreline, and although she stood several yards away, I wondered if she might sense my presence. She didn't move.

For a few moments, I watched her, no longer gripped by the urgency that had sent me looking for her. I wanted to go out and put my arms around her, but I didn't want to intrude. Besides, I didn't feel like taking off my shoes.

"Marlena," I called out.

She turned but didn't smile. As she came nearer, her eyes

glistened, but I didn't notice her pink nose until she stood right in front of me. Now, I realized how unprepared I was for any sort of emotional display.

Trying to preempt melodrama, I spoke offhandedly, "Buck thought you ran out on him. He's hoping for one last dance."

Tears welled. "He would have fought him."

"No, he wouldn't. Derek's not like that. He'd never hurt Buck."

"No—I mean Buck would have fought Derek."

"Marlena …," I suppressed a patronizing grin. "Buck was feeling young tonight, that's all. It made him feel like a kid to defend his date."

"No," she said with gravity. "Buck thought he was twenty again. Don't you see? He was defending *Mary*, not me."

"He was only remembering what it felt like to be twenty, that's all."

"Samuel …," her voice lowered plaintively. "While we were dancing, he whispered to me, calling me Mary." Tears brimmed in her eyes. "He told me how much he loves me, and misses me and … couldn't wait to make love to me …."

Her words, like the rain now pelting our faces, took a moment to saturate. I didn't want to believe that Buck had slipped that far. "It's just tonight and the music and the dance. That's all."

Marlena's grimace forced tears down her face, mingling with rain.

I dreaded the answer to my next question. "It is just tonight, isn't it?"

She looked away. "No. It happens a lot. At first, I thought Mary was a nickname for *me*, but then he would talk about his wedding day as if I should remember it."

"Why didn't you tell me?"

"Samuel, I'm sorry. I assumed you knew how he is." Through her crying, I had difficulty deciphering her next words. "Sometimes he's not sure who your mother is—once he even asked about you—and at first, he didn't know Billy at all. I'm sorry, I thought you knew."

"I didn't know he had gotten *that* bad. I know he gets a little disoriented, and he forgets things, but ...."

Peering back at me through dark ringlets clinging to her face, she must have seen my disbelief turn to grief, and then to anger, but she couldn't have known it was not directed at her. She stood there trembling, and through her tears said, "I'm sorry ... I'm so sorry ...."

I couldn't let her run off this time. I grabbed her and pulled her close against my soaked shirt. Although her body warmed mine, her hair cooled my lips as I swallowed back my own emotion. My skin bristled at the thought of Buck, that I didn't know—didn't want to know how bad off he was. Pangs of regret turned my stomach for having pawned him off on Marlena. I should have known these things. Instead, the burden had fallen on her.

As I stroked her hair, I wasn't sure what torrent of guilt-spiked pleasure rushed through me, but it was so forceful and so incongruous with my grief that I feared I might crush her for the strength of it. Just then, I heard Derek's voice from behind. Marlena withdrew with a start. I wanted to tell him that it wasn't what it looked like, but in reality, it was exactly the way it looked.

Drenched in rain and liquor, he muttered, "If you wanted to have a go at her, you could have just said so."

"Derek," I said, as Marlena moved away. "You've had too much to drink. Let me take you home."

"You're not taking me anywhere." He swaggered toward me. He had been building up to this for weeks and I knew what was coming next.

"I'm not going to fight you." I backed away, wiping my face, trying to get a clear fix on him. I had seen him fight often enough to know never to turn my back on him. "C'mon, Derek, we'll duke it out tomorrow."

Rather than back off, he threw a clumsy roundhouse. I cleared it, but he wasn't so far gone that he lost his balance completely. He charged and tackled me to the ground, shoving air from my lungs. I was getting ready to defend myself when

Billy came from behind and pulled him off. Derek cussed a few times and sputtered something about turncoats. Billy said he would drive him home, that Elaine and Mother had already taken Buck.

Sand clung to my wet body, and as I half-shook and half-wiped it off, I looked for Marlena, but she was nowhere around. Only her rose lay at my feet. It was my turn to cuss, to the backdrop of more thunder. I hurried to my truck, overheated by not only the scuffle with Derek and the jog to the parking lot, but my chest still carried the warmth of her.

Torn between needing a few minutes to myself and thoughts of her walking back to the house in the dark and the now pouring rain, I turned my key in the ignition. Nothing but a click. Of all things, it wouldn't start, wouldn't even turn over. That's when I seriously began cussing. I lifted the hood—everything looked right, but it was dark. I figured the battery had gone dead. I slammed it shut, locked it up, and started walking. Just as well. I needed the time.

I sloshed through puddles and spongy turf in a torrential downpour. Hoping to avoid any well-meaning passersby, I headed for the footpath, down closer to the water. Keeping familiar landmarks in sight and careful of how I stepped, I navigated through areas prone to washing out. Lightning flashed in the distance, answered seconds later by more low rumblings.

I had seen Derek far worse, but I hated that we had pushed each other to that point—that our friendship had come to this. I hated that we couldn't talk it out like men rather than battle it out with fists. Yet part of me would have loved to plant one right on his jaw.

The more I thought about him, the more my anger stoked. Something about his rotten breath—the disgusting combination of beer and gin—turned my stomach. Just the memory of it made me gag. Then, like an abrupt slap, Derek's angry face morphed into my father's.

In that flash, I was a kid, standing at the end of the dock with that same foulness in my nostrils. A blinding bolt split the sky. A deafening clamor charged and then voided every sense. All at once, images and sensations rushed upon me … memories of that day when I was eleven, when my Dad reeked of beer and gin.

Get your tackle, Sammy, we're going fishing, he mumbled, stench belching from his lethargic mouth. He swayed, bracing himself against the post, dropping his bottle on the dock.

I shook my head, *I don't want to go.*

Don't give me lip, boy! He yanked my shoulder. *Get in the boat!*

I backed away, bracing myself, my heart pounding. His hand grazed my cheek in slow motion as I stumbled and fell on my backside, the bottle clattering behind me. I cowered, wishing he would speed away and never come back.

Red-faced and dripping sweat, he stood over me, his fist balled, but it was the toe of his boot that I felt. *Get in the boat! Or I'll leave without you!*

I scooted farther away, picturing us slamming into the jetty or another boat. I imagined both of us floundering in white water. He threw his arms out, waving me away like a madman, and stumbled aboard. As the engine turned over, he swore, swaying at the throttle. He nearly tumbled overboard as the boat lurched ahead, leaving a trail of blue smoke and a crooked wake.

I sat there, my ribs bruised, sick to my stomach, willing him as far away from me as the sea could carry him. I finally stood and picked up the liquor bottle, throwing it at the dot falling off the horizon, leaving me feeling so small and insignificant.

Beside me, stale beer wafted from the beat-up old fish bucket full of cans. I kicked it the way my father kicked me. Its contents hurtled down the dock, clamoring over the edge into the rising tide. I rubbed my cheek, holding back the burn behind my eyes, wishing I were free of him forever.

And yet, here I was, twenty years later, still not free of him. As I made my way along the muddy path, I realized all at once, *That's my last memory of him.*

I struggled to keep my footing and bent over, trying to catch more breath as sweat stung my eyes. My foot gave way on a slimy rock, sending me to my knees. I sat, envisioning my father's twisted face. My own face burned, as if he had just struck me. My diaphragm pushed into my throat—I couldn't breathe. I was drowning—imagining my father drowning, seawater filling his lungs. Was he too drunk to even know what was happening or did he struggle for his last breath?

I had let him go—wished him dead, wished the sharks would eat him, but they didn't—they left him to wash ashore on someone's backyard beach.

My lungs collapsed. When my chest finally expanded, the sky and sea had merged, leaving me disoriented. Which direction was I headed? Where was the boatyard? Was the ocean to my right or to my left? Without bearings, I staggered toward lights, trying to dam the flood of memories.

As I made my way, my nerves jumped with each flash and clamor, the way they did for months after he left. *It's just the shock of losing his father*, they had said. *Too bad no one had been there to stop Bill … It's just a good thing Sam didn't go with him.* When what they really meant was, *too bad Sam hadn't stopped him.* Too bad I had wished the unthinkable and made it come true.

A flash of anger heated my body. A wave of guilt then drained all warmth.

God, it's freezing.

Chapter 27

OFF IN THE DISTANCE, OUR OLD GAS LAMP BECKONED like a lighthouse in the rain, its dull reflection flashing from the hinged Wesley House sign that swung beneath it. I made my way halfway across the dooryard before I spotted Mitch's Buick. Fortunately, the rain and steaming windows obscured the sight of whatever was going on inside. The idea of Mitch and Mother making out tightened the knot in my stomach.

Stumbling onto the deck, I wiped my face and braced myself for whatever awaited me inside. As I stood at the door, Billy sat alone at the kitchen table. In the shadows cast by the hall light, he took a quick swig from his flask. As I stepped in, he slipped it under the table.

I stood on the mat, dripping and exhausted, prying off my muddy shoes. He grabbed a dishtowel from the counter beside him and tossed it to me. Mopping my head, I avoided looking at him.

"I left Derek passed out in bed," he said.

I nodded, rubbing my forehead.

He smoothed his hair. "You look like hell. What happened to you?"

"Truck …."

"What—did it back over you?"

"Wouldn't start."

"I'd have come looking for you, but I assumed you wanted some space."

I nodded again. "Buck in bed?"

"Yeah—"

"He's okay?" I wondered if my eyes looked as bloodshot as Billy's.

"Yeah, but—"

"You seen Marlena?"

"No. Elaine said she wouldn't talk to anyone when she came in. She just went upstairs."

I offered a terse nod and made a move for the hallway.

"We need to talk about Buck," he said.

I kept walking. "Not tonight, Billy."

"Sure ... we'll talk whenever you're ready ...," his voice trailed off.

I grabbed another towel on my way upstairs. My heart throbbed as I labored with the weight of each step. Now, I thought of only Marlena. I needed the reassurance of her in my arms, knowing that somehow she would understand my pain without my having to say a word. I needed her to rouse something that would displace all this agitation and untwist this wrenching knot in my gut.

Only a slip of light from under her closed door lent any illumination to the dark hall. As I approached, draping the towel around my neck, I heard her quiet rustlings inside and knocked.

She didn't answer.

"I know you're up." I leaned at her door.

She didn't respond.

"Can I come in?" I grabbed her doorknob.

"No."

"I'm coming in anyway. You'd better be decent."

I heard her scurry and gave her a few seconds before cracking the door. She bolted to her bed and closed the lid of her little suitcase. Her duffel bag hung over the foot of the bed with a small stack of clothes beside it.

"What are you doing?" Faster than I could acknowledge the

obvious, I spotted the writing tablet and pencil on the bed. I picked it up. As she tried to snatch it from me, I noticed my name.

"You can't read it," she blurted.

"It's addressed to me, of course I can read it."

For a split second, I hoped it was a love letter, but her frantic expression told me otherwise. That didn't keep me from reading aloud the first line.

"'Samuel, I'm so sorry I left without saying goodbye ....'" I could not comprehend her words and I reread them to her, as a question.

I sought her eyes, but she evaded my gaze. She wouldn't respond at all. Everything inside me froze up. She planned on leaving—leaving without a word—just walking away and not telling me. It made no sense. My jaw went slack. "You were going to leave?"

No response. She just tightened her folded arms.

"You weren't even going to say goodbye?"

"Samuel," she pleaded, "I simply couldn't face you after the mess I made."

Heat rose in my neck. I restrained my tone with difficulty. "You'd rather spare yourself a little discomfort than say goodbye to me?"

She looked away through tears.

"Well, you can go ahead and cross out the first line, because this is goodbye." I threw the tablet on the bed and walked out on her before she could walk out on me.

The sound of her crying carried to my room, but it seemed to echo as if it were only some distant noise mingling with sounds of falling rain. She was hurting, but I convinced myself that I hurt worse. She had swapped the twisted knot in my gut with another boot to the ribs. Everything I had been through and was going through amounted to far more than all her melodrama. It had become quite clear that she was an unstable individual, and I did not need one more liability sucking me dry. Better that I saw it so clearly now, before it got really messy.

But somewhere beneath my misery, I hoped she would reconsider, that through all my anger she could see how much she meant to me.

At some point, as the pouring rain turned to drizzle, I drifted into sleep. I didn't know what I dreamt, and I didn't know what time it was when I woke in the dark, but I heard her bedroom door open and then close. For an instant, I hoped she would come to my door, and that she would slip inside and into my bed and everything would be okay. But then I heard creaks of the staircase and her steps on the deck through my open window. She was gone, and my chest caved in. For the first time in years, I wept.

Chapter 28

WITH A SET OF JUMPER CABLES IN THE BACK of Derek's Hummer, I rode with Billy to the fairgrounds parking lot. We had left before breakfast, but I did manage to down three cups of coffee—even then, I couldn't tell if the fog was on the road or in my head. The damp air and ground seemed to have little effect on tourists already emerging for the final day of hoopla. Each bump in the road jarred my aching head. I yawned again as Billy pulled up beside my truck. I pushed myself out of the passenger seat. Every muscle wrenched like a whole-body charley horse. My rust bucket started up with far less resistance than I did, and I followed the Hummer over to Derek's place.

I drove in behind Billy and sat in neutral, waiting as he took the keys up to Derek's apartment over his scuba-diving-sailing-treasure-hunter shop. Paint flaked off his storefront. He should have been working on his own stuff instead of helping me out over the past weeks. He probably would have, had *she* not shown up. Oh, who was I kidding? If it hadn't been her, it would have been some other Girl.

I pushed back images of last night—of my father. Angst added a disquieting edge to my exhaustion as I vacillated between the rear and side view mirrors in case I might catch a glimpse of her. Until Mother brought it up, it hadn't occurred to me that the bus didn't even run on Sunday.

"What's Marlena going to do?" she had asked. "Walk twenty miles to the next town?"

I told Mother I didn't know what her plan was and it didn't matter to me how long she wandered the streets of Wesleyville. Maybe she was hitching her way back across the country or planned to hook up with the carnies tomorrow morning.

"What kind of girl leaves that way, without giving notice—without even saying goodbye?" Mother had asked, wide-eyed and annoyed.

"The messed up kind, Ma."

When Billy enlisted me for the drop-off, I had taken him up on it without hesitation—anything to get out of the house and avoid talking about Marlena or thinking about Dad. Billy hadn't brought up either, but that didn't stop me from thinking about her and the note she left.

After the initial, *Samuel, I'm so sorry I left without saying goodbye*—and I reread it without choking, even though she crossed out the first line, the way I told her to—she had continued, with the predictable, *I just couldn't face you after all the mess I made*. Then the cliché, *I never meant to hurt you ...* followed by the obvious, *or complicate your life*. Next, a nice personal touch with stalking undertones, *I came to Wesleyville to meet you, to get to know what kind of man you are*—and then, finally, the punch line—*before I told you my story*. She then lamented that she hadn't finished telling it and that she had left it for me in the suitcase. Period. Not even a Love, Very truly yours, Sincerely, or even a signature.

I had found her note tucked under the crazed plastic handle of that small suitcase the size of a tackle box that she first arrived with. She had parked it in front of my bedroom door this morning. It nearly tripped me on my way out. I tossed both letter and unopened bag onto my bed with irritation and then headed downstairs.

Even as I recalled it, I steadied my hands on the steering wheel. The muscles across my back constricted, pinching my neck. I took another deep breath, pushing away thoughts of her. How had everything gotten so out of control in such a short time?

After my few minutes of wallowing, Billy descended the exterior staircase.

He climbed into my passenger seat. "He's still sleeping."

That was no surprise. Derek would be out cold until at least noon, and God help anyone who tried to rouse him before then. I took my time putting the truck in reverse, and Billy suggested we go to the wharf for breakfast. Even with all the tourists mobbing our local diner, we would both prefer that over the chaos at home.

Our waitress, Lilly, a frizzy, bleached matron whom we had known for years, snatched us from the cluster of patrons we walked in with.

She squeezed my arm. "Hasn't your mama been feeding you good enough?"

Escorting us to the far corner with menus tucked under her arm, she glanced back and acknowledged my brother. "You're looking fine these days, Billy. You ought to come home more often."

"How are you, Lil? And how's Fred?" he asked, his smile less tense than at the house.

"I'd love to tell you all about it, Hon, but haven't the time." She wiped crumbs and pocketed change from our table. "Sorry about the mess—it's been a zoo. Just thought you two might enjoy the best seat in the house."

She winked at Billy, passed us a couple of menus, and squeezed my arm again. This time I felt it as if she had grabbed hold of a day-old bruise.

It wasn't truly the *best* seat, but the corner booth, partially overlooking the harbor and a few lobster boats, suited me fine. While Billy perused his options, my attention wandered to the boats in the harbor. Lobstermen. So consistent. No distinction of day or season, heat or cold, rain or shine. Glancing around the diner at old lobster traps hanging from the ceiling and picturesque scenes behind glass, I chuckled at how us locals took their trade for granted. Funny, how tourists romanticized the industry, carrying it home in calendars or placemats, rarely appreciating the sweat that went into the lobster on their plate. Lilly returned with a coffee carafe. "What'll ya have, Hon?" I turned my mug upright and she filled it. Billy ordered a full course breakfast.

Instead of inspecting flaking varnish on lobster boats or the usual staring off into space, watching people come and go, or any other thing I subconsciously did with my attention rather than engage him, I looked up from my coffee, directly at Billy. We stared at each other for a long time, yet it was no stare down.

I sensed him wishing he could get inside my mind to unlock whatever it was that kept me silent. For sure, I was upset about Buck. That was a given. I think he even suspected I might be remembering things. But I didn't know how to talk about that—didn't want to talk about it. I doubted he realized Marlena wasn't just a Girl, that although I figured I was better off without a nutjob like her, I would miss her—her every peculiarity—every single day.

I knew Billy wanted to talk about Buck, wanted me to bring it up, probably so that I wouldn't feel as if he were trying to take control. I was, to my surprise, void of hostility. I felt none of my usual resentment.

I asked, "What are we going to do?"

His gaze dropped and came back to mine. "What do you think we should do?"

Lilly showed up with his omelet, and I let him take a bite before answering.

"I want to keep Buck at home for as long as we can."

We easily agreed upon that.

I couldn't stall any longer. "What do you think we're dealing with?"

He swallowed. "Some variation of dementia," he said, without sounding clinical.

Dementia. I hated the thud and then the echo of the word.

"We need to know exactly what's going on with him." He laid down his fork. "I know some very good specialists in Portland—"

I sighed with exhaustion and leaned back in my seat, rubbing my unshaved jaw.

"You've got a lot going on, Sam, why don't you let me take care of all that. I'll line up the doctor, find out what's available for in-home care, and what financial assistance programs Buck might be eligible for. I'll pitch in whatever money I can to make sure Buck gets the best."

I stared into my empty mug and nodded.

The fact was, and we both knew it, if not for Buck, we would have been so much worse off. He had been the primary stabilizer in our childhood, even above Mother, who had been, in her own way, suffering and struggling to keep it all together. Buck loved us, and he had been the one man we could look up to—the one who was always there for us.

Lilly returned and refilled our coffees. "What else can I get ya?" She took Billy's plate.

"We're good."

She tore a bill from her pad and slid it between us. Neither of us went for it. We weren't done talking. Taking a deep breath, I brought my eyes to his. He waited.

"How could someone as good and gentle as Buck raise someone who could be so mean?" I asked.

Billy studied my face and hesitated before saying, "Dad wasn't mean all the time, only when he drank."

"Then he must have been drinking a lot of the time."

Billy could have used that opportunity to gloat over my belated recognition of that truth, but he didn't. He seemed to take no satisfaction in saying, "Yeah, he was pretty messed up."

"But, why?" I pleaded.

Not as the psychiatrist, but as my big brother, he shook his head and said, "I don't know, Sammy. Sometimes it just happens."

I found no consolation in that, and I wasn't planning on some big confession, but I told him, "You know, I used to think that you were the one who made him so mean."

He winced at my words. "I know."

"But you were the one who took the brunt of it for me."

I think we were both taken aback by my candor. He remained silent, searching my eyes.

I needed to say more, and the words just came out. "I used to be so angry that you left and never came home—that you were so selfish." I wanted the profundity of my words to hit hard.

He came back with none of his usual justification. He simply absorbed my accusation like a child used to being punched.

"But you couldn't have come back here even if you wanted."

His gaze did not deviate as I remained silent, begging me to put the pieces together on my own.

My insides stirred with something I hadn't felt for my brother in a very long time. Sympathy. Maybe something stronger. "He screwed you up as bad as me."

He exhaled sharply. "Yeah."

His admission hung out there for a long minute. I thought about last night and all I had remembered. Then I offered a confession I never would have imagined myself capable of. "I was there. On the dock. The day he left, you know … I didn't try to stop him."

He blinked slowly and shook his head. "No, Sam … I didn't know that."

"He wanted me to go with him, but I wouldn't."

He didn't ask me to elaborate. He probably saw the torment all over my face.

I added, "He hit me … I don't think it was the first time."

Now I saw my own torment reflected in my brother's eyes. The tendons of his neck strained as he swallowed.

"I guess you didn't need to come home after he was gone," I continued. "You knew I was safe and that Buck would take care of me … I can see that now."

His jaw remained tense as he exhaled. "We didn't get to choose our father or our childhood, but at some point, we started making our own choices. I just chose a different life,

Sam, that's all. And you've chosen yours too. It may not always seem that way, but you have."

I thought about the decisions that had been made for me and the ones I had made in my adult life.

He kept his eyes on mine. "The thing of it is you can make different choices whenever you want."

I finally saw that and nodded.

Perhaps it wasn't my lot in life that made me restless, but unresolved issues that I had avoided for too long. Too many repressed memories. Like a sea monster below the surface—if it merely bumped my boat on occasion but I never capsized, maybe the monster didn't really exist. But the fear—the utter terror—was always there.

I went to grab the check and Billy snatched it from my hand. As I fished out a few bills for the tip, he asked, "What about the Girl? Marlena."

"She turned out to be flighty. We'll have to find someone else for Buck."

"That's fine for Buck, but what about you?"

"There'll be other girls," I lied.

I WAVED AT BILLY AND ELAINE AS THEIR BEEMER pulled out of the dooryard, past The Wesley House and Help Wanted sign. Mother clutched Mitch's arm as she wiped her eyes. At least I didn't have to offer consolation there. Rather than follow them and Buck into the house, I headed to the boatshed. Blowing out a long breath, I flopped into the moaning chair beside the back doorway. It's where I went when some project had gone to crap—when the wrong cut screwed up something that took two weeks to accomplish. It's also where I hid when my life felt like it was unraveling.

I had figured out a few things since breakfast, but none of that changed anything with Marlena. In fact, so many revelations in such a short time left my insides raw, as if scraped to the bone. As soon as I closed my eyes, they shot back open, landing on the *Mary-Leigh*. I couldn't sit still. Uncovering her hull, I walked beside her. Even though I did pick up a tool, I had no intention of putting it to work. It was midday and I missed the way a shaft of light used to graze her bow before we repaired the roof. I remembered the first time I laid eyes on Marlena—in that same intense light—she and her little suitcase.

At the rate I had been working on the *Mary-Leigh*, it would be years before I re-launched her. Although it tormented me every time I walked past her, as I spruced up or rebuilt someone else's dream boat, she was waiting for me with the patience that only an old wooden vessel could possess. She understood. I ran my hands along the planks of her hull. Light still shone through many of her seams—dried out like an old barrel, begging for water.

For the first time, it occurred to me that when my father had secured her lines before the big storm of '78, he had probably been three sheets to the wind. In reality, my father's negligence had stripped her vitality. As I mourned her, I fully realized that I was also suffering at his hand, even now.

How long would I allow myself to tread water, a project always put off—worthy in theory but relegated to last on the list? I easily drew the metaphor—the *Mary-Leigh* and I had a lot in common—yet it was a concept easier thought about than acted upon. In my frustration, I wrestled the canvas back over her bow and headed to my room.

I never went to my room at midday, and Mother asked if I was sick. I told her I had some bookwork, now that Billy and Elaine had gone, that I needed to take advantage of a few quiet minutes. That was partially true. I booted up my computer as if I planned to accomplish something, as if I were going to pour my heart into another chapter or add an emotional edge to something I had already written, when all I wanted was to read her story. Just the same, I couldn't quite bring myself to open the case.

I pushed back in my chair and spun to face the bed. I thought about the *Mary-Leigh*, about the time involved to make her seaworthy, about my level of commitment. I thought about my father, about Billy's memories of him—about my own. I thought about Buck—about how he was a real father to me—I thought about his stories, about my own. I thought about Derek and our friendship. I thought about anything I could come up with rather than think about Marlena.

I remained aware of her letter, laying there on my bed, right there, within arm's reach. Finally, succumbing to impulse, I snatched it. I wanted only to reread the last part. She printed with no erasures, as if she had known exactly what she had wanted to say.

I reread … *I came to Wesleyville to meet you, to get to know what kind of man you are before I told you my story. I wish I told it to you when I had the chance, because it's your story too, so I left it for you in my suitcase.*

It creeped me out that she had come all this way to meet *me*, just to tell me a story. What had she expected? That I would find her version of *Robinson Crusoe* so original that I would write it for her? What difference did it make what kind of man I was? And it was no more *my* story than it was Captain William Wesley's, as if pinning *his* name on a fictional character transformed her imaginings into my family history. Weird stuff. Delusional stuff. More and more, she was shaping up as someone better left alone. I sighed with relief—cutting her loose had been the right thing to do. Hopefully, by ten AM tomorrow morning, she would be well on her way, far from The Wesley House.

Even still, her small piece of luggage stared at me, begging my attention. I glared back with all the concentration she had ever focused upon me. I couldn't keep from wondering about where she had left off with her story. I had to admit, I was still curious about the girl on the island. I guess it was the writer in me—I couldn't stand not knowing how a story ended. Perhaps it might even answer some questions about Marlena. Unable to restrain myself any longer, I rose to stand at my bedside.

Her old, tan, fabric-covered suitcase with nickel-plated corners lay on my unmade bed. I unbuckled a leather belt that reinforced a sprung latch. I slid the other fastener and lifted the lid. A spiral-bound notebook—its front cover flipped to the back—sat atop what appeared to be more note pads and papers. I glowered at the heap of writing still in its place. Lines of plain and clear print, similar to that of Marlena's note, stared back. Without touching it, I begrudgingly read the top line.

'The first time I ever saw a man was in the fifth winter of my womanhood.'

Chapter 29

I REREAD THE OPENING LINE AND ALLOWED ITS implication to settle.

With that sort of lead, how could I resist the next line? There was nothing tentative about my interest now, but even as I read her next words, I still refrained from handling the notebook.

'At sunset, I spotted something coming out of the sea, way out where the sky and water meet, billowing black and thicker than a waterspout.'

I had to face it. I fully intended to read every word she wrote. With a measure of self-disgust, I took it in hand and sat back in my chair. Resigned, I continued reading.

I had never seen anything like it. Perhaps palm fronds burned on a faraway island, yet it looked nothing like the fires we had built. How could the sea burn? The strangeness of it kept me watching for hours until the sun disappeared below the sea and smoke spread above it in shades of amber. All night, I stayed on the beach, imagining people would come, just the way Mamá said they might. I didn't want to miss the people, but my eyelids did as they pleased. They closed for only a moment before sunlight warmed my face. I sat up, wide awake.

All the black had disappeared in the cloudless sky. The surf rushed in and out and palm trees rustled as if they had never seen the black smoke. Had I only dreamt it? Cormorants flew overhead and darted out to where waves broke against the big rocks, where dead and ruined things often churned in the breakers. Out where the Captain's ship used to be.

I squinted at a black speck on the crest of a wave, out on the horizon. It was the largest bird I had ever seen. At the same time, distant thunder rumbled. As the bird grew larger and larger, noise pounded my ears, louder and louder. I stood and ran into the surf. My stomach felt like the time I ate a bad conch and my skin tingled. I held my breath and rubbed my eyes.

The closer it came, the louder it rumbled. Mamá had told me about airplanes and helicopters, but I could never have envisioned something so large up in the sky. As it flew overhead, I crouched, covering my ears. It flew right over the island and disappeared. The noise went away, but soon it came back from behind. My feet wanted to run, but my knees were too wobbly. I spun around as it circled from the dune to the precipice and back to the beach. It hung in the air, like a gull flying against the wind, whipping sand all over, stinging my skin and swirling hair around my head. It pushed me back and I stumbled toward the brush to get away from the blowing and the chopping noise. I could barely breathe as I squinted, unable to look away. It landed, and two figures in billowing green fabric and smooth white helmets jumped out. That's when I ran to the nearest palm tree and hid, but they must have already seen me because they bent over and rushed toward me like barracudas.

I dropped to the ground with my knees to my breasts, but I didn't take my eyes off them. One had dark skin like Tomas and one had skin the same as mine. They towered over me like trees. Men. I wrapped my arms tighter as the dark one reached out and put cloth over my back. They yelled, but I didn't understand them because of the noise.

The pale man came close to my ear. "Are you hurt?"

My heart beat so fast that it cut off my breath and I couldn't answer. I shivered, but that didn't stop me from staring. He had a sharp nose, thin eyes, and even thinner lips. Still, I said nothing.

The dark man shouted, "Where are the others?"

The light-skinned one put his hand on my hair. "Are you hurt?"

I made myself breathe. "I don't hurt." My voice shook.

"Can you stand?"

I nodded. My legs quivered so much that I didn't know if they would hold me up. He pulled the thin blanket to cover my front and steered me toward the precipice, rushing us away from the noise.

"Are there any others?" he asked.

I thought about Mamá and nodded.

"Where are they?"

"There's only Mamá." My words came out weak. "She died."

"Where is she?"

I pointed toward the gravesite. "I buried her."

The light-skinned man followed me and removed his helmet. He didn't have any hair on top of his head. The other man returned to the helicopter. As we stood over the grave, he kicked at the ground and looked back at me. He rubbed his short hair and frowned. I didn't say anything. I simply kept my eyes on him and pulled the blanket tighter around me. I still couldn't believe what was happening—that a real live man was standing in front of me. I backed away from him, and even though I thought about running, there was no place to go.

"What is your name?" he asked.

I didn't mean to ignore him, but the other man arrived, and when I saw the shovel and the black bag he carried, I stood right over Mamá. Now my voice came out strong, and I put my hand up. "No!"

"We can't leave her here. We have to bring her back to identify her remains." He shook his head. "You'll have to step aside."

Before I even moved, the other man began to dig. I glanced at the overgrowth covering graves of the Captain, Tomas,

Benita, and the others. I didn't want them disturbed also, so I stepped aside, hoping all the brush would keep them hidden.

As he dug, I thought of the day I buried Mamá. I made myself do it sooner than I wanted, so she wouldn't get stiff like the dead rabbit I found in the fruit grove with maggots in its eyes. Or the dead bird that got caught between the rocks. Something had eaten parts of it and it smelled bad. As I dragged Mamá's body, I stared at the track she left in the sand so I wouldn't have to look at her. Soon, I couldn't even see that through the tears. I stopped and started so many times that the sun had set before I reached the gravesite. Then, I sat at her side for another day—I forced myself to cover her with earth, thinking she might suddenly wake up. She didn't.

As the men dug, I stared at them, not Mamá. Their eyes disappeared behind thin slits and their mouths gaped. They had found her decomposed body. Neither said a word as they exchanged grimaces.

The light-skinned man asked, "How long ago did she die?"

I still was not used to his voice. "Soon it will be two springs."

He frowned again. "How long have you been on this island?"

"My mother washed ashore the spring before I was born, all by herself."

He looked at me, but not at my face only. He seemed to be examining every inch of what he could see, the same way I stared at him, as if neither of us could believe the other one was real. "Let me get this straight. You were *born* here?"

"Yes."

The two men looked at each other. Their shoulders dropped and their mouths opened, but neither said a word. The light-skinned man led me away as the other stayed with Mamá. I glanced back as he unzipped the black bag. I answered his questions about what I saw the night before. He held on to my arm and told me I would be leaving with them.

I yanked my arm from his grip and backed away. "I don't want to go with you."

"You have no choice."

So many thoughts and feelings rushed through me that I turned and started to run toward my hovel, but I ran right into the other man's chest. I pushed away from him but his arms around me were too strong. I tried to scratch him, but he gripped my wrists as I struggled and the sheet fell to the ground.

"She's a feisty one," the dark man said.

The pale man stepped closer. "Take it easy."

I kicked the man holding me. He let go of one hand and I scratched his face. He let go of the other and I ran as fast as I could to the precipice. I heard someone behind me as I scaled the rocks to my hovel. Every time I found a loose rock, I threw it behind me. I heard him say, "*Jesus.*"

I didn't look behind, I just ran inside the opening and crouched in the corner on my grass bed. The entrance darkened with the man's shadow. I trembled as he looked all around at my things.

He said, "What the …."

"Get out of here! This is *my* place!"

"Listen, we don't have time for this. You have no choice." He stepped closer and tossed me the wadded-up sheet. "You're coming with us. If there are some things you want to bring, you've got two minutes to collect them and come back down to the beach. If you don't, Evans and I will have to drag you out. Is that what you want?"

I didn't want to go with them, but I didn't want to be left behind, so I shook my head.

"Two minutes," he said and left.

Still shaking, I spread out the cloth, gathered my favorite things, and wrapped them up. I should have taken more time to say good-bye to my hovel, but I ran back down to the beach. I kept the bundle in front of me, covering my breasts, wishing it also covered the small drape of animal hide loosening from my hips. I stumbled toward the helicopter until blowing sand stung my face and legs. I stopped. When I looked for the men, they came from behind, carrying the black bag. I dropped to my knees. I wanted my Mamá, not in a bag and not in a grave. I needed her to hold me close, the way I hugged my bundle and closed my eyes—so close and tight that I couldn't breathe or see.

When I felt a sheet drape over my shoulders, I opened my eyes, but couldn't see through my tears. The light-skinned man put his arm around me and tried to make me stand, but my legs wouldn't work. How could I leave my island—my home? But I couldn't let them take Mamá and not me. I tried to stand. My legs gave out again, and the man scooped me up. I pressed my face into my bundle as he carried me toward the thumping and blowing. I kept my eyes shut and let him and the other man help me up inside. He strapped me into a seat, and I looked at him just long enough to see his sharp nose very close to mine. I cringed.

In front of us, another two men sat wearing the same white helmets with black visors, glancing back at me. I wiped my tears, trying to get a better look at them. Mamá had told me about men, that there were different kinds. I prayed they were the good kind, but I wasn't sure. I did not like any of these men.

We began to rock back and forth and everything shook. I gripped my seat and shut my eyes again. I felt a hand on my shoulder and flinched. Even though we went up, I felt heavy. My empty stomach lurched. I shivered and squeezed my eyes shut so tightly that I saw spots. When I finally opened them just enough to focus, my island teetered below. We hovered near the ground like scavenger birds. As we passed over our little hut in the fruit grove, my eyes burned inside their sockets and tears flooded out. I would probably never see my home again. I wanted to tell the Captain goodbye—that I loved him—but I couldn't speak. I just watched the island turn into a little green speck until it disappeared.

We traveled over the water for what seemed like a very long while and then landed on a gigantic boat. When the pounding noise stopped, the sharp-nosed man leaned toward me.

"My name is Phelps," he said. "Don't be afraid."

"I'm not afraid." And I wasn't, but I couldn't stop shaking. So many things had happened so fast. Every time I tried to breathe, my lungs wouldn't fill and tears kept trying to push their way out.

He climbed from the helicopter first and tried to take my bundle, but I wouldn't let him. With his thick arm, he helped me down onto a surface that felt as firm as a rock and flatter than anything I had ever walked on, but it constantly moved beneath me. The sheet covering me billowed like a sail. Dark water surrounded the boat. It churned like a stormy cloud about to split open. It pushed the boat upward until I saw only the sky, and then it dropped as if it were going to spill over onto us. The ocean had been all around me for my entire life, but I had never seen it look so ominous. I stopped to watch it, but the man held my arm and kept me moving toward one of the looming towers. It seemed almost as tall as the precipice, and was the same cold, gray color. My stomach tingled as if I had swallowed a hundred little jellyfish. I didn't like Phelps hanging on to me, but if he had let go, I might have fallen over.

Phelps led me down some metal stairs and into a narrow hall. A low rumbling vibrated in my ear, and the boat rocked back and forth. We bumped each other, and he squeezed my arm as we walked into a small room. The sick bay. He closed the door behind us.

He tried to take my bundle again, but I wouldn't let him. He shoved some folded fabric at me and patted a tall bed. "Listen, you have to put this on and climb up on here."

I didn't budge until he stepped toward me. I backed up against the wall, knocking things over and trying to pull my sheet tighter around me. "Get away from me!"

The door opened and a new man stepped inside. His hair looked like sand and his eyes were the color of the sea, and just as deep.

"Knock it off, Phelps!" he said, glancing at me and back at him. "Where's your manners?"

He held his hand out to me. I stared at it and then looked at his face.

He smiled and tilted his head. "I'm a doctor. My name is Dave. Would you like to tell me yours?"

Mamá always called me Baby, but I had another name. It sounded strange when I said, "Marlena."

He nodded. "You've been through a lot today. If you want to stand, you can, but you might be a little tired after your helicopter ride. Sitting might feel good." His voice sounded deep and gentle, like waves.

Even though he kept his hand held out, I didn't take it, but I moved away from the wall and toward the bed. He unfolded the fabric and held it up. "Your arms go in these holes."

Still holding my things, I put one arm in and then the other. I set my bundle on the bed and climbed up without help. With my things on my lap, I watched him carefully as Phelps stood off to the side.

He looked me over for a minute and asked, "Does any part of you hurt?"

I wiggled my shoulders and feet and shook my head.

He held out something shiny attached to long, black tentacles. "This is a stethoscope. I'm going to put this part on your chest to listen to your heart. It might be a little cold. Is that okay?"

I nodded.

Each time he checked another part of me, he told me exactly what he would touch and how it might feel and asked if that was okay. I always nodded. I liked his smile. I even started to smile back. He wanted to know my birthday, but Mamá wasn't sure of the exact date. She only knew for sure that it was in late December. They guessed that I was about seventeen years old, but later, when we calculated from the time my parents set sail, we estimated I was probably closer to nineteen. He asked if I knew what a menstrual cycle was, and did I have one yet? I told him I did.

I told him Mamá's name, and I also gave him her nine US numbers, the ones she said I needed to remember in case something ever happened to her and someone found me. Mamá also told me that every place on earth could be located with special numbers.

"Do you know the longitude and latitude for my island?" I asked.

His eyebrows shot up. "Not off the top of my head, but I'll find out."

"And write them down?"

"If you'd like."

"Could I look at what you're writing?" I asked.

Dave chuckled until I read aloud some of his writing.

"You can read?" he asked.

"Of course I can. And I can write too."

He gave me a pencil and a tablet of paper. "Show me."

I studied the pencil and its sharp point. "I only know how to write in the sand or with a piece of charcoal on a smooth rock."

"Just try." Dave put my hand to the paper.

I wrote my name, but I didn't do a good job. He said I could keep the pencil and paper to practice.

They had so many questions. How did Mamá die? Did I ever have any sicknesses? I told them about the conch, and the time I ate the berries that I shouldn't have, but that I didn't ever remember not feeling well. Even after Dave finished examining me, he had more and more questions, but I had to be careful how I answered. Mamá warned me that if people knew about the Captain and the gold, it might make them greedy, like Achan and Judas in the Bible. I didn't tell anyone about the gold.

Soon, I needed to pee. Dave brought me to the head and showed me how it flushed, and then left me alone. Inside, I held on to the door handle. My legs weren't so wobbly in there. I took a deep breath. Mamá told me about toilets, but it looked nothing like I imagined. When I turned toward the sink, my mother's eyes looked at me from above it, but it was only a mirror. I moved my hand back and forth over the smooth glass as the reflection followed. We had the little signal mirror on the island, but it was the size of a shell, and I never saw how I looked, all my parts together. My eyes looked exactly like Mamá's—black dots in a sea of gray, circled in brown. I moved closer to the mirror until tears blurred my face. I wiped my eyes and noticed my snarled and matted hair.

Mamá used to comb her fingers through my hair every evening as we sat on the beach, undoing the tangles from the wind and sticky things I ate. When our hair grew too long, she used Ruby to cut it off. We braided strands of it together for all kinds of things. After she died, I sat alone and ran my fingers through my own hair, pretending she was with me, but I still ended up with tangles. After a while, it made me too sad and I stopped. I didn't care anymore.

I sat on the toilet. It took me a long time before I could go. When I was done, Dave knocked on the door and then came in.

"Are you okay?" he asked.

I glanced at the mirror and shook my head. "My hair looks bad."

"Don't worry about that. We'll fix it later." He smiled and stood beside me. "This is how the sink works."

He put soap in my palms. I went to taste it, but he wrapped my hands in his, rubbing mine together. What looked like sea foam covered the hair on the tops on his hands. He had a gold band on one of his fingers. I turned to his face. He smiled and I touched his rough chin. It felt like dried sand. His eyebrows jumped, but he didn't say anything. He smelled a little like the soap. Then he showed me how to dry off with a towel, and even though I could have figured it out myself, I didn't mind that he helped.

When I came out, Phelps had unwrapped my things. He held the Captain's dagger. I rushed over and tried to grab it from him.

"That's mine!" I said, but he held it up away from me.

"Where did you find it?" he asked.

"Mamá found all these things on the island."

"Have a little respect," Dave said as I grabbed my doll before either of them did. I was mostly concerned they would pick up the Bible, because I had tucked the gold coins in the spine and stuffed some leaves in each end to keep them from coming out.

"May I?" Dave asked, about to put his hand on the Bible.

"Be careful or the pages might fall out." I sounded mad because I was. He left it alone. The Captain's log lay underneath the Bible and they didn't even notice it.

Dave said, "You can keep everything but the dagger."

"I need Ruby!" I talked fast and loud, "I use her all the time to cut up my food and open things and to cut my hair and throw at small animals and skin them and protect myself from snakes."

Phelps chuckled. "We use other things for eating."

"But I need her for protection!"

"There aren't any wild animals where you're going."

I didn't like the way he talked to me, as if I didn't know anything. And why did he think he could look through my things? My whole body heated up.

Dave patted my arm. "We'll make sure you get it back."

I believed him.

Dave handed me soft, stretchy cloth and a pair of sneakers. Dave unfolded the shirt and pants. "Can you figure out how to put these on?"

"Of course I can." I yawned, taking the clothes into the head.

The clothes were loose, but I did not like wearing them. The shoes almost made me trip. I relaxed a little more because Phelps was gone when I came back out.

"You must be hungry," Dave said, leading me through a narrow door. I sat on the bed and he sat in a chair beside a tiny table.

"Yes," I said and yawned again.

Phelps returned and set a tray in front of me. I looked at it and back at him.

"An apple and toast," Dave said. "You'll like them."

He returned to the doorway, talking to Phelps as I bit into the fruit. It crunched, so I stopped chewing to listen. Phelps said something about the "media," and "PR." I swallowed and tore off a piece of toast. I stared at it as I made out the words "special circumstance," and stuffed toast into my mouth. It didn't taste like much of anything, but it made me smile. "All agencies have been notified," Phelps said. He also said something about paperwork and fingerprints as I drank the water. It tasted funny.

Next, Dave put my head over a sink and washed my hair. To finish rinsing the soap out, I stepped into the tiniest room where warm water showered from a spout. I used soap on the rest of my body too. I would have stayed under the shower much longer, but Dave said we needed to conserve water. After I dressed, he sat on the bed and I sat on a chair in front of him while he used his fingers and something slippery from a jar to fix my hair.

"I have little sisters," he said. "I used to comb out their snarls."

He worked on it for a long time and never hurt me even once. Then he brought me to the mirror over the sink and stood behind me. He got most of the snarls out, but he had to cut a little bit. A small clump of it fell to the floor.

"It's good you have such thick hair," he said. "It doesn't even show."

"Do you think it will look pretty?"

"Are you kidding me? It'll look gorgeous." He smiled at me in the mirror. He had straight, white teeth like mine.

Afterward, I lay on the bed. I tried to keep my eyes open, but just like the night before, they wouldn't cooperate. When I opened them again, I was alone and the door was closed. A duffel bag lay on the chair with my unopened bundle on top.

I reached over and grabbed it, hugging it tight. Where were they taking me? Mamá told me she had a sister, a mother, and a father in Kansas. I would probably end up with them. I didn't know too much about my father except that he had been born in Venezuela and his family owned a plantation. I had no numbers for him. Whoever my people turned out to be, I hoped they would be waiting for me when we went ashore.

Soon, the boat rocked me back to sleep.

Chapter 30

S MUCH AS I HAD ENJOYED LISTENING TO THE first parts of Marlena's story, reading her third segment—the more primitive style of her written words—sounded more like Marlena, as if I could hear her voice. My heart ached in her absence. I wished she were sitting on my bed, facing me, so I could watch her expression change as she spoke the next words.

"Wake up," someone said. When I opened my eyes, Dave was sitting beside me. "It's time to go."

I yawned. "Are my people waiting for me?"

"No, not *your* people, not yet."

Several days passed and Dave visited me a lot. He even took me for a walk on deck, and I met some other people. I always carried my new notebook with me, and anytime I met someone, I asked them to write down their name and the date, just like in the Captain's log. I also started writing my own journal about everything that was happening to me.

Finally, we landed in Mayport, Florida, but it took a long time before I could leave the ship. People in uniforms from Departments needed to talk to me, but Dave did most of the talking. After they made my fingerprints and took my picture and I wrote my name on important papers, Dave walked me into a parking lot. We rushed past more people trying to talk to us, but Dave didn't talk back, he just put a jacket over my head and kept me moving to a van and told me to get in quickly.

"Who are they?" I asked.

"The media," he said, but I didn't understand. I just knew I didn't like the media.

My heart beat fast as we drove to a hospital. Riding in a van made me almost as unsteady as flying in a helicopter. I just wanted to close my eyes and sleep, but we didn't drive for very long. When the van stopped, Dave squeezed my hand and said, "Time to go."

More men and even some women rushed past me as we walked through the doors and into another small room. Each person looked different from the others. They had different skin colors, different hair, and unusual shapes, but soon I had a hard time telling them all apart.

I put on another little shirt that tied in the back. New people asked me questions, ones I had already answered. They also stuck things in my mouth, listened to my heart, and hit my knee. Even though Dave stood beside me, I closed my eyes tight to make all their faces go away. Someone grabbed my hand to straighten my arm. When I opened my eyes, I saw a big needle.

I jumped off the table.

When Dave tried to hold my hand, I pushed over a cart. Everything around me clattered. I covered my ears and started to run, but someone caught me. I tried to get away until I realized it was Dave. He held me close.

"Marlena," he said in a gentle voice, "these people don't want to hurt you, they simply need to make sure you're healthy."

I took a deep breath. "How would they like it if I poked all of them with a sharp stick?"

Dave asked the others to leave for a minute and brought me back to the table.

"Marlena, this is something we have to do."

"Then I want you to do it."

"Okay." He quickly tied a string around my arm. Then he

rubbed a spot with something cold and pointed at the clock. "Tell me when the red hand gets to the five."

"Okay."

"Ready?"

As I glanced away, I felt a pick and a tug. I closed my eyes. "Yes."

"Already done."

I cried into his shirt, not because it hurt, but because everything had changed so fast. I wanted to curl up in my grass bed and wake up on my island and not see any more people or answer any more questions. Why did Mamá want to be rescued? This place was much worse than living on our happy home.

After that, Dave brought me to another small room and let me sleep. I woke slowly, listening to voices—a woman speaking softly. She said something about long-term isolation, trauma, and helping me. I just lay there with my eyes closed and listened to the sound of her sweet voice, imagining it was Mamá.

When I opened my eyes, a woman with straight silver hair and brown eyes, and wearing a pretty dress, smiled at me.

Dave said, "This is Linda. She brought you some breakfast."

She placed a tray of food in front of me. I ignored the fork and used my fingers.

Linda smiled a lot, like Mamá. She didn't have a pad or paper or a stethoscope or anything at all. She simply talked to Dave, who told her all about me. I didn't have to answer hardly any questions while I ate. When I finished, she talked mostly to me.

Linda used a soft voice as she asked me what sorts of things I did while I was growing up, what kinds of games I played, how I learned to read, and what my mother was like. She let me talk and talk, the way Mamá used to. She just smiled and asked a few questions every now and then, but mostly, I talked. I had no idea that I had so much to say.

Dave left for a few minutes, and she talked to me about some private girl things. Mamá already told me about that, about the differences between men and women and how babies are made.

When Dave came back, he brought chocolate ice cream. I ate only a tiny bit. It tasted too sweet and too cold.

When Linda left, she and Dave stepped out of the room together. In a little while, he came back alone and sat on the bed beside me. "They found your people."

My heart jumped.

"You have an Aunt Rita and Uncle Bert."

I frowned.

"What's wrong?" he asked.

"I don't like the way their names sound."

"Don't worry," he smiled and took my hand. "They're probably very nice."

"Where will I live?"

"Kansas."

"How far from the sea is that?"

He sighed. "About as far from the ocean as you can get."

My shoulders and chest felt heavy. "Will I live near you?"

"No. My wife and I live in Virginia. Well, she does. I'm not home too much."

"Is she nice?"

Half of his mouth smiled. "Yeah, she's pretty nice."

I frowned. I wished he didn't have a wife.

Dave touched my cheek gently and then stood. "We'll be flying into McConnell Air Force Base. Your family will be arriving the day after tomorrow to pick you up."

"Will you stay with me until then?"

"Yes. I'll even come on the airplane with you."

I could tell he liked me from the way he smiled and how his eyes brightened when he talked to me. He wanted to know about me and my life on the island, but there wasn't a whole lot to say. I did the same things every day of my life. I didn't want to talk about myself. I wanted to know all about everything he had ever done. He probably could have told me many more things, but I kept interrupting with questions. Always more questions. He teased me about that, but I kept asking anyway. I didn't ask about his wife again, but I wondered if she missed him.

On the final day, he was there when I woke up. He stood at the big window and peered outside.

"Can we go now?" I asked.

"Not yet."

"Can we at least go outside for a walk?"

He sighed, still staring out the window with his arms folded. "Marlena, I need to talk to you."

"But I'm tired of this room. The air smells bad."

"Marlena—" he turned to me. "Since you were born and raised on an island with only your mother, it makes you extraordinary. Do you understand that?"

I didn't, not really, but I nodded anyway.

"Because the Navy rescued you, you're a bit of a celebrity."

"What's celebrity?"

"It makes you special. It makes people very interested in you. Some people would even like to show you off to the public."

"What does showing off mean?"

"Remember the people who tried to talk to us when we got off the boat? They still want to ask you a lot of questions."

"The way Linda and you did?"

"No. Not like that. These people want to take pictures of you for television and magazines so the whole world can look at you."

"I don't understand."

He took a small object from the table next to the bed—a remote control—and pushed a button. The television flashed noisy pictures across the screen. I didn't like it one bit.

I covered my ears. "Make that stop."

He shut it off. "'Showing off' puts your face on every television in every hospital and every home all over the world. The media already knows about you. More and more people will be curious, and you won't have any privacy for the rest of your life."

He gestured for me to come to the window. As I stood

behind him, he pointed at the parking lot.

"Tomorrow, people with cameras and lots of questions will crowd that parking lot. They'll all be here for you," he said.

"I don't want to talk to them." I looked up at Dave. He pulled me close and hugged me. It was the first time anyone had hugged me since Mamá.

I heard his breathing in his chest as he said, "I know. I'll figure something out."

That night, after I fell asleep, Dave nudged me. "It's time to go."

He gave me a pretty dress like Linda's. After I put it on, he led me through several doors, down some stairs, and out another door into the dark. There were no people, only a car nearby. I couldn't wait to climb inside if it would take me away from there. I sat on the back seat.

"You can sit in front with me in a few minutes. For now, lie down and be very still." Dave spread a blanket over me, including my head. We drove for a little while and stopped. Dave talked to someone, and then we drove again. Soon, he stopped and let me get in the front and put my bag on my lap. I dug through it. "Where's Ruby?"

"Don't worry about that. You'll get if after the flight."

"Okay."

Before the sun came up, we arrived at the airfield. An airplane took off and flew directly over us. I ducked so that it wouldn't take my head off. Dave laughed, but every time I saw or heard one, I cringed and covered my ears. I could hardly believe I would soon be on one of them, flying way above the earth.

Finally, when the sun turned orange as it rose in the sky, we stood in front of huge windows. It appeared so much smaller than the sun on the island. I pressed my hands against the glass, so smooth and so flat. I looked out beyond the glass at airplanes and sky, and then I looked at the glass and saw myself. I leaned close to it and my breath collected like morning fog. I went to lick it off, but Dave told me not to. He laughed and said I was like a little kid.

He led me out some doors to an airplane not much bigger than the helicopter. We climbed some stairs and smiled at some people and then he buckled me into a seat beside his.

He stared at my face and a slow smile came over his. "You really are special, you know that?"

I liked the way he looked at me. "I don't know. I only know that you're special, because I haven't met anyone like you."

He chuckled. "You haven't met that many people. After a while, I won't seem all that special. I'm actually pretty ordinary."

"I guess I don't know about ordinary. I only know that you're the first man that made me smile. I know I'll never forget how you look and sound and smell." Then I pet the back of his fingers. "I like the hair on your hands."

He laughed aloud and squeezed my knee while he shook his head. Then he put his hand in his pocket and pulled out a candy bar and some crackers. I liked the crackers, but only ate a little of the candy bar. Too sweet.

I heard a voice from overhead and Dave said, "This will be fun."

I smiled and held my breath as we took off. I grabbed my seat with one hand and my duffle bag with the other, but it didn't feel anything like being in the helicopter. As soon as we climbed above the clouds, I forgot all about flying so far away from the ground. I closed my eyes and fell asleep and didn't wake until we landed.

"We're in Kansas," Dave said.

I rubbed my eyes and peered out the window, looking for my people.

"I don't see them," I said.

"They're probably inside the building."

"I don't feel good." I stared at Dave. "I don't think I'm ever going to see you again."

"Maybe someday you'll come visit my wife and me in Virginia." He stood. "And we'll write back and forth. It'll be fine, you'll see. Besides, I'm sure your new family is very nice."

I didn't say anything. I just followed him to the doorway and down the stairs into much cooler air. I shivered as we walked quickly to the building. He opened the door and I stepped in. A very large woman came right up to me and sighed. "You must be Marlena."

I SET MARLENA'S NOTEBOOK IN MY LAP AND CHOKED UP. SHE had drawn me into her delusions and I was starting to believe it. I wanted to believe it. It would explain so much, and there were still many pages left to read. I wanted to know what happened in Kansas. I tried to recall—hadn't there been some preposterous story that flashed across the headlines a few years ago, something in one of Mother's tabloids about some girl raised by wolves or apes or something? It made the headlines for a day or two, and then nothing. I tried to put it all together, trying to make it true. I was in the middle of reading her next sentence when Derek came through my bedroom door.

Chapter 31

DEREK STEPPED INTO MY ROOM AND SHUT THE DOOR. He scratched his bed head.

"Didn't your mother ever teach you to knock?" My arms settled across my chest as I stared at his crumpled T-shirt and shorts rather than make eye contact.

He walked to the side window and glanced out, ignoring my question. I assumed he had already heard about Marlena—that he had only shown up to gloat. An apology would be completely out of character. Without missing a beat, and as if last night had never happened, he said, "You'll never guess who came by my shop."

He waited for me to bite, but I was in no mood. "What do you want, Derek?"

"Come on, Sam. Just guess."

I rolled my eyes and said nothing.

"That's right, *Marlena.*"

"Listen, Derek, if this is about last night—"

"To hell with last night. This is serious. She came to my shop trying to hire me."

"What do you mean?" I sat up and leaned forward.

"You know, for some trans-Caribbean voyage ...."

I hated when he baited me, but I couldn't help prodding, "And?"

"She came in about an hour ago. Get this. She wanted to hire me to bring her to some island way off the coast of

Brazil." He loved withholding information, and I hated it just as much.

I caved with a sigh. "Yeah …?"

"Then she walked over to my globe, studied it for a second, and pinpointed the place."

I feigned complacency and settled back in my seat. "Really."

"You know anything about that?"

My turn to withhold. "I don't know. Maybe." I was thinking, *Oh, God, I actually do.*

"She told me she wanted to leave as soon as possible, can you believe it?"

"And?"

"Of course, I told her there was no way. She obviously has no idea how long it takes to put something like that together."

I waited for more and then checked my watch as if I had better things to do than listen to his drivel.

"Yeah, it was kind of funny. I asked how she would pay for it—Visa or MasterCard?" He chuckled. "And she plunked down a gold specie on my counter. You know anything about *that*?"

I scratched my head and shrugged.

He chuckled again. "I told her it would cost a whole lot more than that, and she pulled seven more coins out of those swim trunks of yours and said she left one with you. *Ring a bell yet*?"

The suitcase drew my attention like a beacon. "She didn't leave anything for me but a bunch of paper."

It took me longer than it should have to come out of my chair and dump its contents onto the bed. Out flopped a large, old Bible, what appeared to be a well-worn leather-covered journal, quite a few newer papers, and something wrapped in cloth. When I unwrapped the bundle, a telescope, compass, pocket watch, dagger, and finally the gold coin tumbled to my sheet.

I looked at Derek, matching his surprise. It finally hit me. *It was all true.*

Derek stared at the collection and then at me. "Where did you get all this junk?"

I picked up the leather-bound journal and flipped open the cover. I read, '*Captain William Wesley, in command of the schooner* Vanessa-Benita.' The first entry was dated January 5, 1867. My eyes probably gaped as wide as my mouth and my legs wobbled. I leaned against my bed.

Derek examined the dagger as I picked up one of the other papers.

"This is some old stuff," he said as I continued reading silently.

Names.

Dates.

Addresses.

The crew she met on the naval ship. All right there and verifiable. At the top of the list, Commander David Putnam, M.D. There in front of me, in his handwriting, were her height, weight, blood pressure, all his observations and assessments, all easily verifiable.

Written across the top of the page, giving me a shudder, were her island's coordinates.

"Come on, man, what is all this?" His question barely registered.

My head and heart swam with remorse. I couldn't believe she had left all these things for me. Yes, they belonged to the Captain, but they were just as much hers.

Even more than that, a gross realization left me stripped of pride. Had I begged her to stay, she would have been right there with me. Instead, I had allowed her to walk away. I sent her away.

It took a second to get a grip and form the question, "What else did she tell you?"

He held the coin up to the light for closer inspection. "When I pressed her on where she got the gold, she wouldn't tell me— would only say that she knew where there was plenty more, and she could take me to it."

My eyes widened.

"Yeah. I know," he said. "I thought she was out of her mind. But, she *did* have a nice cache of pretty rare pieces. You don't see too many of these around, and most of it only on the black market."

I still couldn't speak.

He rubbed his jaw—a nervous tick. "I asked her who else knew about them."

"What'd she say?"

"She said she sold one to a pawnshop in Kansas City to get bus fare. She said she didn't fill out any paperwork in the transaction, which is good, but I told her that she shouldn't be carrying that stuff around as if it were pocket change, that she should leave it in my safe. That didn't go over real well, so I told her that even if the pawnshop didn't know the coin's real worth, by now it was bound to be in the hands of those who did, and they'd be looking for more—willing to do anything to get their paws on it."

"Is that really true?"

"I might have exaggerated a little, just to get her to leave it with me. You know how gullible she is." He let out a quick laugh.

"It's not funny. You probably scared her."

"*Yeah*, I did. And it worked. She let me put it in my safe, as long as I gave her the combination."

"Where is she now?"

"I left her at my place, but I doubt she stayed there—said I couldn't hold her against her will."

"You should have brought her back here."

"Hey, man, I tried, but she was really wigged out—didn't want anything to do with coming back here with me." With a sly smile, he added, "And here I thought the two of you were all chummy."

He stared at me, waiting to hear what I knew.

"Yeah, well, things aren't always what they appear." I turned away and looked out over the bay—at that patch of Cuttermann's Island.

"That's it? That's all you got? Give me a break. What is all this crap on your bed, and why do you have it?"

"It's her stuff." I was reluctant to divulge her personal

information, figuring that if she had wanted him to know everything she would have told him herself.

"So why'd she leave it with you?"

"Because ... it belonged to the Captain."

"Captain who?"

"You know ... Wesley ... William."

"No way."

"I know, it sounds crazy." I lifted her notebook. "But it's all here, all documented."

He reached for the Captain's journal, flipped to the first page and then the last. He looked at me for verification.

I stuck the coin in my sock drawer. "I'll explain it to you on our way to town."

DEREK CLUTCHED HIS STEERING WHEEL AS HE NAVIGATED a sharp left turn in the road, forcing me into the door. He ran fingers through his hair. "So, what you're telling me is that she hadn't even seen a man until three years ago?"

"Apparently."

Derek's eyes bugged, wild with imagination. Then he turned to me with disgust. "And you blew it?"

"Just shut up and drive."

He did, but as we neared town, he reverted to his chin rubbing. The silence grew tense. His uneasiness spurred my curiosity.

"You don't think anyone is looking for her, do you?" I asked.

"They'd have to be pretty motivated. It all depends on how much information she leaked at the pawnshop." He didn't quell my anxiety a whole lot. Given her nature, it seemed unlikely that she would have spilled much. Just the same, my heart began palpitations.

"Don't worry about it," he said. "Probably some fifteen-year-old nephew apprenticed to the pawnshop owner melted it down."

"Or?"

"Or ... even if the owner didn't know exactly what it was,

he's got a guy who deals in coins, who's got connections—who …," he fell silent again. He had that look on his face, the blotchy one that I rarely ever saw. He always got it when he thought about his encounters with the unscrupulous sector of his industry. He ran a legitimate business, but a while back, he had gotten tangled up in some dodgy stuff and he didn't like to talk about it, which meant he was scared.

"You don't *really* think she's in any danger, do you?"

"*Nah.*" His eyes shifted all over the place and his foot weighed heavier on the accelerator. Tourists jumped back onto the curb as we zoomed past.

"Last time I checked, it was still against the law to run down pedestrians, you know."

"Not on the last day of Heritage Week, it's not." He scowled as I grabbed the door to brace myself for the upcoming turn into his driveway. He swung wide and halted inches from his garage door. In a flash, we jumped out, heading around to the private entry as he jingled his keys. The door cracked ajar.

"I told her to lock up if she left," he said under his breath. The light bulb shone overhead and he called out her name as he headed to his safe. With a few spins of the dial, he hit each number and then pulled it open. "They're gone."

"Any of your stuff?"

"No. All my stuff is in a safe deposit box. All except this—" He pulled out a handgun and loaded it.

Now, my heart really started pounding. "You're not serious."

He bit his lip and clenched his blotchy jaw.

"*Nah,*" he answered, disinclined to put it back.

"Put it away, man. I don't even want to see that thing." I shot a glance back toward the doorway. "Maybe she's upstairs."

Before the words left my mouth, that's where I was headed. On my way out, I heard Derek shut the safe and give it a spin.

I climbed the steps of the outdoor staircase, two at a time. As I entered the apartment, I called her name and walked through each room. If I hadn't been familiar with Derek's 'disorganizational' skills, I might have thought thugs had ransacked the place, but it looked normal for his habitat.

"Any luck?" Derek asked from behind.

"Jeez, Derek, if she had come up here, all this crap would have scared her off for sure." I peeked in at the bathroom. "She's not here."

We headed back down.

As we crossed the street to walk the couple of blocks to the fairgrounds, he speculated, "She's probably using her coins for Ferris wheel tokens. I'll head over there."

We split up. He proceeded toward the tents, and I took off for the beach. We would meet up at the carnival. I scanned the thinning crowd for the silhouette of my too-big shorts on her willowy, bushy-topped figure. Nothing in the parking lot—not in the picnic area, nor out by the jetty. As I stood on the beach where Derek had tackled me, I kicked at the ground. A few feet away, sand half-covered a wilted and browning yellow rose. As I picked it up, the petals fell off. Perhaps Marlena had never seen anything so violent—not personally. Without the numbing effects of television, maybe she had never even been exposed to a fistfight. Likely, she did believe she had ruined my relationship with Derek.

And the thing with Buck—it was hard to know how it had affected her, interacting with someone that old and watching him decline in such a short time. It was enough to unsettle me, and I had been expecting it, just putting it off in my own mind.

All her words—spoken and written—came back to me. I placed her in the context of her island with her mother, and then alone, imagining the sort of turmoil she had experienced. I wished I had read the remainder of her story before taking off with Derek. It was my hunch that not all had gone well in her new environment in Kansas. The more I envisioned her struggles, the more I regretted my reaction to her note last night. Remorse stuck thick in my throat as I headed to the carnival grounds.

Derek rested a hand on one hip and scratched his head. "She's probably just tucked in some out-of-the-way place."

"Yeah … or she might have headed to the bus depot."

As he drove, I mustered my optimism, hoping that within minutes I might see her and have an opportunity to explain that I wasn't upset, that I was sorry. But could I persuade her to come back with me?

The sight of the empty bench outside of the closed depot building dashed my confidence. We drove on past for another five miles. Nothing.

Derek turned us around, and we took his Hummer slowly through the streets of Wesleyville. Talk about conspicuous. Faces turned but none of them Marlena's.

We sat at the only traffic light in town. "She doesn't want to be found, Derek. You may as well bring me home."

Before the light turned green, Derek looked at me. He must have detected the weight of everything in my expression. I returned his glance. For a split second, I thought he might offer an apology or at least an acknowledgment of his role in all of it. Not that I expected it. I returned my sights to the road, thinking about how alone and frightened Marlena must be feeling.

Finally, he opened his mouth, though it took a second for words to come out. "I'll hang around the fairgrounds and then check back in at my place, just in case."

"Whatever." I hoped my expression conveyed how little I cared what he did. I was already speculating on the rest of Marlena's story. Perhaps I would get some clue as to her next move or at least some more insight on her thinking.

He pulled into the dooryard and shifted to neutral as he came to a halt in front of the boatshed. Tapping his steering wheel, he stared ahead as I opened my door. I began climbing out.

"Sam … about last night …."

For an instant, I wanted to let him off the hook. Instead, I kept my eyes on him. "Yeah?"

"I really didn't know—I didn't realize—you should have said something."

"And you should have known."

Chapter 32

*A*VOIDING MOTHER, I HEADED TO MY ROOM and went directly to Marlena's notebook.

"Where was I?" I mumbled as I scanned the page and sat. Picking up where I left off, I read aloud, "'No, this is a mistake. You can't be my mother's sister, you're too big.'"

*A*unt Rita stepped even closer and drew me in. I almost suffocated as she buried me in her big, mushy arms. She smelled worse than the hospital, and her short, reddish hair didn't move at all. Then she held me at arm's length and put on a sad face.

"I simply can't believe you exist." She covered her mouth.

I didn't say anything. I just looked at Dave.

He said, "It's time to go."

I swallowed back my tears but they came anyway. I hugged Dave so hard that he had to push me away, but I saw in his eyes that he did not want to let me go. My aunt gave me a coat, took my hand, and pulled me along down a hallway. I kept turning to look at Dave until we stepped through a doorway back outside. I put the coat on in a hurry. The cold air stung my eyes as I wiped my face dry.

My uncle waited at the car. He stood as tall as my aunt, but two of him could hide behind her. His clothes hung from his pointy shoulders, drooping the way his face did, and several dark hairs curved from one ear, up over his shiny head to his other ear. He tried to take my duffle bag. I wouldn't let him.

My aunt squeezed into the seat across from Uncle Bert and she turned to look at me.

She let out a long, slow breath. "Your eyes are exactly like your mother's."

"I know. I have beautiful eyes."

The crease between her brows deepened. "And you sound just like your mother."

I wasn't sure why sounding like my mother would make her frown.

All of a sudden, I remembered that Dave forgot to give me Ruby.

"We need to go back!" I said.

My aunt rolled her eyes. "Simmer down. You can't go back. You may as well get used to it."

Tears streamed down my face as I thought of Dave and Ruby.

As Uncle Bert drove, Aunt Rita whispered at him. He didn't say much. They didn't talk to me, so I fell asleep. When I woke up, it was too dark to see anything but the yard light and the front door. Wind blew my hair and carried whiffs of something sour. Uncle Bert held the door open, and I followed my aunt. The air inside smelled even worse. A plump girl with Aunt Rita's face slouched on the sofa. She peered over a bowl, licking a spoon and squinting at me from my head to my tight shoes.

Aunt Rita said, "This is your cousin Rachel. She's twelve, and you'll be sleeping in her room."

"You look like a school teacher," Rachel said.

I smoothed the dress. "These aren't my real clothes."

"Then, where are *they*?"

I shoved my hand in my duffle bag and felt around for rabbit hair, then pulled it out. "This is mine."

She covered her mouth and laughed.

Aunt Rita said, "That's obscene. You'll wear proper clothes

as long as you live here!"

That night, I climbed between stiff sheets and pulled the blanket over me. I could hardly move. It felt as strange as clothes. My old dried-grass bed wasn't luxurious, but at least it knew the shape of my body, and my rabbit skin sash didn't cover much, but it didn't creep up in my delicate places. I stared at the ceiling most of the night, thinking of Dave.

The next day, I followed Rachel out to the barnyard. I held my breath. It smelled worse than rotting seaweed. My boots nearly came off as we trudged through muck. I would have gone barefoot, but my face and hands were already too cold. As we approached the barn, large animals trotted toward us. I hid behind Rachel.

"They're just cows." She laughed. "You're not afraid of a stupid cow, are you?"

"No. I'm not afraid of anything."

"Go ahead, touch it."

I stepped forward and the cow reached its head over the fence. I poked its nose, and it blew warm, sweet air from its nostrils. I put my palm against its mouth and it licked me.

"It likes me," I said, touching my nose to its nose and staring into its large brown eyes. I had made a friend.

At dinnertime, we sat around a cluttered table in the kitchen. Aunt Rita set a glass of water in front of me, and I poked at the floating ice cubes.

She frowned. "Don't play with your food."

"It's not food, it's frozen water." I caught one and popped it into my mouth.

Aunt Rita said, "Don't be rude."

Rachel giggled as she piled a lot of food onto her plate. I scooped a tiny bit of beans and a potato. Aunt Rita dropped a brown square beside it.

"What is that?" I asked.

"Meatloaf."

"What's meatloaf?"

Rachel rolled her eyes and huffed. "It's ground-up cow meat mixed with a bunch of other junk, dummy."

Eating a wild rabbit was one thing, but I would never eat a friendly cow.

The next morning, I started school at home with Rachel. She sat in front of a computer and tapped the keyboard. I opened her old books and started to read. Rachel called me dummy and dolt and dweeb and geek and lots of other funny names because she had already completed nine grades while I had to begin at grade one. I learned fast because I loved reading so much. Rachel liked reading too, but she said she had no choice because my aunt and uncle wouldn't buy a television. They said it would make her brains rot. If rotting brains smelled anything like the barnyard, I wanted nothing to do with those noisy televisions, either.

I couldn't wait to go to church the first time, even though I would have to ride in the car again. The seatbelt was almost as uncomfortable as the bra and underpants Aunt Rita made me wear.

"Just so you know," Aunt Rita said as she strained to turn and look at me from the front seat, "we're telling everyone you came from Florida."

"But that's lying."

"No, it's not. You flew in from Florida. Besides, we're just trying to protect you. It's for your own good."

I didn't like lying. I decided not to talk to people so I wouldn't have to lie also.

As we walked up the church steps, a man in a dark suit said, "This must be your niece from Florida."

"Yes," Aunt Rita said, "this is Marlena."

"Well, hello, Marlena," he said, holding out his hand. "I'm Pastor Wilkes."

I just looked at his hand and looked at him.

"Don't be rude, Marlena." Aunt Rita pinched my arm. "Say hello."

Even though my name was Marlena, I was not her niece from Florida, so I wouldn't say anything. Rachel came up beside me on her way into the church and rolled her eyes. "She's not very smart. Don't expect her to say much." She kept right on walking and I followed her inside.

Her voice changed to a whisper. "This is going to be the longest hour of your life."

Even though the church had walls and a ceiling, the room felt as huge as outdoors. Light streamed through colored windows and our footsteps echoed. When music began to play, I hardly noticed the uncomfortable benches we sat on. I picked up a book beside me, hoping it was a Bible, but it was only a songbook. I liked reading and singing along, but then we had to sit again and my rear end went numb. I thought we would learn about God, but Pastor Wilkes talked mostly about hell. My mind drifted to the Captain and to making up stories. I had to be careful that I didn't start talking to myself the way I did on my island or I would get a jab in the ribs. As my mind wandered, so did my eyes.

Across the church, a wrinkly man snored. White hair stuck out of his head in every direction. The boy beside him slouched. His dark hair covered the collar of his shiny black jacket with shiny zippers. I liked his blue eyes when he looked at me—they reminded me of Dave's. He kept looking at me, and I kept looking right back, until Aunt Rita poked my ribs. Soon we were staring again. I liked the look of him, especially because he didn't look like everyone else.

After church, he started to walk toward me, but Aunt Rita grabbed my arm and pulled me outside.

"You stay away from that Ed. He's trouble," she said.

I yanked my arm from her grip. "What does that mean?"

"It means I want you to stay away from him."

"Why?"

"I just told you why." She used her quiet yelling voice. "Don't ask so many questions."

"That was only two questions."

"Don't be rude."

I was rude if I talked and I was rude if I didn't, but I knew I had better keep my mouth shut.

The next Sunday, the boy and I stared at each other again, but the best part of the morning was sitting beside a woman with a baby. I saw only its face and lots of dark hair. Without asking, I touched the baby's head. It felt like rabbit's fur.

The mother smiled. "Would you like to hold him?"

I nodded.

I held him close and he stared at me. He had a tiny nose and chin, and even tinier fingers. He made quiet little sounds and I thought about how Mamá must have felt when she held me for the first time. Tears filled my eyes. I remembered the day Mamá explained that as long as we lived on the island, I would never have a baby. I had cried for days. I hoped now that someday I would have a baby of my very own.

After church that day, my aunt said she didn't want me holding any more babies, that they would give me ideas. I didn't know that ideas were bad.

Every day blended into the next, but at least the air started to warm. I helped plant a garden—that was something I knew how to do better than Rachel. She hated working in the dirt and I loved it. I even wrote a letter to Dave and told him all about the vegetables we grew and my first trip to the Farmer's Market. The best part was leaving Rachel and Aunt Rita at home. Uncle Bert hardly ever said anything, but at least he didn't frown at me all the time.

I walked behind Uncle Bert as we passed the vegetable stands on our way to the stables. Ahead of us, I spotted Ed, the dark-haired, blue-eyed boy, standing beside the wrinkly man who sat under an umbrella. Ed was as tall as my uncle and still wore his shiny black jacket, even though it was warm enough for me to wear just a light cotton dress. As we approached, I slowed down. I knew I wasn't supposed to talk to Ed, so I just smiled at him and said, "Hi," to the old man. Uncle Bert didn't even notice that I had stopped at their table.

"These are good looking beans," I said.

The old man picked up a bag with a hand that had only two fingers. "How many would you like?"

"Where are your other fingers?" I asked.

"Buried in the hayfield, I 'spect."

The boy stepped closer. "This is my grandpop, Horace. I'm

Ed."

I looked at Horace, who smiled with rows of big, white teeth. "Why are his fingers in the hayfield?"

"Accident with a bailer."

I heard Uncle Bert yelling my name from far ahead.

"I have to go," I said. I didn't want to, but I hurried to catch up with Uncle Bert. From there, we went to the animal pens. I saw Ed behind the stables smoking cigarettes with other boys, and later I watched him help Horace pack up their table. Ed smiled a lot, even when he wasn't looking at me. As we drove home, I folded my thumb and two fingers into my palm. My hand cramped. I was glad a wrinkled old man without all his fingers had someone to help him.

That evening, we sat at the kitchen table eating dinner.

"You look scrawny," Aunt Rita said and scooped more casserole onto my plate.

Uncle Bert butted right in. "Leave her alone or she'll end up as fat as you."

Aunt Rita turned bright red. She frowned at me as she slammed the serving spoon on the table and stormed out of the room. For the rest of the summer, Aunt Rita never let me and Uncle Bert go to the Farmer's Market alone, which meant I didn't get to talk to Ed and Horace, but I watched them. Sometimes I saw Ed hug Horace. Aunt Rita only hugged me when we first met, and I hadn't ever seen my aunt or uncle or cousin hug anyone. I thought of the times Dave hugged me. I missed hugs. I missed Mamá.

By the end of summer, Rachel complained so much about sharing a room with me that Uncle Bert fixed up a bedroom at the back of the house near the pantry. It was small and dark and reminded me of my hovel. When I couldn't sleep, I snuck out the back door and wandered over to the cornfield. The stalks grew so tall they stood over me. When I closed my eyes, they sounded like wind blowing through palm trees. If I tried hard, I heard the whoosh of surf on the shore. That's when I talked to God about my life and thought about infinity.

Chapter 33

"Samuel!" Mother's voice carried up the stairwell. "Supper!"

Supper would have to wait. I rose from my seat, cracked open my bedroom door, and hollered down the hall, "I'm doing bookwork. I'll heat up leftovers later." The tone of my voice left no room for negotiation.

Only my mother could force a sigh to travel three stories up and land with irritation. The sound of her heavy footfall clacking down several stairs gave me the go-ahead to resume my reading.

I snuck out every night until they harvested the corn, but by then it was too cold to be outdoors. The days shortened and summer flew away with the geese. All the leaves fell off the trees. Stronger winds blew, bringing bitter cold air and sometimes snow. It looked so beautiful, floating from the sky and covering the ground. Frost collected on the windowpanes of my new bedroom, making the prettiest designs. Sometimes I even saw my breath in the air.

In my hovel, I read, practiced writing, and wrote Dave and told him about the Captain and Ruby and about my new life—that I wished he were my family. When I missed Mamá and my warm island, I reminded myself of my loneliness after she died and that I should be happy and grateful to live with people.

One morning, I woke up feeling hot and cold at the same time. I held my stomach and curled up under my blankets as crazy dreams whirled around in my head. I don't remember much about it, but my aunt took me to a doctor. He gave me shots that made me feel worse. For days, I stayed in bed. When I was well enough to sit up, my aunt came into my room and felt my head.

"Your fever seems to be gone," she said. "Is there anything I can get for you?"

"No, but I wish you'd tell me a story."

"I can't think of any to tell."

"Then tell me about Mamá when she was young."

My aunt took a few seconds to answer. "Well, we didn't really get along."

"Didn't you like her?"

She frowned. "I didn't like how she disrupted the family. Your mother was wild, promiscuous, stubborn, and self-willed."

I felt as if my fever came back. "You should be glad my mother was stubborn and self-willed, otherwise she would have died on the island long before I was ever born."

My aunt's lips pressed together as she shoved her hand into the pocket of her apron. "This came for you in the mail."

She held out a small envelope. I reached to grab it, but she didn't let go right away. She stared at me for a moment before she left my room. Even before I looked at the envelope, I knew it was from Dave. He wrote that he worried about me. He wanted to make sure I knew that I was old enough to be on my own and make my own decisions, but that I shouldn't leave my aunt and uncle until I could take care of my own needs. That's when I decided I needed to earn some money. I wrote Dave back and told him I was working on a plan to save money and that I did not have many needs. Only a little food, a few clothes, and not even a bed, just a few blankets would do.

Time passed quickly as I planned my garden. Uncle Bert even said he would buy the seeds, and I could keep half of what I earned when I sold my vegetables at the Farmer's

Market. As soon as the ground thawed, I started preparing the soil. Now I didn't mind the smell of manure as I mixed it with my patch of earth. It smelled like hope.

A few days after my first harvest, I overheard Aunt Rita and Uncle Bert arguing. When I heard my name, I listened harder, but I couldn't make out all the words. I stood at my bedroom door and Uncle Bert's voice rang clear. "If you don't trust me, *you* can bring her to the market and sit with her all day!" Then a door slammed.

The next day, I received a package in the mail from Dave. I brought it to my room and tore off the brown paper. A doll with dark, curly hair lay inside with a note on her long skirt. Dave wrote that he bought her in Egypt because she reminded him of me, and that I needed to be careful because she had a Ruby under her skirt. Right away, I knew what it meant. I hid the dagger with my coins and hugged my new doll. Then Aunt Rita barged in and read the note. She said it was obscene and took the Egyptian doll from me. When I grabbed my doll, her head came off. I tried to mend her, but she was ruined. Every time I looked at her head sewn on sideways, she reminded me that I needed to learn how to take care of myself so I could leave Kansas.

On my first day at the Farmer's Market, Aunt Rita stayed home. Uncle Bert drove me in his big pickup truck and backed it up beside other trucks behind a long row of tables. As he let down the tailgate, I noticed Ed and Horace three tables down, unpacking their produce from a bright red pickup truck with pretty orange and yellow flames on its side.

Uncle Bert wiped his forehead. "You can set out all the vegetables on your own, can't you?"

"Of course I can!"

"Okay, then. If you need anything, I'll be over at the stables," he said and walked away.

I reached for my crate of beets and Ed came up beside me.

"Why don't you get up in the bed and pass me your stuff," he said.

I struggled to climb up on the tailgate in my dress. As I

squatted in the bed, I gathered the skirt between my knees and grabbed some cabbages.

"I know you're not from Florida," he said.

I didn't say anything back. I just held my breath and handed him a box.

He took the cabbages and set them on the table. "Rachel told me."

My eyes must have bugged out of my head.

"Don't worry," he said as he reached for my radishes, "I won't tell anyone."

I looked into his blue eyes. I didn't ask if Rachel also told him where I did come from. We finished unloading my vegetables in silence. When we were done, he grabbed my waist like a crate of collards, lifted me off the tailgate, and set me on the ground in front of him. His eyes stared into mine.

He smiled. "Okay, well, if you need anything, I'll be over there with Horace."

As he walked away, I asked, "Why don't I ever see you with your mother and father?"

He paused a few seconds before he turned back around. "It's just me and Horace."

"Oh. Well, I like your truck. It's pretty."

He let out a chuckle. "Thanks."

That day, and every week afterward, all of my vegetables sold. Every week, Uncle Bert went to the stables, and Ed helped me unload and reload the pickup. Sometimes, when I sold out, and Ed had gone off with some other boys, I sat with Horace and we shared my jug of water. "It's the universal solvent," he would say. "If you're thirsty, you're already dehydrated!" He would also say, "When I was your age ...," and tell me about all the crazy things he did. He didn't always remember my name, but he could remember things from seventy years ago.

One day at the beginning of autumn, I finished my chores at the farm and went for a walk down the gravel road that ran between two cornfields, stretching farther than I could see. The crop stood tall, now the color of sand, and corncobs drooped

like goat's ears. Wind rattled through the dried husks,
reminding me of palms again. I kicked at a stone in the road
and it shot into the field, startling a flock of large, dark birds.
They took to flight all at once. Hundreds of them flew
overhead in waves, moving in one direction and then the other.
They swept one small sparrow along with them. I felt exactly
like that little bird, rushed along by forces much bigger than
me.

I walked for a long time, talking to myself without worrying
if someone might overhear and say, 'Quit that, or people will
think you're insane!' I liked to hear the sound of my voice—
why did that make someone insane?

From behind, a loud truck drowned out my soliloquy. It
didn't take long for it to drive up right beside me. I quit talking
but kept walking.

Ed rolled down his window. "Nice day for a stroll."

"Yes," I said.

"So, where are you going?"

"Nowhere."

"Me too."

"No, you're not. Trucks don't drive nowhere. People in
trucks are always going somewhere."

He chuckled. "I was being ambiguous."

"What's ambiguous?"

He laughed. "It's when something can be taken more than
one way. It's like a joke."

"I don't understand."

He smiled and shook his head. I still didn't understand.

"So, you want a ride into town or anything?" he asked.

"See, you are going someplace."

He squinted at me and pulled his long hair away from his
face. "You're pretty strange, you know."

"Yes, I know. So are you."

He laughed. "Are you sure you don't want to take a drive?"

"I'd better not," I said, even though I felt like climbing in
and driving far, far away, just like the birds.

Then winter came a second time and it was worse than the

one before. I got sick again, but not as bad as the last time. I tried to stay busy with reading and studying the home-schooling books that Rachel finished. I also wrote Dave. All the days blended together, but not the way they did on the island where I kept busy with only a few things to do. I read my new Bible, but sometimes I read the Captain's old one even though the binding started to come apart. I also reread the Captain's log.

After Mamá died, I read his account on my own and discovered parts she hadn't read aloud to me, parts about the Captain's wife and his love for Benita and his jealousy and resentment of Tomas. Only after seeing men for myself did I begin to understand many of his feelings and how Tomas and Benita must have felt about each other.

While I lived on my island, I knew I would never be with a man. I had begun to wish I hadn't read what the Captain wrote about love. It made me feel strange in ways I had never experienced. When I left my island and saw so many men— more than I could have ever imagined—I began to wonder when or if I would ever have a man of my own. I liked Dave very much. I think maybe I loved him, but, just as the Captain already had a wife, so did he. I also liked Ed, but after the Farmer's Market ended, I only saw him occasionally at church. We didn't talk, we just stared.

By the end of winter, I missed my island and Mamá so much that I wouldn't even get out of bed. I couldn't stop thinking about how if I hadn't walked off and left her, the snake never would have bitten her, and Dave would have rescued both of us. After she died, I wasn't always glad to be alive. Many days I wished I wasn't. Some of those bad feelings had come back, and I hardly ate anything. I just stayed in my room and talked to myself. Sometimes, it might have sounded like an argument because I was trying to talk myself into being happy. That's when Aunt Rita brought me to the doctor again. A special kind of doctor, she said, as if I didn't know what a psychiatrist was.

I sat in a chair and the doctor waited for me to talk. I had nothing to say.

He peered over his glasses. "Tell me about your life on the island."

"There's not much to tell." I thought about the time when Dave's friend, Linda, asked that same question. I wanted to tell her everything, but this time I didn't say a word.

"You spent a lot of time alone. Did you ever hear voices?"

I thought about the Captain, Tomas, and Benita. I never actually heard their voices, not like Mamá's when she was alive, but in a way, I did. Just the same, I didn't think it was a good idea to tell him about the conversations I made up.

That didn't stop him from asking many more personal questions, about my childhood, about my feelings, about sex, about Mamá. Even though I didn't answer any questions, he wrote on the pad the whole time.

I asked, "What are you writing?"

"Does it make you uncomfortable that I'm writing?"

"I don't like it."

"Do you want me to stop?"

I did not like how he answered my question with a question, so I did it back. I asked, "Why don't you want me to know what you're writing?"

"Is that what you think? That I don't want you to know?"

"Do you really think that I even care?"

"Do you?"

"You're the doctor. What do you think?"

Then we stared at each other some more until he held up pictures with black splotches. Most of them resembled things on my island, and so I didn't mind telling him what they looked like. Then he gave me papers to read and yes-or-no questions to answer. They were easy and I didn't have to talk to him, so I took the tests, but none of them made me any happier.

By the end of the day, even the soothing sound of my own voice was not enough to make me talk. I wanted to go home—not to Kansas but back to my island. I just stared at the wall.

The doctor said I needed to take medicine and stay in the

hospital. Now they couldn't stop me from talking. "I certainly will not take medicine. I am twenty-one years old and I have legal rights."

"You're not capable of making rational decisions in your state of mind. You should be admitted to a hospital for your own good."

"You're the one who needs to be in a hospital for your own good so you can learn how to treat people nicely."

The doctor turned to my aunt. "Your niece is clearly disturbed."

"I am not disturbed," I said, "I'm unique and extraordinary. You just want me all to yourself so you can figure me out. The only one who will ever figure me out is someone who loves me."

That's when I walked right out of the room. My aunt followed. She never took me back there. She tried, but I wouldn't get in the car.

I received another letter from Dave, telling me about his adventures, which cheered me up. I reread the Captain's log yet again, and then decided to begin rewriting his words in a new notebook so his copy wouldn't be ruined. I filled notebook after notebook until the ground thawed and I could dig in the dirt. Soon I would be earning money again, and I would have enough to leave Kansas. And soon I would see Ed at the Farmer's Market.

Unfortunately, I never saw Ed sitting with Horace at their table, or hanging around behind the stables. Ed graduated high school and had a job at the Wal-Mart, Horace said. He always set up Horace's table before Uncle Bert and I arrived, and we always left before they closed up. Ed told him to tell me, "Hello." It almost made me want to shop at Wal-Mart, but I had been there once and had my heels rammed by shopping carts, not to mention all the big televisions at the back of the store with big faces all saying the same thing at the same time. Nothing could make me go back there.

Chapter 34

CHUCKLED AT MARLENA'S WORDS. I GOT A KICK out of her interactions with the shrink. No wonder she knew how to put Billy in his place. As much as I wanted to absorb all the pages I had already poured through, I was near the end of the notebook and couldn't wait to finish. I would read now and ponder later.

At the end of the summer, everyone looked forward to the county fair, except me. Sometimes I didn't even like sitting at the crowded Farmer's Market. Aunt Rita insisted that Uncle Bert drive up and down isles of cars in the wide-open field to find a close parking spot. By the time we found one, sweat trickled down the side of my aunt's knotted face. Before Uncle Bert turned the engine off, Rachel opened her door, jumped from her seat, and jiggled all the way to a cluster of her friends. I followed my aunt and uncle, lagging behind until they stopped at the cotton candy stand, and I snuck behind a big tent. As soon as they went on their way, I headed back to the car.

I leaned against the dusty bumper and closed my eyes, wishing for a breeze like the one that blew continuously on the island. All I had to do was remember winter, and I didn't mind the heat at all. In the distance, I heard rumbling. Ed's truck approached.

"You look really hot sitting out there in the sun. You want to sit in my truck? I'm going over to park in the shade."

I pushed a handful of curls from my face. "It *is* sweltering hot."

"Then what are you waiting for?"

I thought of Aunt Rita. "I can't go anywhere with you."

"We won't go anywhere. We'll just park right over there." He pointed to a line of trees.

I bit my lip. "Okay."

I climbed inside and glanced at him. He wasn't wearing his black jacket today. Just a T-shirt and shorts. We drove to the edge of the field and parked under a huge tree.

"Are you really from an island?" he asked.

I didn't know if I should tell the truth, but I wanted to. "Yes."

"You have no idea how cool that is. I've never been anywhere."

"I hadn't ever been anywhere either."

"So, do you like Kansas?"

"No. But I have nowhere else to go."

He leaned his head back and closed his eyes. "I wish I could move a million miles away from Kansas."

"If you did, you'd end up back in Kansas forty times."

"What?"

"It's about twenty-five thousand miles around the earth. That means if you went a million miles, you'd pass through Kansas forty times."

He looked at me the way Dave used to. "You're a lot smarter than you let on."

"I know."

He laid his head back again. "What I meant was that I wish *I* could move to some island, or Alaska, or Australia."

"I knew what you meant."

"Then you *do* have a sense of humor."

"Of course I do. It's a special kind."

He squinted at me. "How old *are* you?"

"Twenty-one."

"You don't seem like you're older than me."

"Three years isn't much."

"You're right." We stared at each other for a minute. He smiled. "So, I guess you've never had a boyfriend."

"No."

"Then probably no one's ever told you how pretty your eyes are."

"My mother always told me that."

"That's different. Mothers are supposed to say those things."

"My mother wouldn't lie."

"I'm not saying she would. All I'm saying is that, well … look at me. Look into my eyes again."

"Okay." I looked straight into them.

He moved a little closer. Soft and slow, he said, "You have *beautiful* eyes."

I smiled a little.

His eyes twinkled. "Now, didn't that make you feel different than when your mother used to say it?"

My cheeks warmed up. "Yes."

We stared at each other a little longer, and then he reached behind his seat and pulled out a can of beer. "I can't wait until I've saved enough money to get away." He cracked it open. "Have you ever tasted beer?"

"No. My aunt and uncle don't drink beer or any kind of liquor."

"Here," he passed the beer to me. "Try it."

I took the beer and tipped it to my mouth. It fizzed on my lip.

"Hey," he said, "maybe we could run off together."

I tasted the beer, but as soon as it touched my tongue, I heard Rachel and my aunt yelling.

Aunt Rita shouted, "What are you doing, young lady!"

All at once, the door flew open and she had me by the arm and dragged me out.

"Both of you should be ashamed of yourselves," she hollered, squeezing my arm tight. I yanked myself free, and she slapped my face. I was so mad that I probably turned as red as her. I ran away from the fairgrounds and headed for the cornfields. I ran so fast that they couldn't catch up to me. They couldn't see me through the stalks of corn, and I kept walking a few rows in, beside the road. I heard them calling my name as they drove past, but I didn't answer.

I rubbed my face where Aunt Rita hit me. It stung as I wiped my tears. Dust clung to my sweating neck and arms. The corn stalks scraped my skin and didn't offer much shade. My tongue stuck to the roof of my mouth. I didn't care. I would walk around in the fields all day if I felt like it. Maybe I would just keep walking all the way to the sea.

A car passed by and Uncle Bert called out my name. I ignored it. After a while, I heard Ed's truck. I pushed my way through the stalks and stepped out onto the road as bright red and painted flames zipped past. Before I had a chance to wave, his tires chewed up the gravel and spit dust all over me. His truck stopped and then drove backward. The passenger door flung open.

"Get in," he said, reaching over the seat.

I climbed up inside, wiping my grimy hands on my skirt.

He pushed the hair from my face. "God, you're a mess."

"I know."

"I'll take you home."

"No!"

"Okay, okay. Where do you want to go?"

"Anywhere away from here! I'm just so mad."

He sighed and twisted his mouth. "You need to cool off."

"Don't tell me to cool off."

He laughed. "No, I mean your face is beet red and you're over-heated. When was the last time you drank anything?"

"I sipped your beer."

He shook his head and pushed on the gas pedal.

"Where are we going?" I asked.

"You'll see."

We turned down a road I didn't recognize, in the opposite direction from my aunt and uncle's house. Cornfields gave way to trees that reached from one side of the rutted road over to the other. Already I felt cooler.

He stopped the truck and jumped out, and so did I.

"This is pretty," I said, looking at all the trees, grass, and wildflowers.

"It's the backside of Horace's property. C'mon, there's a creek by the clearing." He grabbed my hand and led me through tall grass and shrubs. Insects buzzed around us. As soon as I saw water, I ran to it. I stopped at the creek's edge and turned to him. "There aren't any snakes in here, are there?"

"No snakes." He laughed, pulling off his T-shirt.

I stared at his chest. It was smooth and white, like his shoulders, and then turned dark brown on his arms.

"What—you've never seen a farmer's tan?" he said.

I just kept staring, fumbling with the laces of my sneakers.

He charged into the water first. I wished I could have taken off my dress, but then I would have been wearing only my bra. Ed dipped into the water up to his chin and watched as I stepped in. I shivered. My skirt ballooned as I waded up to my waist. The water didn't get any deeper than that, so I plunged in, head first, and came up next to Ed. We moved over to where water gushed over some rocks. Ed filled his hands and drank. I did the same.

I gulped again and splashed water on my face. "This feels so good."

He swam over to a large, level boulder in the middle of the creek and hoisted himself up. I followed and sat beside him. Sparkles of light danced on tiny bubbles, and even though the water didn't whoosh like waves, it sang a happy melody that made me smile. Now the sun felt good on my body as I stretched out, my back flat against the warm rock. Ed lay beside me, and I closed my eyes. A while later, Ed said, "I'm going to turn into a lobster if I don't get out of the sun." I pictured him with claws and antennae.

He slipped back into the current and waded over to the shade of the sandy bank as I dangled my feet in the trickling water. Watching me, he sat and combed his fingers through his shiny hair.

I jumped into the creek and waded toward him. My dress clung to my legs as I stepped carefully over rounded stones and then squatted to get another drink. The water tasted sweet. As I sipped from my hand, I stared at Ed. I wondered how he tasted.

When I sat beside him, he pushed hair from my face. We stared at each other for a long time, and I thought of what he said about my eyes. When I smiled, he came closer. His forehead pressed mine as the tips of our noses brushed, and then our lips. His mouth was soft and warm. He tasted sweet as creek water. I liked the way his lips felt on mine and then found my cheek and my neck. His hand moved from my face to my back as we lay down. I held him tight and he rolled on top of me, and even though he didn't feel too heavy, I could hardly breathe. My heart raced and I couldn't kiss him fast enough. I rolled on top of him, grabbed his hair, and kissed his face. He tasted sweet and salty. He moaned, and his hand on my waist moved up to my breast.

I gasped. "Ed …."

His other hand slid up my thigh.

Between breaths, I said, "What are you doing?"

"We're gonna"—his eyes danced around mine—"you know," he panted.

"You mean make babies?"

"Whatever." He kept kissing me.

"But we need to be married first."

He stopped and pushed himself up on his elbows. "Married?"

I sat on him, stroking his smooth chest, and nodded.

"Jeez, Marlena. I'm eighteen years old. I can't freakin' marry anyone, and I sure don't want to be making babies."

I rolled off him. I flopped onto my back and let my arms drop to my sides. He sat up. I was still catching my breath.

"But I thought you wanted to run off together," I said.

He sighed. "Marlena …."

Tears slipped from the corners of my eyes as I stared at sunlight blinking behind green leaves.

"I do want to get out of Kansas, but I can't right now. I have Horace. I'm the only people he's got."

"But I have money and everything. We could take Horace with us."

"This is Horace's home. It's the only place he's ever known. I can't up and move him. Besides, where would we go?"

I thought of Dave. "I don't know yet."

"Well, it sounds like you need more of a plan."

He was right, and so was Dave. I wasn't ready yet. I had a lot more to learn. From now on, I would think twice about kissing a boy again, and I knew that Ed was not going to be my people.

When he brought me back to my aunt and uncle's house, they didn't yell as much as I thought they would. Later that night, before I fell asleep, Aunt Rita came in my room and sat on my bed. Her eyes and nose appeared red and puffy. I sat up and she held my hand. At first she didn't look at me, she just sighed.

"I'm sorry I hit you," she said. "It was wrong for me to do that. It's just that sometimes you remind me so much of your mother, and I'm so afraid that you'll turn out like her."

I couldn't go around being mad at her forever, so I said, "I forgive you." I didn't want to hear her speak about my mother like that, so I lay back down and faced the wall. I thought about Ed and Dave and the life I wanted. I knew I did not want Aunt Rita and Uncle Bert's life. I had a choice. Mamá told me that even if it seems as if we have no choices, we do. Sometimes it's as simple as choosing life over death. I had to think about that almost every day after Mamá died. When men came to my island, I chose to leave, but I could have stayed. After that, I almost forgot I could still choose.

My aunt and uncle tried hard, but nothing made them happy. They weren't happy with each other and they weren't happy with themselves. If I wanted to find happiness, I had to look for it on my own. When I made that simple decision, nothing else mattered.

I wrote a letter to Dave, hoping I could see him, but his wife wrote back. She said I couldn't come to visit, that he was overseas and that I shouldn't write him any more letters. I needed a different plan. Around that time, my aunt and uncle bought Rachel a new computer, and they gave me her old one. I taught myself to type and spent a lot of time copying the Captain's log. I even learned how to use the Internet to locate people and research genealogies. I found Captain Wesley's family and The Wesley House. The thought of traveling by myself all the way to the coast made me nervous, but not as much as running out of money. I would have to sell one of the gold coins. That winter, I did not get depressed because I intended to leave as soon as spring arrived.

I knew I shouldn't leave without telling anyone, so the week before I planned to go, I told my aunt. She yelled and said I was too incompetent to live on my own, and that I was just like my mother. I walked away and didn't bring it up again. I think sometimes it's best to leave without saying anything.

On a warm spring night a week later, three years after I arrived in Kansas, I packed a little suitcase, stuffed a few clothes and my two dolls in my duffle bag, and left a note on my bed. Very quietly, I snuck out the back door and walked to Ed and Horace's house.

Horace answered the door in slippers and a nice matching plaid outfit with buttons down the front. When he smiled, I gasped. "Where are your teeth?"

"Huh. Darned if I know," he said.

I wondered if they were in the hayfield with his thumb and fingers.

Ed came up behind him. Rubbing his eyes, he said, "What are you doing here?"

"I need a ride to Kansas City."

The sun came up as we drove on the highway. By the time we arrived in front of a pawnshop, cars and people rushed all around us. I had been off the island for three years, and still I saw so many new things. Some of it reminded me of the island. The wind blew strong and whipped dust and dirt into little cyclones that danced on the ground and disappeared. I smiled at the way birds scavenged anything they found to eat. It didn't smell like the island, but it still made me happy. As people walked by, they reminded me of sandpipers, scurrying down the street.

Ed and Horace came into the pawnshop with me. The woman behind the counter had bright red lips and strong perfume that smelled like Aunt Rita. I held my breath. While she weighed my coin and then counted out exactly three hundred and ten dollars and thirty cents, I noticed a bunch of knives under the glass counter. Since I no longer used Ruby and wanted to keep her safe, I asked, "May I see that one?"

The smelly woman's eyebrow shot halfway up her forehead as she reached for it. "This ain't no kitchen cutlery. It's a Fairbairn-Sykes Fighting Knife."

I drew the dagger and balanced its weight in my hand. It felt a lot like Ruby.

She shook her finger at me. "You be careful with that, hon."

"I know how to use it."

After that, Ed drove me to the bus station. As everyone else boarded, he took my hand.

"Are you sure you want to do this?" he said.

I nodded and let him kiss me on the cheek, but that was all. He didn't even try to kiss my lips. Maybe the knife scared him.

During the bus ride, I thought about my destination and what new things I might see on the coast. I missed my old friend the ocean more than anything besides my mother. I thought about the Captain and of how he would want me to be strong. And I thought about a shipwright named Samuel Wesley.

For months, I imagined the day I would meet him. Maybe the Captain's family could be my family. I also had things that belonged to the Captain. If he could talk, he would tell me to return them. When I arrived in Maine, I wanted to give the Captain's things to Samuel right away, but first I wanted to know what kind of person he was. I had learned that people aren't always the way we hope they will be or need them to be. At first, he didn't treat me very well. I thought I would leave, but then I met Buck and he reminded me of Horace, except he had all his fingers and his own teeth.

After I had been there a few weeks—it took that long for Samuel to warm up to me—I received a letter from Dave. His wife had given him an ultimatum, and he said he couldn't write to me anymore. I didn't understand and it made me very sad, but at least Samuel started talking to me. He even let me read his manuscript. He said I should write my own story, and so that's what I did, in this very notebook.

Dear Samuel,

I'm sorry I didn't give the Captain's things to you sooner, but I knew you would want to know where they came from and how I ended up with them. I didn't want to give them to you until I told my story. Because those things belonged to me too, I would be giving you a part of me. I would have told you about the Captain before this, but I had no idea how busy you are and how little time you have ... and then the days seemed to fly by and I learned to like you.

Before I arrived, I imagined that once you got to know me, you might even like me enough to ask me to stay, to be a part of your family ... that I would finally have a home again and people I felt were mine. For a little while, I believed that's what I had found, but I was only thinking of me. I never thought about how having me around might upset your life. I'm so sorry for the trouble I caused. I don't mean to cause trouble wherever I go, and wherever I go next, I hope I'll do better.

I survived alone on an island. I survived being with people who weren't sure if they really wanted me or even each other. I can survive on my own, no matter where I end up. Maybe one day I will find some people of my very own, the way you have. I will be happy if I can find even one person, but for now, I have to be happy with only me.

Love, Marlena

Chapter 35

STARING AT HER NOTEBOOK IN MY LAP, I LET OUT A long sigh. The girl I had just read about was Marlena, the peculiar young woman who had been sleeping across my hall for the past two months. All the pieces had finally come together. I shook my head but couldn't shake my astonishment.

I reread the first sentence and then flipped back to her closing note. I couldn't believe that I had played a small part in her incredible story—her incredible life.

Little had changed for me in the past twenty years. It seemed incomprehensible that anyone could have such an extraordinary experience. I had convinced myself that only fiction produced exceptional characters. I didn't even recognize the real thing living under my own roof. How had I allowed my own mediocrity to blind me to who she truly was? Worse yet, I let her slip away.

My stomach rolled with anxiety as I counted off eleven foreboding strikes of the clock. The mackerel sky of afternoon had thickened, obscuring any moonlight as I peered out the window above my desk. Through glass, darkness accused me, reflecting back the image of my guilt-ridden face. Sparing myself, I looked at my watch as if I hadn't just heard the quarter-past chime. Derek hadn't contacted me, and I doubted he would.

If she did leave Wesleyville, where would she go? I had no idea, and it seemed she did not want to me to find her. For the first time, an awful notion struck me. *What if I never see her again?* My chest tightened and my eyes blurred. Pushing back into my chair, I clutched her notebook, refusing to admit defeat.

I laid her story on my keyboard and stared at the last page, as if her thinking—her deepest thoughts and desires—might jump from the pages into my head. I rubbed my temples. Where would she go? Somewhere away from people. Near the water. Somewhere quiet and safe, maybe even familiar. Some place where she could sleep. As if her heart leapt from her penciled words into my heart, I knew she would settle down for the night in the most secure place she could find.

IF NOT FOR THE YARD LIGHT AND THE MERCURY VAPOR lamp illuminating the boatyard and dock, there would have been no light at all—the sky remained clouded, and not even a splinter of the moon shone through. I followed the path, through the shadows, out behind the boatshed where Billy and I had sat only nights ago. In spite of the flashlight, I caught my toe on one of the bottles left behind and sent it spinning, chattering in the gravel. I didn't know why I was trying to be so quiet. In the near distance, bottle rockets whistled and firecrackers peppered the heavy night air.

I stepped onto the dock under another beaming light. Down toward the end, *Trigger's* slip beckoned. Her fiberglass hull reflected fireworks over the harbor as I climbed aboard. Loud streaks of blue and red bursting across the sky shimmered on the water and cast a candescent glow around my shadow as I cleared the hatch. Once below deck, sounds muffled and light disappeared. I felt around for the light switch and flipped it. As I headed toward the bow, toward the berth, I prayed she would be there, that in seconds, I would know she was safe. When I opened the door, I sighed, but not with disappointment. I had never known such intense relief as when light from the galley lit the bed, vaguely defining a small occupant.

My shadow blanketed her as she lay, sound asleep atop the spread, still wearing my shorts. Her body curled around her doll. Slowly, I moved to the bedside, toward her back. She lay motionless as a faint shadow shifted with her every breath. I stood over her. My hand poised only inches from her uncontrollable, beautiful hair. I wanted to touch her, to sink my fingers into her soft curls, to stroke her bare arm, but I refrained. Yet, I dared not take my eyes off her, as if in a blink she might disappear. All outside noises receded. The sound of her breath and of my beating heart filled the silence.

Images of an island, shipwrecks, and cornfields flashed through my mind. Only weeks ago, I had met the most peculiar character I could have ever constructed, and now she lay before me. The embodiment of innocence and strength.

I thought about her quest to bring my ancestor's story finally back to his home, about how the Captain had led her to me. If I hadn't allowed her to wear away my resistance, would she have left, taking her story with her?

And what about her expectations? What if she chose to stick around? What might that mean for me? She had blown in like a fresh breeze, stirring my windless life—a life, I had to admit, I had chosen, even if by default.

I thought about my own loss and how it had affected me, how it had affected all my relationships, particularly with women. The way I kept my distance and made excuses. The way I backed out before someone could walk out on me. Just the thought of allowing myself to care for someone as much as I did for Marlena made me break out in a sweat. The feelings of an eleven-year-old boy, standing at the end of a dock, flooded back. Like a sea monster's tentacles, the memories choked me. Short of breath, I pressed the heels of my palms to my burning eyes, trying to concentrate on Marlena. As I looked upon her figure, breathing rhythmically with the rocking hull, dark images gave way to calm as she came into focus. Perhaps through her eyes I could put the past behind and finally see *my* people, people who had *not* deserted me.

There she lay, dreaming of islands or cornfields or some

uncharted place where she hoped to find someone of her own. Might she be dreaming about me? As unworthy as I felt, I wanted her. I wanted to be her people. I wanted her for my own.

I lowered myself to the edge of the bed to lie beside her, to hold her close. As my body shifted, she roused and rolled to face me. Sitting upright, she clutched her doll and grabbed her duffel bag. Her eyes flashed full of remorse.

"I didn't mean to startle you," I said, still short of breath and drawing her hair from her face. Tears filled her eyes, and without another word, I pulled her to me. She offered no resistance.

I had so many things to tell her. I wanted her to know that I had read her story, that she had exceeded my hopes of ever meeting someone so amazing. That I wanted her to stay with me for the rest of my life—that I would do anything to make her stay.

Instead of all that, I uttered three words. "I love you."

I lay down, enveloping her in my arms as she cried softly into my chest. She never said a word, but her body calmed. I shifted to my side with her as she took my hand, wrapping herself in my embrace. She gently kissed my palm and I knew she belonged to me. As the boat swayed and her body once again gave in to exhaustion, I too fell asleep and dreamed of the uncharted—of islands, voyages, and love.

Chapter 36

WITH MARLENA CLOSE AT MY SIDE, I WOKE only moments before footsteps padded above deck. Not the cautious, sneaky steps of bad men hunting down Marlena, but familiar and decisive movement, headed straight for the berth. In seconds, Derek's silhouette darkened the doorway and I half-sat up. Marlena roused, and then his voice jolted her upright.

"I should have guessed as much," he huffed. "Would have been nice to receive at least a phone call. I've been up all night, worrying." He sounded exactly like my mother.

Marlena glanced at me with alarm, as if perhaps Derek had shown up to finish me off.

"Sorry, man, it was late," I said. "You know how it is." And, of course, he did.

Derek looked at Marlena with his speculative evil eye.

"I know I should have asked first." She leaned into me. "I just didn't know where else to go."

He scratched the back of his neck. "I'm just glad you found a safe place."

She clutched my thigh. "You don't want to hurt Samuel anymore?"

"What would be the point in that?" He smirked and walked away.

Her befuddled brows arched.

"It's a guy thing," I said. I hoped we might have a few quiet minutes to get some stuff out in the open, but her concern quickly shifted.

She gasped. "Is your mother mad at me?"

"A little, I guess."

She leapt from the bed. "I need to tell her I'm sorry."

Before I could offer mediation, she was well ahead of me, on her way to the house. We had no quiet words between us, no reassuring gesture, nor any acknowledgment of anything preceding that moment. I sat for a few seconds, rubbing two-day scruff on my chin. Had any of the past forty-eight hours even registered with her?

I took off, only a few breaths behind her, but by the time I stepped in the kitchen, Marlena had melded into Mother's embrace. Then Buck came in. He seemed blissfully unaware of Marlena's earlier absence.

"Let's go fishing," he said, as if it were business as usual.

"Alright. But I should probably get my things off Derek's boat first."

Becoming acutely lucid, he frowned. "That young man isn't taking advantage of you, is he?"

"Of course not, Buck. You know better."

"Then why are your things on his boat?" It seemed the question sprung more from uncertainty—an inability to clearly assess the situation—than catching her in a lie.

She patted his arm. "I just needed a change of scenery."

Squinting and scratching his head, he nodded. Rather than pursue it to his embarrassment, he said, "I'll meet you out on the dock."

Marlena stepped back outside. As I turned to follow, Mother said, "I'd like a word with you Samuel."

"What, Ma? Can't it wait till later?"

"What's going on with her?"

"Why don't you ask *her*," I shot back, hoping Marlena wouldn't get too far ahead of me.

I left Mother annoyed, I'm sure, but I couldn't let Marlena go about her usual routine as if the past two days had never happened.

She had reverted to her unhurried pace, and I easily caught up as she stepped onto the dock.

"You don't have to help me, Samuel," she said. "I know you need to get back to work."

"To hell with work." I stepped onto the dock with her.

Her stride faltered and she glanced at me with blushing cheeks, but then kept right on walking.

Did she imagine I hadn't opened her suitcase, that I hadn't read every word she wrote? That none of it would have a profound effect on me or my expectations?

"Marlena—" I hoped to rouse some acknowledgment of what she had put me through—what I had put *her* through.

"What?" She stepped onto *Trigger's* deck.

I knew from experience and all she had written that she wasn't the sort to hold a grudge, but wasn't this where most women wanted to hash things out? I hoped she would take the initiative. She didn't.

"Don't you think we should talk?" I followed closely as she ducked below deck. Was she ignoring me? Not until we arrived at the berth entrance did she face me.

"We could talk if you want to, but Buck is waiting for me. Besides, I said I was sorry—you know, for leaving the way I did, without saying goodbye. I know it was rude."

"I'm not talking about that, Marlena. I understand all of that." I was amazed that she didn't get it. "You know, I *did* read what you left for me."

She glanced away, as if my words evoked a sudden recollection, and she moved toward the bed. "You read *all* of it?"

"Of course I did. What did you expect?"

She reached for her doll. "You're so busy. I thought it would take you a few days."

"Did you think your leaving meant that little to me?" I bobbed and wove my way into her range of sight, trying to snag her full attention.

"I don't know. I just …." She carefully placed her doll in

her bag. "It's just that you were so angry."

"But I wasn't angry last night."

"No." She offered a shy smile. "You weren't."

Before I could say anything more, she slipped past me on her way out.

"Marlena—"

She turned. "We can talk about it later, Samuel. Buck's waiting for me."

Not until that moment did I consider the mindset of someone raised in seclusion with only one other person. The relativity of time and a lack of urgency extended dialogue for hours, perhaps even days.

I trailed behind, offering to bring her duffle bag to her room. After that, I went to my own room. From my window, I watched her and Buck fishing. She sent a slender spear into the sand beneath the water. Hadn't I been doing that with my dreams and aspirations, aiming at some illusory thing I hoped to snag? I considered all the options laid before Marlena. If she stayed, would she become bored and frustrated with my life— discontented—as if she were navigating someone else's rudderless boat? Perhaps not immediately, but what about as she matured? How much contentment was possible for someone like her?

For the remainder of the afternoon, I worked on the *Mary-Leigh*. Every so often, I caught a glimpse of Marlena, usually with Buck. From what I observed, her day progressed like any other in the last ten weeks, and she seemed not nearly as preoccupied with my activities as I was with hers.

During dinner, as Buck told another tale of Captain Wesley, I couldn't stop wondering if Marlena had targeted me as a means to fulfill her desire to have babies. Not that I didn't want kids someday, but did she view me as more than a sperm bank with the added perk of having the Captain's genetics? The truth was, no matter how well she believed she knew the Captain, or what fantasy she had constructed around his great-great-great grandson, she didn't really know me.

When Buck finally settled down for the night, when all the

guests had turned in and mother headed to her room, I came upon Marlena in the parlor. I stood close behind her as we paid homage to the Captain.

"The first time I saw this painting," she said as she leaned back against my chest, "it was as if seeing my own father for the first time. I love the Captain."

"Yeah." I remembered that first night. "I walked in on your moment with him."

"Yes. I thought for sure you would guess it all, just from the look on my face." She turned to me, and that same enamored look beamed from her eyes, but was it for me? Or was it for the Captain?

I moved the hair from her face. Light from the hall glazed her cheek, pale and pink as porcelain. Only my own insecurity could keep me from kissing her now. She stared up at me with searching eyes, the way she had done a hundred times before, and smiled with anticipation. She was waiting for me, and I would not disappoint.

Sinking my hands into her hair, I brought my lips to hers, carefully, gently at first, ready to withdraw at her first hesitation. She responded the way I hoped, pulling us closer and pressing herself against me. My tongue first found hers, prompting her giggle, but she was the one who came back for more.

We were completely wrapped in each other when the doorway darkened and Mother gasped. "Oh, my—I'm sorry."

As quick as that, Mother disappeared.

Marlena smiled. "Don't worry, Samuel. She already knows I'm in love with you."

"What!"

"I said, she already knows I'm—"

"I heard what you said—I just can't believe you told my mother—that's something I would like to have heard first."

"I thought you knew."

I shook my head. What else did she take for granted? What else did she assume I already understood?

"You are so peculiar." I kissed her forehead.

"And you're very funny."

I pushed her hair from her face again, studying her expression. After one more brief kiss, I said, "We should head up."

I let her pass me, intent on following her up the staircase. As she moved, I remembered the first time I saw her from that angle, how even then I wanted to reach out, place my hand on her waist, and slide it on down to her hips. This time, as we reached the first landing, I didn't resist the impulse. She took my hand and led me the rest of the way.

"I still have your things," I said as we neared my bedroom door.

She hesitated at my doorway, and I invited her in. She glanced down the hall and then back at me as she slipped inside.

Everything remained laid out on my unmade bed, all except the gold coin, now tucked in my dresser drawer. She faced the bed, stroking the Captain's journal. What was she thinking? Before I could ask, she turned, half-sitting and half-leaning at the edge of the mattress. She held up the looking glass.

"See?" She offered it for my inspection. "It's dented, just like in the portrait."

I took it from her, rubbing the indentation with my thumb, remembering. She stroked Ruby's blade and tested its point with her finger as she looked around the room. Spotting her notebook still lying on my keyboard, she blushed. "So, I guess you did read it."

"Of course I did."

"I wish I knew half as much about you."

"Me too, though I guess there's time for that, isn't there?"

"I suppose so … but soon you'll be back to your regular work routine, and then the summer will go by fast …."

"Maybe you'll decide to stay longer."

"Maybe I will." She smiled. "But you'll probably have to beg me."

I laughed and pulled her to me.

"Then I'll start begging tonight." I was no longer laughing.

"That way you'll be *sure* to stay."

I went to kiss her again but she withdrew.

"I can't kiss you in your bedroom," she said, "or you might think I would make love to you in your bed."

Okay, so she had read my mind. I relaxed my hold of her. Really, her reaction wasn't some big surprise given all I had learned about her.

I kissed her forehead. "Seriously, though—please stay."

"Where else would I go, Samuel?"

Chapter 37

ROMANTIC NOTIONS INDUCED THE MOST pleasurable dreams. I woke slowly, threading visions of Marlena's world through mine, weaving them into everything that had transpired over the past few days. Even when sunlight coaxed my eyes open in my familiar surroundings, Marlena still seemed as much a part of my dreams as my reality.

I rolled over, shielding my eyes, and focused on the clock. 5:49. I hadn't overslept by much and didn't rush—not until Marlena's door opened and closed, that is. Then I couldn't get out of bed and pull my jeans on fast enough.

When I rounded the corner of the second-floor landing, Marlena sat several steps up from the ground floor. She had added something new to her wardrobe—almost as drastic as her last addition.

She stood, smoothing the floral print of her skirt. Technically, it covered as much of her as usual—which was more than I could say for her new tank top—but even in dim light I could see clean through the sheer folds of fabric.

Her face beamed. "I was waiting for you."

"Oh, yeah? Why's that?"

She shifted from one bare foot to the other, wiggling her hips, making the fabric dance.

I grinned. "New outfit, huh?"

"Yes."

She wiggled some more with her hands on her hips. I caught a glimpse of those wispy hairs under her arms. *Au naturel* indeed.

She continued, "Your mother gave me a bag of clothes for the needy. I didn't know I was needy, but when I saw this skirt, I thought, *I need this*, so I guess I am."

I laughed as I landed on the step beside her. "Has my mother seen it on you?"

"Not yet."

"Well, don't be surprised if she says you need to wear something under it."

"But I am wearing something under it. I put on underpants."

I suppressed my amusement—and my imagination—and smiled. I moved to the step below her. We stood eye to eye.

"It reminds me of sea foam. You do like it, don't you?" she asked.

"I do."

"Oh, good."

I leaned in a little, about to kiss her, when Mother called her from the kitchen. Marlena giggled and slipped beneath my arm. Her hips swayed with nonchalance all the way into the kitchen. As I followed, I heard Mother say, "Oh, Marlena, dear, you need to wear a slip with chiffon."

I entered the room in time to see the baffled expression on Marlena's face.

◄❀► MITCH'S TRUCK PULLED INTO THE DOORYARD SOON AFTER I collected the tools to disassemble scaffolding on the *Marjie B*, that sloop that had been in shop since last November. Normally, it took him less than a minute to find his way into the shop. This morning, I waited a half hour, growing more impatient by the minute. I readied myself to start the job without him. As I wedged my shoulder under the plank and reached for the screw gun, he finally showed up.

"You want to give me a hand with this?" I called out.

"Yup. No problem."

"You sure about that?"

"Yup." He glanced back toward the doorway—toward the house.

"The screw gun—" I said with a full eye roll. "Could you man the screw gun?"

"Sure thing," he said, but his aim did not obey. The bit slipped and nearly caught my shoulder. All I could envision was the screw gun or plank gouging into that new coat of bottom paint.

I inhaled restraint. "What's goin' on, Mitch?"

"What?"

"You're all over the place. I can't have you distracted in the shop—you know the liability."

"Take it easy, Sam."

His tone set me off. Before I could censor my words, I said, "So, you plan on marrying her or what?"

"What?"

"Are you planning on making an honest woman of my mother?" I regretted my words as soon as they came out.

His chin dropped. He glanced at the house again and then back at me, but quickly looked away. "Don't know if she'd have me."

"Jeez, Mitch." I didn't know which of us was more uncomfortable. "I really don't want to have this conversation with you. I'm just thinking of my mother's reputation. You owe her that much."

His jaw tightened. The conversation was over.

"Just get the bit in the head this time." I braced myself for the weight of the plank.

As soon as we had the *Marjie B* ready to move, Marlena showed up in the doorway. Bright sun disclosed that Mother had made no headway on the slip issue. I chuckled at Marlena's independence and that swishy little thing she did. She had no idea—at least, I didn't think she did.

"I'm going with your mom and Buck down to the senior center this morning," she said.

"Okay." I grinned. "Um, I hate to sound like my mother, but

if you're going to town, you really do need to wear a slip."

She grimaced. "So what if people can see my legs? Everybody has legs!"

"Trust me on this."

Mother came from behind and shoved a small wad of fabric at her, then planted her fists firmly on her hips. "If you want to go to the senior center, put it on!"

Marlena frowned. "Fine." Right in the doorway, she gathered up folds of chiffon and stepped into the slip, wiggling it up over her hips. Mother glared and I chuckled.

Perfection!

They took off and I returned to work. Launching a boat was not a huge undertaking, but it was best to have an extra guy on hand. That meant I had a few hours to wait before Derek ambled over.

I walked the *Marjie B's* perimeter, double-checked the carriage and cradle, greased the railway, and gassed up the winch. It had been nine months since I fired it up, so of course, the sucker wouldn't even turn over.

I dug through the tool chest, then returned to the winch lean-to and disassembled the carburetor. I messed with the fuel lines and doused the filter with gasoline.

Mitch appeared. "I need to run an errand. Can you spare me for an hour?"

"Go ahead. Derek probably won't show till noon, anyway." I mopped my forehead.

After what seemed like an hour of tinkering and sweating, I checked my watch, but only twenty minutes had passed. Lethargic from the heat, I abandoned everything and stationed myself in front of the *Mary-Leigh*. Drawing the canvas back, I thought about how ridiculous it was that something compelled me to keep her covered. I was always trying to shelter everyone else around me, trying to keep everything under control, as if that were even possible. For all of life's unpredictability, the most unpredictable thing had finally happened. I was in love.

I stood with my arms folded, staring at the *Mary-Leigh*, but imagining how my future with Marlena would unfold.

"Excuse me—"

I turned to the doorway as a man walked toward me. My height. Khakis. Polo shirt. Close-cropped hair. Customer.

"Yeah?" I said.

"I didn't find anyone at the bed and breakfast—" He turned to the object of my preoccupation. "She's a beauty."

"Yeah—pitiable—but a sweet vessel, just the same."

"What is she? Forty-five foot?"

"Forty-six, eight."

"Ketch?"

"Yawl."

He walked the length of her. "Looks like a Rhodes."

"Yeah," I said, impressed with his aptitude.

"Gotta be late '40s or so."

I nodded. "Yeah, '49—a variation on a couple earlier designs."

"Sweet." He extended his hand. "Dave Putnam."

As I gripped it, I recognized the name, but a moment passed before its implication punched me in the gut.

Capt. Dave Putnam. Crete. Navy. Marlena's doctor.

I could have twisted his hand right off his wrist. He must have seen my astonishment. If he hadn't, I'm sure he did when he said, "I'm looking for Marlena. Her family said I could find her here."

I released his hand.

"Marlena … yeah. She's not here right now." Why didn't I say I don't know any Marlena? I scrambled for a way to send him off. "I could give her a message, if you want."

"That's okay. I'll just stick around until she returns. In fact, I was hoping there'd be a room at The Wesley House."

I glanced toward the doorway. "Pretty sure there's a *No Vacancy* sign."

He flinched, drawing in a quick breath with a brusque nod. Was he, in that second, sizing up who I was and how I fit in? Before either of us had a chance to exchange another word, a car door slammed. We each turned our attention to the entrance. Marlena stepped inside.

It seemed to take a few seconds for the sight of him to register, and it wasn't until he started toward her and spoke her name that recognition colored her face.

"Dave—" The word barely slipped from her mouth before she rushed toward him, trampling my heart on the way.

As they embraced, my insides withered. When she pulled away, she grabbed his hand and led him back to me.

"This is *Dave*, the one who saved me."

"Yeah." I strained to breathe. "We met."

"I'm sorry," he said, "I didn't catch your name."

"Sam. Sam Wesley." I uttered the words, but they had no impact. He should have reacted, should have grasped who I was. My name should have wrenched his gut the way his name did mine. As it was, he didn't even break a smile, let alone a sweat. He only nodded, oblivious to my heart, hammering straight through my shirt.

"Come on." She led him away. "Let's go sit on the swing."

They left me swimming in astonishment, trying to keep my head above water. Then, as if it finally dawned on Marlena, she glanced back at me, but I saw no apology in her eyes or comprehension of my predicament.

I slipped off into deep, dark waters.

Chapter 38

As I FINISHED PREPPING THE RAILWAY, THE Hummer's door slammed. Derek stepped into the doorway. "Who's the buzz-top on the swing with Marlena?"

With false composure, I said, "Some guy from her past."

"Really? What guy?"

"The guy who took care of her—the Navy doctor."

He took a couple steps back toward the door.

"Whoa." He folded his arms. "Bad news."

"Yeah. No kidding."

He gaped in their direction. "What are you going to do about it?"

"What am I going to *do*?"

"Yeah, I mean you're not going to just let him step in here and take your girl, are you?"

I eyed him and then glanced at the door. "Maybe he's just here to say 'Hi' and that's it."

"Oh, get real, Sam."

"Besides, he's married." Why hadn't I checked for his wedding ring?

"So where's his wife?"

"How the hell should I know?"

He tossed a glimpse in their direction. "Look at them. You tell me he's not here for her."

I stepped beside him and took in the same view. They sat, more facing than beside each other, and Dave sandwiched his big mitt between Marlena's hand and her knee. She didn't take her eyes off him.

Derek was right.

"And how am I supposed to stop it?" I felt as helpless as a boy on a dock, watching his father speed away.

"Fight for her, Sam. Fight!"

"What? I'm supposed to go punch his lights out?"

"Sure."

"What are we, in third grade?" I walked back to my bench.

"Come on, Sam. I thought she was the one."

I whirled around. "Yeah, well, maybe I'm not the one *she* wants."

"Are you kidding me? She's crazy about you. I mean, she did pick you over me."

"You never had a chance—you were just too infatuated with yourself to see that."

It took a second, but he shrugged it off. "That's beside the point."

"Listen, could we just get this boat out of my shop?"

"Sure, Sam. Whatever you say."

I walked to the rear of the building and shoved the doors along their tracks, opening them wide. I gave them a kick for good measure.

"Great. Where's Mitch?" I muttered, as if I didn't know.

By the time I walked past the yard swing to fetch Mitch from the house, Buck had joined Marlena and Putnam and taken over the conversation. Mitch met me on the deck. I said nothing. I just turned and headed back to the shop with him in tow. I couldn't resist looking over at them. I had never seen her happier, and only one other time in my life had I ever felt so insignificant.

Fortunately, I would be working out at the back of the boatshed—out where Billy and I had drunk a few beers not too long ago—out of sight. From the shade of the lean-to, I worked the railway winch and released the cable, paying it out along the gentle decline as Derek and Mitch walked the *Marjie B* out the back doors, toward the ramp. I had coated the cable, chains, and pulleys so heavily in grease that they couldn't screech or groan if they wanted to. The trucks grumbled on the tracks, crunching an occasional bit of gravel as they crept along the rails with barely a stutter. To my relief, the motor purred without any more misbehavior. As soon as water lapped her keel, I took Derek's place. I figured that if the whole thing were going to crash on its side, it might as well put me out of my misery. At the rate the day had been going, I half-expected it. I would have welcomed it.

I debated whether I ought to step the mast immediately or wait, then opted to go ahead—anything to be away from the house. That shot the rest of the afternoon. All the while, I hoped Marlena and Capt. Dave Putnam had talked things out— that she had set him straight and sent him back out to sea. As I came from around the boatshed, half-expecting to find his parking spot vacant, I walked right into his rental Malibu.

WHEN I ENTERED THE KITCHEN, MOTHER'S BROW SHOT above her glasses as she removed a stack of plates from the cupboard. She said nothing, but gave me a look that implied, *Who is that man with Marlena and what is he doing here?* In fact, it wasn't a stretch to also infer, *And what do you intend to do about it?*

"How soon till dinner?" I asked, heading to the bathroom.

"Ten minutes—would be sooner if I'd had some help this afternoon."

I ignored her for the moment, but after I washed my hands, I set the plates around the dining room table and returned to the kitchen for the silverware.

Mother hadn't quit stewing. "I told them we were all booked up, but Marlena offered him her room."

"What?"

"She said something about staying on *Trigger* for the night. Well, I didn't want to be rude—he seems nice enough—but *honestly*."

"Great," I said under my breath.

"Who *is* he?"

I returned to the dining room with utensils and she followed.

"Just an old friend."

"Well, she certainly is a little mystery, isn't she?"

"Yeah." I practically slammed them on the table. "Where are they now?"

"Upstairs."

Doing what?

I stuck around the kitchen and grabbed a beer from the fridge. When they entered the room, she had him by the hand. I glared at Putnam as he sat beside her at the table. He had no trouble maintaining eye contact with me, though Marlena did.

Lasagna did not improve my mood as she leaned into him the way she had done with me. I would have preferred it if they both kept their hands above the table. Putnam seized any opportunity to look me straight in the eye. I found part of that reassuring—as if his intentions were aboveboard—but I could have easily inferred it as a challenge.

I broke from his gaze. "Please pass the bread, Ma."

Mother handed it over as she let out a terse breath. "So, Captain Putnam—"

"Please, call me Dave."

"Alright, *Dave.* Tell me, how did you meet our Marlena."

He glanced at Marlena, who smiled sheepishly. Before he had a chance to reply, she intervened.

"He rescued me."

Mother's brow twitched. "Rescued you from what, dear?"

I knew the look on Marlena's face—the one she assumed when weighing all her options—when she was deciding how much she should withhold.

She smacked her lips. "He rescued me from isolation."

"Whatever do you mean?"

"It's a very long story, Mrs. Wesley." She gave me the first glimmer of a smile I had seen directed toward me since Putnam arrived. "Samuel can vouch for that."

"Do tell." Mother turned to Buck. "You don't mind if

Marlena tells the story tonight, do you?"

Marlena didn't give Buck a chance to respond. "I don't wish to tell it tonight," she answered with resolve that I'm sure Mother took as rude.

"Oh, honestly," Mother said and carried empty dishes to the kitchen.

It may as well have been only Putnam, Marlena, and me at the table, because any peripheral conversation receded as Marlena's sights vacillated between Putnam and me. My scrutiny shifted between them.

I pushed away from the table. "So, how long are you here for, Putnam?"

He didn't quite look at Marlena, but it would have been hard for him to miss the way her whole comportment responded with expectation when he said, "Just a day or so."

⚓ MARLENA'S BEDROOM DOORKNOB RATTLED. I HEARD HER say, "Goodnight," and then the clunk of the door closing.

I had been sitting at my keyboard, seething, evaluating my options. I could have followed Marlena out to *Trigger's* slip, got on my knees, and begged. I could have helped her understand that a crush on him was perfectly natural given her situation, but that he didn't know her like I did, that what she felt for him was only the illusion of love. But I didn't. She needed to reach those conclusions herself.

Just the same, I needed to confront Putnam.

Seconds later, I rapped on his door. It opened and he stood, shirtless, with quizzical eyes. He looked fit, like he spent a lot of time at the gym. He wasn't built any better than me—well maybe a little. He opened the door wide and motioned for me to come in. I took a few steps, folded my arms across my chest, and squared my jaw. He pocketed his hands and tilted his head in anticipation.

I prolonged my silent gaze for effect. "You're not here simply for a visit."

"No." He kept his eyes on mine. "I'm not."

"You think you're in love with her."

"I may be."

I tried not to flinch. "And your wife?"

"It's over."

"You realize Marlena and I are involved."

"I gathered as much." Each response came without hesitation, as if he had rehearsed this conversation all afternoon.

"And you seem to have no problem with that."

"I'm here to answer something for myself. I know that if I didn't pursue the possibility of a relationship with her, I'd always regret it. I just need to know if I have a chance."

I stepped toward him, riveting my eyes to his. "You don't."

His hands came out of his pockets. "Don't be so sure."

At that point, I wasn't so sure, but I wasn't going to let on. "Marlena and I are serious."

His deadpan expression changed to almost a smile, but not quite a smirk. "Well, then, you have nothing to worry about."

My jaw tensed. "Why don't you just do the honorable thing and back off?"

"You know I have history with Marlena. I can't walk away from her any more than you can." He parroted my tightly folded arms.

"You're not the only one who shares a history with her, and mine precedes yours."

For the first time, he wavered, seeming unsure of what I alluded to. Hadn't Marlena told him about why she came to Maine?

"History is one thing. The future is up to her."

"Have you even considered what's in Marlena's best interest?" His unruffled exterior galled me. I took a cheap shot. "She doesn't want the life you have to offer any more than you're ex-wife did."

Had I not kept my eyes fixed on his, I wouldn't have picked up on his subtle recoil, the way the tendons in his throat pulled. I had struck his insecurity.

"You don't know anything about my ex, and somehow you seem to think you know me." He inhaled deeply enough to expand his chest. "You don't. And you have no idea what I have to offer Marlena." He then stated what we both knew. "Marlena is capable of making her own decisions. She knows what she wants, and if she's undecided now, she won't be for long."

Chapter 39

OR HOURS, I STARED AT THE MURKY OUTLINE OF a light fixture above my bed as I sprawled without a blanket or sheet, listening to the oscillating drone of a fan. The dark of my room and thoughts of my exchange with Putnam consumed me until finally I dozed. I might have slept an hour or two, but then rose before the sun. It still hadn't appeared by the time I ended up in the shop. It seemed to lag in the sky like a weighted balloon.

As light crept across the horizon, I stayed alert for the sound of Marlena heading from *Trigger* to the house. If I had stood vigil at the shop door, I could have caught her, but she managed to slip past the boatshed, and I didn't notice her until she flitted up the deck steps, wearing the little blue date dress. I couldn't stand the idea of Putnam having Marlena all to himself at breakfast, so I put down my scraper and entered the house.

Expecting to see them both in the dining room, I braced myself for the impact. Neither sat at the table, but Mother cast a glance toward the hall. I heard voices beyond the French doors as I approached the parlor, which I did cautiously, intent on eavesdropping for as long as possible.

While standing out of sight, I heard Putnam say, "So *this* is the Captain you wrote me about? And he's Sam's great-great-*great*-grandfather?"

"He's why I came to Maine."

"Okay … that explains it."

I stepped into the doorway. Their backs were toward me. He slipped his hand to her waist and she faced him. It looked as if he might move in for a kiss, but she ruined the moment when she said, "All those things I brought from the island are my history, and Sam's too."

He rebounded, directing her attention to the Captain's portrait, and took her hand. "And that must be Ruby peeking out from under the Captain's coat."

She smiled. "Yes, and the telescope and watch fob."

At that moment, I must have caught her eye.

"Sam." She dropped his hand.

Putnam put on a friendly game face. "Sam." His eyes belied the congenial tone. "I trust you slept well."

"Likewise." I glanced at the Captain and back at Marlena.

"Dave," she said, "don't you think Samuel looks just like the Captain?"

Putnam appeared to study my face, as if he cared the least bit about drawing any similarity between Marlena's hero and me. His head cocked, and with his eyes glued to mine, he stated, "Their features are similar, but the Captain's eyes have that glint of a man who's actually been to sea—who's lived and breathed it. A man with salt in his veins." The subtle flick of his brow landed the insult.

"I doubt that glint lasted very long on the island," I said, still caught in his sights.

"Sam is right," Marlena said. "The Captain paid a very heavy price for his adventurous spirit. I think if he had the chance to do it all again, he would have traded his seafaring ways to be with his family."

"Perhaps." He now focused on Marlena. "But as I understand it, if adventure hadn't landed him on that island, your life might have been quite different. In fact, you wouldn't be standing here today."

She seemed to contemplate his words before answering. "Yes, my whole life would be different, wouldn't it."

"Except, *I* still would have found you." His gaze shot from her to me and back. "And where would that leave Sam?"

Marlena's eyes narrowed as she responded. "But I *did* know the Captain, and he *did* lead me here."

Putnam stepped closer to her. "And exactly what did he lead you to, Marlena?"

To me, Marlena. Just tell him!

She didn't look at either of us as her sight settled upon the Captain. After a moment, she opened her mouth, about to offer her verdict, when Mother stepped into the doorway, hands wringing.

She spoke in gasps, "Sam, I need you and the plunger in the bathroom, right away."

Putnam smirked. Marlena remained expressionless. I exited with Mother.

BY THE TIME I FINISHED WRESTLING WITH PLUMBING-gone-wrong, I had lost track of Marlena and Putnam. When I emerged from the house, his car had vanished.

I indulged myself with the hope that perhaps now things could get back to normal.

Just before ten, I had reorganized my shop, sharpened a few tools, and I may have even been whistling. That's when Derek showed up.

Then it occurred to me. *What's Derek doing here before ten?*

"What's the deal?" he asked, as soon as he stepped inside.

"What do you mean?"

"You let her take off sailing with him?"

Like a gust whipping through the building, his words stole my air. "What are you talking about?"

"I just saw them on the harbor in one of Casey's rentals."

I rubbed my forehead, trying to keep it from exploding. I hated to ask, "The daysailer?"

"Nah, man," he said in a foreboding tone. "His cruiser. The *Layla*."

The legendary *Layla* of unrequited love.

WHILE I HAD DEREK ON HAND, I ENLISTED HIM TO ASSIST with hauling the next project on my roster, a cutter of the *Mary-Leigh's* era. Throwing myself into work was the only way I knew to deal with the situation. I couldn't keep from scanning the bay for the *Layla's* return, but at least I had some control over wood and machinery. I had far less success over my imagination. What were they doing out there? Even from what little I did know of Dave Putnam, I doubted he would take advantage of her.

No matter how busy I stayed, the hours dragged. Between the heat and waiting, I had no appetite by dinnertime. It would be air-conditioned and I wouldn't have to face Putnam at the table, so I made my appearance for the meal. I pushed the food around my plate, and then Buck started in about wonderful Capt'n Putnam.

"I like the cut of that young man's jib," he said. "He's a bona-fide Navy man, and a doctor, you know."

Then it was Capt'n Putnam *this*, Capt'n Putnam *that*. He wouldn't shut up about him.

"Hey, Buck," I said. "Don't you think it's about time to tell a story?"

Of all things, he fabricated some idiotic tale of Captain Wesley and Captain Putnam fighting over a fair maiden.

"What'd you do, Buck, run out of imagination?" I tossed my napkin to the plate. "I'm going back out to the shop."

I missed the predictable old Buck.

I hadn't intended to work until nearly midnight, but in the back of my mind, I thought I would remain out there until they returned. They didn't. Were they planning on staying out there all night? By 11:45, I gave it up and headed to my room, but not before stopping at the liquor cabinet. I didn't bother with the shot glass. I went for the tumbler and the first amber liquid I laid my hands on.

I dropped to the seat in front of my computer and swung to focus on the door. A long swallow burned all the way to my knees, smothering the gamut of screwed-up emotions I had endured throughout the day. I downed the rest of my drink in one gulp, poured another, and then peeled off my T-shirt. Through my open side window, I heard the crunch of gravel and clamshells as headlights reflected off the windowpane, drawing me like a voyeur. The mercury lamps lit the dooryard, providing ample visibility as Marlena and Putnam walked hand-in-hand over to the docks. The boatshed hid the sight of them for a moment, but as they reached the end of the slip where *Trigger* moored, they reappeared. They faced each other and I held my breath, waiting to see if she would invite him aboard. It was difficult to discern, yet they seemed to be talking—but not for long. He moved in and kissed her—not just a peck, either. He had her fully embraced.

How could I have been so certain, only days ago, that Marlena knew what she wanted—that *I* was who she wanted? I watched in disbelief—hating the sight of it, nauseated by it—yet I couldn't look away until he finally withdrew. He headed back down the dock, leaving Marlena standing there in that little dress, fingers to her lips, waiting until he rounded the boatshed. What was she thinking? What did she truly want? The breeze on my numbing chest could not cool my anguish.

I returned to my chair and didn't even bother with the tumbler as I drank down another gulp of bourbon straight from the bottle. Who did he think he was, just sailing into our life, ruining everything? Couldn't Marlena see that he could never offer her what she wanted—not the home and family life she longed for? How could she not see that?

My head buzzed. The sound of heavy footsteps jarred me from a whirl of thoughts. Without calculation, I grabbed the doorknob, pulled it open, and caught Putnam as he approached Marlena's room.

He looked me up and down. "Waiting up for me? How sweet."

I matched his sarcasm. "You missed dinner."

He smirked. "You sound like my wife."

"I thought she was your ex."

"She is."

I stared him down, steadying myself against the doorjamb. I

had no idea what I hoped to accomplish, standing there. I only knew I did not want his last moments with Marlena to linger uninterrupted, to be his last memory for the night.

"You've been drinking," he said.

"Yeah." I tasted the residue of liquor on my lips. "Just testing out a theory."

He exhaled an impatient breath. "What theory's that?"

"That I could tolerate you better after a few drinks."

He didn't give in to a full eye roll, but even in my inebriated state, I knew he was formulating a response. I didn't give him a chance.

"You show up uninvited, go after a girl who's obviously in a relationship, and don't have enough honor to stand down. Fact is, you've overstayed your welcome. This is your last night. I want you gone in the morning."

I stepped back into my room and slammed the door.

Chapter 40

MY MOUTH MUST HAVE HUNG OPEN THE ENTIRE night, because I dreamed that I had washed ashore after a harrowing shipwreck and had a mouthful of sand. The sun was burning my eyeballs right out of their sockets. When I forced my eyes open, I cringed at the glare and rubbed away grit. I flopped over, trying to gain some momentum.

"Eight o'clock?" I sensed that I had missed an important appointment, but it took a moment to remember, for the realization to shoot ice through my veins. How could I have overslept?

Adrenaline did not steady my feet as I staggered toward the window overlooking the dooryard. When I finally focused, the conspicuous absence of Putnam's rental resuscitated the throb between my ears. As I headed for the bathroom, voices and clanking dishes echoed in my head, ricocheting off every nerve ending. I didn't bother with a shower. I needed to know what— if anything—awaited me downstairs. Four aspirin and a pair of jeans later, I stumbled down the hall, pulling a T-shirt over my head.

Faces in the kitchen blurred past me as I made for the door, plowing through guests and avoiding all but Mother.

"I thought you were already out in the shop—you've been up and out so early lately."

I smoothed what must have looked like ostrich feathers sticking out of my head. "You seen Marlena?"

"I'm not sure where she is. She and Buck were up early, and I haven't seen her for hours. Just look for Buck."

My heart leapt, and I braced myself for the heat, visible even at eight in the morning. I grabbed my boots and brought them to the deck, keeping my eye open for Marlena. I hoped she would step into view at any moment. As I tied a double knot, Buck came out of the boatshed.

I met him halfway. "Where's Marlena?"

"Oh, she's been gone for hours."

"What do you mean?"

"She left first thing with that nice Capt'n Putnam."

He may as well have struck me upside the head with a two-by-four.

"Left? Left for where?"

"Don't know."

"Did she say anything?"

"Said she loves me—even gave me a kiss, right here." He rubbed his cheek. "You going with my soup on that job?"

"The usual, Buck." The words left my mouth without thought or meaning. He walked toward the house, but I couldn't move. Minutes may have passed before I ended up in the boatshed, oblivious to anything around me.

She wouldn't leave like that again, would she? Not without saying goodbye. Then again, she was capable of it. She had run away from her family in Kansas without a word. She had disappeared on me once. She was always walking off when it suited her. What prevented her from doing it again? On second thought, maybe they had just gone for another sail. Ironic how, overnight, that option could bring relief.

Inside the shed, Mitch had already begun work on the new job. He offered only a brief acknowledgment of me as I stood there, trying to replace questions with something tangible. Before the boatshed could further bake my aching brains, I pushed the front door wide open for some ventilation and then headed to the rear door to do the same. Aside from improving the lighting, it did little to alter the atmosphere.

The best thing I could do was throw myself into work, but I lacked my usual focus and stood in the back doorway staring down the road toward town. I envisioned the two of them going off together, him making promises and her trusting implicitly. The sight of the Hummer heading toward the boatyard yanked me back. Derek swung in around to the rear. I considered retreating, but lethargy had set in.

He sprung from his vehicle with all the energy I lacked. "Why are you looking like your boat just sank?"

I didn't respond—couldn't come up with anything.

"Capt'n Kangaroo is gone," he said. "Saw his car headed out of town this morning. I thought you'd be doin' the happy dance."

"He took Marlena with him." The words came without a stammer, and even as I said them, they didn't sound real. I didn't believe them.

"Whoa. Seriously?" He drew in a long, sympathetic breath. "That really sucks. Sorry, man, I didn't know."

"Yeah, well." I rubbed my forehead, as if that would help me process the unimaginable. "Listen, I gotta get back to work."

"Okay, sure. Let's have a few beers at The Bilge later."

I gave him the canned, "Yeah—sounds good," but I didn't mean it.

As soon as Derek left, I went to my finish shelf, going through the motions of taking inventory for the project.

Mitch climbed down from the ladder and shook flakes of old varnish from his shirt. "Lunchtime. You coming?"

"Nope. You go ahead." My stomach still wasn't right from last night's drinking. I would be hard-pressed to come up with any appetite.

I lifted a gallon of marine varnish from the middle shelf and gave it a shake. Half-empty. So little exertion should not have put me in a head-spin, but my equilibrium did something funny, and I had to brace myself against the workbench. It was noon, which meant I could add dehydration to my list of discomforts.

Rather than force a strong façade, I dragged the moaning chair inside the back door and planted it in the shade. It was an old metal and plastic office chair with padding that had disintegrated along with its snagged fabric. Its greaseless joints rebelled with a creak as I sat and leaned forward, resting my elbows on my knees and my forehead in my palms. The pulsating in my skull deafened a constant buzz between my ears. I couldn't seem to take in a full lung of air.

Oh, God, she's really left me.

As I stretched backward, shifting the wobbly joints—both the chair's and mine, I tipped all the way back until the doorjamb caught me. With a weight heavier than midday fatigue, my eyelids shut. I wished I could have dozed, found some reprieve, but the image of them kissing kept playing on a loop. I could have replaced that image with the recollection of her lips on mine, but why torment myself further?

I need to accept the truth.

Then, when I opened my eyes, where should my sight fall but upon that place in the roof that we fixed last month, the place where a shaft of light used to beam in. I shut my eyes again, but it didn't hinder the vision of her standing there with sunlight reflecting off every hovering dust particle surrounding her. How she seemed like an apparition, haloed by radiant filaments of wild curls. How even the folds of her skirt glowed. And that quirky little suitcase the size of a tackle box. I should have dropped to my knees.

God knows she has me on my knees now.

My whole body burned and my skin tingled. My every sense heightened and amplified and then sucked into a vacuum as everything around me disappeared. All noise receded until it was only the rhythm of my heart. One thud followed the next, but I imagined that each might be the last.

Face it, she's gone.

A brief, isolated sensation startled me back—an icy droplet splashed upon my arm, hot like a spark.

A sigh cut through the silence.

I blinked.

Another droplet trickled down my forearm against the backdrop of my old canvas shorts, loose on Marlena's hips. Beads of water traced rivulets over the sweating pitcher, nestled amid the familiar curves of her T-shirt. As she bent forward, her eyes smiled through wild curls. Her lips came nearer and I drew her in. As refreshing as the day she came into my life, cool water spilled over me.

"I want you, Samuel," she whispered as the pitcher tumbled to the ground and her lips met mine. I pulled her into my lap, allowing her kiss to convince me of how much she wanted me.

As wobbly as I had felt earlier, her lips on mine made me all the more dizzy. "Marlena." I pressed my forehead against hers as if she might read my thoughts.

Stay. Marry me. Never leave me again.

She smiled, "I'll never leave you, Samuel."

I searched her eyes.

"I thought it all out," she continued. "My mind is set. I'm sorry I made you feel bad. I just didn't understand. But now I do."

I couldn't leave it at that. "I want to believe you Marlena, but what if you change your mind again?"

"I never changed my mind in the first place. Dave helped me see that."

My eyes begged for more.

"I love Dave, but he doesn't make me feel the way you do."

"Then why did you leave with him this morning?"

"I just went to have breakfast with him in town, to say goodbye. It made me sad to hurt his feelings. He wanted me to go with him, but I couldn't. I told him I didn't want to leave my home again, and that I was already in love with you, and he couldn't change that. He said we could still be friends." The corners of her mouth curled. "He said to tell you that you better never hurt me, or he'll come back here and mess you up."

"Is that right?"

"Yes." She giggled and leaned forward to kiss me again and then asked, "When's the last time you ate?"

I shrugged as she wiggled her way off my lap. With my arm around her, we walked toward the wide-open doorway, and at that spot where I first saw her, she tossed her hair the way she always did and glanced up at me with a promising smile.

The End

Epilogue

ON MY WAY FROM THE MAILBOX, I CRAM A LETTER BACK in its envelope while looking for Marlena. As I come around the house, I spot Buck on the swing with his nurse, and Billy with Elaine on the deck. My Marlena is sitting out on the dock. She swings her feet, flicking an arc of droplets at some target—probably some little fish skimming the surface. By the time I snag her attention, the letter is moist in my hand as much from excitement as humidity. I can't remember a sultrier July.

As I walk the weathered planks, she reverts to gently riffling the rainbow film on the water's surface as she smiles at me and then casts a glance down the road.

"Wow, Derek's actually on time," she says.

His hummer pulls in beside my rust bucket. "Yes, well, I did have to promise keg beer and party food."

"Oh, speaking of which." She braces herself to stand. "What time did Mom say she'd be over to help with food?"

I offer my hand and help her up. "Right after she finishes painting her kitchen cabinets, but I think she'll probably just come over with Mitch whether she's done or not."

The Hummer door slams, and I tuck the letter in my back pocket—timing doesn't feel right.

We walk toward Derek as he nears the dock, asking the same question he's been asking for the past two years, "So Marlena, did you remember those coordinates yet?"

"You are relentless." She rubs her round tummy as I pull her close. "I have a launching party to prepare, and you boys better get the *Mary-Leigh* ready before your guests show up."

"Don't overdo." I place my hand atop hers. "Ma will be here in just a few minutes."

"Okay." She reaches for a kiss—and not just a quickie—then walks away, her fingers lingering in mine.

Derek rolls his eyes.

"Oh," she glances back. "What was in the mail?"

I want to wait until later, when it's just the two of us, but I know Derek will be excited about it too.

"Oh, nothing—just a little paperwork." I pull the envelope from my back pocket."

"What sort of paperwork?" She squints at my unbridled smile.

"Just a contract."

"Not *the* contract ..."

"Yep."

"Oh my gosh! You're going to be a published author!" she squeals and runs back at me, throwing her arms around my neck, practically bouncing off my middle.

"Careful—you'll bruise little William," I say.

Derek slaps my back. "So, what's the title I should look for on the best seller list?"

"Story for a Shipwright, of course!"

The Island

IN A PLACE WHERE SEA DASHES AGAINST ROCK, WIND pushes through a crag of hollowed-out earth. Salt consumes smooth and jagged alike. The stiff hinge of a captain's chest collapses under the weight of its lid, and tattered linen, once fringed with finest French lace, billows beside a carved-out window where a haze of light passes through the gloom of an abandoned hovel.

A snake lurches at its prey. Neither acknowledges the wind as the mouse escapes through a narrow fissure onto the ledge. Its twitching whiskers feel the coming storm as it looks windward, toward gathering clouds. A hawk descends from the precipice and snatches its dinner, then swoops over the low mangroves and a crumbling hut. It lights upon a branch in the fruit grove and consumes its morsel. It again takes to flight, circling back toward the precipice, finally landing far above a shallow grave and stares out over the ocean. The bird has no recollection of any shipwrecks, but the Island does.

The Island is alive and changing, yet unchangeable. Its place in the sea as fixed as the foundations of the earth, and as unyielding as time itself. It watches as life proliferates in its lush, secret, and wild places. It even welcomes new life that scampers with the ebb and flow of its surf. Sometimes that surf transports life, gasping for breath, filled with horror and gratitude. Sometimes, the dead wash ashore.

In that surf, an ancient golden face trips aground, flickering as it rolls and tumbles amidst sand and pebbles. Dark clouds loom on the horizon, yet no one is peering through a looking glass, their breath stolen by the sight of sea and sky merging in terrors.

Reader's Guide

1. Samuel feels that his life is caught in a rhythm of mediocrity. How has this affected his ability to see Marlena for who she really is? How would you perceive the inexplicable peculiarities of a new acquaintance? If you were in Samuel's position, at what point might you have drawn the correct conclusions about Marlena's past?

2. Why did Marlena's story about Captain Wesley disturb Samuel?

3. By the end of the story, how did Samuel's perceptions of Billy change? How did your own perceptions of Billy change? At what point and in what way? Have you ever experienced such changed perceptions in real life?

4. What influenced the differing voices in Marlena's three stories?

5. What did Marlena learn about the opposite sex from her relationship with Ed? What did she learn about herself? How did Ed and Horace's relationship influence Marlena's relationship with Buck?

6. In what sense does Marlena rescue Samuel? What bearing did Sam's last memory of his father have on his reaction to Marlena's plan to leave?

7. What beliefs provided Marlena with the courage/ability to leave her family in Kansas?

8. In what way did Sophia and Marlena's regular reading of the Captain's log and the Bible equip Marlena for life on the island, and later off the island?

9. Many of Marlena's behaviors are considered rude. What are some social norms that make little or no sense to you, and why?

10. Imagine you have washed ashore with a handful of strangers on a tiny uninhabited island in the middle of nowhere—stripped of everything. What qualities of character would define you and distinguish you from other survivors? What reputation would you develop?

Other Novels

by

J. B. CHICOINE

❧~❧

Portrait

of a

GIRL RUNNING

ALL LEILA WANTS IS TO GET THROUGH her senior year at her new high school without drawing undue attention. Not that she has any big secret to protect, but her unconventional upbringing has made her very private. At seventeen, she realizes just how odd it was that two men raised her—one black, one white—and no mother. Not to mention they were blues musicians, always on the move. When her father died, he left her with a fear of foster care and a plan that would help her fall between the cracks of the system. Three teachers make that impossible—the handsome track coach, her math teacher from hell, and a jealous gym instructor. Compromising situations, accusations of misconduct, and judicial hearings put Leila's autonomy and even her dignity at risk, unless she learns to trust an unlikely ally.

Straw
Hill
Publishing

Available as a trade paperback and e-book from your favorite online bookstore

Portrait

of a

P R O T É G É

Sequel to *Portrait of a Girl Running*

FOUR YEARS AFTER THE CLOSE OF *Portrait of a Girl Running*, Leila is twenty-two and living on a pretty, little lake in New Hampshire. A new set of circumstances throws her into a repeating cycle of grief that twists and morphs into unexpected and powerful emotions. Leila must finally confront her fears and learn to let go while navigating the field of cutting-edge psychology, protecting herself from the capricious winds of Southern hospitality, playing in the backyard of big-money art, and taming her unruly heart. Even her 'guardian' has a thing or two he must learn about love and letting go.

Straw
Hill
Publishing

Available as a trade paperback and e-book from your favorite online bookstore

SPILLED COFFEE

BENJAMIN HUGHES IS ON A MISSION. He has just bought back the New Hampshire lake cottage his family lost eighteen summers ago, in 1969, just before he turned fourteen—just before his life blew apart.

Still reeling from a broken engagement, Ben has committed himself to relive that momentous summer for the next twenty-four hours.

Every summer as a boy, Ben has gawked at the pretty redhead Amelia, granddaughter to the richest man on the lake, Doc Burns—owner of a Cessna floatplane and the Whispering Narrows estate. During the summer of '69, Ben not only sneaks around with Amelia, but he learns how to fly with Doc, and meets an eclectic cast of characters that will change him forever. The best summer of Ben's life turns out to be the worst as the Burns' family dysfunction collides with his own family's skeletons.

Straw
Hill
Publishing
S H
P

Available as a trade paperback and e-book from your favorite online bookstore

About the Author

J. B. CHICOINE WAS BORN ON LONG ISLAND, New York, and grew up in Amityville during the 1960s and '70s. Since then, she has lived in New Hampshire, Kansas City, and Michigan. New England is her favorite setting for her stories.

When she's not writing or painting, she enjoys volunteer work, baking crusty breads and working on various projects with her husband.

She blogs about her painting and writing, and can be contacted via her website, www.JBChicoine.com and her J.B. Chicoine author page on Facebook.

CPSIA information can be obtained at www.ICGtesting.com
Printed in the USA
LVOW06s1943290915

456197LV00004B/458/P